A CHANCE AT LIFE

JIMMIE WATKINS

To everyone who ever believed in me, even when I didn't believe in myself.

ACKNOWLEDGMENTS

To a very special someone who has helped me become a better person, and my family and friends, of course. None of this would be possible without you.

CHAPTER 1

A FLICKER OF SHADOWS

WITH THE WEIRD dream still clouding my mind, I tossed and turned until my phone's alarm startled me awake. Groggy and disoriented, I arrived late for class feeling like a character in a movie. Settling into my seat, I couldn't shake the unsettling remnants of the dream. No, I couldn't remember the late-night visions I had, but I did recall an unsettling echo that shaded my thoughts for the remainder of the afternoon.

Sitting inside a well-lit classroom on a sleepy Friday afternoon, I listened to the instructor discuss how Native Americans buried their dead. As the teacher droned on, I zoned out, envisioning a rehabilitated home and old friends I hadn't thought of in years. I didn't know why I was thinking of Keisha and Xavier, but I was, and it troubled me. Flashes of guns, money, and big-muscled thugs clouded my mind, accompanied by a grinning male figure whom I couldn't quite remember.

As the class wore on, I wondered if the visions were left-overs from the crazy dream I had last night or maybe warnings. Whatever they were, I pulled my hood tighter and surveyed my surroundings, feeling nervous and out of place.

In the quiet of the classroom that peaceful afternoon, my body trembled with a chill, stirred by the paranoid emotions that permeated the air. I perked up in my seat, gripping the laptop screen from the sides. It felt like someone was observing me, looking at parts I wanted to remain hidden. A couple of students noticed my erratic motions, but I didn't care. Scanning the room, I searched for the source of my discomfort as a wave of awkwardness washed over me.

Odd, I thought, releasing the screen and relaxing in my chair.

The bright fluorescent light hummed overhead, echoing the rhythm of my rising heartbeat. A chill blew from the air conditioner, making the room feel like a meat locker. The soft taps of keys from nearby students on their laptops hit my ears, adding to my growing anxiety.

Out of the corner of my eye, a shadow flickered—a brief darkness hovering out of reach. After checking the room, I saw nothing, still on edge. Returning my gaze to the teacher, I listened, uncertain of what was happening and hoping that I wasn't going insane.

The professor scanned the room with narrowed eyes for an answer to the question he posed, his forehead glistening. After staying up last night reading the required materials, I wanted to put the information to use. I raised my hand, hoping he'd call on me, trying to shake the weird sensation of being watched out of my mind.

However, to my disappointment, he chose another student. Several of us who had raised our hands lowered them as the young woman gave her answer with all the confidence she could muster. She looked deflated when her answer proved to be half-right. The professor corrected her and then continued his lecture.

Just as I started to feel normal, my phone vibrated with a text message, jolting me from my focus on the professor. I ran a hand over my waves, frustrated at receiving a text during class. Shifting in my seat, I typed a discreet response under watchful eyes beneath the desk. Then, I refocused on the teacher, who hadn't noticed my actions.

When class ended, I texted the recipient to meet me outside and to be quick. Being late for practice meant running extra laps as punishment, and the Lord knows I didn't want that. Those additional laps could drain you on top of the intense conditioning the coach made us endure.

Plus, with my hectic schedule, I never had time for myself. Running track for the school and selling weed on the side left me kind of busy. Along with spending time with Amina, I was never in one place for very long. It had been months since I'd called home and checked in with Mom. To be honest, I was enjoying my time away from home.

As I gathered my things and exited the classroom, my mind wandered from the lecture to the text message on my phone. It was a stark reminder of the dual life I led.

Entering the eerily empty, silent halls, the bright lights overhead felt ominous and electric. A cloud of haze gripped my mind as I walked, reminiscent of the weed in my backpack. My legs took me forward as if I were in a dream, being pulled along against my will.

The reflection of the light bouncing off the floor carried a disturbing quality, making everything stand out. With each step, the fluorescent lights bent and distorted, making me feel dizzy. I panicked, looking around. The silence was louder now, with an ear-piercing quality echoing in my ears.

That was when I noticed the other students were nowhere to be found. This place wasn't as crowded as a train station, but it did have people—people who had just left class, people who should have been in the halls.

Fear gripped me by the throat.

In that moment, I ached for a drink, like I had been running for miles. I rummaged through my bag for a water bottle but came up empty. Looking for any form of wetness, I decided to walk to the nearby fountain to quench my ungodly thirst.

My throat was beginning to close in need of water, like someone stranded in the scorching desert. Dogs would sometimes drink from the fountain, but I didn't care; I had to have a drink. There it was, calling me, beckoning me. The water fountain would be my last attempt to satiate my savage thirst. When I threw my hands towards it, it retreated further away from my grasp. This made me feel even more disoriented and lost. I panicked and clawed at my shirt collar, thinking I would die if I didn't reach it in time. When I did, a surge of relief washed over me, like I had been saved.

As I gulped water from the fountain, my arms tingled like crazy. Someone was watching me. Rising, I noticed a short, dark-skinned man standing to the left of me. Wearing expensive shades and several gold chains, his presence was foreboding. With my breath caught in my chest, I froze at his awkward demeanor and menacing glare.

With my hand still holding the lever of the fountain, I stared at him. Locked eye-to-eye with something from another world, I braced, ready to defend myself from his sinister presence and haunting gaze. I stood as still as a statue as he chuckled, his arms folded across his chest, drawing me into his weird aura. Something about this dude wasn't right, but I couldn't quite pinpoint it. With his slick goatee covering his face and jet black skin, he looked like a cheap pimp. Someone out of a film.

"Hey, who are you?" I asked, fearing his response. "Got a problem or something?" I let the words fill the deserted hallway.

At that moment, I wanted answers for his intrusive behavior. A reason for his jarring presence and disturbing, sick grin. Just as he was preparing to speak, I heard something from the other direction, drawing my attention away. The hairs on my neck raised, causing an involuntary twitch as I heard the man make a move. When I turned to face him, the stranger was gone. His presence vacated. The encounter, only seconds long, seemed to stretch like warm caramel.

I scanned the area, taking in everything, and looked around the large foyer. Where did he go? I wondered. And where did he come from? No one just disappeared like that; this wasn't a dream. Now perplexed, I noticed the hallway had people walking out of class or talking to each other. The sound of their voices rose, filling the air.

Standing with a blank look, I was ready to get out of there and forget about the strange encounter. Taking a step towards the exit, my hair stood on end. It was bizarre to admit, but I was uneasy. The short man had to be a figment of my imagination, or I was going insane.

After making my sale, I walked to the parking lot and headed toward my car, happy to be outside under the rays of the sun. With it being a Friday, the whole campus was alive with activity. It was nice and freeing, and I looked forward to practicing. Running was stress relief for me, and the short dude by the fountain had brought down my mood.

I tossed my backpack onto the passenger seat and got in.

The air freshener was dangling and permeating the air, as always. I plugged the phone in to charge it and placed it beside me, getting ready to drive to practice. As soon as I dropped it, I received a call. I jumped, startled. Settling myself, I answered, still unnerved by the strange happenings in the hall.

The screen revealed Amina sitting in what looked like the cafeteria. "Where are you, Travis?" she pouted, using the screen as a mirror to fix her hair.

I gripped the phone tighter. "In my car, about to go to practice. What's up?"

"Are we still going to the party tonight?" She flicked at her hair. "I really want to go."

"I guess. Last time I missed the party, we lost the meet. It's a ritual now."

Her face lit up. "Perfect. I can wear my new outfit. You're going to like it."

"I'm sure I will, and make sure you're ready. You know I hate waiting," I remarked, adjusting the rearview mirror.

"I will," she smiled. "Oh, and thanks for ignoring my calls earlier. I could've been in trouble. I don't like it when you ignore me."

"Ignore you? What are you talking about? No one called me," I replied, confused.

"Boy, you're tripping. I just called you a few minutes ago."

I sat puzzled and wondered how I missed her call. A cold wave of unease washed over me again, but I forced it down. "What's wrong, Travis?" I heard Amina's voice in her thick country accent.

"It's nothing," I told her. "I must've been talking to somebody."

"Well, next time, answer when I call, and I promise I will be ready. Miss you." Then she ended the call.

The air inside the car stuck to me, so I lowered the windows to allow some circulation and took a deep breath. *How did I miss the call?* I thought. Was I that unwound by the weird dude by the fountain? Putting the keys in the ignition, I started the car and drove off to practice. Pressing down on the gas, I sped off to practice, unable to reconcile the strange events that had transpired. Dwelling on the strange, short dude would have to wait until I left the track.

CHAPTER 2

BETWEEN THE LINES

AFTER PRACTICE, I strolled inside the room to find Marcus sitting with his head down, engrossed in his studies. I scanned the tight space, tossed my backpack on the bed, and greeted him lazily. "What's good?" I asked, heading to the closet.

Marcus looked up, his focus unwavering. "Nothing much," he replied, taking off his glasses and placing a finger in his textbook. "How was practice?"

I peeked around the closet door with an armful of clothes. "Rough; the coach almost killed us today. I thought he'd make us run forever."

"Ha!" he said, half-enthused. "I'm sure it was." He continued with his reading, ignoring my presence again.

Marcus was my roommate, and we often got into arguments over people stopping by for me. He wanted time to study; I wanted to live a little. I had to admit, when he wasn't being an asshole, he was pretty cool. But the boy liked his space and wanted to be alone, like a goddamned sentinel, always standing watch and observing instead of living in the moment.

As I looked through my wardrobe, I recalled a time when I invited friends over, and a girl was digging him. That night, I had shoved him, saying, "Introduce yourself; offer her a drink or something. Anything to show you're interested." But Marcus, being Marcus, just complained until they left, as he always did. The Marcus I knew was alright, but he never showed anybody that side of him, which left me wondering what was wrong with him.

Finding my outfit for the night, I sat on my bed and looked around the room. *Now I could relax,* I thought, letting a smile creep across my face. The room was neat, with a few pictures on the wall, with diagrams and whatnot. A double desk and our beds. If you ask me, it looked like every college dorm room I had ever seen on television.

Looking at Marcus, still studying, I felt frustration. This dude was only worried about school and never did anything else but study. I guess it bothered me because college was supposed to be our first chance to spread our wings and be free, without any parental guidance. We had a chance to be adults, and he was wasting it. Always in the books.

At that moment, my phone vibrated in my pocket, alerting me that it was a customer. I looked over at Marcus, who had his head down, and hoped he would understand. Though I didn't want to sell weed here, I was tired from practice and didn't want to drive. After thinking it over, I texted her to swing by to pick up what she needed. She replied, "Twenty minutes."

In the meantime, I grabbed my laptop, put on some music, and began working on my assignment for class. Marcus complained about the loud music, so I switched to earbuds and read up on burial practices and totem poles.

However, I couldn't focus on the assignment, no matter how hard I tried. The strange events of the day swirled around my mind like a tornado: the strange dream, the visions of guns, killers, and old friends, and the way the short stranger grinned at me and disappeared. It all had me tripping. I hadn't wronged anyone that I knew of, so I was perplexed as to why someone would be stalking me. My life was complicated but manageable, and with every second accounted for, I had no time to offend anyone. I was always busy.

While still daydreaming, I heard a knock on the door, pulling me out of my confused state. Marcus eyed me, like he was the police, while I got up to answer. I opened the door, inviting Bianca inside.

"Hey, Bianca," Marcus said, with a nervous look.

"Hey, Marcus, I didn't know Travis was your roommate."

"Yeah," he quipped from his seat on the bed. "He's... great."

She giggled, "He sure is," as she turned around to face me.

I walked over to my desk and pulled out a chair for her, inviting her to have a seat. She sat, crossing her thick thighs over one another. The way she moved was almost too calculated, like she knew the effect she had. Her blue top hugged her figure, complementing the stretchy pants and sandals.

With her voice carrying a hint of mischief, she gazed at me, her stare lingering a bit. "Hey, can I ask you a favor, Travis?"

"Yeah, if it ain't too taxing," I replied, walking over to my stash.

Marcus coughed, irritated at our interaction. If he wanted to talk to Bianca, he could. It wasn't like I'd care. She was a customer, and Amina would kill me anyway.

But Bianca's eyes were fixed on me, watching my every

move. "I need help moving a dresser," she smiled. "Do you think you can lift it for me?"

Here was his chance, I thought. "Maybe Marcus could help you; I'm kind of busy these days," I said, looking over at my nerdy roommate.

Bianca glanced at Marcus, pausing and waiting for a reply, but he just sat there, looking through his wire-framed glasses. After an awkward silence and no response, she continued. "No, I think I want you to do it; you're more fit, and I don't think he wants to help anyway."

I was surprised at her behavior since she had never acted like this before. "Sure, just let me know when," I shook my head, disappointed at Marcus.

"Are you sure?" She looked at me, infatuated.

Bianca's alluring gaze made me think of Amina. "Yeah, I'm sure," I said, giving her the baggy. "Text me, and I'll see what I can do, but no promises."

She hugged me, throwing her arms around my shoulders and pressing her body against me. I stood stiffly, returning her embrace. She was soft, smelled like lavender, and had a whole heap of problems.

She looked at me with a dreamy expression and giggled. "I hate where it sits now." She hit me on the shoulder. "And I need it moved, like yesterday."

I returned her gaze, looking into her soft hazel eyes. "We'll see, Bianca."

As she left, I watched her saunter out of the door, her hips swaying side to side. She was attractive and obviously coming on to me. I bit my lip as her shoes tapped against the floor. Closing the door behind her, I went over my next move.

Marcus sat on his bed with a smirk. "One of these days, all the BS you're involved in is going to catch up with you."

"What are you talking about now?" I asked.

"You know what I'm talking about, and when it does, I'm going to be front and center," he finished, tossing his phone in the air. "Front and fucking center."

Marcus's words hung in the air, but I chose to ignore them, too caught up in the anticipation of the evening ahead. I shifted my focus to preparing for a night of escapism with Amina, forgetting Bianca's gaze and Marcus's nagging presence.

As I sifted through my wardrobe for something to wear, my brain wandered to the curious incidents of the day. The odd, lingering feeling from the encounter at the fountain crept up my spine, sending a shiver down my back. I shook my head, trying to dispel the unease. Tonight was not about strange men, flirting women, or cryptic dreams. It was about losing myself for a moment and preparing for the upcoming meeting with my friends.

CHAPTER 3

THE PARTY

MUSIC PLAYED inside the car as we pulled into the restaurant's parking lot, my head nodding along. With the light from street lamps above casting a cool glow, it felt like the perfect Friday night to chill out with my friends. The spot we were headed to was the local burger joint, where all my classmates went to eat and talk after a long day of class. Amina, who was sitting beside me, wanted a bite to eat, and being the young entrepreneur I was, I wanted to see if I could make a couple of sales before we left for the party.

The strange occurrences of the afternoon were forgotten for the moment, and all I wanted to do was relax and kick it. With my girl, a shitload of weed, and a head full of bad intentions, tonight was all about fun.

Amina reached over to lower the volume, looking at me with her soft eyes. "Travis, when you order, get me a couple of extra sauces. They're real stingy with their condiments," she drawled in her Southern accent, her words dripping like sweet, sticky syrup.

Amina was from Alabama and had dark brown eyes and smooth skin. She was smart, and I liked spending time with her. She made me think, and I dug that. "Before you leave, let me ask you something. Do you ever think about where you're headed in the next few years?" Her voice carried a mix of curiosity and concern.

I paused, caught off guard. "That's kind of out of the blue. What's up with all this future shit?"

"Well," she leaned in, her eyes searching mine, "we had this thing in class today. The professor made us map out our next five years, career-wise. It made me wonder about your plans."

I shrugged, feeling a bit uneasy. "I've never been much of a planner. I'm living my life, you know? Just vibing."

Amina frowned, confused by my response. "But you gotta have some sort of direction, right? I mean, having a plan... It's like preparing for the future."

I could sense her frustration, but planning just wasn't my style. "Look, where I come from, we don't do the whole long-term plan thing. It's more about surviving the here and now. Anything beyond that feels like... I don't know, playing around with fate or something."

She looked at me, shocked. "You really gotta think more about what's ahead, Travis. With your big brain. I'm surprised you haven't thought about it."

I didn't respond to her. Besides this wack-ass conversation we were having, she was legit. Ride or die, as we said. I mean, this girl had gotten me out of some jams before, when my pockets were hurting.

I grabbed her by the thigh and smiled at her. Attempting to lighten the mood, "Need anything else while I'm inside?"

She knew I was avoiding her question with a side-eye that said everything. Letting her apprehension fizzle away, she looked at me with a smile. "Hmm, a strawberry soda, if they have it, and... that's it."

I exited the car while she pulled out her phone and started taking photos of herself. "Oh yeah, don't forget the condiments!" she shouted out of the car at me.

As I walked toward the restaurant, I couldn't help but wonder if I would still be breathing in five years. Where would I be? Ha. Who had time to think about the future when you had the present to occupy your time?

The parking lot was full, with cars blasting music and people standing outside, talking and enjoying the Friday evening. It was a feeling of freedom then. A bunch of kids, away from home for the first time, are out making their mark on the world.

Walking past the clothing store, I stopped in front of the burger spot. It reminded me of some of the spots back in Chicago. A couple of students hung outside, crowding the door, talking about a hookup with some chicks. I walked past them, nodded, and went inside.

The smell of greasy food hit me, bringing some comfort.

Hearing my car horn from the parking lot, I saw Amina telling me to hurry up. Her hands were pointing at her wrist, but I waved her off. I made a few quick sales under the table and talked to a few people. It was Friday, and the atmosphere was charged with anticipation for the weekend.

Eventually, I sold my last bag and ordered, leaving a couple hundred dollars richer. I dapped up my friends and clients, then left with our spoils: two greasy cheeseburgers and strawberry sodas.

Amina perked up at my arrival, irritated at my delay. My hair stood on end, and my senses sharpened. It was the same feeling as before—the feeling of being spied upon.

Time slowed down, and a fear fell over me that I had

never felt before. Like someone had thrown a dark, invisible cloth draped over my shoulders. I dropped the sodas on the ground, and the plastic bottles bounced on the parking lot pavement.

Out of the corner of my eye, I saw someone I knew—a face I couldn't place a name to. I scratched at my arm, thinking a spider was crawling on me. Focusing my eyes, it was the same dude from the water fountain earlier.

I turned to make sure it was him, but when I went to look, no one was there. Was I tripping, seeing things? My mind flashed. Laughing, I brushed it off, but I couldn't get that unsettling smile out of my head. Just his presence alone was frightening, but I had to play it cool; Amina was watching. I forced a nonchalant grin and carried on.

I paused with the greasy bags in my hand and my head cocked to the side. I must've looked odd because Amina asked what was wrong. I said nothing, even though I was cautious. I bent to retrieve the sodas, hopped in, and we ate.

Now, my curiosity was on fire, and I had to find out who this person was. Whoever it was, though, I wished they would leave me the fuck alone. Yet a nagging feeling told me that this encounter was just the beginning of something far more sinister.

When we arrived, it wasn't much of a party yet, with a few people sitting around chatting with each other. The music was thumping at a decent pace, with the lights dimmed. Smoke filled the place, despite the near-empty environment. By my side on the couch, Amina sighed, looking bored. I kissed her on the cheek and passed her an empty cigar and some weed, then asked her to roll up while I went to take a piss.

She complained as I got up, but I ignored her, still piffed about her asking me about my future. A few moments later,

I stood by the bathroom, nodding my head, when the door swung open. Again, my leg twitched, and I felt funny. Looking around puzzled, my eyes landed on this short dude in a track suit, much like the guy from before. His walk was slow and methodical, and all I remember hearing was the clang of the gaudy jewelry he wore around his neck. Looking into his eyes, I recognized it was the same guy as time slowed down to a syrupy crawl.

The music stopped, and the noise from the people near me became silent. Their mouths seemed to be moving, but nothing was coming out of their faces. What the fuck was happening? I thought. Grinning that same unsettling smile, the short guy approached me. When he was within range, he ignored me but bumped me as he passed. A forceful push that sent me back a little. "Hey!" I shouted as I shoved the stranger off of me. "What's your problem?" I asked, mad that he had the audacity to touch me.

Opening my mouth to continue to question him, I got turned around by someone standing next to me. I rotated back around to face the stranger, but he was gone, like a ghost. It was then that the music came back, rushing in, disorienting me. Shaking my head, I felt sick. *Who in the hell was that?* I thought. I knew him from somewhere, and it was bugging me. Deciding to find him later, I used the toilet and returned to the party. When I exited, I asked everybody if they knew who he was. Unfortunately, the people I questioned shrugged, claiming they hadn't seen anyone matching his description. I was confused as I walked back to Amina, thinking the whole day felt strange.

Everything, from sitting in class to the water fountain to practicing, made me feel disconnected. Like a person watching my life unfold on a screen. I shivered as I sat beside Amina, who was live-streaming herself again.

"Here, I rolled it just like you taught me," she smiled, looking at her accomplishment.

I took the blunt out of her hand and found a lighter. I put the fire on the ass end of the weed and inhaled, letting it wash over me.

After coughing, I passed it to her, and then it went around the room. Someone sat down next to me and sent another one around. Then another. Amina and I were pretty much baked for the rest of the night.

I drank a beer or two and kicked back with my teammates, enjoying the get-together. We were going to Campton next week, and most of us were excited. They had some nice runners, but so did we.

Sitting there, I was excited but also a little unnerved by the mysterious man. Why did he push me, and where did he go? It felt strange and out of place. I wanted to at least figure out what happened.

With all the remembrances of races and my friends floating in my head, I pushed the rest of the day into the back of my mind. I felt good and in control again, and I was determined to let nothing ruin my evening.

As we lounged, the night deepened, and the music softened. My mind floated, half here and half there. The strange man's face lingered in my head, but I didn't let it bother me. Life was good, and tonight was about enjoying the moment.

CHAPTER 4

THE FOLLOWING MORNING

ALL NIGHT, I tossed and turned with haunting nightmares that tortured me. I saw visions of unfamiliar faces laughing as I ran endlessly toward the finish line in a race against myself. Each time the race ended, someone would push me back to the starting point, forcing me to begin again. Huffing and puffing, I'd make my way back near the beginning, and then the same thing would happen. It felt like a thousand hands were pushing me repeatedly for hours.

Exhaustion gripped me as I struggled against the powerful forces of my mind, my heart thudding relentlessly in my chest at each futile attempt. When I finally woke, I was drenched in sweat, breathing hard, and overjoyed with relief that the torment had ended.

With my eyes trained on Amina's ceiling fan spinning slowly above, I felt the warm, stale air blow against me. Each rotation of the blades reminded me of that horrible dream. *Time to get up,* I thought, turning my head and hearing her soft snores.

A strong smell of greasy food still lingered, making me

feel nauseous and restless. Getting up, I sat on the side of the bed, yawned, and reached for my phone on the nearby dresser. It was 10:27. Late, but not too late. Seeing my jeans on the floor, I slipped them on, feeling the rough texture of the fabric against my skin. "Time to drain the snake," I mumbled, heading to the bathroom.

Being a Saturday meant a day to chill and make more sales. Despite the previous day's strange events, I felt good about the approaching day. *It was over,* I thought. A new day, a new start. Forget the grinning bastard, the dreams, all of it.

Finished in the restroom, I walked down the hall toward the kitchen, still dazed from my slumber. Feeling off balance, my arm rubbed against one of the decorations along the wall. "Whoa there," I said, grabbing it before it fell.

Upon reaching my destination, I glanced around the space, idly scratching my leg, thirsty and a little hungry. Pulling the fridge handle, light flooded the room, casting an orange glow over the shadows. "There we go," I said, grabbing a can of grape soda and cracking it open.

The cold contents of the beverage were so refreshing that I drank the whole can in seconds. Taking sip after marvelous sip, I let out a fierce belch before it was empty, feeling refreshed. Shaking the can, I tossed it in the trash. Ducking back inside the icebox to find a snack, I rummaged around the fully stocked fridge. "Throw a little something on my stomach, then get back to bed," I said under my breath. Maybe an apple or an orange will give me some energy.

Deciding on something else to eat, I grabbed the bread and smoked turkey to make a great big sandwich. I'd run it off later, I supposed. That was when Amina's roommate exited her room and opened the curtains.

Light shone around the room, making me shade my eyes with my arm. "Damn, it's bright," I said. "You trying to blind me or something?"

"No, I'm not, Travis." Her sarcastic comment filled the room. "And good morning. Get any sleep?" she asked.

"A little. Your friend's stingy with the covers. She hogged the sheets the whole night. But what's up with you this fine morning? Are you about to make a run?"

"Yeah. I'm on my way to the gym, and then who knows."

"Trying to stay in shape, I see," I said, going back to grab the ingredients for my sandwich.

She looked at me strangely. "I'm surprised you have an appetite. If Amina pulled something like that on me, I'd be too upset to eat," she said.

Confusion gripped my face. "What are you talking about?" I asked over the sound of my phone vibrating in my pocket.

Looking like she was holding back a giggle, she turned the knob on the door. "You haven't seen it? The video of you that's going around?"

"No, is it bad?" I asked, letting the refrigerator close.

Standing halfway out the door, she looked amused. "You better see for yourself," she laughed bashfully.

Without a second to spare, I pulled out my phone. I was confused at first by what I was watching. "Huh?" I mumbled, but then it all became clear.

Her eyes were glancing at my phone. "Well, I'll leave you to it, and don't use all the mayo like you did last time. See ya," she said, slamming the door.

My eyes couldn't believe what they were seeing. It was

shaky and filmed from a poor angle, but there I was, bagging and selling Bianca the weed. The glaring brightness of the phone screen made the details unnervingly clear—every illicit exchange, every nervous glance. And then, to top it off, Marcus had tagged the school's administration office. I was royally cooked.

How could I miss him filming me? Was I that distracted by that girl's shape? But there I was, ogling her with my eyes. "Shit," I said. "What am I going to do now?" Here I was, thinking he had that goofy smile for Bianca, and he was recording me the whole time. I slammed the phone against my chest in frustration, still in disbelief.

Filming me unaware and then posting it on Instagram was low, really low. I flashed back to my friends cracking jokes when they visited, or the occasional sock on the door when Amina visited our room. I wasn't out to make Marcus's life miserable; I was just being me. Was his life so unbearable that he would pull something like this? I was the one pushing for him to live his life and even suggested that he help Bianca with her furniture.

I guess Marcus was angrier than I ever imagined and decided to get some payback. Why he would go to such extremes was beyond me. But after the fear left, I was pissed.

I read the comments, and they were all bogus. It only took reading a few before I knew where this was heading. Quickly gearing up, I left Amina's place, bracing myself for the confrontation with Marcus.

On the car ride over, I had to untag myself from the post to give my battery a rest. Alert after alert, from video calls to Facebook notifications. "Ding" never sounded so unpleasant in my life. And to make it worse, on campus, other students would point and whisper under their breath as I passed. Damn, this shit is spreading faster than COVID, I meditated.

I opened the door to my room, ready to pummel my roommate for pulling this. "You little shit," I said, marching inside. "I'm about to beat your ass."

My eyes deceived me, however. Looking perplexed, I found Marcus's side of the room emptied, his belongings gone. The drawers on his desk lay scattered, with little scraps of paper lying inside.

I stood there for a minute, with students gawking and talking under their breath. Grabbing the door, I slammed it as hard as I could. The vibrations shook the room, and the picture of Amina and me fell to the floor. I started to pick it up but decided to leave it where it fell. She's going to be pissed.

After some online investigation, I learned that Marcus had posted that video and left school. I was so enraged that moving away was the best thing he could have done because, at that moment, I wanted to beat the living shit out of him.

How could he pull a sucker move like this? Then not be a man and flee. "FUCK!" I yelled out into the empty room. As mad as I had ever been. Students knocked on the door after my outburst, but I ignored them. "Leave me alone," was my only reply.

Inside the dorm room, alone with my seething anger, my mind raced with choices. I knew not to sell out of my room, but I was running late, and now I could possibly be expelled.

I still didn't think it was a big deal, but the whispers I heard outside my door made me feel different. "They're going to kick him out; watch," someone said as they walked by.

"He's on scholarship for track too; I hope they let him stay." Some sympathetic voices rang out.

Amina was sending paragraph after paragraph, asking why Bianca was so flirtatious with me. Throwing around accusations like fastballs. Blaming me for things I hadn't done.

Women were an enigma to me, but I didn't text that back. In fact, I didn't text anything back. In the solitude of my dark room, I reflected on my plight. Overwhelmed, I lay on my back and drifted to sleep.

When I got brave enough to venture outside my room, I went to the restaurant, ordered some nuggets, and sat in the parking lot, trying to forget my problems. Tossing a nugget in my mouth, I knew I had messed up royally.

The messages flooding my phone were outrageous. One hundred fifty-four notifications and counting. The school would no doubt request a meeting on Monday.

Nine times out of ten, I would be kicked out. Shaking my head, I needed somebody to talk to. When I called Amina, I was sent directly to her voicemail. I left a brief message, telling her to call me back, which she never did.

I didn't want to deal with her mouth at the moment, but I needed to explain myself. Hoping she'd believe me, I left a voicemail. "Please call me back," I begged. Taking a long sip from my drink, I laid back in my seat. "Well, Travis, you win some, and you lose some," I said, feeling like shit.

The situation was fresh, and I needed to figure it out. When I called my friends, all they had were jokes and weed when I needed answers and a plan.

What would I tell the faculty? How could I explain it all? With no immediate answers flooding my brain, I just accepted it. Time to pay the price.

I was alone, it seemed, and I had never felt so abandoned before. Back home, I had my brother and granddad, before he passed, to give me advice. He and his euphemisms were always filled with wisdom. Here, I had no one to guide me. If I wanted to, I could call home, but I felt so bad that I just drove back to my room and sulked for a few hours while watching TV.

When things looked like this, I usually ran, and that's what I did that night. I needed to run away from my problems and my stupid decisions. Maybe the feel of the wind blowing against my face would help me feel better.

I went to the track and ran until my legs felt like linguine. Every lap I ran brought more distance and some clarity. I had made a mistake like many kids do; maybe the school would show some compassion. I could only hope, right?

When I was finished, I was damn near cramping when I saw that guy from the party—the one who bumped into me. It was still early Saturday evening, and the place was deserted. Everyone was out enjoying their college life, and this asshole had appeared to fuck with me. I'd take my frustrations out on him, I mused.

The silence of the locker room was eerie and haunting that night, with sounds of things settling throughout. The sudden pressure from a pipe or blurt from the fire detection system filled the air. It all had me on edge.

The bright lights were almost sickening with their intensity. The room was filled with hundreds of lockers with metal benches before them for resting and changing clothes. I slowly rose and walked toward the showers, where the stranger had gone.

"Where are you?" I sang out. "You picked the wrong one tonight."

My feet stuck to the moist floor as I looked for the creepy fucker who had been following me, and I wanted answers. Stupid pranksters trying to get views were about to get much more than internet traffic. While searching each row of lockers, I heard something close by that echoed out. A voice or a whisper. "When I catch you, it's on," I shouted. "I don't know who you are, or what sick game you're playing, but I'm going to fuck you up when I get my hands on you."

Leaving the locker room, I went toward the showers. The fluorescent lights were dim here, with the light shining down with an ill-looking pale glow. The walls were lined with showers, all sparkling clean and gleaming in the sickly light.

As I walked deeper into the room, I heard a noise. Something was scraping across the floor. A long, screeching sound that racked my nerves. I put my hands to my ears. "Who's there?" I called out into the empty shower, but there was no response, and the screeching came to an abrupt halt.

After a few seconds, I heard footsteps running. More than one. Then a shower, spraying water. I crept forward, intent on finding out who was behind this and exacting my revenge. Behind me, I heard more footsteps, closer sounding and almost on me. When I turned my head, all the showers came on, one by one, in sequence.

Shh, went one shower. *Shh,* went another, until all I heard was water cascading out of the spouts. It was deafening. The sounds of all that water rushing out caused fear to grow inside me.

The cool breeze brought by the ice-cold liquid was

freezing me to the bone. "Aye," I said, and I saw my breath before my eyes. "You're only making it worse for yourself," I said half-heartedly, with my voice rising.

The showerheads nearest me started pouring faster, the sound growing louder as more and more water gushed out. I stood frozen. When the final showerhead turned on, it drenched me. Then the drain started spitting water out from the floor like a geyser.

What was happening? If someone pulled a prank on me, they got me good. "Yo!" I called out. "Who's playing games with me?"

Standing there, waiting for a reply, I started to get fearful.

I braced up, cocked my fist back a little, and walked out of the showers, looking for whoever was trying to prank me. Behind me, the showers stopped. I was ready now. But after a minute or two, nothing happened. No one sprang out or tried to scare me.

Soaking wet, I grabbed a towel and dried myself off. These goofy college kids were always playing. "I hope you had fun, 'cause I didn't," I yelled.

"It's time to get out of here. Fuck this shit," I continued, grabbing my bag. Before I left, though, I looked around a bit, still alert. Unable to discern who was playing around, I cautiously exited the facility and went back to my room.

CHAPTER 5

FACING THE CONSEQUENCES

THE REST of my weekend was terrible. On Sunday, I stayed in my room and tried to study, even though my mind was distracted. I knew the school would contact me soon, and I dreaded it. Needing an excuse for what the video showed, I tried to come up with something, but I couldn't think of anything. "Travis, you got caught red-handed; it's time to man up and accept it," echoed in my mind.

The entire agonizing transaction was caught on camera. When I did step out of my room, girls were calling me a cheater, even though I hadn't cheated, which infuriated me. All the guys were calling me a "player" or a "ladies' man," like I had done all of this on purpose. Smiling and trying to keep a straight face, I accepted the false accolades and carried on, but inside, I was embarrassed. When I did call Amina, she told me to talk to Bianca because we were done.

My feelings were hurt and bruised. Along with that, there was trouble with my plug, the guy I got my weed from. "Dude, you're too hot to do business with right now. Maybe later, when the heat dies down," was all he texted.

So I was dry on the herb side. No girl, and about to get

kicked out of school. All of this felt so sudden and out of place, like someone had planned it. The one thing I still had was my car.

With the window down and the cool air blowing against my face, I cruised around the whole town until my gas tank was empty. The situation from earlier moved through my mind like a ghost. I knew the choice to sell weed on campus was risky, but a few others had done it, and nothing happened. Marcus had screwed me over big-time.

It appeared that I was going back home soon, a place I didn't want to return to without fulfilling any of my goals. My mom and brother would welcome me with open arms, but my feelings of being a disappointment to them were strong. I did have a car, but I got it through selling weed, something I could have done at home. I wanted a piece of paper that said I could follow rules and produce. Going home without having a diploma ate at me.

It was 6:39 a.m. when the email from the school's administration pinged my phone. I dug it out, read it, and continued on. Forget it, I thought. I'd deal with it later, as I exited my room and went on a jog. Maybe running would make me feel better about my upcoming meeting with the school administration.

Sitting in that office, waiting to meet with Mrs. Hernandez, was torture. It was cold and bright, and it felt like a ball was in my stomach. My two years at the school were replaying in my mind on a loop. Sitting there with my legs bouncing up and down, I knew I was screwed. I had gotten into trouble before, but never like this. All night I lay in bed, tossing and turning, dreading this moment. *Dumbass*, I thought to myself. What would my mom or brother say? Would they expect this, or would they treat me differently, you know? There were so many things in my head fighting for attention that I yearned for something to calm my nerves.

My mind shifted to Amina and our relationship. How she always was there for me, or fooling around with her after practice. That girl was there for me, and I had let her down. I went over the last serious conversation we shared, where she asked where I saw myself in five years. Well, Amina, this wasn't in my plans.

When Mrs. Hernandez opened the door, I was pulling down on my ear, lost in my mind. My body tensed with anxiety as I stood and entered her office. She was short, wearing burgundy-colored pants and a blouse, her hair tied back with her lips pursed. "Mr. Johnson, you do know why you're here, don't you?" she said as I took a seat.

The room was dull, full of wood and plants, with a large printer in the corner. On her desk were pictures and a nameplate with her name emblazoned across it. All I could smell was ink, with her loud, flowery perfume assaulting my senses. "No, I do not." I tried to act ignorant, even though her look let me know she had already seen through it.

"I'm sure your Instagram account was very busy over the weekend," she said, tapping at her phone. "Um, I don't know what you're talking about. I hardly check."

"Drop the act. You're not fooling anybody but yourself, Travis, and well, I'm disappointed," she interrupted.

"It was some weed; half the students and even some of the faculty smoke. It's legal." I pulled out the one excuse in my arsenal, hoping it would be enough.

She looked over at me from her desk, shaking her head.

"But the distribution or sale of psychoactive materials on school property isn't, and you know that."

I knew it was over when I heard that technical talk. I slunk back in my seat, turned my head, and waited for the rest to unfold. "I looked up your record, and it says you are a good student, competing to be on the dean's list, and a star athlete. Can I ask you a question?"

I shrugged. "Why didn't you get a job?" she asked.

I turned to her, with my dreams crushed. "Because I wanted a life too. Working at some coffee shop, or picking up after the basketball team in the evenings, would've killed my social life."

She sat up in her chair. "That's the problem with your generation; it's all about you and some perpetuated image you have in your mind. Living in some make-believe world. News flash—it's more complicated than that. 'That place' you've imagined doesn't exist."

"I don't believe in a made-up world, Ms. Hernandez. It was about having some time to myself to think. I tried a job, and I couldn't do it with school and having a girl. It was driving me crazy. Wake up, rush to practice and class, and all the while, my girl is fussing about spending time with her. Selling weed made my days easier." And it did. Working all the time was terrible for my mental health. Selling weed was way more manageable, and it let me socialize.

She shook her head and looked down at a picture on her desk. "I have a child your age, and your generation acts as if you have extra lives. Like you're Mario or some damned body. Let me tell you something, Mr. Johnson. There aren't any second chances, and in the 'real world,' when you die, that's it." Her voice was stern, but it also sounded like she cared a bit.

"Well, you know I have to expel you, but your record is so good, it's almost a shame," she said, looking at the computer screen. "I should follow the book, but I like you, and I want to try to help you."

Now I sat up in my seat.

"How about you leave our university and continue somewhere else?" she added.

"Huh?"

"I don't want to expel you," she explained. "But I can't have you stay on campus after it was recorded for the faculty to see." She placed her chin over her hands. "You're a good kid, you're just misguided. My advice is to transfer to a different university, and I won't damage your record. Just do me a favor, Travis."

"What's that?"

"Stop bringing your past with you. Leave Chicago behind, or at least the street part. It's too much at stake."

Her words were truthful, and all I could do was offer a bullshit excuse. "But it's hard, Mrs. Hernandez. Japanese kids are jumping off buildings from all the stress and expectations your generation places on us. I did what I did because it was all I knew," I said, hoping she would understand.

Eyes can tell a lot about a person, and Mrs. Hernandez's eyes let me know she was sympathetic. As she leaned back, thinking about the situation and staring at me, I felt like a lab rat.

"Maybe if it wasn't broadcast over the campus that way for the faculty to see, I would understand, but as of now, you have to leave, Mr. Johnson. I'm sorry."

The center of my chest caved in, and I zoned everything out after that. All those books and classes, combined with track meets and parties, were gone, finito as they say. I stood, head hung low, and exited her office. "Mr. Johnson, have a good day... and if you see Bianca out there, please send her in."

I walked up to Bianca, furious. "Did you set me up?" I asked.

Her face took a defensive look as she stepped back at my question, just as upset as I was. "No, Marcus planned all this by himself," she held her head down. "He even suggested I flirt with you, telling me you said I was cute. I figured you were interested."

"That fat fuck," was all I could muster.

Thinking back to how he was playing with his phone and that little speech he gave, it all made sense. Marcus was more clever than I gave him credit for. "Sorry, I just knew you set me up, and I..."

She placed a hand on my chest, pushing me aside. "Save it. I have to go inside and try to convince this lady to let me stay. I'm so pissed right now, I could scream."

I wished her luck with her appointment with Mrs. Hernandez, and exited the building, clouded with thoughts of the future and returning home.

With each agonizing step toward my car, my mind replayed the choices that led me here. I tried to find excuses, but the truth was a bitter pill. I knew what I was doing, and I chose the easy path. Sure, Marcus played his part, but the responsibility was mine to bear. My feet dragged along the pavement, kicking a rock or two as I walked, depressed. The cool air had no effect on me after receiving the news. "Maybe I should've gotten that Starbucks job and toughed it out," I said to myself.

I hopped in my car, feeling dejected. I blazed some weed and drove around to think. Hitting all the hangouts, I talked with my friends, never letting them know I had been kicked out. Every laugh was fake, and every handshake was false. I wondered if they could tell as we smoked and played 2K. While smoking, I decided to leave in the morning. Fuck this school, and fuck Marcus. I was going back home. So, after hanging out, I went to the gym, talked to the coach, and said my goodbyes.

My phone received a notification, alerting me out of my sleep. Reaching over to pick it up, I saw it was Marcus. I sat up, steaming, ready to read it and see what the fuck was going on. Because after disappearing without a trace, I wanted an answer to why he snitched on me in the manner that he did.

Call me, and I'll explain. That was all it said.

I called him and waited for him to answer. A few seconds later, a voice sounding frightened answered. "Hello? Travis," he whispered. "Before you start snapping, it's not like you think. You have to let me explain."

"I'm all ears, because as of right now, I've been kicked out of school, and I'm pissed. How could you film me and post that shit on Instagram?"

Silence for a few moments, then footsteps, followed by erratic breathing. "Are you okay?" I asked but didn't get an answer. I hung up the phone wondering what was happening, then another notification.

Meet me at the burger spot in 20 minutes, followed by another. *And don't be late.*

What the fuck was that? Was Marcus running from someone? Or was I tripping? In any case, I left for my car and went to hear what he had to say. And if I didn't like it, I'd beat the shit out of his bogus ass.

I pulled into the parking spot, surveying the area, not sure if it was safe. With him running from someone and that weird short dude stalking me, I didn't want to take any chances. After seeing that it was just me and a few students on a calm afternoon, I got out of my car and went inside the restaurant.

I saw him sitting at a booth from behind, recognizing his sweater and odd-shaped head from a distance. I pulled the door handle, letting the metal cool to the touch, and entered. My eyes were still peeled for any newcomers or anybody looking to cause me harm.

The smell of French fries was heavy in the air as I approached the bench across from him and took a seat. "Yo. What's up?" I said, taking a fry from his untouched tray of food. "Everything alright? You sounded like you were being chased earlier."

He picked up a fry and tossed it in his mouth. "Oh, I was trying to catch the professor and wanted to handle that before I met with you. Did you think something happened to me or whatever?"

"Kind of. The last few days have been interesting, to say the least," I said, looking around the restaurant. "What happened, bro? Because right now, the one thing keeping me from whipping your ass is my curiosity. Why film me and post that shit? I need an explanation, and it better be good, or else." My voice carried the threat.

He inched back with a concerned look and began to explain himself. "I'm so sorry about that, Travis. I didn't want to do that to you, but the person who told me to do it scared me, dude."

I inched forward and folded my arms around the booth. "What dude?" My face screwed.

"This short black dude, with all these gold chains and a tracksuit on, looked... evil to me and wouldn't stop grinning." He explained.

It was the same dude from before, the same man who bumped me at the party. "Did he have a goatee and shades on?" I asked, growing alarmed.

"Yeah. How did you know?"

"That motherfucker has sort of been stalking me." I rubbed my chin. "What else do you have to say?"

"The dude knew shit about me and my family. Telling me what my mother last spoke to me about and threatening my sister. I was scared as hell of him. So when he told me to arrange for Bianca to come through to the room, I filmed you as he suggested and posted it. I'm sorry, Travis, I didn't know what else to do." Marcus explained it in a breath. "Please forgive me."

"Dude, they kicked me out of school, and if it wasn't for Mrs. Hernandez, it would've been worse." I shook my head.

"Like I said, I apologize, but he knew shit no one could know but me. I had to. And then I rationalize everything. My conscience got the better of me, that's why I left like that." He said taking a bite from the burger in front of him.

I watched him chew his food and had another of his fries. Thinking. "So, have you seen him since? I want to talk to him. And don't trip about the filming stuff; he used you."

He paused, with a bit of bread falling out of his mouth. "You sure? Because this has been on my mind the whole weekend."

"Yeah, it's cool." I said standing to leave. "Just do me a favor."

He nodded. "Let me know if you see him." I said. "Now I have to go back to our room and pack."

━━

Later, when I returned to my dorm room, I called Amina and told her what had happened at the administrative office, and she rushed over, concerned for me. After the conversation with Marcus, I knew what happened and wasn't as mad as before. She wasn't even mad at the whole Bianca debacle and was quite sympathetic to my problems.

The closet's contents lay strewn across the bed, a jumble of jackets and shirts draped haphazardly, awaiting their turn to be folded. Bottles of cologne lay scattered among a sea of unworn jeans, their scents mingling in the air. Among it all, old socks and discarded underwear contributed to a musty undertone; creating a pungent aroma in the room.

"So, you're leaving," she murmured, sitting on my bed.

"Yeah," I turned, grabbing a trash bag.

"That bitch, Bianca, didn't have to leave school," she exclaimed. "They put her on academic probation. Why did they kick you out?"

"I told you, Marcus set her up too. Don't be mad at her. Be mad at me for lacking," I said. "I never sell weed out of the dorms anyway, because of that reason. Marcus just had it out for me."

"Why are you defending her?" she snapped."

She looked at me with an attitude and said, "Okay, I'm just saying, I don't like other women on my man."

I picked up a pile of shirts, feeling deflated. "And now you don't have to worry about that at all, for a while."

"Don't say that. We'll stay in contact, won't we?" She insisted, shoving the clothes aside.

"I suppose, but you know how that goes."

She looked up at me with tears playing in her eyes and hugged me tight, making me drop the bundle of shirts on the floor. I knew she liked me, and I must admit, it felt good to have that effect on someone—to be loved. But what was stronger were the feelings I felt back. I had never said those three words before to her, but the feelings I felt in the moment were strong. What began as a simple embrace grew with intensity as our bodies locked around each other like puzzle pieces over piles of clothes. In each other's arms, the world's complexities faded into the background, leaving us grunting and panting over each other like animals.

CHAPTER 6

FAREWELL

WHY DON'T you ever remember the start of your dreams? Why do you just find yourself inside a world, not knowing how you got there? You have no idea that you're no longer awake and have transitioned over. As the lights brighten, you find yourself in a different world, with different rules. Inside a dream, the lines between rationality and logic blur, and the impossible becomes possible. You might find yourself eating rock soup, or conversing with lost loved ones as if they were still alive. At the moment, it's easy to forget that none of what you're experiencing is real—just subconscious chatter from the depths of your mind.

The rock soup might symbolize your stubbornness and visions of your grandmother's regret for something you overlooked during the day. My dream, while lying next to Amina, wasn't like a typical dream. It had a distinct beginning; I didn't just become aware of this strange world. As soon as I closed my eyes, I felt like I was falling for eternity.

Plummeting through an endless black space. My lungs should have been raw from all the screaming I did, but to my surprise, they felt fine. That was the moment I knew I was dreaming; the moment I stopped yelling and let myself fall forever.

The sensation was euphoric as I dropped into the dark abyss. I felt freer than I ever had. Here, I could be without fear of consequences and embrace the weight of the surrounding blackness. Eventually, I saw the earth rushing towards me, and braced for impact. The wind whipped around my face as I plunged to the bottom of the cavern.

The pavement rushed to meet me, and unlike other dreams of falling, where I'd wake up with a fluttering heart, this time, I landed hard. Kicking up a cloud of dust shaped like a mushroom, I checked my body for pain. After realizing that there was none, I stood, dusted off my clothes, and looked around.

After I settled, I found myself on a track field under a giant moon, its enormous craters staring down at me. As I walked, it followed me like it was attached. I paused to look at it, and it swelled to encompass the entire sky. It was breathtaking. Juxtaposed against the track field, with the haunting moon above me, I felt like a character in a video game.

It felt strange to be 'awake' in a dream, using my rational mind. The craters looked real, and the stars shone next to them, like glittering drops of light. "What is this place?" I breathed out into the silence.

I stood there, feeling the wind of the dream world fold around me as I moved. In the far distance, I noticed a store that didn't exist in reality. With each step propelling me on, I ran towards the store, driven by a strange curiosity. When it felt like I would never reach it, I did what every lucid dreamer does. Flew. I leaped into the air, moving like I was swimming in soup. Colors swirled around me as I sped, and soon, the store was right in front of me. I glided down like a bird in the air that caressed me.

Landing, I grabbed the door handle, feeling its familiar coldness. Through the door's glass, I saw him—the unsettling guy from the party and the parking lot, his smile too wide, his eyes too bright. He felt off, like a whisper would make him disappear. As he waved, a rush of blood went to my head, I let go of the handle, recoiling.

I turned to escape, but froze. There he was again, right before me. How could he be both outside the door and behind the counter? My thoughts spun, struggling with the impossibility.

Then, reality snapped back. I woke up, the dream fragmenting into wisps of memory. Disoriented, I noticed Amina slipping out of the room, her silhouette moving with quiet grace. Confusion and concern mingled within me. Was she leaving because of something I did in my sleep?

Reaching for my phone, I saw that five minutes had passed since I last checked, but it felt like hours lost in that dream world. My mind was full of questions. Was this just a bizarre series of dreams, or something more troubling? The line between dream and reality blurred, leaving me in a state of uneasy wonder. Should I be worried about these dreams, or was my mind playing tricks on me?

—

After a night of restless dreams, I began packing. I went to the local big-box store and bought contractor bags for my belongings, a bag of chips, and a water bottle. I planned to call my mom on the way home and drop the news on her about my expulsion. She'd understand, but I didn't want to break her heart. A college degree meant something to her.

She knew about the illicit activities I was doing to get by but didn't fuss. Our neighborhood gave us a unique worldview —winning at all costs. College life had opened my eyes, but I was still naive. More than anything, I wanted to avoid disappointing her.

In the self-checkout line, the feeling of being watched returned. Pain shot down my leg, making me wince. The lady in front of me turned and asked, "Are you alright?" "Sure, it's just a muscle I pulled while running track," I lied, as the feeling of being watched intensified. She offered advice on muscle care and rest, then resumed waiting. The pain worsened, but I didn't want to show it. My eyes scanned the store for the man from my dreams. As the pain subsided, I stepped forward, growing more frightened by these unexplained pains and dreams.

Something was happening here. It had been two days since the last episode, and I'd forgotten about it. But standing there, buying more trash bags, the sensation returned with force, blurring reality with dreams. As I left the store, I couldn't get my mind off the pain that inflicted me a short while ago. My hands trembled on the steering wheel, my gaze darting around the empty parking lot. Was this all a mistake—an illness playing tricks on my mind? With the radio playing, I drove back to Amina's place to say goodbye.

As I walked toward her, I felt a pang of regret over the loss of our relationship. She stood outside her apartment, hugging herself, trying to contain her emotions. After my conversation with Mrs. Hernandez, who made the consequences of my staying clear, leaving seemed the only option. My days at the university were ending. I could stay at Amina's apartment for a while, but then what? Being a local dealer and driving around making deliveries all day with no real plan? That didn't appeal to me; I didn't want to be a nobody.

Amina fidgeted with a napkin, her voice shaky. "I can't believe you're leaving already," she murmured. "Just... can you stay a few more days? Maybe you can sort things out; stay here. Katrina wouldn't mind, you know?"

"I've gone over this a million times in my head, Amina. Staying... it's just not an option. I'd feel... well, you know." I hesitated, touching her cheek. "I've got things to sort out, stuff to figure out about myself. It's hard, but I need to do this alone. You understand, right?"

Her eyes brimmed with tears as she threw her arms around me. I could feel her small body against mine, trembling and struggling for breath. I wrapped my arms around her, holding her close, feeling the reality of our separation.

"Goodbye, Travis. Don't forget about me," she whispered into my chest.

Turning away, my steps heavy, I felt the weight of our time together, making each step difficult. I glanced back once, seeing her framed by the doorway, before forcing myself to walk away.

Driving off, my head was filled with memories— meeting Amina, our conversations, my time at school, and all the remarkable people I'd met. At the start of my junior year, I had made a mistake, and now I was saying my farewells. I stopped by a few friends' places to wish them luck at the meet tomorrow. It was a bittersweet experience that would shape many of my future decisions. At that moment, I think I understood what it meant to be an adult.

CHAPTER 7

HOMECOMING

IT WAS 5:14 pm as I parked my car in front of Mom's house. Tired, but happy to be finished with the long drive. While positioning the car in the space, I looked up and saw my brother and mother sitting on the steps, enjoying the mild weather. It felt familiar and warm to see them together on the porch like that. Like, nothing had changed since I left, and I was welcomed.

Looking at the house, I felt melancholic. The place was a duplex-styled home, which my grandfather left my mom when he passed. The fence was rickety, the grass was browning, and the old hose lay curled on the lawn. I thought of games we played and family gatherings. Running with cousins, fighting, and playing hide and seek. Deep down, it felt good to be back, though I tried to hide it at the time.

Calm, whose real name was Malcolm, started dancing down the steps to the thumping music I was playing. I raised the volume even louder and hopped out, giving my brother a big, proper hug and shaking his hand about a hundred times.

"Welcome back, little brother." He jumped around. "How have you been? You doing alright?"

Looking at me in a cheerful mood, I chuckled and grinned at seeing my brother for the first time in a long time. "Yeah, man, no complaints from me."

My mom was looking from her seat on the porch, in her nurse's uniform, with tears in her eyes. "My boys are back together," she shouted, smiling. "Now come and hug your momma, boy." She continued, sounding like an old lady.

Feeling bashful for some reason, I ducked my head and said, "Sheesh, here I come."

Mom was in her fifties and wore a ponytail tied to the back. A workaholic who was rarely at home, I was pleased to see her. Calm and I kept doing our goofy dance for a few more seconds, then I ran upstairs and gave her the biggest hug I could.

A car drove by, and I peered down to see Calm sitting inside my vehicle with his fingers twisting every knob and dial like a mad scientist. "Aye!" I screamed out. He looked up for a second, chuckled, and kept doing what he was doing. He was a year and a half older, but let him tell you, he had years on me.

Mom, on the other hand, couldn't stop smiling. It had been a while since I'd left, and she was overjoyed at my return. I scanned the neighborhood, seeing that it had changed a bit while I was gone; most of the vacant lots were filled with new homes, and a couple Mercedes and Cadillacs were parked out front. It looked funny to me and unfamiliar. *I guess I'll get used to it*, I mused.

We hauled armfuls of clothes and my precious keepsakes across the lawn, piling them up in the vestibule. Dust filtered through the sunlight beaming in from the screen door, as if no one had set foot in there for months. Calm coughed into his hand until Mom swatted him with her dishrag, telling him to "quit his foolishness." The familiarity of their silly banter wrapped around me.

As we worked, we fell into reminiscing about misadventures from our youth—close calls with cops, lucky wins shooting dice, dreams as big as stadiums during hot summer nights. With each memory, the years I'd been away melted further into the dark corners of the room until the space itself welcomed me back like an old friend.

"Yo, remember when you were scared of the police, nigga?" Calm cried out.

"They had just taken away Unc." I laughed, the memory turning bitter in my mouth. "I thought we were next."

My eyes darted out the window, watching a patrol car creep by, and the laughter caught in my throat. Nothing had changed. In this neighborhood, the police still lurked around every corner.

Calm noticed my tension as the cops rolled down the street and made a joke. "Travis, nobody's looking for your brainy ass... relax."

His tone shook me from my thoughts. I forced a grin. "Well, what about the time you lost the light bill money? Ma almost killed you," I mused.

"Somebody took that, not lost, little bro."

"Yeah, right, you dropped it at the store. The man said it."

Calm stopped laughing, getting serious. "Aye, that's enough," I heard my mom say, hitting me on the arm.

We dropped the last of my things on the floor and went inside. Forgetting about our brief spat and enjoying each other's company, I strolled around.

I couldn't believe it. Everything was as I remembered it.

The living room, with the couches still in plastic, sat against the wall. The picture of Jesus near the door. A white clock sitting on top of a shelf filled with crystalline angels. The rug, the table, everything.

At that moment, something delightful hit my olfactory nerves. Taking a deep inhale, I picked up on my mom's home cooking. It smelled like those good Sundays when she had a day off and would cook feasts for us as kids. I rushed through the house to see her stirring a pot of something inside the kitchen.

On the stove was a tin foil pan of baked macaroni, a pot of cabbage, and some cornbread with big hunks of butter. Besides it, there was a bowl of her famous fried chicken, looking as crispy as any restaurant. I licked my chops, hugged her again, and sat. The smell made my mouth water. Looking at all the food my mother had cooked for my arrival, I felt blessed and loved. No dreams or strange men with haunting eyes invaded my thoughts. Being around my family made me forget it all. And the look in my mother's eyes—well, that was what I needed at that time.

She placed the bowl of chicken on the table, and I reached for a crunchy piece. "Eh eh," she said, tapping my arm with the spoon. "Wash your hands, first. You know better."

My big-headed brother walked in and washed his hands beside me, pushing me like he used to when he was younger.

"Stop fooling around and sit down and eat before I have to go to work," I heard my mom say while shoving Calm back. "I missed a shift making this food for you I hope you like it." She dragged her chair against the floor. Getting settled, she made her plate. "Now what happened at school? And don't leave out anything."

I put my head down. Even though she knew I was selling herb, I was still embarrassed. "Can we talk about something else, please?" I groaned.

Ma's facial expression softened when she looked into my eyes. I guess she saw the regret I felt and cut me some slack. "Later," she smiled.

It felt good to see my family and to be back home. Hearing my mother fuss was like music to my ears. I ate, devouring as if I hadn't eaten in a while, and was going back for seconds. The macaroni was so cheesy, I couldn't help myself.

Ripping a chicken wing in half, Calm looked at me with fat, greasy lips. "Glad you're back, little brother. It was getting boring without your sad face ass around." Before grabbing a napkin and wiping his mouth.

"Yeah, yeah," I grumbled, shoveling mac and cheese in my face.

Setting down the napkin, looking satisfied, he asked. "What's on your mind?"

"You know, bro, I wish I-"

He cut me off. "Man, fuck those teachers at that bullshit school." He paused, thinking about what he wanted to say. "Man, listen, they don't know how we live around here. The struggles we deal with. Every time you leave the crib could be your last." He said. "When Ma told me what you did, I said no big deal. You're a fighter, always has been."

Calm was practical and a realist. Always seeing things in their raw form and expressing them. I thought about it, but disagreed. I knew being back was a mistake, but I kept it to myself.

"I know, but I still wish I was still there. If you knew how sweet I had it, you'd wish you were there with me."

After a while, Ma got up, scraping her plate into the

trash. "Boy, you're back, and that's all that matters," she said, walking over to hug me. "Don't worry about it, pray, and don't sit on your ass. An idle mind is the devil's workshop." She grabbed her phone off the counter and hugged me one last time. "Talk to you later." Then she was off, not giving me a chance to respond.

We sat and talked further. I told him what college was like, and he told me about his kids. Eventually, Calm wiped his mouth and stood, leaving his plate behind. "Yo, bro," I said, pointing at the plate.

He looked back, "I ain't finished yet, and plus, I got something to show you." He motioned for me to follow him.

But as we walked upstairs to where our bedrooms were, the way that railing felt under my hand gave me this sinking feeling, like I was here for good.

With him leading, he turned and went into his dungeon, as he called it. A place he never invited us to when we were younger. It was dark, musty, and messy. Clothes were everywhere. It looked like a bomb had gone off—real talk. Eyeing the closet, he went inside, the creaking hinges adding to the suspense. With deliberate care, he pulled out a uniform covered in plastic and lifted the protective covering.

"Dude," my brother said with his eyes glistening. "I got a little promotion at the gig." Looking like he was exposing top secret information, in a quiet voice, he spilled his news. "I might be able to pull some strings and get you hired." He grinned, his earrings reflecting the light coming through the blinds.

My eyebrows raised as I thought about it at that moment. I could use a job, I thought, but I was determined to return to school. Being in the hood wasn't healthy for me. Being away at school gave me bigger ambitions and the means to achieve them. Meeting different types of people opened my eyes to the world.

Still, I smacked his hand and shook it, happy for him. "Congratulations! One of us has some good luck around here." I held my head down.

Sensing my apprehension, he just smiled, pulled out a blunt, and offered me a hit, which I declined. "Well, the offer stands. Just let me know, and I'll do what I do. They love me at the gig," he grinned.

We stood talking for a bit before I decided to go reacquaint myself with my bedroom. I left him there, blowing weed smoke onto his new uniform, and shaking my head. "That dude's a trip," I said to myself, and I disappeared to my own dungeon.

CHAPTER 8

GETTING REACQUAINTED

THE FAMILIAR SIGHTS and smells overwhelmed my senses as I stepped into my childhood bedroom for the first time in years. The closet door still hung open, unchanged since the day I'd packed my bags for college. Even the crumpled pack of blunts lay in the exact same spot by the trash, as if frozen in time.

I sank down onto the creaky mattress, bouncing, and chuckled under my breath. Judging by the layer of dust coating every surface, my workaholic mom hadn't set foot in here since I left. My brother Calm never had reason to poke around my room either. Why no one had bothered to clean my space bewildered me. Maybe they wanted to leave it as I did, which gave the impression that I hadn't left at all.

Feelings of awkwardness rushed over me as I sat. Attempting to shake the mood, I walked over to my desk and computer, rubbing my hands across the surface of the screen. It was outdated, but it had some old games and a copy of Fruit Loops on it. I dusted off the accumulated grime, turned it on, and laughed at my desktop wallpaper.

Some anime characters greeted me, making me feel nostalgic for simpler times.

On the desk next to the screen was an old watch. The bezel faded, and the quiet tick that accompanied it was silenced. Disappointed, I held it to my ear, realizing that it had stopped functioning. It was my dad's, and I cherished it with its chipped paint and worn band. I found it in a shoe box when Ma redecorated after Granddad died.

Speaking of my dad, the little information I did know came from the streets, which wasn't much. They said he was a heartless individual who made a couple bad choices. My grandfather, on the other hand, hated him because he got his daughter pregnant and was working for the local dealer. Marriage was what he wanted for her, but that never worked out.

I put the watch on and strapped it, fastening it tight and secure. I remembered daydreaming about what my dad was like when I was younger, wearing the watch. The things he liked, or foods he preferred would fill my mind while watching TV. Turning it over, it looked good on my wrist, so I kept it on. Maybe I'd go to the store and buy a battery, I mused.

The story was that my dad was killed before I was born, and like I said, I didn't know much about him. Mom would always get dramatic when we brought him up, threatening tears or anger. "He died in the army," she'd say, but that was a lie. It didn't mean much to me as a kid, but as I got older, it irritated me that she wouldn't talk about him.

With the timepiece snug on my wrist, I brought up the rest of my things, not bothering to unpack. I didn't plan on staying that long, so I slung the bags of my clothes into the closet, along with my other things. If everything went as I figured, I'd be out of here in a month.

Calm slipped around the corner, still smoking his blunt, the pungent trails funking up my room. "So, Travis, how does it feel to be back? Talked to X yet?"

X, or Xavier, was my best friend from high school. We hadn't spoken to each other in a while, but hearing my brother bring him up, I got curious about what he was up to.

"Nah, not yet," I said. "Is he still 'wild' like before?"

"And you know it, that fool always be in some shit. If you do link with him, be careful," he said, taking a big pull from the blunt in his hand.

"Bro, I already know."

Calm glanced at me with a serious look, blowing the yellowed smoke out. "For real, he's always hanging around questionable cats. The hot headed kind too. Protect yourself when you're with him, and watch yourself."

The grim realities of being home had set in as I looked into his concerned face. The constant threat of violence was heavy, and everyone had to be protected. Hell, staying around here was like a Clint Eastwood movie. The only things missing were the whistle and tumbleweed.

"It's like that?" I asked.

Calm was protective of us and wanted to make sure we were safe. "Hell yeah. You gotta be safe, little brother," he let out with a hint of caution.

After the warning, my brother dipped out and left me to ponder what I had returned to. See, the streets of Chicago were always wild, but it seemed that in my stint away from home, things had gotten worse. Despite the nice cars and rehabbed homes, violence was still prevalent, and I'd have to navigate it with precision if I wanted to survive.

I dug out my trusty old Bluetooth speaker, played some tunes, swept, and made my bed. I retrieved some clean sheets, putting them on the bed, and I felt a little better about returning home. I missed school and whatever, but I'd be good here until I could get back to school.

After tidying up, I ran downstairs, looking into the 'fridge to get a drink. Pulling out an empty container of Kool-Aid, I'd have to make some more if I wanted any. After making it, I poured myself a tall glass, adding cubes of ice, and then made my way to the front porch.

It was the beginning of fall, and a few trees were turning brown. Neighbors were out on their porch in the near evening, in jackets or sweaters. The wind was starting to pick up, but I didn't mind. Sitting out here brought back a lot of memories—some good, some bad. Like when my granddad would sit out here drinking a beer, reminiscing about earlier times.

Sipping my drink, I scrolled through my phone, searching for Xavier's number. I knew I hadn't talked to him since I graduated, but I was trying to move on and focus on my future, and holding onto the past wasn't helping. It was how I coped with being away. To gain something, you sometimes have to let go of things that hinder you. It was sad in certain instances, but to build something, you sometimes had to destroy what was in its place, or move it out of the way. All those old relationships with people who weren't around me felt something like that.

With the phone on speaker, I called and hoped that it would ring. Dun dun dun dun, it repeated before the voice-mail came on.

Ending the call, with a smirk on my face, I sent him two texts, one after another: Hey, it's Travis. Answer your phone.

Then I waited, watching neighbors wander by, bundled up against the early autumn chill. I missed so much being away at college, I thought while waiting for a reply. But part of me was also dreading all the old drama and danger that came with this place.

My phone buzzed with an address and an emoji telling me to come to where he was. Though it was a few blocks away, I was not apprehensive about going. Thinking it over, however, I decided to slide over and see what my homie had been up to since school.

Calm was standing by the refrigerator when I told him where I was headed. He handed me some weed and a Budweiser for my journey and told me to be careful once again. With a nod of thanks, I secured the offerings and said my farewells, reminding him to take care as I stepped out into the night, keeping my head on a swivel.

When I arrived, Xavier was waiting by the curb with a cup and a cigarette in his hand. The look on his face was pure mischievousness. He was dressed in black with tan boots on and a small gold chain, with a picture of some deceased friend or family member. I couldn't tell which from this far. "Travis, is that you?" Xavier called out as he walked across the sidewalk, carrying a red cup. The streetlights were silhouetting his lean frame against the night. I flashed the headlights twice, and he angled toward the idling car, a surprised grin breaking through his hard expression.

He wrenched open the passenger door, the overhead light revealing his black bomber jacket and the glinting chain around his neck. As he collapsed into the seat, the sour stench of weed and liquor washed through the car.

"Damn boy, I almost didn't answer the phone with your ghosting ass." Xavier's voice rang inside the car. His bloodshot eyes watched me from the passenger seat, awaiting some explanation.

I rubbed my chin, feeling the words catch in my throat. "You know, if I hadn't bounced like I did after graduation, I might've never made it out."

Xavier snorted in disbelief. "You could have at least picked up the phone every now and then? Lots of wild shit has been popping off since you dipped on us." His gaze held mine for a moment before sliding away toward the row of run-down houses lining the block.

In the brief silence, I followed his eyes down the dark street. A faint bass throbbed from an unseen party, while shadows of locals passed beneath the yellow glow of street lamps. This neighborhood hadn't changed. But Xavier had. The laugh lines I remembered were replaced by a wary tension around his mouth and hardness in his eyes—subtle shifts that spoke of dangers I'd been shielded from while at school. A pang of regret pierced my relief at seeing an old friend. I had ignored more than his calls over the past few years while focusing on my future.

"No doubt, we have a lot of catching up to do," I replied.

I didn't have any other explanation, so I rolled up the weed my brother gave me. The silence was awkward and filled with unspoken angst. We hadn't seen each other in two years, and we both didn't know what to say. His aura, if you will, was somehow darker, like he had seen something. "You picked a good day to come back, bro," he said, sipping from the red cup he carried in his hand.

"Oh yeah," I said as I sprinkled the weed on the cigar.

"Yeah, nigga. This little get-together is bananas, bro. You should come in for a bit and see everyone; they're going to trip when they see you."

I licked the leaf, looking over at the building. "Let me finish rolling up, and we can slide inside," I said, fumbling with the blunt.

As soon as I entered, I blazed up, and Xavier stood by my side with a menacing look. The music was playing, a card game was going on, and most people I grew up with were enjoying themselves. It felt just like old times. The room was big, with a gang of people inside. Music was blasting, and people were talking and enjoying themselves. It felt like old times.

I blew the smoke out, waiting for somebody to notice me. Xavier cleared his throat, trying to get everybody's attention. That's when a young woman threw a balled-up piece of paper at Xavier.

"Sit your corny ass down, Xavier," was all I heard, followed by laughter.

Xavier, smiling, walked toward the girl, yelling at her, and started laughing as well. I followed behind through the thick room, bumping into people while the multicolored LED lights flashed and pulsed. No one recognized me as of yet, and I was disappointed when I heard a voice shouting, "Is that who I think it is?" followed by a bunch of "Oh shits" and "Get the fuck out of here's."

"What's good? How you been?" followed by the occasional "Nah," was my reply. I swear, I must've shaken a hundred hands that night at that gathering. I saw all the guys from track, mirroring Xavier, who was aged and hardened. I also saw a couple girls I went to school with and a few new ones I wouldn't mind getting to know. It was the most fun I had in two years. Don't get me wrong, college was new and intriguing, but this hood shit was on a different level.

Anything could happen at any time. Just being here was

like a drug. This was one of the main reasons I left. Every day can't be a party, not if you want to do something impressive with your life.

Eyes low and high out of my mind, I stood on clumsy legs when I noticed Xavier's brother waving at me to come holler at him. The weed we'd been smoking was like thunder, pounding my senses. I stood on my feet, letting the dank air wash over me, then walked a few steps. Rubbing my chest like I was smearing on Vic's Vapor Rub, my free hand met his with a loud crack.

We talked a bit, with him asking about my mom and what I was doing in school. I responded by not telling him much but listening as he detailed his adventures in the hood. Xavier's brother was the real thing in the streets—a legit hustler. When he was around, we all felt safe.

Seriously, this dude showed us how to maneuver as kids. When we didn't know up from down, he showed us the ropes. He used to hang out with Calm, but they fell out a while ago over some chick. I thought it was goofy to let a girl come between them, but Calm ended up getting her pregnant. Not once, either, but twice.

We stood near the back of the room when someone entered, and all in attendance turned to look at who sauntered in. Keisha, my ex from high school. With more curves than the letter 'S', she was legit, in my eyes. A couple of dudes looked at her with lustful eyes and thoughts of having her. She was still attractive as hell and looked older as well, wearing a skintight body suit and Jordans. The shy Catholic schoolgirl I once knew had disappeared, leaving a confident beauty in her wake. The same eyes and cheerful demeanor remained.

She wore her hair in short locks now and wore makeup; something she never did in high school. We locked eyes, and we both smiled. Keisha turned her head with a manufactured attitude, almost daring me to follow. I went after her, but Xavier's old brother held me back and called Xavier over.

"Holler at your boy first; she'll be around, trust me," he said.

━━

Later, I sat on the back porch, smoking a cigarette with some of the guys. I don't smoke often, but I was stressing about school and listening to what they were up to while I was away. The young men were my age or younger and savage.

The stories they shared with me were gruesome and made my stomach turn. They thought they were impressing me, and I almost hurled. House robberies, murders, and baby mamas were all they talked about. I had changed too much—learning about finance and running for the school. Their problems were life and death, and mine were petty in comparison, or at least it felt that way. Maybe Mrs. Hernandez was right, and I was taking unnecessary chances.

While they were catching me up, I detached myself from the conversation; it didn't feel right. When Keisha came out of the screen door, I said my goodbyes and approached her, happy to leave the small gathering.

Standing under the porch light with a cup in her hand, she glowed. to me. My mind flashed to the past and how she hurt me, but I stuck the images in a box and buried them for the moment. By the time I got to where she stood, she had sat down and crossed her arms under her breasts. Her curvy body brought back good memories, and her smile almost made me forget about my issues with her.

I tried to hug her, but she balled her fist and swung at me. "I should kick your ass, Travis," she grumbled under her breath at me. "Why did you leave like that? Huh?"

I moved out of the way of her weak punches and grabbed her arms. "Calm down, shorty, before you hurt yourself," I said to her.

I looked into her light brown eyes, and she started giggling. "Ooh, I hate you," she said, snatching her arms back in a fighting stance.

"Let me explain before you start swinging again with your feisty ass."

The music was bumping in the background, with drugs and bad decisions all around. I couldn't chill here; there was too much going on, and it was low-key dangerous. Thinking that one of these guys did something to somebody, I was ready to leave.

I looked around, eyebrow's raised, and asked, "Wanna dip? My car is right out front. We can talk and get caught up."

Keisha looked me up and down, considering my offer, her eyes hinting at other things. After a few seconds, she picked up her drink and followed me inside.

She said she had to tell her friends that she was leaving with me first, and use the restroom. I nodded, and I went into the living room, looking for Xavier. He waved at me as soon as I entered. "You look like you just saw Keisha," he said.

"Yeah, we're about to leave," I smirked.

"I knew you were going to reconnect or something," he said, looking disappointed. "Y'all finna leave?"

"Yeah, bro... It's kind of crowded in here," I said.

He shifted on his feet. "Well, don't be a stranger, dude, and hit my line. We got a lot to catch up on."

Our hands came together, doing a handshake that only we knew. A series of complicated gestures we made in school. "I got you, Xavier. And don't worry, I'll hit your line."

I leaned against the wall as he disappeared into the crowd. Scanning the living room, I waited for Keisha to emerge, feeling a bit impatient. Laughter and lively chatter filled the room as people mingled and drinks flowed. Out of the corner of my eye, a figure caught my attention—one that made my chest tighten.

It was him—the strange man—that had been following me. Here, he looked out of place in an immaculate tracksuit and flashy watch, his smile somehow both magnetic and chilling. I watched, transfixed, as partygoers flocked around him, hanging on to his every word.

"Who is that guy?" I asked a girl refilling her cup beside me.

"That's Lucky," she said, raising her eyebrows. "You heard of him? Dude's a legend around here. And he's loaded. Want me to introduce you?"

"Nah, I'm good," I said.

However, I couldn't pull my gaze away from his hypnotic presence. Some instinct told me to turn and leave, yet I felt myself drawn closer through the crowd, as if in a trance. Before I knew it, I stood face-to-face with those penetrating eyes and a too-wide grin. "Well, well, well. Hello there, Travis," he purred, his voice lyrical. "So nice of you to join our little gathering."

My heartbeat stuttered. "How do you know my name?" I stammered. "And why do you keep showing up around me?"

With a casual wave of his hand, the people surrounding Lucky dispersed as if on cue, leaving us alone. "Come now; there is no need for suspicion," he said, almost inaudible. "Did I not mention we are old family friends? You must have me confused with someone else."

Lucky's smile didn't falter. "Our eyes play tricks sometimes, do they not? I can assure you, I am no stalker." He leaned in.

"Nah, they don't, and my eyesight is straight." I steadied my nerves, glaring into those hypnotic eyes. "What are you doing here?"

"I'm well known around here, or haven't you heard? The neighborhood loves me," he said. "We need to speak. I have an old friend who's dying to meet with you."

"I'm not meeting anybody. As a matter of fact, I didn't want to meet your spooky ass," I said.

"You have to calm down, Travis. All that apprehension isn't healthy, you know."

This man was beyond irritating, causing the hairs on my arm to stand the longer he spoke. From behind, I heard Keisha talking with her friends, and I was ready to end this conversation.

But before I could disengage, he grabbed my arm. "I don't want to hold you up, but later, I'll explain everything. Now go, enjoy yourself before that pretty girlfriend comes searching."

I trembled with adrenaline, fear, and fury, warring within me. I wanted to grab Lucky by his expensive lapels and punch him, but I held back. As if reading my raging thoughts, Lucky chuckled.

"No need for violence, my friend. Rest assured, we will chat again soon." His gaze bore into me. "But for now, I think we should part ways."

Before I could respond, Keisha's voice cut through the din as she emerged from the hallway. His attention shifted from mine in an instant, his unsettling presence evaporating into the pulsing crowd. But questions still screamed in my mind as Keisha took my hand, guiding me outside. I felt Lucky's smiling eyes follow me out the door, as unease swirled in the pit of my stomach. Our encounter was far from over.

Keisha's presence shifted the air. I felt her hand; firm and reassuring, grasp mine, pulling me back from the edge of confrontation. Without a word, but with a look that spoke volumes, she guided me away. The background hum of the party seemed to swell as we moved, putting distance between us and Lucky. His presence lingered like a shadow, but in Keisha's determined grip, I found strength. We left, not in retreat, but in a silent pact of defiance.

"Everything alright?" She questioned.

I didn't answer her.

As I walked out of the house, his eyes locked on mine as Lucky continued to tell his legendary story. It was like the world slowed down as he paused and smiled. I grabbed the doorknob to leave, and he smiled deeper and more sinister. Keisha called him a creep and went out the door, unaware of the intense conversation I had just had with him. I asked her if she knew him, and she shook her head.

At that moment, I knew something wild would go down, and I didn't want to be around to witness it. The neighborhood had changed since I left, but much of it stayed the same. If you got that feeling that violence was about to erupt, it was best if you listened and got the hell out of the way.

CHAPTER 9

THE DRIFT

BEFORE I GO ANY FURTHER, let me tell you how Xavier, Keisha, and I first met. How we all met each other and became friends, and as far as Keisha is concerned, much more. It was a turning point in our lives, and for the story to be understood, it has to be told in detail.

It all began during my freshman year, an experience that turned out to be alright now that I look back on it. So much has changed since then, and we have all done things and matured. But back then, we were fresh-nosed, with milk behind our ears.

As I transitioned from grammar school, I was inexperienced, almost like a novice. I'd never had a girlfriend and never ventured into the world of smoking weed, or anything, for that matter. I guess you would call me a nerd. In my younger days, I watched anime and read books. Getting lost in the world of authors was what I thought of as fun. That, and video games. The world of gang activities and the like didn't interest me.

Most people in my neighborhood were already playing with the police, which my grandfather advised me against.

"Boy, don't hang with those bad-ass kids; they're trouble," he'd say. Or "that's because nobody loves them." At the time, it was strange. But later on, as I got older, I knew what he meant. Any other kid would've rebelled, but I listened. My grandfather had been in the army, and I respected him like a father.

So I stayed to myself, reading and trying to defeat the last boss of whatever game was popular. By the time I got to high school, I was a shy, observant teen. Kind of tall and lanky, with a temper.

I remember getting off the bus the first day. It was rainy, and stepping off with a gang of students felt like lining up for an amusement park ride. Or a nightclub.

I had never seen so many kids all at once. The seniors seemed almost like adults, wearing makeup and high-heeled shoes. It was all so new to me. With their expensive clothes and gang signs everywhere, it all made me feel inadequate.

During this time, my mom was just getting clean and starting her new job. So that meant she couldn't afford the latest fashions. Lucky for me, I had Calm's hand-me-downs. With him being a hustler and going to a different school and all, I could wear all the nice clothes that he deemed out of style.

On the second day of classes, lost and in need of directions, I asked a skinny kid where the restroom was. He pointed me in the right way, and I was off before I peed myself. I rushed, determined to get there before the second bell rang.

As I entered, the smell of piss and weed smoke engulfed me. While trying to get to the stall, I bumped into this short, dark kid, Xavier. The dude must've had an attitude because he pushed me back with aggression. Now, as I said, I wasn't a fighter, but I'd heard from Calm to fight, or I'd be picked on. I didn't want that to happen, so I punched him in the face. Quick and powerful. Man, that sent it up.

With the second bell about to ring, the halls were deserted, giving us free rein to whip each other's asses. In my mind, it wasn't just a fight, but a message to any other student who might challenge me.

He'd throw a punch, and I dodged it; I'd lunge, and he'd push me off of him. When we finished our gladiator's bout, we'd both have bloody mouths and noses. When the security guard grabbed us, we looked a mess. Both of us were huffing and puffing as students peeked out of their classrooms, watching as we were escorted to the administration office.

After the woman in the office reviewed our records, embarrassment was written all over our faces. Oome to find out, we had more in common than we thought. Looking him up and down, I felt bad for punching him like I did. The woman cut us some slack, opting not to suspend us, and I was surprised. That fight worked out for both of us, though, because the other students knew we'd fight if we had to.

Over the next few weeks, Xavier and I became inseparable best friends. We refused to tolerate disrespect from each other or anyone else. We bonded and never saw the need to join gangs or cliques. I discovered that he lived not far from me, and that was perfect. I would walk to his house before school, and his mom would prepare me a quick breakfast.

We'd eat and hop on the bus to school, talking about anime or a girl we thought was cute. It was like I was coming out of my shell and experiencing life for the first time. Sometimes we'd even ditch school, if it were a half day, and head to the video game store or downtown to laugh and goof off.

Looking back on it, it was one of the nicest times of my life. Growing up like I did, I yearned for just that type of thing—to be free and rambunctious, as they say. To this day, I'll never forget it.

Something crazy happened one morning as we walked to the bus stop. If I recall, it was a fall morning, and it cemented Xavier and me as friends. It was bogus to witness, but I had to save the woman, right? The victim was an older lady on her way to work, and the dude was a drug addict we referred to as a "clucker" because of their erratic movements.

The lady was waiting for a bus when the disheveled man approached and tried to snatch her purse. I grabbed a hefty rock and hurled it at him. "What the fuck?" he cried out, holding his head.

It was then that he looked in Xavier's and my direction and ran towards us. Like I said, I wasn't a fighter, but seeing that shit bugged the hell out of me. My adrenaline was boiling, so I rushed in to tackle him, with Xavier joining in. We whipped that old man's ass, dealing blows to his face, until he fled. The grateful woman thanked us with a twenty-dollar bill before continuing to wait for her bus.

Xavier questioned my motives on that day, but I couldn't answer. I had acted on instinct, believing it was wrong for someone's mother to be subjected to such an ordeal. To be honest, I saw my own mom in her position and felt I had to prevent it.

From that day forward, our friendship was solidified. We had been cool before, but now we were like brothers. And when my tall, lanky ass tried out for the track team and made it, Xavier did the same.

While we were sophomores, he pulled off a feat that was beyond me, however. Getting a girlfriend. It ate me up inside, but I hid it well at the time. I tried my best to hide it, though the first few weeks were brutal. And boy did he rub it in my face.

"Nah, I can't hang out today. I have to see my girl. Maybe later," he'd say, reveling in it.

I'd kick a rock on my way home, daydreaming of having a girl to call my own. Someone to spend time with and talk on the phone with, like he did. But that all changed one day at the restaurant by our house.

One afternoon, Xavier and I were at a spot near my house to order some food. The kind with chicken wings, gyros, and mild sauce on everything. He was there buying some fries and a drink for his girl as I sat there minding my own business, feeling a bit left out. I walked up to the man behind the counter and ordered an Italian beef, dipped without peppers, and fries on the side, thanks to my mom's new job.

My clothing game was more on point, and I had developed a style, so to speak. "Yo, I told you to hold the peppers," I shouted through the bulletproof glass.

"Sorry, sorry," he replied, then gave me a pop for messing up my order.

Xavier's girlfriend was eyeing me like she was figuring something out. She pulled out her cell, still looking me up and down, and decided to call up her friend. "Her name is Keisha," she told me. "She's my friend. Want to meet her?"

That was all I needed to hear.

On the walk to Keisha's house, I planned out what I would do and say. Through the BDs and by the Vice Lords, we walked, hoping no one would fuck with us. Having Xavier's girl with us helped in that regard. Those guys seeing us with a girl made them think we were cooler than we were.

When we arrived, Keisha was wearing a jacket and jeans with alluring lips and soft eyes. A dime in my eyes. I tried to be cool, but my adolescent brain was a mess. I stood against the banister, doing my best not to stare at her, although I couldn't help myself.

I'd peek at her, and then she would do the same.

Xavier and his girl kept laughing at me and cracking jokes all while we chilled that day. Despite this, Keisha liked me. A lot. When it was time to get back, she added her number to my phone. I stood there, stunned in silence, as I had said anything to her the whole time. Girls remained a mystery to me then, and they still hold the same enigmatic allure.

Keisha had both her parents at home, which was unusual then. Growing up in a two-parent household, she had a different upbringing than most other girls. I'm not saying Keisha was "better," just different.

All the girls I knew went to public school and wore regular clothes. She had a bedtime, just like in those TV shows, and she couldn't answer her phone when we started hanging out. I don't like to generalize her, but she was a good girl. On the other hand, with my mom at work all the time and my granddad being granddad, I had free rein to do as I pleased.

I was intelligent and responsible, unlike Calm, who was a 'wild' teenager by this time, always getting in trouble. So I couldn't help but look up to Keisha's family and how they handled things. She admitted they weren't perfect, but from the outside, they seemed like it.

We spent so much time together, Keisha and I, sitting on the porch when it was nice out. It was hard to separate us. When the temperature dropped, we spent all night on the phone with each other, falling deeper in love with each other. This was the first relationship for the both of us, and we were in 'love.'

Keisha and I dated throughout our school years. She was my introduction to the world of love. When I left for school, it broke me, and she was one of the main reasons I didn't keep in touch with everyone. Even though Xavier broke up with his girlfriend, we'd still spend our afternoons together on Keisha's porch after school, kicking it and cracking jokes.

When Xavier introduced that bag of weed into our lives, everything changed.

I was sixteen and entering my junior year. I had gained some from my time on track. I was fit and lanky, while Xavier, a couple of inches shorter, exuded a confident aura. We were popular at school, and nobody dared to fuck with us.

One day, Xavier sprinted up the steps with an evil smirk. "Here," he said, tossing me a bag of weed that filled the air with its pungent, green aroma. I opened it and took in the scent. I knew Calm used to smoke and leave blunts lying around, but I had been trying to maintain a healthier lifestyle. I was different, or so I thought I was.

I shook my head when Xavier asked if I knew how to roll. "Nah, man, I've never smoked before."

"What? Not even a joint?"

"Hell nah. I'm trying to stay fit," I replied, watching Xavier snatch the bud back.

As we stood there, Keisha walked up and sat in my arms as I leaned on the banister. My eyes couldn't help but follow hers as I watched Xavier's clumsy attempt at rolling a blunt. After he messed up the blunt, Keisha took the second one and the weed, heading into her hallway to roll the perfect one.

We were surprised and laughed, not expecting her to roll it so well. She said she learned from watching her parents. They were married and seemed like a well-put-together family, so that surprised us. I guess it goes to show you that you never knew what people did behind closed doors.

The three of us sat there and smoked, experiencing it for the first time. The sticky marijuana made everything seem slower, and I couldn't stop laughing. Everything around us, from the old man with his cane to the beat-up cars in the neighborhood, all seemed so amusing to me.

It felt like being at a carnival, but without riding any of the rides. Keisha leaned forward and handed me a Now-and-Later. I reached for it with clumsy fingers, almost dropping it. It was like I was underwater.

"Watch it," she yelled, but I caught it. Xavier just sat there, observing my amateur attempts at handling the herb with a grin.

"Boy, you tripping," she said.

I didn't care, though. All I understood was food and snacks. "I'm so hungry, I could eat anything," I said, rubbing my stomach.

Keisha invited me in to get a sandwich, and we fooled around, which was incredible. That day stood out the most when I thought about our friendship. I wish we had stayed like that, but life never stays the same. From what I noticed, it moves and changes constantly. Pieces were removed, new characters were added, and through it all, you must keep your head tight. Because at any given moment, you could lose it all.

This next incident marked a major turning point in our lives, filled with regret that we all shared. We were seniors, getting ready for our prom and graduation. Though our futures were unwritten, we all felt like the world was ours for the taking.

I remember my mom was happy for me, and so would have been my grandfather had he lived. Granddad, the father I never had, moved on. I guess all the cigarettes and drinking caught up to him, and he passed away after his birthday. The funeral was small and neat, with a few relatives coming. Mom didn't get along with her. family anyway. I didn't care, and I cried for days about the old man. We paid our respects and moved on with our lives.

But for me, my mentor had transitioned, and I was feeling lost for a couple weeks. Who would yell at me for drinking all the orange juice or forgetting to take out the garbage? It was difficult to get used to not seeing him sitting at the kitchen table or out back on the porch, listening to his radio.

This one particular morning, a few months after he passed, we stood in front of the store after school, waiting for Keisha to get off her bus. We had our track uniforms on and were pretty sweaty from all the laps we had run. Going into his bag and pulling out a bag of stinky herbs, he held it to my nose.

"Smell that nigga," he snickered. "We about to get blazed."

I took the weed and gave it a proper smell. "Oh, really?" I said, grinning.

"Yeah, once your small-neck ass girl gets here," he said, pulling a blunt out of his pocket.

The conversation died as we waited; both of us were irritable.

I stood in the street looking for the bus, but Keisha wasn't on either. Where was she? I wondered. Concerned, I called her, but my calls went to voicemail, and my texts went unanswered. Looking at Xavier, we decided to wait on her porch for her to return from school so we could smoke.

The wind was blowing, a calm breeze, and I crunched on some Doritos as we talked about Xavier's ambitions after school, which I found a bit outlandish.

He wanted to be "the man," just like his older brother, who had a reputation for making things happen. Although Xavier excelled in school and track, his brother's street cred overshadowed his achievements. I wasn't fond of Xavier's brother, finding him unpredictable and associating him with bullshit. He and his crew always wore R.I.P. shirts to honor their fallen soldiers, which struck me as odd. Since Calm had warned me about him, I had heeded that advice and kept my distance.

Anyway, while we were shooting the shit, the doorknob of Keisha's door twisted. I turned my head, expecting to see her, but instead, a light-skinned guy walked out. Dreads swinging and wearing new Jordans, I stood up. "Hey, homie, who the fuck are you?"

His response was dismissive: "None of your business," he said as he bopped down the stairs.

Who was this light-skinned dude coming out of my girl's front door? I grabbed his arm, and Xavier moved in closer. Suspicion grew as I asked, "Who were you in there with?"

The guy laughed at us, a disrespectful gesture that made me cock my arm back. But as I got ready to swing, he lifted his shirt, revealing the handle of a pistol. I was mad, but not stupid.

As I released him, though, Xavier snatched the gun's handle out of his waist, delivering a forceful blow across the back of his head. "I hope you heard my friend," he said.

I was stunned. I had never seen anything like this up close. This was my first full assault. Xavier's grabbing the gun out of his waist was unreal. I looked at Xavier, and he looked like a different person. His face snarled, and he bit his lip. He looked like a real thug. This charged me.

I grabbed the dude's collar, and as he whimpered like a girl, "Keisha," he said. "I'm seeing Keisha," he bawled out like a child. But it didn't make me any less angry. I turned my back, my anger reaching a climax. "What the fuck?" I snarled before returning to deliver a punch right into his punk-ass face.

Xavier cheered me on as the dude staggered back, clutching his jaw. "Don't be here when we get back," he said, running down the block. I wasn't concerned about his return; however, I wanted to know what he had been doing in there with my girl.

I was amped up and pissed off. I wanted answers . I rang Keisha's doorbell more than twenty times before she answered. Xavier warned me to be careful, as he planned to tell his brother about what went down. Keisha answered and claimed she had been showing the guy something for class, but I found it hard to believe. We argued for hours, and though we smoothed things over, my trust was shattered, and my feelings toward her changed.

I felt violated for real. I hadn't had any other girls in my room but Keisha. She was extra-bogus, and she knew it. Every time I looked at her, in the back of my mind, I was angry with her. How could she do something like that? Did she have feelings for me, or was I just a sucker?

After the incident, Xavier found himself further into the streets. He had always had street connections, but this event enhanced his reputation, marking a turning point in our trio's dynamic.

Things had changed us, and, I stopped hanging around Xavier so much and focused on school. Keisha and I continued dating, but it wasn't the same; it felt forced. She kept the same story, even though I was suspicious.

The guy we confronted never returned, but our days of hanging out after school, smoking weed, and laughing ended after that. It was a bitter but pivotal situation that made me realize that sometimes the people closest to you, even your girl, could end up being straight-up poison.

CHAPTER 10

LATE NIGHT REFLECTIONS

WHEN I LEFT HOME, I didn't know I was setting off a series of events that would change everything. I just wanted to catch up with an old friend I hadn't seen in a long time and have some fun. Fate has a way of bringing things together, though. A phone call here or a rejected advance there—all of it was connected; all of it made sense in the larger scheme of things.

The neighborhood was different. I felt tension, combined with a sense of hopelessness, in the air. When I was younger, it didn't feel like this. Now that I had returned, it felt like I was locked inside a prison filled with the worst killers and thieves.

Keisha and I exited the party and walked towards my car. The sedated, empty streets welcomed us with open arms. The short dude, Lucky, had me spooked, and I was trying to distance myself as much as possible. His identity and origins troubled me. There was something familiar about him, yet I couldn't quite put my finger on it.

I unlocked the car and climbed in, and my eyes lingered

on Keisha. I was trying to reconnect with an old friend rather than worrying about some creepy short dude. Forget him, I thought. It's just a weird coincidence that the man who had been stalking me since Oregon was attending this party in the hood.

I felt shaken, but I hid it from Keisha as she sat beside me. Sensing something was off with her, I asked, "What's wrong?"

She turned to face me. "Nothing," she replied, her voice holding something back.

We sat in silence before I pulled out the weed Calm had given me. "Wanna smoke?" She nodded, and the mood began to lighten.

I wanted to hang out with Keisha like old times and see what she'd been up to. Nothing more or less. As I went to roll a blunt, she tried to snatch the bag, joking she should roll it herself since mine were always loose.

"Oh, so you've got jokes now?" I said, snatching it back. She fake pouted, knowing I'd cave and let her roll it. I liked that playfulness with her—I could be myself.

I reclined my seat as she broke down the cigar. "Stop watching me, you're making me nervous!" she said when she noticed me studying her technique. She crumbled the herb inside and shaped it into a perfect blunt.

Once lit, the smooth smoke filled the small space. We passed it back and forth, and as we smoked, we opened up, reminiscing about old times.

"So, what have you been up to?" I asked, watching the smoke hit the steering wheel and spread out.

"Right now, I've got a job doing customer service. I tried the college thing, but it didn't work out. Isn't that what happened to you?"

Her voice was small and light, like a whisper that brought back good memories. I had told her about my weed-selling business, Amina, and how it all ended. When I finished, she was almost as mad as I was. "And you didn't kick his ass?" she asked, growing more animated.

"Marcus left after that. The whole situation is so fresh; I still get mad thinking about them. If I had caught him, it was over." I bit my lip, my anger seething.

She reached over and rubbed my back. "And your girlfriend left you? Poor baby," she said, calming me down.

"Sort of. Amina was one of those streamer girls who was always online and shit. It was a 'thing' for her."

I re-lit the blunt, took a deep pull, and asked her under my breath, "Do you have any kids?"

"No, Travis," she said, mad that I had asked. "I ain't having kids until I'm married." I felt relieved.

"What about you?" she asked.

"Nah, the only person I dated after you was Amina," I said.

"Yeah, yeah, yeah."

The blunt burned out, leaving a lingering sweet aroma in the car. We were both high and mellowed out, enjoying each other's company. And then, Keisha turned to me and asked if I could take her home.

Instead of heading straight to her house, I cruised along Lake Shore Drive. It was something that I had always wanted to do since I was a kid. High and carefree, I savored the moment with the girl who used to be mine. For a brief moment, all was right with the world.

We parked at McDonald's and ate burgers and fries, stealing glances at one another. She smiled, and I laughed out loud at some of our antics. With our stomachs filled, we let our guards down, reminiscing about the good times. The conversation grew quiet, and we started wondering where we went wrong.

"Why did you break up with me after graduation?" I asked.

She shifted in her seat, putting her hand on my chest, suggesting we not spoil the mood. At that moment, I received a call but ignored it without checking who it was. I was about to hear the truth about our failed relationship.

"Just tell me, and then I'll drop it. You owe me that much," I insisted.

She placed her fries back in the bag, took a long sip of her drink, and sat there, not saying anything.

"Never mind," I sighed, shifting the car into drive. "I'm sorry I brought this up." But before I could leave, she grabbed my arm, stopping me.

"Wait, I'll tell you, but you already know," she said.

I settled back, curious for an explanation. This had better be good, I thought.

She looked at me with those soft brown eyes. "I was angry, okay?" she admitted.

I raised an eyebrow, encouraging her to continue.

"I was mad that you were leaving and wanted to get back at you. You weren't supposed to leave, Travis."

A tear rolled down her face, then another.

"But we had discussed it and planned to keep in touch. We were fine. You didn't have to do what you did."

"Boy, I wasn't going to sit around waiting for you, and I was pissed. You just couldn't see it," Keisha responded.

"So you just go and sleep with that guy?" I asked, shaking my head. "You're crazy; you know that, right?"

"It was because of you," she said, still teary.

"Enough, I'm taking you home."

After thinking about what she was implying, I asked

one more question: "How are you going to blame me for your cheating? Make it make sense," I said.

She attempted to answer, then stopped. Wiping her eyes, she crossed her arms and looked out the window. "You wouldn't understand," she said.

And I couldn't.

After a silent drive back to the neighborhood, I arrived back at her house. She told me to call her to finish our conversation later. I told her to be cool and began my way back to the house.

But before I drove off, I sat there, feeling like I should've pursued her harder. We were both stupid kids, and I did still have feelings for her, but thoughts of her treachery were at the forefront of my mind. My phone flashed with a call. I looked down and saw it was Calm. What could he want this late? I played with the thought in my mind.

"Where are you?" he asked, sounding worried. "I have been calling you like crazy, bro. Somebody shot up the party, and I wanted to check on you." Now, he sounded relieved that I was okay.

I knew something would go down if I stayed. The dude Lucky was bad news, and I sensed it. "Damn, anybody get hit?" I asked.

"Yeah, but not seriously. Get your ass back here; the streets are too hot, bro."

I hung up and went back home. In the morning, I would call Xavier and ask what had happened. For now, I was glad I survived the first day of being back in my wild-ass neighborhood. I hadn't been back for 24 hours, and someone's shooting up a place I just left.

After driving into town and catching up with my old friends, my high ass parked the car in front of Mom's house, exhausted. I was in zombie mode as I entered the crib. It was 3:47 a.m., and the streets were empty. I exited the car, surveyed my surroundings, and headed inside.

The trees were beginning to brown, and leaves littered the ground. Our yard, in particular, was covered in them, and they crunched and crumbled under my feet as I stepped through the front yard.

As I walked, my mind focused on my problems, causing that familiar warm yet sharp feeling in my chest that creeps in when you feel trapped. If I wanted a decent life, I'd have to leave again. Getting out of the city was the best option, and going back to finish school was all I had left. The hood had become even wilder and crazier since I left, more unpredictable. Perhaps it has always been messed up, but I couldn't see it when I was here. In any case, I needed to find a way to escape.

I walked up the stairs like a zombie, ready to hit the sack. Tomorrow, I thought, I would wake up and run, get some air in my brain, and work through this mess.

As I put the key in the lock, I heard leaves rustle. A slow, steady drag through the yard caught my attention. I turned my head and saw a cat jumping across the fence.

Feeling relieved, I unlocked the bottom lock. I twisted the knob, but the door didn't open. While fiddling around with my keys, I dropped them in front of me.

High, tired, and depressed, I sighed and bent down to grab my keys. That's when I heard someone across the street saying, "Aye," trying to get my attention.

I rose and focused on the sound, seeing a figure draped in darkness. I couldn't make out their face, but I didn't want to take any chances.

"Who's there?" I said, reaching under my shirt as if I had a gun.

The figure stepped forward to stand under the streetlight, revealing his face. From that distance, it was still hard to see. I stepped down the stairs, allowing my curiosity to get the best of me.

Who was this mysterious figure? Was it the guy who had been following me, or someone else?

"Who the fuck are you?" I shouted just above a whisper.

The mysterious person just stood there, staring at me. I turned to walk away when he said, "Follow me."

His voice was ragged and old, carrying the weight of decades. I approached him, expecting to smell sweat and filth. However, to my surprise, he had a clean, antiseptic-like smell, much like a hospital.

"I'm not about to follow your old, weird ass anywhere, homie," I said as I got closer.

He appeared to be of Mexican descent, maybe even Native American, draped in oversized garments that seemed to swallow his frail frame. With all the wrinkles around his eyes, he looked ancient, standing there under the street lights. His face was covered in nicks and cuts, like he had just shaved.

His Adam's apple moved as he spoke. "Just like my grandson," he mumbled. "Just like him."

He was covered in freckles and those age spots that old people have on their skin. I looked him up and down with scrutinizing eyes. He was holding a can of beer, wrapped in a paper bag, and wobbling from side to side.

"Get lost," I said, and I jumped at him, not to injure him but to scare him. Such people could get wild and try to rob you or something. I wanted him to get away from me.

Feeling frustrated, I wanted everything to return to normal. First, it was the short dude from the party, and now, this.

He didn't flinch and stood there, mumbling under his breath, with a distant look in his eyes. I said forget it, left the old man under the streetlight, and went inside.

CHAPTER 11

COMPLICATIONS

IT WAS EARLY in the afternoon when I awoke, with the events of the previous night still clouding my mind. As I lay there, the morning's grogginess gave way to a sense of urgency. I knew I had to focus on finding a new school today. I peeked into Mom's room and saw her sleeping, her light snore echoing. Even though being home sucked, seeing my mom and brother felt reassuring.

I returned upstairs and hollered at Calm for a few minutes. He went through what he heard about the shooting last night and told me to be careful around Xavier. "Things have changed," he said. And they had, but not much. Shootings and such had been going on for a while. What was different was that I was involved, and he was concerned.

My big brother was talking about how everything was different when he was the one who had changed, as he now held a steady job instead of running the streets. I felt proud of his transformation. He said he would bring his kids to see me on his day off. I said, "Cool," then went into my room. I did a few push-ups and listened to music.

When I stepped downstairs, Mom was up, making something to eat. The smell of bacon had grabbed me by the nose, like in those old Tom and Jerry cartoons on YouTube. She was cooking up something fierce, whipping the eggs and pouring them into a skillet with butter.

"How was your night? You didn't get into too much trouble, did you?" She asked, scrambling the eggs with a wooden spoon and scraping the skillet.

"Nah, I didn't; I just saw a couple of friends," I said, standing over her.

The scent of frying bacon filled the room. It smelled so good that I couldn't resist trying to grab a piece. She popped my hand with the spatula, stopping me. "Wait until I'm finished, boy. You're going to get germs on everything."

She looked at me with a sour face. "Wash your hands and set the table. I want to talk to you before you start running those streets."

Over breakfast, we discussed her job and the recent trouble my cousin from the suburbs had found himself in after getting caught stealing iPhones. After a while, the conversation turned to me and what I had planned to do.

"Ma, don't worry," I said. "I'm going back to school. It's too wild around here."

"When? Because if you stay around here and start messing with these little girls, you'll never leave."

With tears welling in her eyes, my mom grabbed my hand, trying to save my life. "I've got a little money saved to help you if you need it," she said. "But boy, there's nothing around here but pain and death, and I want so much more for you."

It was a heartfelt moment that we rarely shared. The look in my mother's eyes stung a little bit and made getting enrolled in school more of a priority.

We ate, and she cleaned off the table. My mind wandered to thoughts of my dad. Thinking about what I planned to do made me wonder if my dad had gone through something like this.

"Hey Ma, was my dad a screw-up like me?" I asked.

She turned toward me and shook her head. "Travis, not today, please."

"Why not? He was a part of me, and he helped make me. I'm old enough to know," I pleaded with her.

"Son, he died not too long after I got pregnant. I don't remember much else," she said, leaving the kitchen.

She was acting like she had been hiding something—some type of pain. Whatever it was, it was time to let it go and talk to somebody. Holding a kid's father's memory hostage was wrong.

We sat there at the table, staring at each other. Her eyes were defiant, like she had already made up her mind, and there was nothing I could do to stop it. I looked at her, but she scraped the chair against the floor, stood, and cleaned off the table.

I shook my head, went upstairs, and pulled out my laptop to get my mind off our discussion. After conducting my research, I narrowed my choices to four potential candidates. I would decide in a couple of days and try to enroll for the winter semester. My mom offering me money felt good, but I wouldn't take it.

I had saved quite a bit while selling weed in school and could now support myself until I found a job. I filled out Pell Grants and other forms I needed to get the loan. With all that done, I took a shower and headed out for a run.

As I walked downstairs, I noticed my mom hadn't come out of the kitchen in a while. I went to grab a bottle of water, and that's when I saw her slump over the chair. This was odd—quite odd. I tapped her arm, and she didn't respond. Growing concerned, I shook her harder, and she rolled over, dazed, with a line of saliva running from her mouth.

I called Calm downstairs, forgetting he was at work. Taking my phone out of my pocket, I called 911 and told them how I found my mother. They told me not to move and that they'd be on their way.

I sat in the living room, waiting, afraid to look at my mother like that. Every time I saw her, I broke down. When the emergency workers arrived, I followed them to the hospital, swerving and emotionally vacant. My mom was my everything, and without her, I was lost.

Waiting in the emergency room for the doctors to diagnose my mom, was hell on my nerves. The bright lights and clean floor amplified my anxiety. The hushed conversations around me filled me with more feelings of dread as I waited to see my mother. I couldn't look at any of the people waiting, so I kept my head down and hoped for the best. Many had sad expressions on their faces or tears in their eyes, waiting to hear about their loved ones. It was a horrible feeling that I tried to ignore. With my mother getting tested, I didn't want to hear about their worries. The woman next to me sobbed, tears streaming down her face, over her son, who had been shot. I got up and moved to an empty area with less turmoil.

She was moved to a room with machines running and monitoring her, while she lay unconscious. Tubes and IV bags were hooked up to her arm, injecting her with vital fluids and nutrients, reminiscent of Frankenstein. She looked peaceful for a minute as she slept in the dull hospital room. I kissed her on the cheek, held her hand in mine, and prayed that God would deliver her. Sure, she had a rough period in her life, but God wouldn't mind that. He was a miracle-maker, and I believed my mother would be okay. Mom was too young to be going through something like this. Many were surprised and said that being a nurse was a stressful job. The demanding hours, and constant pressure were the culprits. They said stress killed, and now I knew it was true, looking at my mother sleeping with a pleasant look on her face.

When the nurse offered coffee, I accepted and called Calm again. He said he was on his way and would call me if anything changed. He was working and couldn't leave today; his promotion made it necessary. I was mad at first, then realized he was just like his mom—always on the clock. We were all hard workers, never wanting to sit still for too long, without seeing something get done. It was in the blood.

Sitting in the waiting room gave me time to think. If Mom died, what would I do? Go back to school? Or move back home and try to find a job? I had already lost my grandfather before I left for school. With my grandfather's recent passing and now my mother being admitted to the hospital, it was all too much.

The coffee was warm, attacking the sleepiness and eating at the mind. It was late, and the doctors still hadn't performed any tests, so I went to find a vending machine to eat away at my hunger. Something to distract me from my worries, even if just for a little while. The hall was quiet as I walked past rooms of people huddled under white sheets, writhing in pain, or facing TV screens, unconnected from what they were viewing. After asking around, I was directed to turn a few corners to get to the regular vending machine, or I could get on an elevator and go to a favorite late-night machine to get snacks from. Being a lover of sweets, I took his advice and went in search of this 'banging' machine, as he said.

I navigated my way to the elevator, still depressed from what my mom was going through. I prayed as I walked for God to look after her. I looked at the room numbers as I strolled through the hospital, feeling lonely. Hospitals were places of finality, and I didn't like the feelings they gave me. Up ahead, the elevator door was open, and I sped up to catch it. I looked around inside, when I caught it and saw no one. I pressed the button to go to the floor with the late-night treats. It was a short ride, and the elevator was decent, making my stomach feel even more empty. The elevator made a sound, and the door opened. When I stepped out, I felt like someone was staring at me from behind. I turned around, and that's when I saw him. Lucky from the party was grinning and coming towards me.

Before I even realized what I was doing, I found myself running. Past the vending machine, past the attendants, and past the janitors chatting by the desk. They called after me, but I kept running, as if I were Jesse Owens fleeing from the frightening man. I had never felt such fear before, and the hallway lights sped by as I ran down the hospital corridors, making me feel dizzy. I stopped at a junction, getting lost in the maze-like structure. The walls changed to school and then to my home. The smells and sounds of all those places washed over me, leaving me disoriented. College professors, my mom's cooking, and my grandfather's laughter, all descended on me. I was overwhelmed, panicking amid a disorienting melange of sensory overload. I was running backward, it seemed, and now I felt myself coming apart.

As I rounded the corner, reality began to blur, plunging

me into a surreal encounter with Lucky. He wore the same outfit from the party and smelled like old, decayed earth, or maybe a cemetery. I couldn't decide which, but they were dank and dark. I couldn't move because I was frozen in my tracks, paralyzed with fear. His breath was warm and foul as he grinned into my face. His eyes reflected all the poor decisions I had made. He reached out for me, and that's when I was startled awake by Calm walking into the room with a big, forced smile, that betrayed his concern. Our mother's breathing was steady, and she had fallen asleep. The rise of her chest was a reminder that she was still here, and that meant something. Calm sat by the bed in the sparkling light, with machines beeping, and said a prayer. It was touching and poignant; I don't know where he heard it from, but it brought me solace and made me think that everything would be okay. I watched as he slumped into a chair, closed his eyes, and went to sleep.

When I awoke, I heard the familiar yet strained voice of Calm, which soothed me in contrast to the sterile hospital environment all around. I rubbed the sleep from my eyes and propped myself up, anxiety gnawing at my insides. "Is everything okay?" The words tumbled out, heavy with worry.

Mom, looking frail but stronger than yesterday, replied with a weak voice, "They're still waiting on the test results, but it's not bad." Her words, though faint, carried a note of resilience. She was sitting up, her eyes more alert, and engaging in the conversation. An empty tray, with a half-drunk cup of coffee, rested beside her. She sniffed the aroma of the coffee—a small gesture, but one that signaled a return to her usual routines. It was a subtle yet reassuring sign of normalcy returning.

My heart felt lighter, as the weight lifted. We chatted for a while, the conversation meandering from mundane hospital routines, to updates on family matters. Despite the sterile hospital backdrop, our conversation was warm, highlighting the enduring bond between a mother and son.

I decided it was time to freshen up. The hospital's atmosphere, laden with the scent of antiseptics and the undercurrent of countless untold stories, had a way of clinging to you. After a day at the hospital, melancholy clung to me like an inescapable fog. At home, the quiet was jarring. Calm called, his voice strained over the phone, mentioning additional tests. He advised me to rest, but rest was elusive.

In the stillness of my room, restlessness took hold. The night was too quiet, and my thoughts were too loud. Keisha's presence in my thoughts was a balm, a reminder of a time less complicated. I texted her, driven by an urge for connection and for a grounding presence, during the chaos.

Keisha walked through the door and gave me a fierce hug, which broke the loneliness I had been feeling that evening. After inviting her to my room, we sat and reminisced about memories that gave way to more serious reflections.

With a heartfelt look in her eyes, she grabbed my hand, her voice filled with concern. "Your mom is sick, but she's tough," she said, trying to squeeze the hurt I felt away.

Looking at her at that moment, the old emotions I felt for her in high school came to the surface. Eyes locked on each other; no other words were needed. Our hands intertwined, forming a bond, as our foreheads came together, which led to me kissing her on the lips. A peck, really. It was brief and unplanned, but it had a profound effect on me during the remainder of the night.

Her genuine response was all I needed. It was then that I knew what we had was special, and maybe I could forgive her for what she had done to me in the past. Pushing the masculine street shit aside, I was happy she was here in my time of need.

As the night deepened, our conversation turned solemn. "I just hope she pulls through," I murmured. The uncertainty of the situation casts a shadow over us. Keisha moved closer, her warmth a stark contrast to the cold fear gnawing at me. "She'll be okay," she assured me, her voice a soft whisper, against the backdrop of my fears.

"What if she's not?" The question hung in the air, heavy and unspoken. "What am I going to do, Keisha? If Mom's sick, can I even think about going back to school?"

Keisha's response was gentle but firm: "Don't worry about that now. Just focus on your mom. Everything else can wait." Her words, simple yet profound, offered a momentary respite from the storm of thoughts raging inside me.

The night unfolded, with us lost in each other's company—a temporary escape from the relentless march of reality. As Keisha drifted off to sleep beside me, I lay awake, the events of the day replaying in my mind. In all the uncertainty and fear, one thing was clear: my future, once a path I thought I had mapped out, was now a road shrouded in fog.

CHAPTER 12

THE DOOR

MOM WAS out of the hospital and taking it easy. The doctors told her to lay off the greasy food and to get some rest. Calm and I waited on her every need, hand over foot. No one had planned this far, and we all needed to sit back and assess the situation.

In between caring for my mom, I was on the phone with admissions offices, asking about transfer policies and obtaining transcripts. Navigating the red tape was a nightmare. I found out I'd have to wait until the winter semester, in 2 months, to transfer. So it looked like I'd be stuck in the hood until all the paperwork went through.

Leaving her so soon after her health scare weighed on me, but after discussing it, she insisted I carry on with school as planned.

Going back to school meant not being able to check my mom's health, and she'd need somebody around to help now. I was paralyzed with indecision. She was already up and moving around, talking about returning to work, but who knew if that would ever happen? The doctor told her to wait a month, and then he'd see. I was glad she was returning to normal.

During this time, I kept having disturbing dreams that some would call nightmares. They were about the old man I saw after that night at the party and a mysterious two-story house. I couldn't make out what the old man was saying, but he was pointing at the house, trying to get me to go inside. There were children playing outside, and Lucky was there, grinning.

In the dream, I'd start walking along the sidewalk to the gate, gazing at the building and wondering. Whenever I'd put my hand on the old fence, I was jolted awake, sweating, and out of breath. It was horrible to experience. The dream had visited me once a week and made me dread going to sleep.

Over the last few weeks, I tried to stay in the house for those few weeks. I mean, I really tried. I exercised, watched a gang of TV shows, and talked with Calm when he was around. Still, I couldn't contain it any longer. That's when I decided to call Xavier and ask him to meet me at my mom's house.

We were sunk in my car's leather seats in front of my house. My father's watch was on my wrist, while I tapped my finger against the bottom of the steering wheel. The air freshener, a faded Christmas tree, was dangling from the rear-view mirror, doing its job, as Xavier smoked a menthol. Wearing a plain black jacket and a black skullcap, he looked like an assassin by my side. The radio was playing at a decent level, the smoke was thick, and we were laughing.

As we were kicking it, he pulled out his phone and

flicked through some pictures. I leaned to the side to see, and he pushed the phone into my hand, happy for me to take a look.

"That's my girl, Maxine," he announced, looking and sounding proud. "I met her out in the South Suburbs... I'm going to marry her one day."

I handed him his phone back. "You serious, dude. This young? Are you sure?"

"Yeah, I'm sure. She has everything we never had growing up: a mom and a dad with private schools and shit. She's cultured, dude. And I love her."

I sat in my seat, thinking about getting married at a young age. "That's some real devotion, my dude. I don't think I'm ready."

"Not even to Keisha? I remember how y'all used to be before she pulled that shit. And I saw you at the party. all lovey-dovey... I swear it looked like somebody shot y'all both with Cupid's arrow. You can't tell me you haven't thought about it."

"Hell nah, I ain't thought about it. She's cool and all, but I don't know if I want to be tied down to her just yet. And besides, we're just kicking it, nothing serious."

"Well, I'm serious about mine, G," he trailed off.

Getting married? What was this fool smoking? I'm going back to school, finishing my education, and thinking it through this time. Amina had the right idea about planning for your future, and marriage wasn't in mine... yet.

Xavier's eyes lit up, and he fired up another cigarette, ashing it. "Yo, stop around the corner from the old spot," he exclaimed. "We gotta get some more buds, 'cause I'm almost out."

Watching over moms for the past couple of weeks was getting to me, and more weed sounded good. "Bet," I said.

It was a short drive; the neighborhood flew by, as he gave directions, even though I still knew the old terrain. Two flats and vacant lots, liquor stores, and dilapidated churches surrounded us. The few denizens were mostly kids, wearing little jackets against the chill. Many were wearing face coverings and looking much older than their age, probably carrying guns under their clothes. This environment seemed much different than college, with academics and teachers walking to class. Looking at the neighborhood as it whizzed by, I was amazed at how some blocks looked like a bomb had hit and others were pristine, with well-manicured lawns and new vehicles parked.

Waiting at a red light near the corner store we used to frequent, I saw the old man from the night of the party. His haunting eyes lay on me, making me twitch. Upon recognizing me, he waved his arms to get my attention, but I ignored him and drove off as soon as the light turned.

Feeling funny and making a few turns, I parked the car, and Xavier texted his brother. Fumbling around with his phone, waiting for a reply, he looked over at me. "How was school, Travis? Was it like Drumline? Did you get your Nick Cannon on, nigga?" He laughed jokingly.

"Fuck you, and nah," I said, pushing his arm. "That shit was hectic. Always studying and busting my ass practicing, running drills for the coach. I barely had the time to think."

Xavier received a text just as we were about to dive into a deeper conversation about my college experience. "It looks like we'll have to wait a few more minutes," he said.

We sat in silence for a minute before he continued with his questions. "So, how were the ladies? I know there were some bad ones out there. You meet any?"

"It was, but I was with Amina while I was down there; she was from Alabama. Thick as hell, bro."

I pulled up her Instagram, and he looked at a few pictures. "Damn, nigga, she's bad as hell. I know you were pissed you had to leave that." He eyed my phone.

"Hell yeah, she was cool as hell too."

"Aye, you never told me why you left. What happened? I figured you were through with the hood."

Marcus flashed in my mind, with his thick glasses and chubby cheeks. "Man, my nerd-ass roommate filmed me selling weed to this bad-ass chick and put it on Instagram—once the school saw that shit, they kicked me clean the fuck out. I was pissed. I almos-"

He interrupted me by stopping me with his hand. "Hold on, let me get this straight: you, Mr. College Boy, sold weed on campus? Get the fuck out of here. I would've never guessed it."

"Man, I had to. I couldn't work at some coffee shop, practice, or attend class. Then I had Amina, with her fine ass, always wanting to spend time. So, being the young, enterprising man I am, I managed to find a way to earn money and create more free time. It was genius."

He looked at me, nodding his head up and down. "My nigga," he said, shaking my hand. "The hood raised you right."

I held my head low, embarrassed by his comments. Maybe if I had found a little gig, I wouldn't be here. Next thing, his phone went off, and he read the text. "A few more minutes," he said. "Then we're good."

Just thinking about school dampened my mood. Annoyed by his questions and pissed at myself, I was ready to drive off. "Who is this we're waiting on, by the way? We've been out here for ten minutes; I'm getting antsy." I looked at Xavier, who still had his head bent over his phone.

"Look at all the big words," he said, raising his eyes at me.

"Antsy ain't even big; you're tripping, bro," I replied, leaning against the steering wheel.

"You know what I mean, using those fancy words we never use in the hood, 'antsy'," he laughed out.

I didn't know why he was antagonizing me, but I brushed it off. Ignore the ignorant, I thought.

Xavier must've seen my face and tried to lighten the mood. "I'm kidding, bro." He paused before continuing. "Ease up, and the dude from the party has the weed."

"Which dude?" I asked him, brushing off his comments.

"The short dude who was flexing at the party," he said. "Everyone was listening to his stories. I think I saw you talking with him. Big bro said he had some gas."

My mind flashed to the party, the shower on campus, and outside the restaurant. It had been weeks since I had thought of or seen the stranger, but I remembered his creepy ass.

I put the car in drive and tried to peel out, but he stopped me with his hand. "Hold on, bro," he said. "We gotta get the weed; what are you doing?"

Looking shaken, I blathered. "I don't want to smoke that short, creepy dude's weed. From what I remember, he was weird as fuck. I don't care how good it is. I'm out."

He got a text, which paused my departure. "Lemme run in here, right quick, and get the weed; you won't even see him," he pleaded with me.

Xavier had a way of convincing me to do stuff I never would do. I'm talking about how, no matter how much my inner voice said no, he always made me laugh and reconsider.

My hand was already shifting the car to drive off.

"Don't be like that, with your scary-face ass. I promise it'll be good," he said one last time.

Putting the car back in park, I took my foot off the gas and waited. A smile lit his face as he opened the door. "Just chill and lemme go grab this weed, and then we can bounce."

I took a second and looked at the spot we were parked in front of. It was old, with scaffolding and signs of renovation. Something was odd about the house, but I couldn't put my finger on it at the time. It was the house from my dreams, but I couldn't make the connection at the time. Dreams are like that. It had a fence around it and patches of unkempt grass sticking up in places. The only 'new' thing was the front door.

Looking at the expensive door made out of some kind of expensive-ass wood, I shivered in my seat. Something was off here, and I sensed it in my bones. If I had made the connection between my dreams and the house, I would've driven off.

Watching Xavier open the fence and walk the steps in a few leaps, I hoped to God he wouldn't take long. What happened next was something so strange that it shook me to my core.

———

Next to the house, on both sides, were homes that had already been renovated but were eerily vacant. New windows and sandblasted brick made the block look like it was on the come-up, but other than that, it was a ghost town —a lost block that nobody visited.

I waited for Xavier for ten minutes before I tried hitting his phone, which went straight to voicemail. This whole scenario felt like another of God's mysteries. After 30 minutes, I was steaming. Anyone else would've been left, but me; never believing in leaving your friends behind, waited.

I mean, I didn't want to leave my homie behind, but he was pushing it. Feeling foolish for waiting for so long, then angry at him for ignoring my calls, my mind raced with worry. Should I investigate or drive off? I could be at home or with Amina instead of waiting in front of the house. Taking a closer look, I noticed the windows were all black, like someone had put something up to them. Xavier, I hope nobody kidnapped your stupid ass, I thought.

Despite the block being quiet, my curiosity got the better of me. Especially about the dude named 'Lucky,' who had been following me for weeks. Popping up at strange times and smiling, then running off. All of it was spooky. First, in school and now back at home. I wanted to find out why this 'Lucky' character was messing with me.

I stood before the rehabbed house, and it looked even more ominous and frightening. The dust from the sand-blasting was still on the porch, covering everything with a cloud of red-like dust. I looked down and noticed Xavier's footprints leading up the stairs. His clunky feet led me to my destination.

Here we go, I thought, and I made my way up the stairs. The scaffolding groaned in the wind, ropes swaying above the door frame. Trash blew by my feet, and a cold breeze crossed my face. Always getting me into shit.

My hair stood on end as I walked on, taking my time and being a little fearful of what I was walking into. My breath caught in the air, hovering before my face. It wasn't that cold, or was it? Staring at the door, I couldn't even remember what it was.

The entrance stood before me, pulling me toward it, calling my name and inviting me in. With its mahogany wood and intricate carving whispering. I knocked on it first but didn't get an answer, but curiosity got the best of me. I put my hand on the knob and gave it a turn, hoping, by some force of luck, that it was open.

The knob was freezing cold, and it felt like a layer of my skin stuck to it as I snatched my hand away. "Damn!" I jerked back, rubbing my hand, and looked at the damage. Red and swollen skin looked back, sore, yet, in a strange way, almost pretty. A little ointment and I'd be straight, I thought.

Whatever was behind the door didn't want me in. And I was happy to be denied access. I turned around, perplexed, wondering where Xavier had disappeared. I stepped down the stairs when I heard the lock disengage behind me. It sounded like a gun cocking. By the time I turned around, it had creaked itself open.

Now, I was spooked. My heart was pounding against my chest so hard that I heard it against the insides of my temples. What the fuck? I thought.

Taking a cautious step toward the mysterious door, I braced myself. Then, out of the shadows, runs Xavier. His sudden appearance sent a jolt of fear through my veins, and I jumped back. He stood there, grinning. "You're not going to believe this," he said, "but look at what I found."

In his hands was a ziploc full of weed, about a pound's worth, and I could smell it from where I stood. I walked closer to get a better look when he grabbed me by the jacket and pulled me inside the vestibule. I held the heavy door open, allowing the light of the overcast afternoon to illuminate the tiny area where we stood.

I looked around, and it appeared that we were inside

the building's entrance—an ample square-shaped space with unfinished drywall begging to be painted. An empty bucket stood to the side, along with a few tools and wires hanging out of places. A door stood before us with a rectangular glass pane, showcasing nothing but darkness.

"What the fuck?" I said and shook his hands off me, almost slipping from the dust on the floor.

"Bro, I don't like how this feels. Put that shit back and let's leave," I urged, my concern growing.

"Are you nuts? This may be our chance," he said.

I turned to leave, weed or not. This was too much for me. All I thought of was school and getting out of this neighborhood.

Spinning me around and looking at me with an expression and a face of empathy, he spoke in a shallow voice, almost whispering. "The place looks empty, and all the lights are out. You're not curious about what's inside?"

"Not really; they are still fixing it up."

"Nah, this place is furnished." He said, peeking through the glass, inside the darkened house. "I see something."

"Man, I'm out of here," I said, turning around. "Niggas could pop out blasting."

He lifted his jacket, revealing a gun. "We straight, bro; trust me. But if you want to leave, then leave. The door is wide open."

I weighed my options. Staying until December, I couldn't risk him telling everyone that I'd chickened out and abandoned him. If I were older and more mature, I would've just ignored what people thought of me. Still, being a 20-year-old kid, reputation was everything.

I let the door close behind me, and it swung shut fast—almost too fast. I felt something tugging at my ears, threatening to pull out my brains. Eyes shifting to Xavier, who had moved his hands to his ears, grunting in pain. Just when the sensation became unbearable, it stopped. Standing there feeling relieved, I heard a soft, subtle pop in the center of my brain, as if it were pulling in on itself. It felt like my mind had split in two. The sensation was so intense, I felt as if it might implode.

When the pressure subsided, Xavier pulled out his pistol and turned the knob on the door. I put up my guard and followed him into the unknown, uncertain of what might lie ahead.

CHAPTER 13

INSIDE THE HOUSE

AS XAVIER AND I ENTERED, we looked around, uncertain of what to expect. Bumbling into each other, we searched for the light switch in the pitch-black darkness, unable to see anything. It was so dark, I thought someone had hit my head and knocked my eyes out of their sockets. "Dude, I can't see shit now that we're inside. Where did all the light go?" Xavier whispered from somewhere in front of me.

Running my hands along the wall, I found the switch and flicked it on. The interior of the place was astounding. "Whoa," I blurted out, looking around at the trappings. Taking a few steps across the floor, I looked down at the plush white carpeting. "This place is decked out," I noticed.

Further study of the room revealed large painted scenes on the walls, with scenic vistas and exotic fruit, like something from an art gallery. "This Lucky dude is loaded," Xavier remarked, and at the sound of his name, I tensed up.

As we walked further inside, we were greeted by expensive furniture and widescreen TVs that hung like specters, blank screens watching us. Art adorned the area above the fireplace, and the walls were covered in expensive wallpaper. I strolled around, nodding in admiration, feeling like the trespasser I was.

"You couldn't wait for me? I was gone for a few seconds," Xavier said, picking at the Ziploc of marijuana beside me.

"A few seconds? More like half an hour; you've been in here for 30 minutes," I replied. "And where did you find that?"

"I found it lying on the floor as soon as I stepped inside," he said of the weed.

This whole situation was becoming unsettling with each passing moment. The discovery of the weed lying there and the mysterious time discrepancies had my nerves on edge.

The air was warm and smelled like air freshener and emptiness. Small lamps beside the couches gave the room a soft glow. This place felt like a home that was lived in. In my mind, I doubted if Lucky even stayed here. Someone had lured us here, and I was alarmed. Who could have anticipated that getting kicked out of school would lead to this?

I put the weed back and finished scoping out the home, running my hand along the stripped wallpaper as I walked, letting the smooth surface ground my feelings in the present and out of my disturbed mind.

Outside the living room was a staircase that led upstairs. I looked at Xavier, then back at the stairs. He left me to explore upstairs while he searched the rest of the house.

I walked the stairs, bracing myself for anything. Halfway up, I felt like a fool. Nobody was here, and I was just panicking about nothing.

But still, I wondered why I was here. I was a college

student, for Christ's sake, majoring in philosophy, breaking into someone's home in the middle of the afternoon. Determined to look around and maybe peek in a couple of drawers, I continued up the stairs like a filthy, no-good-for-nothing thief.

Feeling ashamed, I reached the landing and found the light. More elegant decorations greeted me. There were two bedrooms and a bathroom. I peeked inside one of the bedrooms, which was unfurnished, with a pair of curtains hanging in the room.

I crept to the next, and this one was fully furnished. It had a king-sized bed, a widescreen TV on the wall, a half bath, and a double door. Spotting a lamp, I pulled the string, illuminating the room. Stepping on the tips of my toes, I crept towards the closet.

The doors slid open. There was nothing inside but clothes and shoes. It was a walk-in, and everything was organized and neat. There were a couple of suits. I looked at the labels and was surprised to find designer names with satin insides and monogrammed shirts. This guy was loaded. If Lucky truly stayed here, he was even more mysterious than I thought.

I exited the closet and opened a few drawers of the dresser along the wall. The top one had a few photos and panties inside—trophies of whoever stayed here from romantic conquests. I pulled out a pair, and they spread out like silk. Nice, I thought.

I closed the drawer, rummaged around the next one, moved the folded clothes aside, and saw something peeking at me. Shining a little, like plastic or something. I grew excited at what I thought I saw. I pulled it out, and my mouth dropped.

Underneath the arranged clothes, a sealed bag of bills caught my eye. I ripped open the plastic, and stacks of money spilled out into the drawer. My hands shook with excitement as I pulled out more stacks and a pristine .40-caliber handgun. Playing with the gun and the piles of money before me felt like I had won the lottery. Next, I entered the closet, poured the contents out of a Neiman Marcus bag, and filled it with the money.

As I stuffed the money into the bag, a wave of guilt washed over me. But then I remembered the endless debt, the struggles of my mom, and the dreams I had to put on hold. Just this once, I told myself, trying to silence the voice of conscience.

I stepped back outside the room, rich. As I pocketed the money, a pang of guilt struck me. Is this me? I thought. Or am I justifying greed? I held the bag open, looking at the sight of all that cash, and it silenced my doubts. It's just this once, I rationalized, though the unease lingered.

Standing on the landing, I called out to Xavier with a sense of triumph. "Yo, check it out; I think I found something," I shouted.

Breathing like running up the stairs had winded him, he looked bewildered. "What's up, playboy? You find anything?" he said, leaning against the wall.

"Yeah, I did, and it's way better than a pound of weed," I said, lowering the bag and showing him the money.

His eyes lit up like a stovetop. "Holy shit!" he said, pulling out one of the stacks of hundreds. "How much is it?"

I shrugged. I didn't even count it, but it was more money than I had ever held. With this much money, a whole lot of opportunities opened up. I felt terrible, but growing up poor and struggling gave me a different outlook on life. He put the money back and ran past me in search of more. I ran behind him and stopped him. "Let's just bounce, bro," I said, grabbing his jacket. "There's no telling when that Lucky character will be back."

He thought about it for a second, with a serious look, but shook his head and continued on. I followed behind, holding the bag and dancing on my feet, ready to leave.

"I checked everything; come on," I croaked out from behind him, but he ignored me.

Running into the room, he tossed every drawer and moved every piece of clothing. When he finished, it looked like a whirlwind had been inside.

I stood against the wall, thinking I had hit the jackpot. Ready to escape, I ran to the window to look out of it and to see if the coast was clear. I moved the heavy curtains to the side and saw nothing but darkness staring at me. The window wasn't painted or taped. It was blackness like I'd never seen. Looking out into it made me feel disoriented and uneasy on my feet, like I was on a boat.

I let the window close and called Xavier to follow me. Next stop, my car, and then counting all this cash.

We ran down the stairs, our arms holding the walls.

Remembering the doorknob had frozen my hand, I used the jacket's cuff to open it; it was stuck. My pulse quickened as I gripped it again and gave it another, firmer tug with more strength, but it didn't budge. Xavier moved me out of the way and screamed out as he, too, was frozen by the cold- ness of the knob.

"What the fuck?" He grabbed his hand. Face twisted in anger, he turned around and lifted his leg. Powerful. Boom boom, it went. Each kick shook the house's foundation, and still, it wouldn't open. "Why. Won't. It. Open." Each word was accentuated by another mighty kick.

"What is this door made of?" he panted.

I ran throughout the house and entered the kitchen. The counter tops were spotless, with all the appliances glistening in the light. I looked at the fridge, which had a large blinking screen showing weird dashes and asterisks.

Huh, I thought, but I had no time to ponder.

I disregarded all the shiny gadgets and ran to the back door. The same thing. It wouldn't open. I, too, kicked and clawed at the door but had no success.

I ran back to the lavish living room and saw Xavier trying to lift the window. Sweat was falling from his head. He put his foot on the ledge and pulled so hard that he broke the lever off.

Sitting back on the couch, he was defeated, breathing hard with his eyes popping out of his head. He was scared out of his mind. "Travis, what the fuck is going on?"

I pulled out my phone to check the time, only to find that all the numbers displayed asterisks and dashes, like the refrigerator. I felt cold and alone, even though I was with Xavier. "Huh?" I muttered, urging him to check his phone as well. He retrieved his phone, and to our shared horror, it revealed the same cryptic symbols. We were stuck in a drug dealer's home with his stash. Today turned out to be the worst day of my life.

As one last effort to get out of this spooky house, I took the .40 cal from my pocket and cocked it. Xavier looked surprised and asked where I got the cannon from. I aimed it at the window, telling him "upstairs," before I pulled the trigger. He stood up, and I turned my head as the barrel blazed and released the shell. We both ducked as the bullets ricocheted and planted themselves in the wall. I dropped the gun, sat on the floor, and screamed out into the silence of the house.

━━

"I'm smoking," he said, sounding irritated. "I'm lucky I bought a couple of packs earlier, or we'd be fucked."

Being locked inside the strange house had Xavier on edge, and he needed the herb to calm him. I was wary of the weed but didn't voice my concerns. It had been about an hour, but I couldn't tell because all the digital clocks were going haywire.

We had tried everything to escape, even trying to throw a set of ten-pound dumbbells at the window. They just bounced off like plastic. The one thing we had yet to try was fire, but trying to set the door on fire didn't feel safe. Burning alive inside wasn't on the agenda.

Sitting on the fancy couch, Xavier had a plate and a weed pile. Green goodness was funking up the room. He was smashing the buds between his fingers, breaking down the flowers.

We tuned in to an old TV show from my childhood; an anime series about space pirates. Cannon blasts and space engines blared out of the entertainment system. Despite searching for other options, this was the only channel with reception, so we decided to watch 'Heist Boys.'

"This used to go so hard," Xavier said, twisting the blunt.

I couldn't focus on the show; my mind was racing for a way out. "Man, we need to think, not watch TV," I said, snapping the TV off.

Xavier's glance shifted from irritation to realization. "Hey, dude. Can't you see I was watching that?"

"Fuck that cartoon; I want out of here," I said. "How can you be so calm when we don't know what's happening?"

"I'm not calm or happy about this bogus house we're trapped in, but I ain't about to stress either."

I was pacing in front of the TV like a crazy person. "What if Lucky comes back and finds us here, holding his cash and smoking his weed? What are you going to do? Blow smoke in his face and apologize?" I asked.

"I already decided... I'm going to start shooting at whoever comes through the door. Get my Keanu Reeves on," Xavier said.

"Get your corny ass out of here," I said. "You haven't killed anybody before. Have you?"

His demeanor changed, and his brows furrowed. "A lot's changed since you left, Travis. A lot. I know whoever enters will come in guns blazing, 'cause I'm blasting."

Xavier was always a hothead, and his accentuating that he'd killed someone stunned me a little. It was a war zone; however, I didn't expect my best friend to have killed someone. We both grew quiet. When I looked up, he had finished rolling the blunt. I tossed him a lighter and then sat down on the couch.

I sat in disbelief. My best friend was a killer, and I was on my way to being like him, or something similar. The information made getting back to school no longer a want but a necessity, and I wished I had never hung out with him.

I watched as he lit the blunt, thinking about the person he killed. As I sat on the couch, my mind was filled with questions. Was it an opp, or was it someone in a drive-by? Was it even a man? Could it be a woman? The hood could turn the most upright man into a caricature of himself. Hyper-masculine and temperamental black men portrayed the role shown by the media and sung about in music. Why did the hood massacre your humanity?

His eyes pinched together at the first inhalation. Trying to hold the smoke, he let out a series of coughs. "Damn," he said, wheezing, passing the herb to me. "Be careful; this is some flame."

This Lucky dude had some good weed. I couldn't take more than a few pulls before I passed it back. It was extra potent. The smoke twirled and coalesced in the center of the room, creating a strong, pungent scent that reminded me of skunks or cat piss.

Our eyes were red and low, and we were slurring our words a bit. The high-strung energy we felt earlier disappeared, replaced by the calm presence we shared.

Second by second, I felt myself sinking into the couch, unable to worry or lift my arms. "Yo, he had it coming, just to make you feel better," Xavier said under his breath, firing up the roach.

"Huh?" I said, high out of my mind.

"Earlier, when I said I killed someone, he had it coming. Punk had killed a girl still in school. Split her head to the white meat." He removed his skullcap and sat it beside him. "She was one of the guys' sisters; we rode down and handled our business. I don't know if any of my bullets hit him, but I was shooting." His voice was cracking with regret. "I ain't crazy or a psychopath either; I'm just tired." He trailed off and hit the last of the blunt. "So you ain't got to be looking at me all strange. I'm still the same. Still human."

In Chicago, that is how it was for young black men. Killed or be killed. It was one of the reasons I was trying my hardest to get back enrolled in school. This place felt like a vacuum of evil, waiting to suck you in and spit you out. Bones and all.

After pondering in my high state, I looked at Xavier, who was fast asleep, with his head hanging over his jacket. Unable to think about anything anymore, I leaned my head back in a magical wonderland, brought on by the potent marijuana. It was like the minute I blinked my eyes, I was asleep. Unable to open them, I dozed off and slept.

CHAPTER 14

THE DREAM SEQUENCE

THE LIGHT from the window shone on my scrunched-up face, waking me. It was a Tuesday morning, and I was on summer break with the whole day ahead, to do whatever I wanted. I made my way downstairs, on legs like springs, and prepared a big bowl of Frosty Toast with my favorite spoon, then settled in front of the TV in my tighty-whities, to watch cartoons.

Placing the bowl on the old, matted carpet in front of me, I zoomed in to watch anime for the remainder of the morning. The carpet, if you could call it that, was old, with soft and hard spots, making my legs scratchy as I sat and watched my favorite show. Despite the discomfort, this was my spot to watch TV, and I'd spend hours glued to the screen.

Today's episode was another installment of Heist Boys on Netflix. Our heroes were embarking on another thrilling, action-filled adventure. Slate Nightshade, the villain, had infiltrated the Heist Boys' base and sabotaged all their weapons, unbeknownst to them. It was epic, with laser fire and smoke everywhere, and I couldn't take my eyes off it.

Our hero, the indomitable William Foster, the abandoned child who would become the galaxy's most well-known thief, was on the brink of victory.

Standing before Slate, he gave a speech that was defiant and true. The music, sounding triumphant, was filled with tension and strife as he stood in his bulletproof suit. "Though I'm not a goody-two-shoes, I still hate to see scum like you walk over little people, and trample over the innocent, you know. It's okay to be badass, but you, Slate, are just plain old bad and despicable."

Slate, who laughed at the words being spoken, welcomed his demise. The camera zoomed in on William, then his weapon, and then back to Slate.

"You may wipe me out and destroy my base, but the seeds have already been planted," he said, still laughing. "But evil will live forever, William, and my defeat will allow my name to live forever."

The screen held on William's hand cannon for a bit, and then they showed his fingers pulling the trigger back in slow motion, each second filling me with anticipation.

I sat cross-legged in front of the TV with my spoonful of sugary vitamins and artificial flavors, splashing milk on my legs, as Slate was about to be defeated, his reign of terror ending. This was the moment I had been waiting for. I sat there, feeling the cool air blow in through the window, with my heart pounding. However, when William pulled the trigger, it was sabotaged and blew up in his face.

A thick cloud of black hid everything and everyone. All they showed was the smoke coming out of the barrel. I couldn't sit still as I waited to find out. What would happen next? Who would emerge victorious? The words shot across the screen: All those questions will be answered in the next episode.

There were more episodes to watch, but I decided to wait till later to find out. For now, I had to take out the garbage and clean up. I was ten, and cleaning up and putting things back where I found them was what grown-ups did, and I was aching to be older than I was. And the upcoming episodes would be even better after I had a snack to watch them. I got up, went to the kitchen, and passed my mom's room. She was in there with the door closed, "think-ing," as she called it, but I knew what she was doing. My older brother knew, too. Netflix and the neighborhood I lived in taught me about drugs. Kids talked and learned things, and I knew my mom had a problem.

The smell of burnt eggs and body odor was intense as I passed her room on the way to the kitchen to straighten up. I sprayed some air freshener by her sealed door as I passed, feeling a bit sad for her, before putting my bowl in the filthy sink.

The sound of beers clinking drifted in through the open window on a bright morning. My granddad was out back, listening to the radio, and drinking a beer. He and his friend would sit out every day in the summer, discussing the White Sox or how bad the Bears management was.

I peeked out and got yelled at. "Put on some pants!" my grandfather shouted before returning to his friend. "You're getting older and need to act like it."

I ran up the stairs, entered my dimly lit room, grabbed a pair of dusty jeans, and jumped into them before heading out to take out the garbage. At that age, I didn't care about hygiene; all I wanted was to enjoy myself.

I went into my secret stash to ensure nobody was look-ing, and I got my last $3. My brother had stolen my money before, and I didn't want that to happen again. Calm was a year and a half older than me and was hanging with the bad kids, as my granddad called them. He borrowed my money, as he called it, to do something he had no business doing. I didn't tell my mother or grandfather, but now I couldn't trust him. Calm was becoming a menace.

You see, my grandfather gave me money to take out the trash some days, and I'd save it. A quarter here, sometimes a dollar. Or when he got his social security check, a whole five dollars. It was a good time. Looking at the money in the messy room, I felt like I was taking care of myself.

I scraped the two bills and loose change into my sticky hands and secured them in my pocket with a tap. Today, after I took out the trash, I'd ride my bike to the store, pig out, and watch TV. What else were summers for?

I walked past my grandfather with two trash bags, hoping he wouldn't yell at me again. The smell was horrendous. I walked down the porch, to ensure the bags didn't touch my legs.

I held the bags like a tightrope, balancing on an invisible beam. The area wasn't big, but it wasn't small either. I walked down the walkway, bumping trash bags against the garage with Granddad's old Cadillac inside. He said it still ran, but Calm said it didn't, and he just liked to hang on to old stuff.

I reached the gate and threw the trash into the bin. As I turned to go into the garage and grab my bike, I heard some kids playing nearby. The voices sounded familiar. I pushed the old, rickety door, which scraped against the floor due to poor hanging. I walked around the old bucket of bolts, grabbed my bike by the handlebars, and opened the garage.

"I'll be back!" I yelled to my grandfather, who replied, "Close the darn garage."

My bike was the best in the neighborhood. It was a dirt bike, blue with red wheels. All my friends used to ask to ride it, and I'd always say no. The last time I let someone ride it, they tried to steal it. My brother had to fight half the neighborhood to get it back. I had learned my lesson.

I sat my bike outside the door, ran inside, and hit the switch. Running out before it closed, I hopped on my bicycle and rode toward the groups of kids.

They were huddled in the back of an abandoned building. Bony arms and ashy legs moved erratically, arguing over who would venture inside. "Stanley's a bitch, and so are you," said the little girl to the bunch of street-smart kids. "None of you even made it past the fence. Y'all are some pussies."

I slowed down and listened some more. "I bet you that there's some guns inside or a bag of money," one shouted.

It appeared that someone had torn the bolted door down and given access to the block kids. The "no trespassing" sign didn't exist to them, even though it was in plain sight. Most of them were bad as hell, always fighting and cursing. They weren't bad if you grew up with them, like I did; it was just how we lived.

I never rode my bike down the alley because I didn't want to catch a flat, but today, I felt adventurous.

I looked at the backyard, which was overrun with trees and branches. The gate was made of wood and was rotten. It was broken in places and looked like it would fall any day now.

"I'm telling you, that dog is going to get whoever goes inside," said one of the kids, with his front teeth missing.

"It's the biggest, most vicious dog I've ever seen," a child from overhead said, dangling from a tree limb. I turned up to his voice and said, "It's got to be watching something."

They argued amongst themselves before one of them walked toward the fence. You could hear a fierce growl from behind and a chain rattling, as the dog pulled and thrashed against it.

He jumped back and went back to the group. "What's up, Travis?" they shouted out to me.

I nodded, with my bike between my legs. They played rock, paper, scissors to see who would go next, while I hopped back on my bike and rode to the store. The girl was right; they were pussies.

I rode down the two blocks and bought a quarter juice, a bag of chips, and a piece of beef jerky from the Arab guys who ran the store. They were arguing when I went in and arguing when I left. They were fiery and mean-spirited. The one reason I came here was because it was close.

I sat on my porch, ate my chips, and drank juice alone, on a dull Saturday afternoon. My friend, the next-door neighbor's kid, was coming over to play. He was a year older, chubby, and always hungry.

"Got any more chips, Travis?"

My selfish reptilian brain crunched up the chips, and funneled them into my mouth. With one eye peeping, I watched his whole mood change. I'm talking about his shoulders slumping and his facial expression shifting. I felt a bit bad and gave him the last of my pop. It'd hold him enough for his next snack.

After sitting there for a few minutes with nothing to do, I had an idea.

"Follow me," I said, and I hopped on my bike.

He was a pest, but he liked Heist Boys and even had the action figures, so I put up with his relentless questions.

After dismissing the first few, I told him where we were going.

"On a heist," I said. "Just like William Foster."

In minutes, we were in the back of the alley, standing by the gate the kids were in front of earlier.

My friend walked toward the fence, and the dog leaped up, pulling his chain.

He ran back, his eyes filled with fear. "Why didn't you tell me?" he shouted.

I asked him to watch my bike and not let anyone ride it. The Fosters were expert thieves and masters of stealth. I would get past the dog, like William would.

I crouched toward the old, decayed fence, listening for the dog. "Get behind me, and don't make a sound."

I went into my pocket and brought out the package of beef jerky I got from the store. I put it in my mouth, and I ripped it open. I tore it into pieces and tossed it over the fence. You could hear the dog run to it. The pit let out a fierce growl, but I threw another piece, silencing him.

We approached the fence, rolling my bike inside and beside it. I went into the package and threw another piece of jerky at him, and I called him a good boy, just like on TV.

"That's it, fella," I encouraged the vicious dog; who was softening to our free treats. If I knew any better, the pooch was smiling. The dog's ears perked as he waited for another treat, with a newfound look of curiosity, on his once-snarled face. I threw one more, and we rolled my bike inside, out of the dog's reach, toward the steps.

Now, we could see what was in the old abandoned building.

Looking at the decrepit home, I felt a bit scared and unprepared. William Foster always had a weapon. All I had was the short, chubby kid. Regardless, I felt just as adventurous. We were surrounded by tall weeds, broken furniture, insects, and old trash. The bushes were overgrown, making it look like a miniature jungle. Spider webs on the leaves and broken bottles underneath our feet.

We stood in the shadows of the old building, about to see something that would haunt us for years. Something was so gross that we never told anyone.

I crept up the stairs, me and the neighbor. The old wood was bending under our weight. On the fourth step, it gave, sending my leg through. I held the banister and saved myself from injury. After breathing out loud, we carried on with the remaining steps. The Heist Boys were on another adventure.

We entered through the door and found ourselves inside a kitchen, or what used to be the kitchen. A couple of walls were missing, and the floors were destroyed. Trash bags and vomit lay in a pool by the stairs, and a stink that made me gag filled my nose.

We called out inside the dark, nasty house but heard nothing. Walking by a bathroom, a giant rat ran across my foot, making me run further inside.

What I saw next did, in fact, make me vomit.

In a room with the door closed, we heard grunting and moaning. We got closer, with me grabbing the knob. Every fiber of my being said to turn around and go back outside, but the curiosity in me said to open it.

I turned it and saw the old man. The same old man I saw at the red light. This was different. I was dreaming, and I was no longer a child, and what I remembered happening —two drug addicts involved in a vulgar act—was replaced by a vision of the old man from the night of the party. He had the same demeanor and the same lost look in his eyes.

The dream, now a nightmare, flashed in and out behind

my closed eyes. I struggled to wake up but couldn't. The short, creepy dude, Lucky, was also here, grinning as before with bloodshot eyes. Daggers that shot ice along my veins.

The old man's face had a look of familiarity to it as his gnarled hands gripped my shoulder and gave me a powerful shake. He was pulling me from my dream, it appeared. When I opened my eyes, he stood before me, smelling like a small distillery, with a serious look on his face.

My breath was jagged, and with my heart in my throat, I struggled to focus on his face. Was I still dreaming? I thought as I sat there, wondering what the fuck was going on.

CHAPTER 15

ECHOES OF THE PAST

THE OLD MAN stood over me, looking into my eyes with a look that made me sit up in my seat. The same old man I had met after the party a couple of weeks ago. He was focused and clear, unlike the night we first met. There weren't any signs of drunkenness or drugs, and he still had the scent of fresh laundry about himself.

I was alarmed and concerned for my safety upon seeing the strange old man. I knew I could overpower him if needed, but I didn't want to beat up an old man. The thought still remained, however. Who was he, and where did he come from? With Xavier and I locked inside the strange house, seeing him standing above me freaked me out a little.

I looked over at my friend, who was knocked out from the potent marijuana and, by the looks of it, having a nightmare. I wanted to shake him, and pull him out of the dream, but the old man was staring at me, making me feel even more uncomfortable.

"Are you coming?" the old man whispered, his warm whiskey breath, wafting into my face.

With a look of disgust and curiosity, I obliged. Moving like death itself, I got up from the couch and followed the old man wherever he was taking me. Almost by instinct, or something that was pulling me towards his destination.

He strolled with a severe lean, like he was suffering from some type of pain or discomfort, grimacing at almost every movement. He would put his hand on the wall to brace himself. All I knew was that my senses were on high alert, ready to grab him if he fell. Even though I didn't know him, something inside of me said to protect this old fellow. I guess, on some level, he reminded me of my grandfather.

The vivid dream I had just experienced clung to my thoughts, enveloping me in nostalgia as I trailed him down the endless hall toward the kitchen. I hadn't thought about that time in years and wondered why my subconscious had dragged it up for me to remember. The light illuminated the narrow walkway with pictures of scenic vistas and oceans.

As we entered the brightly lit kitchen, I noticed a door I hadn't seen earlier, which perplexed me. I remembered the large refrigerator; its clock was still behaving strange. The range and appliances were still sparkling, and the floor was spotless. But right next to the stove was an old door that stood out from the rest of the modern home.

The door was raggedy, splintered, and hung as if by hope on rusted hinges. Right above the knob, the paint had faded from years of use. To be honest, seeing the old door brought me some comfort. The faded paint meant people used it often, and I liked that.

With his severe limp evident, he made his way to the door, his wrinkled fingers curling around the knob. As he pushed it, the door swung open, exposing the darkness and an unknown presence from within. Turning to me, he leaned against the frame before venturing into the abyss.

Like a specter, I followed, ready to support his frail body, which wouldn't withstand a fall.

"Is this the way out?" I asked him, my voice soft and weak. "Hey, old man, where are you taking me?"

"It's not too far," was all he said.

In the darkness, the only sounds were the creaky steps we descended, with each step threatening to give away at any moment. The old man moved with extreme caution, taking slow steps; that heightened my anxiety. Would he hurry up? I thought. The more time he took, the greater the risk of an accident.

I heard a squeak, and the old man paused, causing me to bump into him. "I think I stepped in something," he said before leaning against the wall again.

Coming to a stop, I felt something wet and sticky on my shoes, but that felt wrong. When we reached the bottom, I heard him fumbling around in the dark before being drenched in a stale orange light.

We were standing in the basement of the home. In front of us was a spacious room with a closed door. The air was cool and stale, and it smelled of dust and liquor. The warm overhead light created shadows that normally wouldn't have alerted me. But there was something about how they hid the side of his face that made me feel timid.

"We made it," the decrepit man said before turning around and walking further into the room.

I looked around, still curious about who this old man was, and why he told me to follow him. Xavier and I were locked inside the house, and I wanted some answers, so I let the old alcoholic lead me further. Maybe he had the answers to my questions and could provide an escape.

When I took a step, I nearly slid and fell from whatever I had stepped in on the steps. I looked at the old man's foot and saw a trail of blood, which made me look down at my own feet to see crimson splashes on my shoe soles.

My eyes went to the stairs, and that's when I saw the carcass. The dead rat's eyes had popped out of its head, and its abdomen lay smashed and bloody. The hairs over its skin were falling from the flesh.

"Disgusting," I thought, sliding my feet on the ground to remove any trace of the vermin that still clung to my shoe.

I looked around for a rag or something to clean off my shoes, still keeping my eyes on my immediate surroundings. Just knowing that I had dead rat guts on my shoes was revolting and made me want to retch. Spotting an old cloth, I couldn't get my hands on it quick enough.

Bent down and wiping the blood from my shoe, I took a closer look at the new room we were in. It was mostly empty, with newspapers and power tools lying around. I should've never followed his old ass, but I did, and now I had to face the consequences.

Getting all the blood off the side of my shoe made me feel cleaner and more stable. I threw the rag back to where I got it and felt a mix of emotions wash over me. Alarm was the most powerful, but a strong sense of regret and loss hung over me as well.

It felt strange, combined with the weird feelings the dream gave me. Where before it felt like I was being pulled along, now it felt like something was pushing me towards the unknown.

What did I get myself into? Following Xavier inside this house had been a mistake. Agreeing to check out the inside is a nightmare. The old man stood in the middle of the room now, holding a half pint of cheap alcohol, rocking back and forth. Eyes looking over my shoulder at something with a grin on his face.

The hairs on my arm stood on end as I felt a dark presence behind me. I don't know how I knew who was shadowing me, but I knew it. Maybe it was the gold chains I heard rattling on his chest or the subtle chuckle, but I turned around to see what the old man was staring at.

Standing before me was Lucky, the foul man who had been following me and wedging his way into my life for the previous month. The man was like something conjured from the darkness, with his relentless pursuit and menacing grin.

"What the fuck is he doing here?" I turned and asked the old man, who still had not told me his name.

"Don't be alarmed; he's a friend," the old man shouted out, sounding drunk.

I inched back from Lucky's immediate presence, with watchful eyes. I didn't care what the old man said; I didn't trust this smiling fucker one bit. How he stood on the back of his feet was imposing.

During my retreat, my eyes never left him. His sinister smile spread to his eyes, as if he were amused by our actions. He wore the latest fashions, with rings and jewelry shining off his fingers and neck. I couldn't determine his age, but I guessed he had to be older than he looked. He had a mothball smell to him, like old people's cologne.

The whispers that danced behind his eyes gave me shivers. His gaze lingered, eating the defenses of my mind. Thoughts of walking through the mall flooded my mind—images of mannequins and marionettes—and I thought he looked like a disturbing puppet or an avatar being guided by something ungodly.

Lucky's voice broke the awkward silence. "Well, well, if it isn't Travis! How's it going? Find any crazy secrets in this nuthouse yet." He laughed out loud.

The cackle made me think back to the pistol, which was in my waistband. The money was an afterthought, but I imagined the hefty pistol in my grasp, at that moment.

I shifted my stance, ready to pull out the pistol at a moment's notice. "Not really; more of the same," I said, letting him know I didn't trust him a bit with my voice. "How do we get out of here?" I asked.

"Whoa there, let's not get ahead of ourselves. The old fella's got quite a tale to tell," Lucky said, patting the old man on the back. "It's a doozy."

I looked at 'Daniel,' fired up. "What is he talking about? You two motherfuckers have been following me for weeks now. What do you have to say, and if it isn't about getting out of this house, I don't want to hear it?"

The old man crept towards the bucket at a measured pace and flipped it, making me angry.

The old man's voice dropped a few decibels. "What are you doing?" Now sounding more raspy and breathing hard. "Take a seat. I must tell you something that may seem absurd, but I want you to listen," he said before kicking over a smaller bucket at me.

I watched as he bent his old knees and rested on his makeshift stool, with my hand on the pistol. He took his time, and I think I heard his joints pop.

Meanwhile, Lucky stood to the side, with his hands clasped as if his prayers were being answered.

Small bugs, which I hadn't noticed before, scampered towards Lucky's presence, their minuscule bodies running across his fashionable shoes. I felt the cool air become hot and humid inside the room, the shadows concealing something evil and sinister. I stood straighter, as if my posture could protect me.

The scene felt surreal, like a nice framed painting or

photograph. Lucky was dressed in the latest trends—designer this, antique that—and an ancient man like Daniel sat on an empty paint bucket in an open basement. The overhead light illuminated the subjects, with the old man in the room's shadows. Lucky's gold chains still shone, despite the limited light. Banksy couldn't draw it better, or maybe he could; I don't know. But however you looked at it, it was a stunning scene to witness, and I wanted to capture it.

I took out my phone to snap a quick memory of Lucky and the old man. Why not? I pondered. I could try to document this entire situation or, at the very least, record the old man's story. It could serve as evidence for some of the bizarre shit that was happening.

I switched the phone to film mode and started recording, but Lucky grabbed my phone and told me not to record. He said he couldn't be filmed. "Whatever," I said, sitting on the bucket, but not before declaring that I would only do so if they showed me how to leave the house.

Meanwhile, upstairs on the couch, Xavier wakes from his sweat-inducing slumber with a start. He pats himself down and calms his breathing. He's panting, out of breath. He had just dreamed of running forever down the same street, where turning a corner led him back to where he had started. He had his old high school track uniform and pistol in his hand.

Remembering that he's trapped in this freaky house, he first looks for his friend. The spot I was sitting in was empty. "Yo, Travis," he calls out while standing and grabbing his crotch.

After not hearing a reply, he takes a leak upstairs and returns to look for his friend.

He walks out of the living room and into the hallway. Up ahead, he sees the kitchen. He takes a right and heads upstairs. He runs upstairs to reach the landing, looking around for the bathroom. Visiting the toilet, he goes inside, and drains the snake into the gleaming porcelain before hitting the light switch.

With a flick, the interior is revealed. It is up-to-date, with multicolored tiles and a stand-up shower. As Xavier shakes and zips, he peeks into the shower and sees a dirt trail. He squirts green hand soap from the fancy dispenser, washes his hands, and dries them on the designer dry clothes, hanging nearby.

He goes into his pocket and grabs a cigarette and some lights. Calming his fraying nerves begins, and he feels a little better. He even felt optimistic.

Just as he was leaving, the lights flickered. First, then a dozen times or more, before going dark.

The only thing he can see is the lit cigarette in his hand, in the reflection from the mirror. He puts it in his mouth, takes another drag, and walks toward the light switch. He flicks it several times, and it doesn't illuminate the room.

Turning to leave the bathroom, the light flickers back to life, revealing an outdated bathroom instead of a modern one. Something that reminds him of his childhood. An old-school bathtub and low-to-ground toilet; cheap shit used by slumlords.

"What the fuck?" He says this, and a woman behind the curtain screams.

His eyes bulge from the sockets, and he turns and runs out into the hallway. When he turns around and looks back, he sees the regular bathroom. No old bathroom fixtures, and no woman screaming. He drops the cigarette on the plush carpet and stamps it beneath his heel.

Looking around, he grabs his pistol from his waist and continues his search for Travis.

He walked up the stairs and went into the living room, searching with his gun. "Yo, Travis, stop playing and come out."

He walked down the long hall towards the kitchen and didn't see Travis or the door. Looking inside the fridge, he grabs a water bottle, and places the gun on the counter. Scared out of his mind, he opens the bottled water, spilling water droplets onto the clean floor.

"Where did he go?" he asks the silent house, knowing it wouldn't answer him. He was just speaking to himself in fear and confusion when he heard footsteps and giggles from the living room.

The water falls from his hands, and he grabs his gun from the counter.

"It's on," he said, running to the room.

When he gets there, he stops and puts his hand in his mouth. What he sees can't be possible. They had searched the house, and it was empty; no one was home.

He puts the gun into his waistband and approaches two kids with long black hair sitting on the couch. They were playing when he entered, but now they looked at Xavier with eyes of wonder.

"Who are you, and where did you come from?" he asked the children, who seemed to be fading in and out.

They ignored him and kept playing among themselves.

He took a cautious step forward, focusing his eyes on the tiny bodies.

He whispered, "Can they see me?"

From behind, he heard a voice. "Yes," and he almost jumped out of his socks.

"Papa is going to fix everything; just relax."

Unable to hide his fear, he ran to the front door, beating on it like a madman. Things like this shouldn't happen. Inside the vestibule, he claws at the door until he rips one of his fingernails off. The adrenaline coursing through his veins ignored the pain. Later, the pain will blossom, but it is forgotten as he tries to open the locked door.

CHAPTER 16

PULLED INTO THE UNKNOWN

MYSTICISM AND RITUALS were subjects I researched in school. Some of it remained fresh and easy to recall—details about how certain cultures believed in spirits, enabling communication with the dead through dances and symbols etched or carved into wood or the ground. Others asserted that life was a reflection; the other side was the real world—a place visited during sleep.

Shamans sent acolytes on vision quests to communicate with lost ones or used a combination of herbs and flowers to pinpoint their long-lost ancestors in the world beyond. I found reading about these topics fascinating, exploring how ancient people turned humanity's inability to understand nature into superstitions.

For example, an eclipse could trigger violent reactions in some ancient societies, such as the Aztecs or Mayans. I didn't believe in spirits at the time, but sitting here with this old man and his strange companion made me reconsider my philosophy.

In any case, here they were before me: one so old, I thought he might shatter on our journey downstairs, and the other dressed like a character straight out of a book. If I stared at Lucky for too long, his darker-than-night skin looked translucent with its murky countenance. Like, if he wanted to, he could peel it off.

The old man cleared his throat and bent to grab his drink near his foot, scraping the bucket against the floor, causing me to look in his direction. "Now, you're about to see a vision—a spiritual window into the past. I wish I had time to explain, but to detail how all this works would take weeks. But for now, just know that time is like a stream moving in a certain direction. Without a ship or a boat, we all drift in the direction that it takes us. Start here," he motioned with his hands. "And end up here. The waves are just too strong for our mortal bodies to fight against them. But say, for instance, that you have a vessel with a strong engine powering it. Then, Travis, you may fight the current and go to any point that you choose. Lucky is that vessel. A powerful steamship can take you back to an earlier time."

"What are you?" I turned and asked Lucky. "Are you some type of spirit? Or something else?"

Lucky moved closer to us. "Let's just say I'm a traveler. Something the universe spat out for variety's sake. A visitor is here for a short while. A gift with a curse."

My heart was thudding against my chest. A gift with a curse? I mused. I sat there, pondering what I had heard. It didn't make any sense at the time. "A traveler?" he said. More like a demon, to my young eyes.

"While you're inside," the drunken man continued, "you cannot drift from him, you hear? And you are bound by certain constraints. The powers that have been granted to him are boundless, but they have their limits." The old man steadied himself and took a drink. "Just know that it all happened, every instance... And you must remember everything it shows you. It's important," the old man said, wiping his mouth with his hand. "I've already begun the first part of the ritual, and now to continue, I need your help for the second part. I want you to be calm and don't overreact. For us, it'll be mere minutes. But to you, let's just say you'll have more than enough to experience everything."

Something told me to get up and demand to be free, but another part was curious about what I was hearing. Going back in time, seeing things, time being like a stream. It all sounded rather mysterious. "I just want to go home. My friend and I found a lot of money and some of the most potent weed I've ever smoked. This thing you're asking of me is too much."

"Who do you think planted all that? Lucky did, that's who. It had to be something enough for you to stay, while I performed the first part of the ritual."

"You're playing games? Is the money even real?"

Looking at my pleading, the old man's voice was very convincing. "Of course it is. Lucky is powerful, as I told you. He can do things that even I cannot explain, and I called him."

I was still unsure about this, but had to ask one more question. "Will I be able to touch things while I'm on this... quest?"

"Will I be able to be hurt? No, not for this part," the old man said.

"No, you will not. You will, however, experience things as if you were there in person. It'll be like watching a movie, so to speak. Just ride the current, and you should be okay."

I sat without saying a word, yearning for this conversation to be over. "Yeah, yeah," I blurted out, annoyed. "All this sounds good, but I find it hard to believe," I said, shaking my head. "You and your strange friend must be high on something."

Lucky chuckled, "High, you say? We're creeping you out? Young man, this isn't the time to be making accusations," he laughed. "He told you that time is a liquid. Did you not hear what he said? I think you should be quiet and be prepared," he said with his gold chains rattling against his chest.

I was now in a situation that frightened me on a different level, but I had to play it cool. These figures would no doubt exploit my fear if they sensed it.

I turned my head and scraped my bucket closer to the old man's seat, while he went into his shirt pocket and pulled out a joint, or so I thought. Trying to avert my eyes from Lucky, the old man bent down in front of my face. Before I could move or push him away, he opened his toothless grin and blew smoke into my face.

The thick, pungent cloud clung to me like a heavy cloth draped over my face. The smoke was translucent but carried a weight that attached itself to my psyche as I tried to breathe in the vapors. I started coughing and gagging, realizing that the stuff I inhaled wasn't weed at all. It was like I was being suffocated by a poisonous breath, bent on pulling the life out of me. I coughed so hard that I fell from the bucket, clutching my chest. Gasping for breath, I thought this was the end.

"This shit is killing me," I thought as I lay on the floor, squirming, clutching my chest.

"It'll stop; just be patient," was all I heard.

The pain was shooting through me in waves, scorching my body from the inside out. My lungs felt like hot asphalt, with the pulses of pain, on the brink of collapsing. Then it all left in a rush. The smoke, the room, Daniel, and Lucky all disappeared, leaving me in the blackest darkness I had ever seen.

I was in between worlds, wandering around, waiting for something to appear, inside a pitch-black area with a thread of light off in the distance. I followed the light with its weak shine, welcoming me. I touched my body, running my hand along my abdomen and feeling my abs underneath my shirt. What is this place? My feet followed the light.

A dense fog was forming as I got closer. Something about this place was familiar and warm. It was almost like I had been here before. I don't know how much time passed, but it did feel liquid, like Lucky said. As I got closer to the illuminating spot, a door formed.

With hands that felt all too real, I tapped the door open and heard the old man's voice speaking in a low tone that I had to strain to hear. It was the wildest feeling I had ever had. Did they drug me and leave me sprawling on the floor, hallucinating, or was I here in the flesh?

I focused on the door, the fog lifted, and two hands gripped me by the shoulders, pulling me inside. I closed my eyes, accepting my fate. And when I opened them, I was in another place and time, wondering if I was still alive. Watching, as well as listening to, a tale that I couldn't discern, from truth or falsehood.

CHAPTER 17

IDRISSA'S STORY PART 1

AUGUST 10, 2002

He woke up early to get a head start on his day, having a busy schedule and significant responsibilities after dropping out of high school. He was always on the move. Idrissa, a very industrious young man, would always do odd jobs for people in the neighborhood: making a run for a dope dealer, smacking up opposing crews, or shaking down small fries.

Many would call him an enforcer, but in these times they just called it 'handling business'. Making sure no one got away with anything slick for his 'boss'. Yet, 'boss' was a term the young kids had discarded as well. The new generation thought making up a new term or phrase changed everything, but it didn't. It signaled the merry-go-round-like choices humanity had been making since the dawn of time.

Under the gritty exterior lay a man who loved his family and did everything in the streets to ensure their well-being. He wasn't wealthy but connected, and his reputation was solid steel. He always came through for the block. Always.

Like the time he had to lay down a few people for robbing the boss's lady. It was gruesome what he did to the dumb fucks, but necessary. Tying them up and dropping them from the ledge was spoken about for months.

Standing beside Idrissa as he gave the orders to drop them from the six-story housing complex, head first, was Victor. Idrissa didn't want to do it, but he liked how people treated him now and the extra money Victor would some-times pay him.

This morning, as he woke, he planned out his day—a ritual Idrissa performed each time he rose. The watch that was wrapped around his wrist ticked like an insect, with his arm near his head. Opening his eyes, he reviewed what he had to do based on the previous day. It was methodical and mapped out.

If Idrissa dropped off some drug money, for instance, he'd follow up with the big boys to ensure it was straight. He measured his movements twice, sometimes thrice, so that he only had to cut once when he acted. It was how he moved up in the organization so fast.

Everyone started calling him 'surgical' because when he sliced, it was with lethal accuracy. Like that time, he had to go handle some kids a block over for selling dummy bags of cocaine. I won't get into it here, but it was pretty messy. After that, Victor always brought him along to enforce his words.

Underneath it all, Idrissa was just playing a role, a char-acter he built to survive the wicked streets. You had to be aggressive if you wanted anything in this city, and Idrissa wanted a lot. So to get all the things he wanted, he had to put on the face of his peers and do things that others would view as savage.

Now that he had gotten older, he had started to look

back at his actions with remorse. A person changes a lot over three years, and in this environment, time was hyperactive, which is to say that he had changed a lot over the 3 years since he had been down.

Victor had given him a package last night to deliver and pick up some money. It was at 11:00 a.m. One of the guys with him would make the exchange, and they'd return with the cash. The other guy was Victor's brother, already a familiar partner for jobs like this.

Today, he would finish the delivery and spend time with his kid's mother. It was Sunday, and he wanted to chill and sort out his life. He was close to making a significant achievement and wanted to share his plans with his family.

Getting out of bed and wiping his eyes, he let out a long, rigid yawn, ready to begin his day. Idrissa's room reflected his no-nonsense, disciplined lifestyle. The faded blue walls seemed to absorb the bright morning light, with a tattered poster of Muhammad Ali standing over a downed opponent as the sole decoration. In the corner, an old wooden chair held his worn-out gym bag, ready for his next mission.

A simple metal pull-up bar hung against the opposite wall, aligned with the door frame. Each morning, Idrissa would grab the cold bar and lift his body with the precision of a seasoned gymnast. His muscles worked in harmony with his body, making him move like an instrument.

Beside the pull-up bar, a faded mirror reflected Idrissa's disciplined figure. The mirror showed his sweat-slicked body, veins pulsating with possibility. As he sat on the edge of the bed, winded from his workout, the wooden frame groaned under his weight. He glanced in the mirror and saw his girl half asleep with his little boy, Malcolm, and then back to the gym bag, his partner for the day's tasks.

"Gloria, get up, babe," he said, his voice a quiet reminder of the world he lived in. "I've got to make a run."

"Okay," she said, still half-asleep.

She was like a picture, lying in bed with his son. Her plump belly is showing signs of another addition.

"Later on, I want to barbecue," he said, rubbing her stomach. "Take my folks' van and get some meat and charcoal. I should be back in a couple of hours."

She answered with one eye open, "Okay, but for what?"

"I want to have a BBQ and tell y'all something. Something that may change our lives."

Gloria sat up, wiping the crust from her eyes. "Huh?"

"I don't want to spoil it. Just go get some ribs and some chicken. I'll be back later."

He kissed her and left the room.

As he exited the room, all he smelled was breakfast and opportunity. He took a quick shower and got dressed, grabbing the gym bag as he went downstairs, ready for today's hustle.

The front door was open, blowing a cool breeze through the quaint home. "Granny, I've got to make a run," he shouted, leaving out the front door.

"Wait," she said, hurrying into the room. "Don't be running those streets without putting anything on your stomach. Sit down for a bite; I'm making your favorite."

He dropped the bag and let the screen door close. He followed his grandmother's every word, like scripture. She was the beacon of the family and the closest thing to a true mother.

"Okay, granny, but just a bite. I've got to take care of some business," he said.

He followed her to the kitchen, down the long hallway, and past his grandfather's study filled with books and pictures of his family from the south. Some were black and white or yellowed, while others were newer inside picture frames. It showed his family's legacy, which he always felt when walking down the hall.

"Where's Granddad?" he said, sitting at the table. "I haven't seen him in a few days."

The old lady yelled loud enough for him and his grandfather to hear her. "In that dang on basement of his."

"You know how he is, granny; that's why you married him," Idrissa said, chuckling.

Idrissa hastily assembled a sausage, eggs, and cheese sandwich. His grandmother tried giving him a bowl of grits, but he declined with a kiss and headed out, ready to handle his business for the day.

He paused for a second before leaving, sensing something. His grandmother asked him what ailed him; he said nothing and left the door.

Juanita, his older sister, was sitting on the steps, enjoying her morning cup of coffee. "The dead have risen," she said while sipping from her cup.

Pausing on the steps and biting his sandwich, he said, "Yeah, I've got to handle something for Vic. Then... I'm relaxing."

"Don't you relax every day?"

The sarcastic heifer got on his nerves, but he loved her. "Stop it; I'm always working," he said, taking another bite of the sandwich. "I'm getting paid, sis; stop hating."

"Yeah, you may be getting paid, but all money ain't good, little brother. You need to be careful."

"I'm always careful; stop worrying."

"Granny and Papa might not understand what you do here, but I do. Be careful, please," she said.

A bit of syrup ran down his arm as he threw the last bite

in his mouth and walked down the steps. "Stop stressing so much, and while I'm gone, call up the family and invite them over; I'm barbecuing and celebrating tonight. It's going to be off the hook," he said to his sister as he opened the gate to his world.

The neighborhood was decent. Not the best, but many raised families around here and sent kids to school or the military. A church was across the street, surrounded by apartments and a corner store.

It was Sunday, and a few people washed their cars or watered their lawns. Further up the street were parked cars, Dodges, and Cadillacs with bad-ass paint jobs and 22-inch rims.

He looked at his car, a fiery-red Cutlass Supreme. It was an old-school car Victor gave him to go on runs for the gang. He was an excellent driver, and he felt he earned the vehicle by being loyal.

Throwing the last bite of the sandwich into his mouth, he licked at the sweet liquid running down his wrist and fumbled out his car keys. Waving at his sister, he got in his car and drove towards his destination.

When he picked up Derek, Victor's brother, he looked forward to making the exchange and returning home. The news he wanted to share with his family was big and could be life-changing.

Derek entered the car, closed the door, and shook Idrissa's hand. "Id, my guy, how's it hanging?" He said before continuing, "Where's the work?"

"In the back," he replied, pointing to the backseat at the bag of drugs.

Derek nodded and went into his pocket, pulled out a pack of menthol's, gave him a cigarette, and lit up one for himself.

Idrissa grabbed it and lit it, relishing the toxic smoke. Derek was talking about some party, but he was only half listening because he was still thinking about the news he was about to share with his family later. *They're gonna trip the fuck out,* he thought while Derek droned on.

"Dude, are you even listening to me?"

"Huh, yeah, yeah, man." Focusing on the conversation again. "You said you went to a party and got it on last night," Idrissa said.

And Derek went back to telling him about his exploits in the hood. Idrissa listened, nodding his head and driving to the location. They'd done this plenty of times, and it always ran smoothly. Go inside, make the drop, and come back.

They were nearing the location, and Derek was fishing a bottle from his pocket. He took a small half-pint of cognac and tipped it back, emptying it down his throat.

His face grimacing, he leaned back and asked, "Yo, after we do the job, I need you to drop me off at my baby mama's crib. She doesn't stay too far away from here."

It wouldn't be a problem, so he told him he would do it, and the two continued. Seeing the place a couple of blocks away, Derek grabbed his pistol, checked the clip, and put it back in, cocking it.

"Maybe I should go inside this time, man; last time you started gambling and shit. I ain't got the time today, dawg."

"No worries, I'll be in and out, and then we can go. As a matter of fact, you can keep the car running," he said as Idrissa pulled up to the house. "Give me five minutes."

Idrissa waited for his acquaintance to make the drop,

listening to the radio and smoking a cigarette. The window was down, and the wind was blowing while the sun beat down from overhead. A few minutes passed, and Derek returned with the money.

"Told you," Derek said, closing the door.

Putting out the cigarette in the ashtray, he said, "You get the money?"

Derek held the bag open for Idrissa to see. After nodding, he drove down the block, ready to return to the hood, barbecue, and kick it with his family.

CHAPTER 18
CALM'S RETURN

AS TRAVIS ABSORBED the old stranger's story inside the basement, on the outside, his brother was making every attempt to locate him. Calm drove past the block where his brother's car had been parked when he and his friend went missing. Wearing his security uniform, he looked like a cop, on a case. He had passed by this block every day on his way to work, and he stopped and looked for his brother every time. When people disappeared around here, it was one of two things: they were either dead or in jail. Calm couldn't see his little brother going to jail and not contacting anyone. The other thing was something he refused to accept. One of these days, he hoped, his brother would return.

Today, as he passed the building, his mind focused on the argument with his mother the previous night. They yelled and screamed at each other, and said things they shouldn't have. She was still recuperating, and he felt terrible afterward, but he had to say how he felt. Knowing that their father was demanding on him and Travis growing up and being met with the same sad story every time they asked, infuriated him. "Your dad died in the military," with no description of how he looked, what he liked, or anything else. The least she could do was tell them his favorite dish or what sports he liked. Little boys, black boys in particular, needed something to latch onto besides the streets. They needed a dad to show them how to be men, how to fight, and how to protect themselves. It's why he made sure he was there in his son's life.

As he and his brother grew, they heard stories about what happened in the neighborhood. Still, it was all foggy, with no one sharing accurate information. The story was that some drug dealers killed a whole family. Nobody survived the tragedy, and people didn't want to bring it up, so it became a hood legend. Their granddad knew what happened that day, but he kept his mouth closed out of respect for their mother. Calm didn't understand, but whatever happened had to be messed up. With their granddad in the grave, that font of information was no longer available to him.

At Travis's 8th-grade graduation, he and his brother decided to squash it, and let Mom be. Whenever they brought it up, she damn near had a panic attack. His mom was a recovering addict, and they didn't want to trigger her. She was doing well, and they wanted her to keep it that way.

He was lying on his bed, thinking about Travis and hoping he was safe—he and Xavier. Twisting over on his back, he thought about what it would be like to grow up with a dad. Would his brother be missing, or would they have different lives? His own son lay next to him, curled, with his hands balled under his chin. The smell of the shitty diaper was lingering around the room, muffled by the air freshener he sprayed. The boy wasn't even a year old and was already making full-fledged assaults on his nose. He looked at his boy and kissed him on the cheek, rubbing his pudgy stomach.

"Son," he whispered. "I ain't going nowhere. Believe it."

At 23 years old, he held a job and cherished his nagging baby mom, whom he valued. On his off days, he watched their little boy while she worked. Looking down at his seed brought up powerful emotions that he thought he had swallowed. What would he tell his boys when they asked about their granddad? The same bullshit story he had heard as a kid? Or make up some tale about a mythical figure and hope they believe him?

Getting up from the bed and making sure he didn't wake his son, he went downstairs to speak with his mother. After all these years, and her near brush with death, he thought he would hear about his old man, in her words. Her silence on the matter had done more harm than good and it felt right.

He gripped the old banister as he walked downstairs, his mind occupied with how he should approach his mother. Should he be gentle and ease into it, or outright and explicit with his questions?

His hands were wrapped around the steering wheel, still frustrated at the conversation he had with his mother. With tears in her eyes, she had almost told him something about his father last night, but she chickened out, the pain too great for her. After pleading with her, he later raised his voice. "Drugs and trying to forget what happened almost killed you, Ma," he screamed at the top of his lungs. "And you still won't tell me anything. Not even what he looked like. What color were his eyes? And who did he live with? Just tell me anything... Even a lie will do?"

The TV played in the background while she sat on the couch in the living room, ignoring his questions. She wouldn't look at him; she was so unbothered. Sipping her black coffee and eating her morning breakfast, she held onto her story like a villain in a story.

Calm, on the other hand, was pacing around the room, pleading with her.

"Please, Ma. I need to know."

"I can't; it's too painful to dredge up. Let old dogs lay, Calm. It's too much for me." She looked up at him. "Maybe later, when I feel better..." Her words came out in a huff.

"What? When you're dead?" he asked, without thinking.

She froze on the couch with her mouth open, not moving or saying a word. When he quieted himself, he looked and noticed her eyes. Seeing for himself the pain his words had.

Anger has a way of making you blind to others' conditions, and he wasn't special in that regard. In the heat of the moment, enraged and emotional, he was oblivious to his mother's feelings on the matter. Tears were streaming from her eyes, and a blank look was displayed across her face. What had he done? "Shit," he said aloud, feeling ashamed.

His hands went to comfort her, but she just stood and went to the kitchen with her now tasteless breakfast and unfinished coffee and tossed them in the sink. Pecking her on the cheek as she stood at the sink, he hoped he hadn't gone too far with his questions. Despite her silence toward his father, she had done a good job since her bout with addiction. Even making sure one of her kids went to college. She wasn't a super mom, but she did have special powers, and he prayed he hadn't damaged them.

Oh, well. He did apologize before returning to his room and playing with his now-wide-awoken son. And to his surprise, Malcolm Jr. had taken another dump, stinking up his room.

▭

Three weeks.

He spent three long weeks hoping his brother wasn't dead. The police knew nothing, and nobody in the hood had seen anything. But still, after all this time, he kept looking for him. He thought of himself as his protector, and knew deep down, that his brother was still alive.

Xavier did get down in the streets, but not enough to get kidnapped or killed. Even though he had left the streets, you still had to be connected, to survive here.

Calm heard things about Xavier, but none of it was too bad. Rumors were that he shot his gun at a large crowd and didn't hit a thing. Despite the tough guy exterior, he was still little Xavier—smart as hell and fast on his feet.

They were all trying to survive in a place that ate kids alive. Make a wrong step or shake hands with the wrong guy, and your life could change in an instant. Chicago had a healthy appetite for young black men.

Peeking out of the car's window, he sees a familiar face looking at the house under renovation; where his brother's vehicle was found. She was standing and staring with a determined look in her eyes. Making out who it is, he calls out her name.

"Keisha? Is that you?" he yelled.

She swiveled her head, smiling, as he leaned out the window. With his arm hanging over the door, he beckoned for her to come to the car.

Travis's ex, whom he hadn't seen since he went missing, wanted to see what she was doing in the area.

"What's up, Calm?" she said, walking to the car, scraping her feet against the ground.

"Nothing much, just on my way to work. What are you doing over this way?" he asked her.

She had a heavy jacket on, and earphones in her ears. "The same as you," she said. "I'm looking for your big-headed brother." She said it with a hint of sadness. "I know he's still al-" she caught herself saying.

The wind was blowing, causing a few leaves to blow past, as she shrunk inside her jacket to avoid the bite of the air. She continued, "You guys still haven't heard anything?"

"Nope," he said, feeling a twinge of hopelessness. "What we can do is pray and stay vigilant." Just thinking about his brother made his chest tight with the unknown. What had happened to his brother?

The two stood in silence for a moment before she peeked inside the car. "I don't have to come down this block to get home. I come by every chance I get," she muttered, breaking the silence. "But still, I worry. Xavier is involved with all types of shit and got Travis into something."

Calm invited her inside the car to get out of the brisk wind, but she declined. "I'm cool, and Calm, believe it or not; I enjoy the weather, and I want to finish looking for your brother."

Calm shook his head, thinking she was strange but loyal. Her eyes looked puffy, like she was crying, by the way, but he disregarded it. Feeling awkward over her tears, he wanted to give her space to feel her emotions. "Well, I have to get on my way to work. Be safe, Keisha, and if I hear anything, you'll be the first to know."

And he was off. He turned down the corner and proceeded to go to the gig. Crying was contagious, and he had to leave before he started bawling. He had held it together for three weeks and wasn't about to cave because some girl couldn't control her feelings. Optimism would deliver his brother and bring him back home safe and sound. Now, trying to forget everything, he prepared himself to do his 8 hours and just work.

As Calm drove off and left her by the curb, Keisha returned to stand in front of the house. Her eyes were locked on it, and the strange door stood out like a missing plank in a broken fence. The uniformity was somehow 'off,' when looking at the other houses. The door didn't belong here. It was new and made of some type of mahogany wood. It was a door from a mansion or something, she supposed.

Her allergies were bothering her, making her eyes watery. She had hoped Calm didn't think she was crying; Keisha shed those tears that she felt the first few days Travis and Xavier went missing. Today, Keisha was investigating, as she does every day. The house struck her as peculiar, not due to its architectural design but for some other puzzling quality.

She knocked on the door multiple times, but there was no response, causing the hairs on her arms to stand on end. When she inquired with the neighbors about the building, their responses were identical, explaining that it was undergoing renovation.

The block was a 'lost' one, as she heard described by the boys who lived near here. No one tried to hustle or make any money on this strip, and it had been like that for years. They said it was cursed, but who believed that? Old ghost stories were just that: stories. Whoever said that cursed nonsense, had to be smoking.

Today, she had a bad day at work and felt frustrated looking at the house. This pent-up contempt towards her bosses gave birth to an unwavering resolve to uncover clues about Travis's baffling disappearance.

Ever since Travis had gotten back from college, she had become attached to him. Having grown a little since high school, she hated what she had done to their relationship. And now it felt like it was meant to be.

A simple car ride between them had caused fierce emotions to bubble to the surface, and when his mom got sick, they bonded stronger than ever. She kept remembering his toned arms above her as he pounded his body into hers. The feelings she felt were strong, and she almost shed a tear, staring at the building. Travis was more than Travis to her, if that made any sense.

Travis's choice to hang out with Xavier was dumb, in her opinion. Once reckless, always reckless. He had changed since they had all been in high school. Gang-banging, having kids, and shooting. He had become everything her dad said to avoid. "Thugs caught slugs," as her dad used to say around the house, and he wasn't lying. A lot of the young men from around here were dead or trying to be dead.

Standing before the rehabbed building, the wind started picking up again, making the empty branches contort and bend. She had lied to Calm about liking the weather before. It *was* cold out here, but Keisha had seen something she wanted to check out. An occurrence that baffled her. She didn't want to say something so strange out loud for fear of being laughed at. *Who would believe it?* She thought.

She narrowed her eyes, scrutinizing the porch. There, wedged under the door, lay a piece of mail. She was blinking rapidly to ensure her vision wasn't deceiving her, pulse climbing. Yet the envelope exhibited bizarre behavior, zipping back and forth at a speed quadruple the norm.

Initially, she wondered if her eyes had betrayed her, but studying the erratic movements only confirmed her suspicions of the uncanny occurrence unfolding before her.

The envelope was old and bent, and whenever the wind blew, it jittered way too fast. With her breath quickening, she waited for a large gust to blow again while moving closer. Nature was so unpredictable, but all was well on time. She thought it would blow when it felt right, and she crouched in anticipation.

Then it happened. A large gust blew, knocking Keisha back with its force. She stood against it and watched the envelope, and there it was. The edge of the envelope moved too fast, almost as if it were flickering, like one of those movies her grandma had on VHS. The envelope looked fast-forwarded. Her eyes narrowed on it as the wind calmed down.

She walked up the remaining steps, taking her time. Scaffolding and rusted tools littered the porch, with an old, empty bucket of paint sitting on top of the steps. She stepped over a loose brick and put her head to the blacked windows, trying to peer inside. It was darkness inside, like before when she was here, like someone had sealed the windows against the light. Her hand went to knock on the window. For some strange reason, her heart pounded against her chest this early evening. Was it the envelope making her frightful or the black void she had stared into?

When her hand left her jacket pocket to tap against the window, a passerby spoke out, shattering the silence and making her jump with fear.

"Excuse me," he said from the sidewalk. "Do you live here?" he wondered.

Blood rushed to her face. Realizing it was just a stranger, she calmed down and replied. "Huh? No, I was just looking for somebody, I suppose," she said, walking down the steps, looking behind her at the envelope.

Keisha spoke with him, her mind still on the envelope. The man looked at her with a strange look before leaving her alone in front of the building. Looking at the weird door, she thought about going back upstairs but changed her mind. The events of the day were too much. She would wait until later, she thought, when she wasn't so scared.

As she looked back at the house, she knew it held some mystery. Some information about Travis and Xavier's whereabouts. Swallowing her emotions, she was done with it for now. After the hard day she had, she pushed the curious thoughts aside and hurried home.

CHAPTER 19

IDRISSA'S STORY PART 2

"YO, leave the money with me, and I'll take it to Victor tonight," Derek said from the passenger seat of Idrissa's car. The radio played a muffled groove in the background, and Derek's voice was hushed as if sharing a secret.

Idrissa listened, glancing at his watch. The words being shared made him doubt his career choice. In the drug trade, you followed the rules or got dealt with, as they said. He had seen lives cut short for failing to pay attention or obey orders, and now he was caught in something that could end his life. Going back home without the money, was not an option.

"Man, your brother would kill me, dog. What are you trying to do?"

Derek fell silent and ordered, "Make a left up here," pointing with his finger.

Idrissa was growing worried over Derek's suggestion to leave the money with him. "Hold on, family. I might not drop you off anymore. You're acting crazy."

Idrissa was worried about what Derek might do with the money. Derek was a gambler and liked to blow large amounts of cash on dice games and sports games; there was no telling what he might do.

Idrissa had even won a few bets wagering on a Bears game. With him, it went beyond just gambling—he had a legitimate problem. The young man would bet on any, and everything.

As Idrissa drove, Derek's face twisted in response. "Nigga, I wasn't asking; I was telling you. You better know your place, little nigga. Just tell Victor I've got the money, and go on home. There's nothing to worry about... I promise you."

Idrissa was worried and wanted no part of this endeavor. The car began to slow, and Idrissa weighed his options. If he went back without the money and no Derek, Victor would probably lay into him. Even though Victor 'liked' him, he would still want his money. Forty-five grand was nothing to play with.

Pointing at the corner where Derek's whole attitude changed since coming out of the house, his somewhat darker and more calculating eyes made Idrissa wonder what was going on. Derek had never acted this way on their previous trips and would be cracking jokes or talking about one of his latest come-ups, trying to convince him that riding back with him was in their best interest. He looked at Derek, "Come on, man. You know your brother will lose it and might kill me if I show up without the money. Give me the bag, or ride back, like we always do."

"You think I'm playing, don't you? Park the car and do as you're told before I lose it. Right now, you're worrying about the wrong motherfucker," he said, pulling out a pistol and placing it under Idrissa's chin. "You need to be worrying about me."

Idrissa froze, his shoulders tense, as he parked the car.

"At least call him and tell him what's up." He paused. "If I go back and tell him that flimsy-ass story, I'm as good as dead."

Derek leaned closer, letting the weapon fall. "Victor likes you, and, you know, you'd be doing me a favor." He poured it on thick. "When I win, which I always do, I'll hit you with a couple thousand, for being a stand-up guy."

"Derek, don't play around with the money, and have me take the fall," Idrissa pleaded, gripping the steering wheel harder.

Strapping the bag around his chest, ignoring Idrissa's pleas, he looked adamant. "It's a sure thing. Just don't tell Victor what I'm doing. Capiche?"

They were in the North Suburbs, with picket fences and lawns everywhere, huge homes, and quiet streets stretching for miles. Derek relaxed a bit and put on his biggest smile. "Now get home, and remember, keep your mouth closed."

Before Idrissa could protest, the car door opened, and Derek walked to a house with a slim young woman waiting on him.

"Fuck," Idrissa's voice rang out into the silence of the car.

After hitting the steering wheel and regretting not going inside and doing the pickup himself, he knew that he was doomed.

▭

The ride back home was silent, and Idrissa's hands fumbled at the dial to lower the volume. With his eyes darting between cars and beads of sweat running down his face, he was frightened. Big, bad, tough Idrissa, was now shaking in his seat. What would he tell Victor when he got back around the block? Where Derek was unpredictable and loose, Victor was an absolute madman. Would he believe that his brother left with the cash and would return? Or were they setting him up? They said the truth would set you free, but dealing with people who told lies for a living posed a different challenge.

Idrissa maintained the speed limit at 65 mph, not wanting to rush home before he dared to confront Victor about the missing money. Derek had played him and ran off with the money. He was so nervous that he chain-smoked, considering whether he should have fought Derek, grabbed him, or even punched him. Derek wouldn't shoot him in broad daylight, would he?

He looked in his rear-view mirror at the police. Breathing in and out, he tried to regain his composure. His grandfather had taught him breathing exercises as a kid to control his fiery temper, which helped. His hands were placed on the steering wheel in the ten and two positions, and he was seated upright. Focusing on the road and breathing to calm his nerves was his best bet. Out here in the suburbs, the police loved to fuck with black people, especially with braids.

"Lord, let them leave me alone. I got too much going on for all of this drama."

The police followed him for two miles, almost tailgating him. As he looked in his rear-view mirror at the shaded faces, he knew they were about to fuck with him. In that instant, they sped off with lights and sirens, in pursuit of someone else. Idrissa wondered if his prayers had been answered. Under his breath, he whispered, "Thank you, God."

If the police had stopped him, he would have been

involved in a high-speed chase or ended up in jail. Carrying a gun and a few bags of marijuana was asking for trouble. And although he was tossing rocks at the penitentiary, the risks seemed worth it at the time. Maybe Derek would hit a lick, and come through with those few grand he had promised. And he could use the extra money for his latest endeavor. Because if everything went as planned, he might be exiting the heartless game sooner rather than later.

Having one kid and another on the way made him think about the future. The cold streets of Chicago were no place to raise a family. His own mother was dead, to the wickedness that made him. His grandparents took him and his siblings in, but they couldn't keep him out of the streets. They were naive to his devilish ways, or maybe they were turning a blind eye. Either way, he knew his life was headed toward disaster if he didn't fix it. But first, he had to figure out how to tell Victor that he didn't have the money.

Hours passed, and he was waiting in one of Victor's spots in the living room, enjoying a drink. It was close to three, and he had to be back to start cooking. A TV played reruns as two men sat at the table, bagging up drugs. Victor would be here in a few , they said. Sit down, roll up, and chill. They had some females coming over later and were excited.

"You wanna chill, Id? It's more than enough," the one with the coffin tattoo said.

Looking over at his guys with a hint of worry, he said, "Sorry, gents, but I'm having a little barbecue at the crib. Y'all could slide, if you want. I'm going to have a couple slabs, chicken, and all the smoke and drink you can handle. It's going to be off the chain."

They looked at each other with smiles and nodded. "We just might. They did say they were tired of sitting around here. Maybe we can entertain them at your spot before bringing them back here."

Idrissa nodded, trying to make himself feel better. When Victor heard about his money, he would flip out.

Checking his watch, he sat there, nervous. If Victor had hurried up, he could still return and? barbecue with his family. The news he was about to drop would change everything. He leaned back in his chair, looking around the primarily vacant room. A TV, a few couches, and the kitchen table. Frayed curtains and empty liquor bottles all around.

He stood up and went over to the window, peeking through the curtains like Denzel in Malcolm X. Turning his head, he asked about Victor again and heard the same response. Getting tired of waiting, he walked toward the door, but one of the men met him at it. "You gotta sit still, Id. He'll be here."

Now, he was scared. These men were his friends, but they were loyal to Victor. Murder was always an option, but he didn't want to endanger his family. Victor was ruthless, and there were numerous people who were eager to fill his shoes. Wearing his poker face, he returned to his chair and checked for his gun. It was under his jacket, in a hidden compartment. If he needed it, he could have it out in a flash. Having been awake since the crack of dawn, smoking weed, and now drinking liquor, his eyelids felt heavy. Unable to stay awake, he fell asleep.

When he awoke to Victor's face twenty minutes later, he was surprised and caught off guard. After looking around and becoming familiar with the sparse room, he stiffened up and remembered why he was there. He was nervous and couldn't sit still.

Victor was menacing, with a scar down his face from a drug deal gone wrong. His dark skin shone as he spoke in a calm and relaxed manner.

"Idrissa, how are you, man? Did you drop off the work, as you were instructed?"

He froze at Victor's question. "Yeah, I did, but..."

"Okay," he said, pulling up a chair and taking a seat. "Rodney here says you didn't bring the money back with you. Is this correct?"

"Yeah, but your broth—"

WHAM.

One of the dudes who was bagging up the drugs hit him on the side of the head, right by his temple. Then another blow, this time to his stomach. He doubled over and groaned. Light flared as another punch knocked his head to the side like it was on a string. He started grabbing for his head but decided not to; appearing weak was a sign he wanted to avoid.

Victor was a big boy—6 feet tall and all muscled. He said this before leaning into Idrissa's face.

"Your brother is crazy, Vic," Idrissa explained, but his 'friends' hit him again. This time, in his groin, making him fell out of the chair.

"Ah, if his story doesn't check out, he's going to be dealt with too; believe that," Victor said, kneeling down to peer into his face. "Talk," he said.

Idrissa explained what happened after they picked up the money, leaving out no details. "I rushed back here to tell you face-to-face. I swear I wasn't on bullshit with you, Vic. I promise," he pleaded. One of the henchmen stood with his foot on Idrissa's back, planting him on the floor like a roach.

Victor bent and held his face like a mother might cradle a child who had been misbehaving. His gold fronts glistening, making sure he was understood, he said, "I believe you, but not completely. If my brother doesn't bring me my money, you're dead. Gang or not." He said this, letting go of Idrissa's face in disgust. "Get out of here, and by tomorrow, if I haven't heard from Derek or gotten my money, it'll be nice knowing you."

He let go of Idrissa's face in disgust, while the two henchmen mused and laughed beside him. "Oh yeah. Can we still bring our girls though, or nah?" They said as they left him to squirm his way up, hurt and embarrassed.

CHAPTER 20

IDRISSA'S STORY PART 3

THE RIDE to his home was short and filled him with worry over the missing money. Victor always kept his word, even if it was wrong. Last year, he was shot at by some dudes a couple blocks over—real nasty cats with a bad rep. While ordering a turkey burger at the local food spot, he thought he saw one of those responsible.

Victor had followed him back to his spot and texted Idrissa to come and handle business and to prepare to get dirty. When he sent those types of texts, he wanted the person to suffer. Normally at the hands of Idrissa, while he watched.

This time, when Idrissa arrived, everyone gathered told him that this wasn't the guy, but he was adamant about it and wanted his revenge. "He looks close enough, and this will send a message," was what he said as Idrissa went inside his home on some guerrilla shit and dragged him out.

For the next two hours, behind an abandoned building, Idrissa tortured the skinny man with a gang of different tools. Retching in between pulling off his fingers, Idrissa did everything Victor suggested.

At times like this, Idrissa zoned out and imagined himself doing something else. Beating a man between the eyes with a hammer was too brutal, even for him. After that ordeal, Idrissa didn't have to do stuff like that anymore, but still. It all painted the picture of a very unstable man who you always wanted to keep happy.

Derek had better come through with the money, or his life was over. Idrissa wasn't even all that brutal; he was just imitating what he had seen. Motions and actions—he saw all black men portrayed in the media. Thug or pimp. Killer and addict. He never thought it would get this bad, however, and now he feared for his life.

Idrissa cradled a small knot on the side of his head from the blow he took from Victor's goons, his former friends. He smoked a cigarette and parked in front of his grandparents' home, praying that it wasn't noticeable.

Looking in the car's rear-view mirror, he mumbled, "I'm good," before taking one final drag and smashing the finished Newport into the ashtray. "Won't nobody even notice it... It ain't that big." He groaned at the lump.

Getting out and feeling the pain in his ribs was a different story. He'd have to feign an injury that wasn't serious. Every time he moved, he wanted to wince at the throbbing sensation emanating from his side. But he was a big boy and would play it off as long as he had to. Gloria would flip and ask questions, and he didn't want to scare her.

Stepping onto the curb, he looked around, breathing in the scent of fresh cut grass that came from somewhere nearby. Standing tall, he took a measured breath, fighting through the pain. It was a lazy, late Sunday afternoon, and the kids played a game of 'it' on the block. White folks called it tag, but in the hood, they called it 'it.'

A kid ran up to him in a bright orange shirt and grabbed

his leg. "You're it," the little crumb snatcher said. Being so frustrated with Victor, the kid's interaction didn't even register.

"I said you're it, Idrissa." The kid spoke louder. "You are supposed to chase us." His chubby hands still clutching Idrissa's jeans.

Idrissa looked at him, smiled, and continued walking.

Any other day, he would've chased him, laughing, but today, his mind was elsewhere. "Maybe next time, little man, maybe next time." He said with a voice of sorrow.

The sun beat at the little kid's back as he ran to his group of friends without missing a beat. Idrissa missed those days of doing nothing and having fun with his friends. Hanging out and getting into trouble. Now 'fun' took on a whole new meaning. Where playing 'it' with his friends was a game of life and death.

The old screen door sounded, and when he walked inside with an old, soft slam, that was familiar. When he left, he smelled eggs and sausage in the air, in the morning. When he returned, the scent of vinegar and spices drifted to his nose.

He entered the kitchen and saw slabs of ribs, bowls of chicken wings, and other ingredients for the barbecue, all sitting on the table. It was a lot. On the 4th, they'd have even more, but for what it was, it was a feast.

Gloria, his child's mother, sat at the table, seasoning a bowl of ground beef and holding his son, with his sister mashing potatoes for her salad. "You're back," they both said, looking up.

"Yeah, I am," he said, looking at the pot on the stove. The ribs were boiled in vinegar to tenderize the meat and hurry the cooking process. The smell coming out of the pot was strong and stung his nose.

His grandmother was still at church, and his grandfather was no doubt in the basement, drinking as he always did these days.

"I was just about to fire the grill, but Malcolm wouldn't let me." His son was fidgeting, trying to grab anything his little finger could grasp. "Could you do it? I'll be out with the ribs, and you can start grilling," Gloria said, beaming at him.

He kissed her and his big-headed son and bent down to grab the bag of charcoal from the floor. A set of multicolored keys fell out of his pocket onto the floor, echoing. He grabbed them up before anyone would notice; this was part of the big surprise he wanted to share. Something he had been saving up for a while.

Walking out to the backyard, he surveyed the area and went over to the grill after he spotted it. And now that he was alone, he let out a groan and continued on. The grill was right where it always had been, under the tree, sitting in the shade. He tossed the bag of coal down, opened the Weber, and looked inside. They barbecued all the time in the summer months, and he didn't have to scrub it down; he just rubbed it with the wire brush hanging by a string, on the side.

As he scrubbed the grill in pain, his mind drifted to his situation with Victor and Derek. Two brothers who were insane and out to destroy his life. The drug game was unpredictable, but he didn't think it would be something like this that would take him out. Gambling.

Derek ran off with that money, which put him in a perilous position, and he was stressed. The lighter he produced was a refillable kind and was old and knotted with dents. Flicking the top, he patted his pockets, found his cigarette, and lit it.

The smoke brought relief as his lungs filled up with the poisonous fumes. After he finished sucking down the toxic vapors, he wiped down the grill, feeling a little optimistic.

"He'll come through... I know it," he said under his breath. As a matter of fact, he started to feel triumphant. The news he was about to share would change their lives.

Later, his girl would wobble down the stairs with her round stomach, and he would begin grilling, and when everybody was together, he would lay it on them. He prayed and asked God under his breath to protect him and his family with a hodgepodge of words he heard from his grandmother. Church wasn't his thing, but his grandmother had instilled the Lord in him when he was young.

Though he hadn't prayed in years, he knew the power it held.

With the grill ready and his silent prayer in God's ear, he pulled out the keys and started to twirl them around on his finger. Regardless of how the situation with Victor played out, he was sharing his news as planned tonight. He had saved up enough and leased a house in the suburbs. The money was obtained through the streets, but the real estate agent didn't care.

Five years of hustling with the guys and he had paid itself off.

Gloria, Malcolm, and the one in her stomach would be protected from the harsh realities of the ghetto. Yup, Idrissa had done the unthinkable. He'd bought a house in the 'burbs. Although he'd have to get a legit job, it was worth it in his eyes. Saving his family from the harsh realities was all he wanted to do. Getting so close to the violence that surrounded the environment made it a priority.

The whole household would come with him. Chicago had proven to be too vicious to raise a family. The house was big enough, with a full basement and four bedrooms—more than enough room. And maybe his grandparents could rent out their old home to some good tenants, or even sell it if they wanted to. Granny would jump at the opportunity to move to a better neighborhood.

Thoughts plagued his mind of the fucked-up shit he did in the streets, and he was tired of losing sleep because of it. The new home would be a unique platform to jump off and live, sending his kids to better schools without the pressures of gangs and violence around every corner.

As the day wore on, his grandmother came home from church, and his grandfather walked up from the basement, drunk and smiling. A couple of his close friends came by, and even a couple of out-of-towners. They had a real celebration that day with drinks, spades, and food.

When he told everyone the good news, everyone cheered and congratulated him. It felt good. It might've turned out better if he'd done this a week prior. Being in the suburbs would mean he wouldn't have to do the pick-up with Derek and all the drama with Victor.

That night, when he had time alone, he thought about all his immediate problems, said another prayer, this time out loud, and asked the Lord to protect him and his family.

When he woke, he planned his day in his head, and this time, it was hard because, in the past, nobody wanted him dead. Rules and regulations were always easy for him to follow; he even excelled at it. Loyalty to the guys, and all the other codes he knew and would practice for life, were good precepts to live by. Waking up and not having a job to do, or an idea of where the money was, was different for him this morning. This was the first time he hadn't planned his day in a long time, and it made him feel funny.

Getting out of bed slower than usual and he exercised. Each chin-up painful, and a reminder of the ass whipping he was given the previous day. When he finished he showered and returned to his room where he saw his girl rocking his child to sleep.

When she eyed him, she was gushing with love, happy to be moving away from the violent neighborhood. Looking at her, he turned his head, unable to hold her gaze. Words started to form, but he held them back like a dam. Because once he started to tell her, they would rush out in an unrelenting stream. Seeing her dreaming of their future, he couldn't burden her with the fucked-up news. Feeling the guilt, he sat on the bed beside her and held her in his arms, thinking about how today would play out.

Derek had his string of luck before and paid off his debts, but lately, he had been unlucky, and Idrissa swallowed a lump and continued to worry.

"I was thinking next week we could be gone from around here. Last night was the going-away party. Are you excited?" He whispered, with Malcolm sucking on a pacifier, fast asleep.

"Yes, I am, and Malcolm will love it, and the little one," she rubbed her protruding stomach. "I knew you were up to something, but not this." She said, lying the baby down. "You think the guys will be okay with you up and leaving?"

He stood up and moved towards the door. "Why wouldn't they? This is why we hustle, right? To live better and make moves. Shit, I wonder why they haven't moved yet." He looked around the room.

"I don't know. You shouldn't have had that barbecue yesterday, telling everybody. Victor might be mad," she said, walking over to him. "You know him and his brother are crazy."

Just hearing the name Victor made him freeze, and his girl felt something. It could've been the look on his face, but she asked what was wrong.

He shrugged and turned his back. "Nothing."

Grabbing a shirt, he left the room, leaving his girl in the dark about his problem with Victor. "I got class later on; you'll pick me up?" She called out to him from the bedroom.

"Yeah, like always."

Running down the stairs and ignoring his grandmother's calls to get something to eat, he almost tripped over his sister. Outside and walking towards his ride, he hopped in, intent on finding Derek and inquiring about what the fuck was going on.

As the morning progressed, he smoked cigarette after cigarette, and his nerves frayed all morning. Coffee always annoyed him, but this morning, he stopped at McDonald's and got a cup so that he could be more alert in his pursuit. He hit all the spots they frequented—the gambling spots, the lounge, everywhere. He even went to Derek's mother's house and couldn't reach him.

The car was sputtering on the corner, down the street from his house. The cigarette from his lips had gone out, and he was frustrated. He had scoured the land and didn't hear or see anything. All the guys looked at him funny when he asked about Derek. Some wouldn't even come talk to him. It was like his reputation turned to shit overnight. Hopping on the expressway to pick up his girl from nursing school, he was beginning to get scared and out of options.

CHAPTER 21

IDRISSA'S STORY PART 4

GLORIA WAS THE COOLEST, most down-to-earth female he had ever dated. She was smart, stayed out of the streets, and had goals and dreams. When they first met, he couldn't believe how lucky he was. While hanging at the corner store with friends, goofing off, he fell in love as soon saw her.

It wasn't love at first sight, but a deep 'like' that grew over time. Gloria was the first person to ask him hard questions about his future and follow up with him. He liked that a lot. Since his mother passed away when he was younger, his grandparents sort of just shut down from the grief for a while. And his dad was a typical no-show, so her showing attention meant something to him.

This gave him and his siblings a 'me against the world' attitude,' which was basically a real loner-type vibe. Glo, as he sometimes called her, made him feel like he wasn't alone, and that was important to him.

It was amazing how a span of a few years could change a person. They had been dating for four years, and yet it felt like he had known her his whole life. In the beginning, he cheated a few times, but they survived, and after she got pregnant with Malcolm, he has been faithful ever since.

If fate and destiny are real, then he and Gloria were as solid as the concrete beneath your feet.

Another thing he liked about her was that she wanted something from life. Having met in high school, she graduated with honors and had big plans after school. She wanted to go off to college. But life has its own plan for you sometimes, and dreams get pushed to the back burner.

Two young lovers are going to express it, and Gloria ended up getting pregnant, destroying her dreams of going off to college. Then, after suffering a miscarriage, she was depressed and forgot about it.

It wasn't until her second pregnancy and successful birth that she began to smile again. When Malcolm started walking, she enrolled herself in school, determined to pull herself up and do something with her life. When she found out about the little one, carried, it emboldened her to finish.

That alone made Idrissa want to do better, even if it was in the streets. Being a petty hustler who used to play football was cool, but Idrissa had dreams too at first. After dropping out of high school to sell drugs, he was focused on becoming the biggest drug dealer Chicago had ever seen. After working for Victor, though, that dream turned out to be a steaming pile of shit.

The drug trade was too difficult to master and not end up being killed. Every story he heard ended the same way. They were all either killed or in jail doing long-ass bids. By the time he figured it out, it was too late for him. If the cops ever found out about any of the things he had done in the name of his gang, he was out there. To be honest, he was surprised he wasn't dead or arrested already.

Luckily, seeing the birth of his son changed him,

though, and made him think about his future with fresh eyes. Gloria and his naive grandparents turned a blind eye to the stories they had no doubt heard by now. They were blinded by how he acted when he was home, which was loving and kind.

Today, driving through traffic, he thought of his future again. All the stupid shit he did in his teens would be forgotten, and this time he would move in a different manner. The only thing he had to do was fix the whole Victor situation, and then he would be free to be the dad he never had.

See, when his days were empty, he would always pick Gloria up from school, and they would talk and go get something to eat. He was proud of her for doing something productive. At least twice a week, they'd do this, and it was their thing. The conversations they had prompted a lot of their major decisions in life. The sound of her voice mixed with her smarts was all he needed to hear to motivate him some days, and today was one of those days he needed it.

A few students were leaving as he pulled up to the community college. He had circled the block twice because it was downtown, and it was a hassle to find parking at this time of day. When he spotted his girl walking down, her face perked up a bit, and by the looks of it, she'd had a shy day.

With his best smile after a long day, he hopped out of the car, grabbed her bags, and helped her in. She was 7 months along, and he wanted to make it easy on her; she was carrying his seed.

As they settled inside and headed back home, Idrissa was contemplating how to break the news that Victor might be after him. He hadn't spoken to Victor since yesterday, but he was sure he still wanted his money.

The radio was playing, and the bass was vibrating the

car. Gloria had her hands folded on her lap, looking out the windows with a pleasant look. The wind ruffled her braids in the afternoon sun. She looked so beautiful and calm that he didn't want to shatter her mood with his negativity. He opened his mouth to speak but said something about the house he'd just bought. She lit up, discussing everything, her eyes reflecting her hopes and dreams.

Throughout the conversation, he had a sinister feeling that made his replies sound shaky. His laughter was false and melancholic. He kept it up, and Gloria didn't realize what he was hiding, but he felt small for not being brave enough to share his concerns.

As they pulled up in front of their home after a couple of burgers, they spotted a small group of men surrounding the house. Victor and Derek were standing side by side on top of his porch, looking heated. Eyeing Gloria rubbing her stomach, he almost drove away.

But before he could, Gloria got out of the car, questioning the young men's position. "Who told y'all you could stand there like that?" With her pregnant mid-section protruding. "Mrs. Johnson don't play about standing on her porch," she said as she walked towards the fence.

Idrissa walked behind, praying that things didn't escalate. "Idrissa, where's my bags?" She said over her shoulder. "Are you stuck on stupid or something?"

Idrissa stood there frozen for a second.

"Well?" she said continuing to stare.

He tried to turn but was interrupted by the voice he dreaded. "He'll grab 'em later," Victor snickered from the porch. "I want to... holler at him real quick."

Idrissa eyes focused on Victor who was wearing a tank top, showing his muscled arms and tattoos underneath. In his front pocket was a pack of cigarettes, the crinkled box smashed against his thigh.

His heart danced inside his chest as he stood there. Each beat threatening his resolve. Many of the young men brandished pistols at him as he paused behind his girl. Grabbing his stomach, he felt sick for a second, but then took a big gulp and decided to take whatever came his way. Did he deserve this? Of course not, but he wouldn't act like a bitch after all the dirt he did for the guys. What he deserved at the moment was their respect.

Taking Gloria by the arms and looking very worried, he spoke, eyes shifting around. "What's up, Vic? Derek, bring you the money." He said, walking up the steps.

Victor halted his movement as he stepped to the to the porch's landing. With a hand, he poked Idrissa in the chest. "I can't believe you showed up," he chuckled, looking over to Derek. "We have to talk about something."

Gloria stiffened up and tried to speak, but was silenced with a deft backhand to the face. Sudden and violent, it made Idrissa grab for her.

The words that came out of Victor's mouth halted his action, however. "Tell your shorty to have a seat; I don't want to fuck up a pregnant woman, but Wacko down there don't mind. Do you, Wacko?"

Idrissa didn't even turn to face Wacko; he knew he was thirsty to do the dirt and get his name ringing. Idrissa looked at his replacement with eyes of fury. Everyone here was a snake. Some would put a slug in their own mother to advance in the streets. Looking down at Gloria's bloodied lip, filled him with rage.

Heart pumping like gasoline, ready to be unleashed. "I'll explain everything; just go inside," he said to his girl between gritted teeth, but the other men standing in front of the door halted her. "What's going on, fellas? Let my girl go inside," he continued.

Victor hit Derek on the arm. "She doesn't want to go in there." He laughed. "It's nasty."

Idrissa's eyes widened as he tried to force his way into the home. Grabbing one of the young punks and throwing him aside. Pushing his way forward like a linebacker, he almost made it inside. Almost. From his blindside Victor caught him with a nasty right hand to the jaw.

Red pierced his vision as he took the blow, but he didn't fall. Instead, he punched Victor in the face with a vicious blow of his own. While Victor stumbled, he grabbed for Derek, who side-stepped and hit him on the side of the neck with a weak punch.

He ate it like a big boy and began to choke Derek so hard that he thought his eyes would pop out. Victor hit him in the ribs and followed it with a cross to the face, which dropped Idrissa to his knees, forcing him to let go of Derek's puny neck. Gloria rushed to his side, screaming; she, too, was hit in the face, silencing her.

"Idrissa, my boy, where is my money?" Victor said, breathing hard. "I asked you yesterday, and you told me some bullshit about my brother running off." He breathed down hard. "That was a lie," he punched Idrissa again. "He said you dropped him off at his girl's house in the suburbs and left with the money."

Idrissa looked at Derek, but Derek couldn't hold his gaze. "You little lying motherfucker," he shouted from the floor but was caught with another vicious punch by Derek. Blood was sprayed everywhere.

"What did you do with the money?" Derek screamed, holding his bruised hand.

Everyone gathered began assisting Victor and Derek in

pummeling poor Idrissa as he grunted out in pain. Once an enforcer but now a victim of Derek's lies, it seemed as if it was over. It was in no way possible that he would survive this.

After several seconds of carnage he looked unrecognizable. Breathing ragged, it was over. Gloria crawled to hold Idrissa in her arms, crying. "Please stop, Victor." She sobbed, her face a picture of agony and surprise. "God, please stop!"

Victor took out a cigarette and lit it gasping for air. "Tell me where the money is, and I'll let you go, Idrissa." He panted. "You put in a lot of work for the guys, and I think we're even for what I did to your family."

If Idrissa's eyes weren't swollen, they would've widened at the words. "What are you talking about?" He said through damaged lips. "Did you fuck with my family?"

Victor, now bent down, hands on his knees. "Yeah, I did. I hope you can forgive me."

Idrissa wasn't crying, but now tears started falling from his bruised face. The men let Gloria run inside to see what happened. After a few seconds, Idrissa heard a scream, followed by a thud.

"Gloria," he sputtered up between globs of thick blood. "Gloria!"

The men who stood and watched dragged her limp body back to the porch. "Wake the bitch up; I don't want her to miss this," Victor said to Gloria.

Derek, following orders, slapped her on the face and shook her awake. Idrissa looked at them with eyes of regret. Preparing his last words.

It appeared that Idrissa's whole family was massacred over money his brother had lost gambling. A dumb habit that would cost him his life. Taking labored breaths on the ground, Idrissa was at the end of his rope.

"I'm tired of repeating myself. Where. Is. The. Money?" Victor said, his voice filled with rage.

"I told you yesterday, Victor, your brother ra-"

Derek wasn't a killer; he was the party animal, addicted to gambling and loose women. However the event was too complicated and too heated, and someone had to die. Raising his shirt, Derek went into his waistband and pulled out a 45-caliber automatic pistol.

Two shots crackled through the air, hitting the bloody and broken Idrissa square in the chest. Gloria, almost caught one of the bullets, but using the last bit of strength, he pushed her out of the way.

There was no music, no last words. Just bloodshed and lots of it.

After the brutal backstabbing, the men walked down the porch like nothing had happened, leaving him to die in a pool of red liquid. Gloria ran inside over her his grandmother's and sister's dead bodies and called the ambulance.

The paramedics, with sirens blaring, arrived and rushed Idrissa's unresponsive body to the hospital, where he was pronounced dead upon arrival. The story spread in the hood the following day, but no one was arrested. Victor and the guys had killed everyone, including his sister and younger siblings.

All who witnessed it were too scared to repeat it, but still, the story would become a legend. It was too vicious not to. All that was left, they said, was Idrissa's watch lying on the porch, still ticking.

What was funny, however, was that Victor didn't live long after; he would die a similar fate. Gunned down by the men who wanted to collect his brother's debt. You can live by whatever code you want, but in the end, if you lived by the sword, one day, you'd have to fall on it.

CHAPTER 22

THE PROPOSAL

I LAY on the floor in the dim, dusty basement, fiddling with my dad's watch on my wrist. The old man stood before me, speaking in a slurred tone of voice, exposing it all to me. "Twenty-something years ago, and I intend to get some revenge," Pops said from atop the bucket in the empty basement. "If you'll help, that is."

I rubbed my ragged chest from the smoke that Pops blew in my face as my senses began to return to normal. My eyes were gummy, and my vision was still hazy, as if I'd been sleeping for a month. Rolling onto my stomach and returning to my seat, I looked around the room, upset that this part of the experience wasn't a dream.

Grandpa looked stronger after telling his story. His chest lifted, and his countenance was rejuvenated. I, on the other hand, felt surprised and maybe exposed. This Idrissa person, if I had seen correctly, was my father. The same father, my mom said, died in the military. The same father I had never met.

This news was too much for me, and I forced myself to stand and pace around. I looked down at the watch my father had worn and felt that connection between us. *How in the fuck did this happen?* I thought, rubbing the band.

I was in a state of disbelief. The old man who kept a beer or pint glued to his hand was my great-grandfather. Somehow he was still living here in the flesh, walking, talking, and drinking like a lunatic. What did he want, and why did he blow that damned smoke in my face?

I now studied him, looking for any similarities between us. Looking at how he sipped his warm beer or sat with his legs bent under him, I hungered for their resemblances. His milky brown eyes and style of dress all intrigued me. I touched the edge of his sleeve and just wondered.

I couldn't wrap my mind around it and shook my head in disbelief. "So you're telling me that we're related?"

"Were you listening? Of course? You have that Johnson blood in you. Can't you feel it running through your veins?" He asked me, looking into my face for some type of recognition.

Lucky, your spiritual guru from God knows where, with his empty eyes locked on us like lasers, nodded along to our every word. Just then, I witnessed an ant crawling along my arm, drawing my attention away. I went to knock it down, but Lucky reached over and balled up its tiny black body between his fingers, placing the insect inside his mouth. We both shuddered, Pops and I. The way his hand felt against my skin reminded me of a hot breeze on a humid day.

Looking back at the old man, I didn't have anything to say. The proverbial cat had escaped and ran off with my tongue, leaving me speechless.

The bucket skidded across the gravelly floor as I sat back down and thought about the story my great-grandfather had just shared with me. My father was murdered, and my mother witnessed it all. Thank God Calm wasn't there and was with my now-dead grandmother.

Looking at his wrinkled face, at all the deep lines etched in his face, spoke multitudes. Inside my mind, I saw everything and even felt the emotions of everyone involved; it was almost overwhelming. I eyed Lucky briefly and was mystified by his powers. Not only did I feel my father's pain, but that of my mom and even Victor and Derek. He caught me snatching a look, and a grin spread across his face like he was reading my mind.

I closed my eyes and saw Idrissa's face seconds before Derek ended his life, the sparks from the barrel, and the pieces of lead that were pumped into his body. And my mother almost destroyed me. When I opened my eyes, I had to fight back tears.

"How did you do that? It all seemed so real, and the feelings were so intense. I experienced everything. Even the thoughts of the thugs in attendance."

Pop's had an answer ready. "That's one of the gifts of our friend Lucky. Some of his magic, I suppose. You're not going to believe the next phase." He eyed me up and down.

"I felt the bullets as they entered and the remorse and guilt... I'm so pissed off I can't even sit still. Victor and his brother were snakes, and my mom," I gasped. "Now I know why she never told Calm and me anything about our dad; that was a complete bloodbath."

Emotional and distraught, I wanted to murder both Victor and Derek with my bare hands for taking my chance at having a father and putting my mom through that. No one should experience that; it was no small wonder why she found solace in drugs for so many years. I turned my head up at Pop, who was still standing over me. "Was it all true?

Like, did it happen? Did my dad buy a house and everything?"

"Yes, and we didn't even get a chance to step inside it. Victor took a lot of my loved ones that day. My wife and I knew what Idrissa was involved in, but we ignored it," he said on the verge of tears. "It's strange what one will overlook for wealth and convenience. With his mom being dead, we didn't know how to cope. And being an alcoholic, I loved not having responsibilities. I could sit in my basement and drink myself senseless."

"Why show up now? Huh? Knowing this doesn't change anything for me. Congratu-fucking-lations, I know the history of my shitty past. It's not going to bring my dad back or the rest of my family," I said, letting my words sit.

Lucky walked over without making a sound, the white of his eyes translucent. "What if your father did have a second chance, another opportunity to give you the life you always felt you needed?" he said, almost whispering in my ear. "You know I can do that, right? It's one of the things I was called for."

My face rose to meet Lucky's, tired of the games and spooky occurrences I had been dealing with.

Granddad stood with Lucky and looked down on me like a teacher. "Lucky is a force we explained, for the lack of a better term, that deals with time and redemption. A deity once worshiped but now forgotten."

"A deity, huh?" I laughed, then thought about everything he had caused and stopped.

"I tell you no lies, boy. This is the real deal—a little malevolent but obedient," Pop said, putting his arm around Lucky. "It was difficult, but he's bound to me." He added before growing quiet.

Was the old man telling the truth? Was Lucky a spirit following his orders?

"He was bound to me years ago to save my daughter but that chance has passed and another opportunity has been granted. Do this and he goes back to where he came from." The old man explained.

The whole thing sounded far-fetched, but it all made sense when I thought about it. The sightings, the incident in the shower, and even being locked inside this madhouse all led to the old man's story being legit.

"I don't like this. It seems... wrong somehow."

"We have a tremendous opportunity, son," he muttered as he bent his ancient body to kneel face-to-face with me. "He can take you back 20 years in the past and save my grandson and my whole family." He added, trying his hardest to convince me. "This is a tremendous opportunity... don't squander it."

Calling me son was doing too much, but it felt good, I must admit. However, the cold, vicious streets and being away from home taught me that blood didn't make you family; it was going through the mud with each other and coming out clean that forged bonds.

This brand new parental figure stared at me with cloudy eyes, "Say yes, and I'll begin preparing the ritual. Say no, and you and your friend upstairs can leave, no strings attached."

I contemplated the choices before me but also thought about how I got kicked out of school. Hearing about Lucky's powers made me question the whole situation. Marcus was a pest but not a snitch.

Gathering my courage, I spoke. "Did you cause me to be kicked out of school? If you did, that was messed up. I was coasting."

Lucky chuckled. "The old man here needed you back, and I did my best to arrange a couple of events that led you to be standing right in this spot. Marcus was just a pawn. His mind was easy to manipulate, and Bianca, well, she didn't get expelled, did she?" He explained. "You are looking to blame someone; blame him."

Desperation leaked from my great-grandfather's voice. "I told him to get you here; I didn't know he would do that, but he may be able to fix it... Maybe he can fix everything. What do you have to lose? My family didn't deserve to die that way. Please, son."

"But this thing could backfire, and then I can lose my life. Something tells me that if I die in the past, it sticks. And from what I saw of Victor, he's a fucking madman."

Pop paced back and forth, "You already know the outcome; that should help you, and your friend is a killer; I heard him say it. All you have to do is kill Victor before he kills my family, and it's finished."

"You want to send Xavier too?"

The whole situation was a mess. Going back in time? Messing with destiny? It all sounded out of my league, and I thought I might be dreaming this whole episode.

"Bullshit aside. Can you send me to the past? Do you think I can save my family?"

Lucky walked towards me. "Yes. Matter isn't as solid as you think it is. To me, reality is happening all at once. The past and the future make no difference. Agree to go and find out for yourself if this thing is real or not."

"What about Xavier?" I reiterated. "Is he coming too?"

"Of course. When I perform the ritual, anybody in the same vicinity will make the trip," Pop said in a rush.

Asking to involve his friend was going overboard. "Look,

old man or grandpa, you are asking for too much. Xavier didn't ask to be here."

The old man was growing more convincing. "Are you sure about that? Who dragged whom inside? Was it him or you?"

"Him," I said, thinking it over.

"So he's involved, and I want my family back. I was too much of a coward then to do anything. If I could go back, I would. My age prevents it, son," Pop's said. "Do you know what I sacrificed for this moment? Do you?"

I was stuck. On one hand, I wanted to leave and get on with my life. I was enrolled in school and waiting for the new semester to begin. On the other was my dad. I closed my eyes and envisioned his face one more time. What more could I say?

I nodded my head.

"So you'll do it?" The old man asked.

"I keep hoping someone will pop out and tell me it was a joke?" I shook my head. "You're talking about sending us back 20-something years. You got to be kidding me?"

"This is no joke, Travis. It's as real, and I can prove it," he said. "Lucky, do me a favor."

Lucky walked towards us. He moved so fast, I didn't see him move his legs. All I heard was the sound of the ridiculous chains, accompanied by the presence of a subdued wind.

I jumped back. "What the fuck, old man?"

My mind flashed back to the water fountain at school. When I first saw Lucky. How he had vanished. It all made sense now. I was frightened and wasn't scared to admit it. This being was something only heard of in stories or old myths.

Backing up further, I mumbled a half-remembered

prayer. The distance was what I wanted at that particular moment. I turned to run away from Lucky's freakish presence but was stopped by my grandfather's hand on my shoulder.

"Get over here so he can show you," he said. "Nothing bad is going to happen to you, I promise."

Lucky had the widest grin I had ever seen in my life. It was cracking his face in half. Like someone had grabbed his mouth and opened his head. I was breathing like a maniac, clawing at the old man, but somehow his old fingers dug into my shoulder, making me stand still.

"It's all a show," he whispered. "Watch."

Standing there with half his head leaning down his back, he reached his hand inside the maw that opened and started digging and pulling up smaller versions of himself. First, it was a handful, then armloads of miniature Lucky's were running around the dusty basement floor.

They were fighting, laughing, and having a good time. The little gold chains reflected the orange light overhead. Their little voices sounded like birds chirping, and they high-fived each other and ran around the dusty basement floor.

Lucky kept reaching into his mouth and pulling more of himself out, growing smaller with each handful. When he finished, he was the same size as them. The little Lucky's were clamoring over each other, melting and blending into a shape. I was transfixed by what I was witnessing.

"It's entertaining, don't you think," Pop's said, releasing my shoulder.

They began to dance and shuffle on the floor in sync with each other. A hundred little men doing dances I had never seen. It was entertaining, and I couldn't pull my eyes away. When they finished their routine, they stopped and bowed. I almost clapped as I looked at my grandfather and smiled.

Then they all came together, melted, and merged into a dark glob that oozed across the floor.

By the time he had finished, he had made a new version of himself. This one, a little younger but still menacing,. I wanted to leave, but I was also curious. This being was unlike anything I had ever witnessed.

"What was the purpose of that?" I asked.

"I told you, a demonstration. He's got a million of 'em. He's my pet, so to say. I conjured him years ago to help with a loss," he said. "Now, he's going to send you back to save my grandson."

CHAPTER 23

THE RITUAL

A LOT of things are too far-fetched to believe, too weird to be true. Like the Lochness or Bigfoot stories I heard as a kid. But the shit I just experienced blew my mind. Whatever strange smoke the old man blew in my face made me a believer.

From my seat, I watched as he went into a room and retrieved a shopping cart filled with trash and empty 40-ounce bottles. One of the wheels was spinning as he pushed it into the room, making small, squeaky noises that annoyed me.

Lucky grinned, his hands rubbing together like a fly. The look on his face teemed with emotion and expectancy. He couldn't wait for his chance to perform for me and Pops.

As I inspected the cart, I saw that it wasn't trash at all but pictures of his family and other keepsakes that he had gathered. By the wrinkled paper bag, I spotted a photo album containing a picture of his family jutting out from the side.

I went inside his movable place of remembrance and pulled it out. Flipping it around before settling my eyes on it, my mind raced with images from my episode on the floor. "Ha, there's Idrissa and my mom. Smiling." I said to myself.

The old Polaroid felt flaky and brittle in my hand, as if a strong gust of wind could turn it to dust. The words were faded around the white border and hard to make out. The smeared ink of forgotten memories.

Idrissa + Gloria, written in a faded blue pen. I recognized the handwriting as my mom's and ran my finger across the indentation. My mother looked so young in the photo, and seeing my dad with my own physical eyes filled me with a warmth I had never known.

"Don't damage that." The old man's voice rumbled like stones from the side of me, filled with regret. "I need that to perform the ritual. Without it, you won't be going anywhere," he snatched it out of my hands.

"They looked so innocent," I said, in stark comparison to the things my dad had done. The murders and killings I witnessed still echoed inside my brain, but in that photo, I saw the love they had for each other. "Also. What was that you blew in my face earlier? Should I be worried?"

"Boy, that was just sage, whiskey, and some herbs. Lucky gave me the making of it; there's no need to worry. Pops dusted off the photo. "Now sit back and watch, I don't need you asking any more questions, to distract me. You're about to see them in the flesh and help them out of the mess my grandson made," he said. "If you'll agree, that is."

"Hold on. What do you want me to do? Do you have a plan, or do you expect me to go back and kill somebody? And how do I get back? Before you begin, I need some answers."

Lucky glided swiftly towards me, as if pulled by magnets, before coming to a sudden halt. I jumped back, surprise all over my face. "Kill this Victor person and save your father... After that, everything will change for you," Lucky slithered.

"Just like that? How am I going to get a drop on that lunatic?"

"That's not my concern. You and your friend must figure it out, but know this: fail, and you both will return with no recollection of the past events."

His words hung in the air.

"Are you sure?" I said.

"Yes, I'm sure," Pop answered. "Are you still doing this? Because once I start, I can't stop."

Mystified, I still couldn't believe that I was about to go back into the past and wondered how it would all happen. Would I be plucked from the present right now, or would it happen over time? And what would Xavier think of being thrown 20 years into the past with me? We were close, but this may be too much, even for him.

My mind swam with possibilities while sitting on that bucket's hard surface. The decision weighed heavily on my mind. I weighed it over, or as much as I could understand. Saving my father was all I thought about. Having him back from the dead would be miraculous. The intricacies and other problems never occurred to me.

I looked at Lucky, ready to make my decision. "Yeah, I'm sure. Saving my dad is important to me, and losing my other family members is too, I guess." I nodded my head, convincing myself.

Lucky smiled a toothy grin and shook my hand, sealing the deal. "Remember this, though, to get back, you must carry out the mission. If the old man here dies in the past, you're returning to it. It's over and let's just say you don't want to happen."

"Sure, whatever you say. I can handle it. I'm positive." I said with all the confidence I could muster.

"Well, I have to begin and get things situated. Gimme a minute," Pop interrupted my conversation with the specter.

Standing there, I felt like a kid in line for a ride at Great America, each second bringing me closer to what lay ahead. As I waited for the ceremony to begin, a fear rose and gripped me. *Should I be messing with time like this?* I wondered. But the chance to fix my family and save my dad was too good to be true.

The thoughts of the great-grandmother, uncles, and aunts I had never heard of before helped ease my fear. It would be hard, but I was sure of myself at that moment. And with my best friend with me, I was guaranteed success. Xavier didn't go off to school and stayed in Chicago, which at times was like a third-world country. Surviving this neighborhood and running with the type of guys he hangs out with would come in handy. Going back in time and pistol-playing with Victor was nothing to a bunch of streetwise kids like us.

My leg tapped in anticipation against the floor as Grandpa rummaged inside the cart. He tossed papers and other mementos to the side or placed them on the ground before him. When he had gathered all the necessary pieces, he disappeared into the room again and returned with an armful of candles, and later with a medium-sized bag filled with what smelled like fresh soil. Earthy and fragrant, it reminded me of my youth as he waddled with it.

I rose to my feet. "Need any help?" I offered but was shrugged off.

The overhead light shifted from side to side, casting shadows all around. Pop's movements were deliberate and unhurried in the dim, cool basement. Soon, chalk emerged from his shirt pocket, and the bag of dirt settled onto the floor.

"Lucky," he said, passing the chalk to the spirit man. "You're up."

Lucky proceeded to get on his hands and knees and draw a series of shapes that covered the whole of the room. What started off as squiggles and odd-shaped lines developed into a mosaic of the photo I had just held.

It was beautiful, and it was all done in a matter of minutes. With skilled hands, he drew on the ground in quick, deft movements like a Rembrandt on Adderall. With a flick of the wrist, he captured the trees and, with a curved arch, the house. All of it was done with a realistic approach that mirrored reality. I wanted to tell him, 'Good job,' but I knew all I would get in return was that evil smile. Around my parents' depiction were six divots that would later hold the candles that the old man now held. Each one made a subtle thump as they melted into the ground before me.

Then, a thin light shot from one candle to the next in succession, making a six-pointed star. "What the fuck?" I muttered as I slid the bucket even farther back.

"No outbursts... We need you quiet," Lucky warned, rising to his feet. "The things I'll be summoning are dangerous, and I don't want anything to go wrong."

"What could go wrong?" I asked.

"Plenty," Pops interjected. "Just stand over there out of the way and be quiet."

Walking away, I made my way to the bottom of the steps and watched them continue setting everything up. The star was illuminating the drawing with a frightening light that made me shiver. "Holy shit. This is amazing. It looks so real. like they can open their mouth and talk." I said. "Everything looks so real."

Bending down to run my hand against the drawing, I was impressed. I didn't have a rational explanation for what was going on and had stepped over the threshold of reality and dream. The longer I looked, the more 'alive' it seemed.

"It's... something," I said over the rendition, amazed by his skill.

Lucky's head snapped with speed at me. "I need silence for the next part," he demanded. With a hand, he pointed towards the candles. "Stand over there and say the words," he instructed my granddad. "You," he said to me. "Give us room."

I shuffled back and let the old man do his job. As he began to mumble words, I couldn't understand. Lightning struck from the ceiling without making a sound, and a fierce wind blew through the space. I shivered. A cloud formed inside the room, crackling with rain and hovering over the depiction on the floor. My eyes were filled with wonder at what I was witnessing. In seconds, the intricate picture of my parents was washed away in a sea of colors.

The old man mumbled the words that sounded like something I studied while in school. I listened with attention, trying to make out what he was saying. It was all short phrases punctuated with vowel sounds. My mouth hung open when I recognized what he was saying. A dialect I'd heard in my anthropology class on the Lakota Indians.

The language was a blend of old native speech and modern slang, which sounded weird but familiar. My arms tingled as I looked on, hypnotized by what I was hearing and seeing. It had the cadence of a rap song, but unlike a rap song, this rhythm didn't make me want to bob my head. No, instead, it made me want to run as fast as I could away from this occurrence.

Lucky then took off his chains and, with a swift motion,

hurled them into the sea of colors. As they descended, they ignited in a burst of purplish flame. The room was engulfed in a thick, billowing smoke, reminiscent of those little snake fireworks I played with as a kid.

The old, dusty shopping cart began rocking and moving towards the whirlpool that was forming as dirt and gravel rushed toward the center. The force was pulling at everything that wasn't nailed down, including us. To save myself, I ran toward the steps and grabbed the banister, while Pops ran toward the door and gripped its knob. Lucky, the spell caster, stood in the middle, inviting the spectacle with outstretched arms and his head thrown back.

"When will it stop?" I yelled but didn't get an answer, shielding my eyes from the debris. The spirit man's body transformed into a great eagle with the body of a buffalo. My feet lifted off the ground as I was pulled into the maddening center. Lucky was more than a mere spirit but something from legend; he was a force beyond comprehension.

I screamed a guttural sound that was drowned out by my grandfather's yell as he dangled from the doorknob. I don't know how Pops held on for so long, but he did with his scrawny arms that carried a hidden strength. Just when my grip on the old wood was failing, it stopped, and Lucky, with his transformed body, lifted off the ground and blazed like a furnace.

Pops and I fell to the floor, and Lucky disappeared, leaving us worried and confused. I rushed to my great-grandfather's side and checked for injuries. "Are you alright?" I breathed, hoping he hadn't broken anything.

"I think so... where is Lucky?" He asked, dusting off his clothes.

"Your guess is as good as mine. Is it the past, or are we still in the present?"

We scanned the room for our spirit friend. "Look around you, son. Didn't anything happen. I think we failed," Pops said before falling silent.

Defeat was etched on his face, and his shoulders were slumped. I had just learned of our relationship, but I felt the pain as well. Grabbing my great-grandfather by the shoulders, I walked him toward the steps.

A rattling halted us in our tracks. "YOU HAVEN'T FAILED... THIS TAKES TIME." I felt every word in my body vibrating against my rib cage. "GO UPSTAIRS TRAVIS AND WAIT. YOU," he addressed the old man. "YOU STAY HERE."

CHAPTER 24

A SMOKE BREAK

AS I WALKED up the steps, a feeling of dread gripped me. Each agonizing approach made my stomach flip with worry. Apprehension was thick, and I feared telling my best friend about the situation I had gotten us both involved in. Why I had agreed to something so reckless was beyond me. And now, standing before the door, I almost feared opening it.

I crossed the threshold, the bright lights and spotless surfaces making me wince. After the spirit-inducing sights in the dark, empty basement, the calm, boring interior of the kitchen was welcoming. Taking a deep breath, the door closed with a thud behind me with an air-sucking quality, reminiscent of a Tupperware bowl sealing shut. I jumped and stumbled the rest of the way into the kitchen, looking around confused.

Looking over my shoulder, the door had vanished, without a sign of it ever being there. I ran my shaky hand along the wall and thought it might all be just a dream—a figment of a stressed-out young mind. That's when Xavier ran towards me, screaming with bug eyes, startling me.

"Where the fuck have you been, fam?" He said shifting

around on his feet. "This spooky house got me tripping, Travis. Tell me you've seen those little kids."

"What are you talking about?" I asked, looking around and seeing nothing.

"Two little kids, a boy and a girl," he explained. "They looked... weird and said something about their grandpa fixing everything."

What Xavier was referring to was the old man, Daniel, my great-grandfather. Lucky did say it would take some time to finish, and the children he was referring to meant the ritual was working.

"I don't know what you're talking about, dawg. I think you're hallucinating. That weed we smoked was powerful." I said withholding the information. "Let's go have a seat, raid the fridge, and put something on our stomachs."

I opened the refrigerator door and found some packaged sliced turkey, along with a few condiments. Setting everything on the island in a jumble.

Xavier held up a tomato with one hand. "Where were you? When I ran in here earlier, I couldn't find you. Did you find a way out?" He said, placing it on the table.

My eyes shifted around the room. "Mm... what? I've been inside this creepy ass house the whole time. We must've missed each other," I lied.

Xavier cut his eyes and looked at me. "If you say so."

Locating some somewhat fresh bread in a box near the sink, we sat in silence and crafted sandwiches while contemplating our next moves. Our jaws mashed the ingredients together, and our eyes never met.

The taste of the sandwich brought back thoughts of school. Flashes of Amina's laughter and my needy roommate's constant requests filled my head. I should've stayed and tried a little harder, I thought, shaking my head. Now, I was wrestling with how to tell Xavier about my great-granddad and his spirit buddy in the basement.

Eating the sandwich next to Xavier was far from where I wanted to be. Maybe I made the wrong choice when my grandfather asked me to fix his problems. How could I regret something I never even experienced? My dad was an afterthought, and the others I hadn't even known of before today.

I looked at the last bite of my sandwich, with its tangy, expensive mustard and wilted lettuce, and tossed it down on the plate. I was engulfed in a whirlwind of problems, questioning my decisions. I washed it down with Dr. Lemon, and Xavier and I returned to the living room.

My mind raced as we walked down the long hallway with the bright overhead lights hanging from the ceiling. It felt even more empty now, more lifeless. In a few moments, we would be snatched and placed 20 years in the past, something I still couldn't believe. Now, it felt like an empty theater with the way the light shone down on us.

As Xavier led the way into the living room, the end table remained upturned from our earlier attempt to break the window. I walked over to it and set it upright, and that's when I looked out the window, peering into the black void. It seemed even darker now, with blacker, emptier areas swirling like liquid or smoke in the abyss. It was hypnotizing. Xavier ran to the window and closed the curtains, ending our visions of nothingness.

We both sank on the couch, defeated but satisfied, with the hearty sandwiches we had made. Xavier pulled out an empty cigar and began rolling another blunt. I asked if he was sure he wanted to smoke again, and he replied, "Hell yeah." I declined and walked around the room, trying at the door and windows one last time.

Even though I knew they wouldn't open, I had to play my part. When I returned from my fruitless mission, Xavier had finished rolling the blunt and asked me for a lighter.

He placed the blunt in a makeshift ashtray and looked at me with a serious expression. "Bullshit aside, why did you leave for school like that? And don't give me any more crap about it being because of some girl. I want the truth," he said, looking at me. Then he broke into a smile and said, "The hood was pretty boring without you."

The question stunned me. We were trapped inside a house with guns and money, and he was asking me about our failed friendship.

I returned his stare, but without the smile. "You know why, dawg," I said. "After that situation with Keisha and that guy, you changed. I didn't want to be thugged out. After you left the track team, I drifted, and you did too."

"Man, you know how it is here; I had to. I thought you would understand. The streets put food on my table, and the running track didn't. I'm surprised I lasted that long."

"I stopped coming around; I was trying to pursue my dreams, and you and your brother would've fucked it all up. Running was my ticket out of this shithole," I told my old friend, shaking my head.

We had shared a lot of experiences and even went out of town together with the track team. A first for both of us.

We learned how to be men together, or at least what we thought men were. Xavier was my best friend, and I felt terrible, but he should too.

"I didn't see you trying to be my friend like that. Every

time I ran into you, you were with your new crew. After graduation, I bounced and didn't look back."

We both grew silent, mulling over the words we just shared.

After neither of us spoke, he grabbed the fat cigar from the table and lit it. The smell was thick and pungent, filling the room with its dense smoke.

The way he looked as he inhaled made me think of how I looked when I smoked. Did I have the same expression, like it was refreshing? How could inhaling burning weeds look enticing? But the smell was inviting and pretty damn tempting. I reached for the blunt and inhaled, forgetting my indecisiveness about hitting it, and enjoyed myself. "Might as well," I thought, because in a moment, all hell would break loose.

The weed slowed down my thinking, and I was still pondering our conversation. We had drifted apart, but it wasn't my fault. I wasn't upset. I just accepted it and moved on. I looked at Xavier, and I could tell he was thinking about it as well.

With the herb clouding my mind as I sat on the couch, dazed, I declined when he tried to pass it back to me and closed my eyes, thinking about what I had done in the basement. Things about my father and my other family members, all killed in this very house.

I shivered, and Xavier perked up in his chair. "Are you alright?" he asked, putting out the potent marijuana.

"Yeah, I'm good, just thinking about something," I replied.

I closed my eyes once again and leaned against the couch when he coughed, "I forgive your big head ass for real. Underneath it all, you were a real friend." He looked at me seriously. "And you may not, but you taught me how to succeed, my nigga."

I looked at him, surprised. "How?"

He went on to explain how my going away to school lit a fire under him. About how he started hustling and following through on his plans. Success wasn't his yet, but it was coming.

When we finished the conversation, we brought out the money I had found upstairs and counted it. Most looked like it came from a bank; all the bills were crisp and smelled of new cash.

The new bills were like a gift from God. I considered paying my college tuition and forgoing a loan, as we counted. I'd get an apartment by campus, have enough money to study, and not worry about anything.

When we finished, we had counted $1.3 million. Xavier was surprised by how it all fit on the couch. I told him he had to look at it with a clear mind. The money was significant—hundreds—and in stacks of ten thousand dollars, it could easily sit there, with room to spare.

I split it between us, and I went to find another bag. When I returned, Xavier unwrapped one of the stacks and made a fan of the bills. "Man, if we get out of here, we are rich," he said, grinning and waving it in front of his face.

We pulled out our phones and took pictures of us playing with the money, posing with it like a telephone to our ears. Xavier even burned one of the bills to light a cigarette.

When we finished playing around, we put the money back inside the bag and sat again. We were having so much fun that I forgot about my plans. The journey into the past would wipe all this away—my friendship with Xavier and

Keisha, all of it. If I pulled it off, I would grow up in Naperville, of all places.

I looked at Xavier and felt terrible for him and for me as well. Did growing up with a dad mean so much that I was willing to throw half a million dollars away? I had turned out pretty well despite not having a father around. I was misguided, sure, but I had figured it out.

I had a sweet car and was determined, on my way to being enrolled in school again, and ready to finish my goals. Despite a few setbacks, I was doing pretty good.

While I pondered my existence, Xavier had the bag of cash on his lap, recounting the money. "Dawg, I can't believe it," he said. "We hit the jackpot."

The smirk I had on my face said a multitude of things. The one thing I wished it hid was my disappointment. I threw out a fake laugh and talked about my plans as best as I could. My future was as cloudy as the room would soon be, as Xavier flamed up the remainder of the blunt to celebrate our find.

Sitting on the couch, able to withstand the potent marijuana a bit better, Xavier turned on the TV and watched 'Heist Boys,' laughing and chuckling, while I sat shaking, awaiting to be whisked away to the past. I wondered what it would be like but also feared not telling my friend, but it was just too wild, and I still hadn't found the correct words.

"Yo, Travis, remember this episode?" when his pesky friend betrayed him, but our hero saw it a mile away. I always dig this one a lot." He said.

Now I felt terrible. I don't know why this was the only show we could watch inside this home, but I hated it at that moment. It mirrored my current dilemma. Looking at Xavier laugh and joke about the situation was the worst feeling in the world.

CHAPTER 25

SEARCHING FOR ANSWERS

KEISHA SAT at her desk with a headset, before a computer screen, with a look of disgust on her face. Feeling sick to her stomach and quite chilly under the blindingly bright lights, all she wanted was for this day to be over. She glanced at the clock, hoping time had sped up in her nauseous state.

Next to her, coworkers chattered on phones, trying to secure more customers and more money. "Something, something industrial; buy this and sell that-" as the coiled wires crisscrossed their voices across massive distances.

In this fast-paced workplace, assistants brought coffee to their bosses while computers sent data to printers. Inside the large room were sixty-five telemarketers and thirteen specialists, all trained and equipped with a script and rebuttals. Keisha was one of the sixty-five telemarketers and a pretty efficient worker. She almost always made sales of whatever it was she sold. Her voice was light, and her professional tone was calm and understanding. She had a knack for convincing little old women to trust her and give her service a chance.

Today, however, she couldn't get a sale for the life of her. Even the new guy, with his unsure tone and muddy voice, made a few sales before her today. What was wrong with her? Was it that Travis and Xavier were still missing, or was it her late period that distracted her this afternoon? Looking around, she felt depressed.

Picking another number on the screen, she called and waited for the person to answer, hoping that this time she would be successful. Her neat little cubicle, with a cup full of pens and sticky notes on her computer screen, seemed empty today. A picture of her Skittles, her late cat, sat to the side, as well as a small fan that blew air in stuffier times, silent as a stalking man beside her.

Sitting at her desk, she thought of the last person she slept with and grinned. Although she told Travis that she had one of those pills to prevent such a thing from happening, she looked forward to the possibility of keeping the child. Carrying his child would be an honor if he was never found. The history between them was long and difficult to describe, but she rubbed her stomach, feeling blessed.

While thinking of baby Travis, the person on the line answered, startling her. "My mind is everywhere today," she thought to herself. Regaining her composure, she sat up straighter and focused. "Yes, something—sold, buy, repeat," she fumbled through the call.

As luck would have it, she made her first sale of the day despite feeling sick. The man on the line even sounded thankful. With a half smile, she grabbed her cup and took a big sip, leaving a smudge on the rim. Even though she felt better, the thought of her missed period weighed on her thoughts.

Would she keep it? Travis would make a good father, but he wasn't ready. He was focused on school and wasn't here to advise her. Her father, for sure, would disapprove, and her mother was like a mirror image of her dad.

Twisting at her desk, she felt lost and alone.

Suddenly, heat blew down on her, making her nose itchy and stuffy. After a few seconds, she removed her sweater and grabbed a Kleenex. Holding the quilted napkin to her nose, she blew it with a soft breath, and then took another sip of tea. Looking back at the list of numbers on the outdated computer screen, she made more calls and more sales.

When her break came, she went to the bathroom and cried into the palm of her hand. She didn't know why she was crying, but she was. A long, silent sob that wracked her. After five solemn minutes in the stall, she exited and went to the vending machine, where she got a bag of potato chips to fill her stomach, and a cold can of grape soda.

The tears she shed must have helped her because, when she returned, she made five sales in a row—a monthly best.

The next thing she knew, her supervisor appeared at her side. "Great, Keisha," he congratulated her. "Keep up the good work; you're killing it." Then he disappeared, as he had arrived. Unfortunately, there wasn't a bonus for achieving that many sales consecutively, but it would look good on her record when she left this place, and that meant something, right?

The day unfolded at its regular pace, with her forgetting about Travis, her pregnancy, and her tears. As the workday drew to a close, Keisha's thoughts drifted back to Travis and the mysterious house. She grabbed her things at 4:30 pm, signed out, and headed toward the elevator, determined to investigate further.

She marked today as a bad day, still thinking emotions were a bitch when you were pregnant. Why did just thinking about her problems make a stream of tears shoot from her face, like a fire hydrant? She counted herself lucky that no one walked by and caught her sobbing. Picking up her jacket along the way, she threw it on and ran to the elevator before the door could close.

"Hold it!" she shouted while catching her breath. "Thanks," she said to the man who held the door open and rode to the lobby.

Ding and the door opened onto the large foyer, with overcast skies reflecting onto the lobby floors. They hadn't had any sun in weeks, and it was affecting her mood. Looking out into the streets and feeling like the gray clouds that hung overhead, she put on her best smile and continued on. The soft click of her heels filled the air as she walked and nodded past the security guards and receptionists by the door.

Exiting, she walked a few blocks, dodging between, and sometimes through, the crowded downtown streets. The wind was picking up, pushing against her back with its shrill sound, shooting between Chicago's massive buildings. She lifted her collar and threw her hood over her head, to keep the wind at bay. Panhandlers stuck bent, out-of-shape cups at her, as delivery men rode by on the street. She ignored them all. She went through this twice a day, five times a week, and learned her lesson about giving these dejected men any attention.

The last time she had, the homeless person tried to go inside her jacket's pocket, forcing her to hit him with the mace. A stream of pepper, and god knows what else, straight to the eyes of the silent man. What made it bad was that no one tried to help her, and they were standing right by her. Chicago was cruel like that sometimes.

After her long walk, she entered the underground train

station, maneuvering through piss and blunt wrappers littering the ground. She gripped her nose as she walked down the stairs, strong vapors stinging her eyes. Though the city cleaned it daily, it still smelled of something terrible.

Waiting for the train brought pleasant vibes from the band playing nearby. A Jamaican man rhymed in patois for Instagram likes and loose change, while filming his performance. She let out a slight smile and tapped her foot in rhythm, her phone tucked away in her pocket. The music emanated from a cheap speaker, sounding thin and tiny despite its loud volume.

Her thoughts drifted to her friend's disappearance. Finding Travis or anything about his disappearance would make her a helluva lot happier. She could tell him she missed her period and get some input on the situation. Being pregnant by a man who's gone missing was devastating to her.

The first train to arrive was in the opposite direction of the one she wanted. When it blew into the station, the train on the tracks sounded like thunder, as it rumbled to a stop. An admirer tried to get her attention, but she kept her head low and eyes forward, oblivious to his advances.

When her train arrived, a crowd of people clamored to get inside, knocking into each other. She ducked her head and entered the train, looking for a seat. Moving like a true Chicagoan, she plopped in the vacant seat before anybody could. As the train carried her closer to her destination, Keisha's resolve to uncover the truth about Travis's disappearance grew stronger.

Taking a long breath, she waited for the train to leave while looking out the window. She had her phone in her hand, scrolling through her timeline. She liked or hearted a few pictures and stole a few memes until she stopped, while a few young men blew potent weed smoke into the air.

She longed for a car, but couldn't afford one with her meager salary. The public transportation system had deteriorated over the last couple of years, and you had to pay attention or become a victim. Some days, she took the bus to avoid the rowdy atmosphere that surrounded her, but today wasn't one of those days.

After a while of riding, the train wobbled and jostled her before emerging into a gray, overcast day. Glancing around, she returned her attention to her phone, keeping an eye on her fellow passengers. As the journey continued, she stood near the entrance, holding onto the overhead strap to maintain her balance. When the train reached her stop, Keisha stepped out onto the platform, ready to confront the mysteries that lay ahead.

When the train stopped, she exited, walked down the stairs, and turned onto the street. Blocks passed by her as she walked at a brisk pace, propelled by her curiosity. The south side was far different than the bustling metropolis of downtown. No tall buildings adorned the sky or panhandlers. Only strife and hopelessness.

She couldn't shake the thought of Travis's car being found near that house. The image of the envelope stuck under the door haunted her, flickering and moving too fast in her mind. If that man hadn't startled her, she wondered what might have transpired. She found herself yearning for Travis to burst through the door, enveloping her in his arms, making everything okay, and securing her. She knew it was foolish, but she still thought about it.

As Keisha walked through the familiar streets of her neighborhood, her mind raced with questions about Travis's disappearance and the strange house. She didn't live far from the train stop, so the house she wanted to investigate wasn't too far either. With each step, her excitement grew, fueled by a desperate need for answers. There was something about that house, and today she would find out.

Turning the corner, she saw the home standing unfinished, still under renovation. The rickety scaffolding gripped the building like an old person's fingers. The windows were still devoid of any light, and the door looked as weird as before.

The mahogany door stood like a foreboding figure before her, beckoning her to investigate and see what secrets it held. She placed a foot on the step, the nippy air biting at her neck. An empty potato chip bag crinkled under her feet as she walked up the stairs, and an empty can rolled her way. She dodged it and felt a shiver across her body. Why did she feel like someone was watching her, waiting to see what she would do? Gathering her courage, she knocked on the door with most of her strength. *Doom, doom, doom,* she pounded the mahogany door, with its lavish designs and too-new exterior.

No one answered, but she didn't stop her pursuit. Boom, boom, boom—she thought she heard something from her side. Thinking it was the window, she crouched forward to peer inside. Unease unraveled her. What was that in the background? Did she catch a glimpse of something inside the inky abyss? A TV, perhaps?

Tapping on the window and yelling as loud as she could, she jumped at the sound she heard. It was the door unlocking, but it resembled a gun cocking.

"That was strange," she mumbled, her voice shaky and weak.

As she walked toward the sound, she heard it again. She stared at the doorknob, and her heart leaped into her throat as she noticed what appeared to be frost emanating from it. "It's not that cold out here," she said. "What would cause the door's handle to be covered in a thin sheet of ice?"

There were all types of papers and debris scattered on the porch, so she grabbed a piece and covered the knob, turning it. The chill reached her, froze her to the core. She let out a breath that hung before her face.

To her surprise, the door swung open, welcoming her inside. She peeked back onto the vacant sidewalk behind her, half expecting someone to halt her progress. Turning to face the dark interior of the building, she stepped inside, beginning what would become the most harrowing experience of her life.

CHAPTER 26

THROUGH THE LOOKING GLASS

AFTER DOZING off from the powerful marijuana, I woke feeling groggy and out of it. Wiping my eyes, trying to erase the fog that clouded my mind, I looked around the room, dazed. The Heist Boys were still playing on the big screen, and Xavier was still knocked out on the couch. A long spool of drool ran from his mouth to his jacket, making me chuckle.

Reaching forward, I grabbed a smoke, lit it, and then sipped from my drink. A million thoughts swirled through my mind, filling me with regret over my decision to help my grandfather. The bluish-gray smoke blew from my lips, bringing some much-needed relaxation. When I put the drink in my mouth, I noticed it was warm and unappetizing, but the smoke from the cigarette made me disregard it. Going back in time? What was I thinking? I shook my head at the thought, taking another long drag from the menthol cigarette and sinking my head back against the couch.

The television flashed images of 'Heist Boys'. The faint volume helped drown out the silence. "This shit is getting too hectic," I said to myself, watching the protagonist on the screen.

I looked at the bag of money tucked under Xavier's arm and sighed. Just the thought of being locked inside a house with a million dollars and pistols sounded insane to me. Finding out my best friend might be a killer was no better either. Xavier busting guns into crowds was wild and confusing, but expected. Our neighborhood was known for wild shit, and why should we be an exception? I let out a chuckle and put the cigarette out in an empty can, the sizzle sounding across the room.

Standing to stretch and loosen my muscles, I let my arms extend as far as they could, hearing each joint snap and pop. Sports had kept my limbs nimble, and I appreciated my fitness, but laying on that couch bent and contorted had made me stiff. And I hate to admit it, but the confines of the house were getting to me as well. I sat again and folded my arms, thinking about the approaching event. "Fuck!" I screamed on the inside.

I was unable to sit still, so I walked to the kitchen. Glancing at my half-eaten sandwich from earlier, which I almost picked up and took a bite of, I passed on it. The bread was already hardened anyway. But something said to check the cabinets above for some reason, and I did. Throwing the doors open, I found a stash of goodies enticing me.

There were cereal bars, chips, candies, loads of caramels, cakes, fruit rolls, and microwave popcorn. If this stash belonged to Lucky, he must have had a serious sweet tooth. And may need to be checked for diabetes.

While rummaging around behind a bag of skins, I stumbled upon a large box of sweets. With steady hands, I pulled it out, mindful not to knock over anything. A cartoon character made of cake, complete with a lasso on the front and soft white crème hanging out of its mouth, greeted me. I smiled and dug into it, savoring the contents, fending off the munchies produced by the weed I had smoked earlier.

I plopped down on the couch, hard enough to rouse Xavier awake. "Get your punk ass up, dude," I said, tossing a Twinkie at him.

Xavier sat up and grabbed the delicious treat, wrinkling the wrapper between his fingers and looking around.

"We're still trapped?" he asked, wiping the thread of drool from his mouth.

"You know it," I replied before ripping the plastic off the cake with my teeth.

We didn't know how long we had been asleep, due to the broken clocks, so we calculated by how many episodes of Heist Boys played through, while we slept. We figured they had been out for two hours.

Two hours was a lot of time, and we were still in the present. The spell that we cast downstairs must be powerful, for it to take so long. I wondered if Lucky did it right, while Xavier wolfed down his Twinkie.

"Damn," Xavier complained. "If we don't figure out how to get out of here soon, I'm going to go crazy," he said before opening up his Twinkie.

My great-grandfather and I had made a pact with a devil, and I was nervous sitting on that couch, like a hooker in church. I looked at Xavier and felt guilty for not telling him. It was just too unbelievable to explain, and not appear insane.

As I ate the Twinkie, I heard someone knocking,

shaking me from my concerns. Powerful sounds coming from the front door.

-Doom, doom, doom-

Looking around confused, my buddy sat up. "Now what?" he said, as I rushed to the front door, with my heart percolating against my shirt.

I put a hand on the knob and turned it, unsure of what to expect. As I stepped inside the vestibule, I saw Keisha, letting the door shut behind her, with that sick suctioning pull.

She was dressed like she had just come from work, with her hair styled and makeup on. Her long jacket was pulled tight and her bag was secured under her arm. A warm feeling filled me as I looked at her, followed by a sense of dread. This wasn't good at all.

Her eyes were wide with surprise, as she grabbed her ears from the feeling the door made, as it closed. "Like a kiss from a demon," I thought.

It took her a moment to process what she saw, and then she broke into a nervous smile.

"Travis?" she stammered, as her voice wavered. "I knew I would find you here. I knew it." She pouted. "Where have you been?"

Falling into my arms and giving me the biggest hug she had ever given me, I felt a mix of emotions inside. I was happy to see her, but also mad that the door had closed behind her, sealing us inside.

"We've been here all day," I said, before leading her inside. "Were you worried?"

Xavier stood, as they entered, his frustration all over his face. "What's she doing here?" he asked.

"I've been looking for you and Xavier for weeks," she said, but the words didn't sink in with me.

"Fuck," Xavier yelled. "Why didn't you hold the door? We could've gotten out!"

Keisha paused and looked him down. "Who are you yelling at? I ain't none of your hood rat bitches, Xavier; I'll fuck you up," she fired back, shifting to her back feet.

Her face screwed up, as she looked at Xavier like he had stolen something, the look in her eyes smoldering with anger.

The situation had turned sour, making it hard for me to think. What was she doing here and why was she upset? *We had been gone a few hours,* I thought. With speed, I instructed them both to have seats while I explained our predicament.

Inside that living room, there was an air of volatility that clashed with my somber mood. Keisha with her attitude, and Xavier with his street shit, were too much. With what I knew was coming, I didn't have time for this. Whether they knew it or not, I had agreed to help my grandfather and go back 20 years in the past. And now it looked like Keisha would be returning with us, ramping up everything.

I hesitated for a second, then gathered my breath. "This house isn't what it seems, Keisha," I explained, looking at her with soft eyes. "I don't know how to say this, but to make a long story short, we're trapped here."

Keisha looked at me in disbelief. "Stop playing, Travis. This isn't funny... The door's right over there."

Nervousness ate at my voice. "There's no one playing games," I said, pleading with her. "Something's wrong with this house—something supernatural, I think. I can't tell you what, but... we can't escape."

Her look of playfulness turned serious. "I don't know if I believe you," she admitted. "I'm calling Calm to tell him I found you... Your mom is worried sick."

"What are you talking about, with this missing shit?" I asked her.

"It has been a month since anyone has seen you," she said.

Something wasn't adding up. We had only been inside this house for a few hours. What was she talking about a month ago?

"You're bugging me," I said, as she went into her purse and dug out her phone.

Her face was puzzled, as she looked at the asterisks and dashes in place of the time. "What's wrong with my phone?" she asked, looking at the strange symbols.

"He tried to tell you, but your smart ass thinks you know everything," Xavier said. "We're trapped and now you are too."

Keisha looked at me in disbelief, her eyes searching mine for any hint of deception. "Travis, what is he talking about? This isn't making any sense."

I sighed, my shoulder's heaving, and ran a hand over my head. "It's a long story, babe. But the short version is that we're stuck in this house and can't get out. I don't know how or why, but time seems to be... frozen or something. We've only been here a few hours, but you're saying it's been weeks."

Xavier chimed in, his voice laced with frustration. "Yeah, and now that you're here, you might be stuck with us too."

Keisha's eyes widened in alarm. "Stuck? You mean, like, trapped? How is that even possible?" She shook her head from side to side. "No, no, this can't be happening."

"Believe me, I didn't want this either," I said, trying to remain calm. "But it's the truth. We can't leave this place."

An uneasy silence fell over the room as Keisha

processed this information. She spoke at last, her voice small and rigid. "What are we going to do?"

I took a deep breath. "For now, we wait and see if my grandfather's plan works. He's trying to send us back in time, to prevent all of this from happening in the first place."

Xavier scoffed. "Yeah, like that's going to work. We're screwed, man."

Ignoring him, I turned back to Keisha. "I know it sounds crazy, but you have to trust me. We'll figure this out, okay?"

She nodded, clutching her arms, still looking shaken. "Okay, I trust you. But you better have a good explanation for all this."

I pulled her into a hug, trying to reassure her. "I promise, I'll tell you everything. We're going to get through this, together."

As I held her close, I couldn't help but feel a sense of dread. Our situation had just become way more complicated with Keisha's arrival. But I had to stay strong, for her sake and my own. Whatever happened next, we would face it together.

CHAPTER 27

STEPPING INTO THE PAST

SITTING AROUND THE TV, I explained what had happened, since entering. The search of the house, the finding of the money, and Xavier spoke about his encounter with the two ghostly children. I kept my discussion with the old man and the fear-inducing Lucky to myself, still unsure of how to break it to them.

Not knowing how to explain the situation without my emotions becoming involved bothered me, and sharing that news, well, I just figured I'd handle it when it came. Lucky said it would take some time for the process to begin.

While Xavier told Keisha about the children, I thought of what it would be like to grow up with both my parents. As a kid, it's what I wanted to do most. Watching those sitcoms where the kids had both parents did something to me growing up. Even though I had my mom and her dad, having a father would've been everything to me.

I half listened to their conversation, until it died down and sunk into the couch. "So, it's been three weeks on the outside?" I asked Keisha, twiddling my thumbs. "That's kinda hard to believe."

She sat up. "Yeah, Travis, I spoke to your brother the other day about how long you have been missing," she hesitated. "He and your mom are worried sick, and Xavier's folks think you're both dead."

I could imagine. Three weeks without a word from either of us must've been hectic. Looking at Keisha, I saw the hurt and joy in her eyes. "I'm so glad I found you," she said.

I didn't know what to tell her at the moment, and I was choked up. We were about to be warped into the past in a few minutes, and I contemplated telling both of them. Xavier would believe all the wild shit we had seen since entering, but Keisha would take some convincing.

Xavier stood and walked to the kitchen to get a drink, leaving Keisha and me alone on the couch. Since coming home from school, she has been a lifesaver. I kept my head busy and provided comfort, while my mother was hospitalized. Sitting there with her, I felt closer than ever to her. I gripped her hand between mine and looked into her eyes.

"I don't like this, Travis; you always let Xavier influence you, and now look." She said this, gripping my hand. "Why did you let yourself be sucked into his petty world?"

"I keep trying to explain to you that we've only been inside this house for a few hours. Whether you believe me or not, this house isn't normal. Time might be sped up in the outside world, but inside, it's moving normally," I said, as she snatched her hand away from me.

"Stop, please. It's too much going on, and I need to think," she expressed, as I got up and stood by the window.

The curtain was closed, but I opened it and stared into the darkness. Keisha got up and came to my side.

Her mouth fell open. "What is that?"

I gripped the curtain, opening it wider. "I tried telling

you that this house isn't normal and that something is going on," I said. "That... blackness... that void is a part of it, and in a second," I stopped myself from telling her about my great-grandfather and Lucky. "Just believe me when it happens. Can you do that?"

She gripped the curtains and closed them. "What are you talking about? Help me understand, Travis," she said, taking off her jacket and sitting it down.

Xavier entered the room, holding a Dr. Lemon and another sandwich. This one was just bread, meat, and cheese. "What's going on?" he asked before taking a bite and returning to his seat.

Here it goes. My chance to bring some clarity to our situation. "I have something to tell you that would explain all these crazy occurrences. The missed time, the darkness beyond the window, the children, everything."

"Well, I'm all ears," Xavier said, sipping the warm soda. "And for the record, I'm not splitting my money with your girl."

He was confident and not moving an inch in his decision. His face was smeared with mayo, as he held the warm Dr. Lemon. His scowl was the same as when we raced against Hilden, and he had come in first.

I noticed Keisha tensing up, about to snap off at him, but that was when the lights began to flicker and a deep rumbling shook the walls of the rehabilitated home. The art on the walls began to shake, and the mount that held the TV gave way and sent it crashing to the floor. Xavier dropped the Dr. Lemon on the already-stained white carpet. "Not this again," he said, looking frightened.

"What's happening, Xavier? What have you done this time?" Keisha shouted at him. "Who did you shoot this time?"

The flickering lights caused our movements to appear jerky and out of sync, resembling the atmosphere of a rave. The air we breathed felt heavy in my chest, like beef stew. It was so hard to breathe, in fact, that I clutched my chest.

After a few seconds, the air returned to normal. "Stop jumping to conclusions," I shouted to Keisha over the ensuing chaos.

The TV, when it fell, turned on and played a series of different sounds, all bleeding into each other. Sounds that melted into each other, mimicking screeches and bleeps, forced me to hold my ears.

Xavier balled himself up in a corner, suggesting Keisha and I do the same, with a voice of horror. That's when the cacophony of sounds fell to a whisper. I heard snatches of conversations between people of all kinds, from arguments and discussions to celebrations and heartache. Keisha screamed out, but I held my hand over her mouth. Her body shivered under my embrace, as I kept her calm in the swirls of madness.

This was the event that I watched Lucky and Pops perform in the basement, the ritual I had agreed to be a part of. The whole thing played back in my head, giving me second thoughts. Somehow, we were being transplanted back in time, but there were no DeLoreans and silver-haired men with intricate machines and flux capacitors. It was some metaphysical, mystical sideshow that threatened to drive us insane.

The dimly lit, flickering lights cast long shadows, and the conversations that filled the air only added to our bewilderment. We were traveling through millions and millions of seconds to save people I had never seen—a family I had lost before I was born. I found myself questioning my sanity as the sights and sounds rose to a crescendo. *Could I really help my murdered father and his family? Was this even happening?* I thought.

We were confined to a haunting silence as the room plunged into darkness. Keisha kept shaking under my grasp, sobbing. I hesitated to rise, but then I saw a weak flicker. Something that casts a light. Focusing my eyes, it grew brighter and brighter, until it gave way to the outline of the room's furniture.

The space felt different now, unfamiliar and unsettling. I couldn't begin to explain how it felt to be 20 years in the past, but we were. The air was... cleaner and lighter, like the problems of the present hadn't happened yet. Like everything was purer and not as toxic from the mistakes we had made as humans.

The myriad of voices had subsided, but in the distance, I could have sworn I heard someone speaking. A voice that was light and innocent. I strained to catch every syllable, attempting to decipher the mysterious conversation. My eyes were adjusting to the past.

The distant voices continued to murmur, as if veiled by the passage of time itself. Their words bounced around a poignant narrative, centered on someone's granddad, who resided in the enigmatic basement. The conversations ebbed and flowed, and the puzzle pieces began to fall into place as I strained to listen. Amidst the murmurs, a name emerged, like an echo from a long-forgotten past: "Idrissa," my father.

I closed my eyes to focus on the distant sounds, lost in my father's voice. When I opened them, intent on hearing more of the voices, I found myself in what seemed to be a different room. It had the same suctioning, solid feeling as before but was much more substantial. It felt like my brain was pulled through my ears, accompanied by a feeling of disorientation that threatened to make me lose consciousness.

Although the physical space appeared the same, the furniture now looked cheaper and more worn. The flatscreen TV had been replaced with an old tube-style set I hadn't seen in years, and the floor was old and cracked. The room looked like a photograph of my childhood.

I looked to where Xavier sat behind a door, bug-eyed and breathing hard. I put a finger to my mouth, indicating him to be quiet. This wasn't the time to mouth off and alert anyone. He looked at me, gaining some of his composure, and nodded with wide, frightful eyes. The bag of money was still in his clutches.

I held out both arms, instructing him to chill, but he ignored me while Keisha crawled out of my arms and mouthed, "What the fuck is going on?"

I looked around the room with eyes of wonder. The light shining through the window, the dull paint, and the old soda cans amazed me. I was sitting behind a couch in 2002.

We sat in our positions until Idrissa left the kitchen and walked into the room we were hiding in. Just like in my visions, he was in shape, with muscles and veins popping out everywhere. He stopped, and I got a complete look at him. Standing at an average height with light skin and an army jacket on, he was as I had envisioned in our present.

With his eyes going over the room, Idrissa was perplexed. "What do you hear?" An elderly voice said. "Nothing, Grandma," Idrissa replied, grabbed a bag, and left through the screened front door.

The floor was in bad shape and cracked, while the screen door bounced shut. We now had the room to ourselves.

The sun shone, and I could hear Idrissa speaking with his sister. His voice was deep and rich, like Calm's. It was an unusual sensation to be transported to 2002, filled with excitement. The world around me felt lighter, as if it were less complex. I knew the tragic events that would unfold here tomorrow, but now it was peaceful.

Belief left me. This was the day before my father was murdered, inches away from where he now stands. I looked over to Keisha and Xavier, and they were looking at me, puzzled and scared.

To explain, I'd need a quiet space, somewhere no one would hear me. I waited for Idrissa to drive off to pick up Derek and see what his sister did after. Also, from what Xavier said earlier about the children, I knew we'd also have to be on the lookout for them as well.

Speaking of the devil, I turned around and saw one of the children standing in front of Xavier. I almost made a sound.

"Hey, I know you," the little brown-skinned boy said, pointing at Xavier. "You came back."

Xavier hushed the child and looked at me like I could do something. I met his questioning gaze with one of my own, a silent exchange of uncertainty that hung between us. That was when the little girl, with her braids swaying, materialized out of the shadows and reached for Xavier, taking his hand as if she had known him all along.

Keisha looked at me, frightened, and Xavier just went along, carrying the bag of money. This was too spaced out for any of us to believe. The little girl walked past the front door, to the steps in the hallway, and led us upstairs.

I couldn't believe I was following these little children inside my father's home. Keisha and Xavier both asked what was going on, but I told them to hold the questions for a bit. They reluctantly agreed, but I knew I had to give them an explanation sooner than later.

My eyes scanned the room we were in, noticing the house was lovely upon further inspection. With trinkets around and biblical verses on platters on the wall, it reminded me of my own home. It felt warm, like an oversize sweater or a comfy blanket in the winter.

We approached the second-floor landing and went inside what appeared to be the children's room. The little girl, wearing braids, said, "Granny doesn't like strangers."

I grew serious and had no time to play games. "Who are you?" I asked with curiosity, expecting nothing less than the truth.

"My name is Kearah, and this is Sam," she said, tugging her brother to her side. "He said a bad word," pointing at Xavier.

"Hey, I was scared," Xavier whispered.

"Could you help us?" Keisha took over the conversation, while Xavier stashed the bags of money under one of the beds in the room. "My friends are kind of dumb, but can you help us get out of here before your grandmother gets upset and you get in trouble?" Her tone was even and gentle, and she felt comforting.

Kearah just ignored Keisha's request. "I like your hair," the little girl said, touching Keisha's hair that fell to the side.

The little boy, Sam, followed Keisha's every word, on the other hand, and opened a window. "This is the only way I can think of. It's not too far. See, Granny will never see you."

"Can you do us a favor?" I said this to the children.

After waiting for their nod, I asked them to keep quiet about our arrival and gave them the Twinkies I had shoved in my pockets.

We looked out, and it wasn't that far down; it'd sting our ankles, but nothing serious. I went first, climbing out and dangling from the ledge. When I fell, it was just as I supposed. I bent down to check my ankles, as the pain shot up my legs.

"Shit," I mumbled, looking around to see if someone had seen me.

After the pain subsided, I stood underneath the window to help catch Keisha. She dangled, but I caught her by the waist, saving her from the pain I had experienced. Next came Xavier, who crouched and sustained some of his weight from the fall.

It was bright and sunny, with a nice summer breeze blowing through the yard. A few birds chirped as well, lightening my mood. Maybe I could do it, along with Keisha.

As we moved like shadows, we made our way to the narrow alley, away from the enigmatic house frozen in the past. My friends cast expectant glances in my direction, their faces etched with curiosity and apprehension. The weight of the unknown events we had just experienced hung heavy in the air, and the urgency to provide an explanation weighed on my shoulders.

The mysterious meeting with the two children and the seeming journey across time had thrown us into confusion, desperately seeking explanations and grappling with the consequences of our strange new situation. Yet, as I began to piece together the events that had transpired, I knew I had a grave responsibility to reveal the truth and guide my friends through this inexplicable journey, even as we continued our escape into the unknown.

CHAPTER 28

LOOKING FOR ANSWERS

WE HAD BEEN WALKING for a few minutes when Keisha gasped. "I can't believe this," she said, eyes wide. With her jacket tied around her waist, she looked hot and tired. Xavier and I looked at each other, startled. She explained something unsettling—unbelievable.

Gripping my arm and digging in her nails, she said that things would become the same whenever we reached a certain distance. I called bullshit but noticed when I scanned the area that we hadn't traveled that far, which seemed odd.

Looking around, perplexed, I couldn't see a reason for Keisha to lie about something like that. To ease her mind, I decided to go for a short run. Not to hurt her feelings either, but to give her proof so she would calm down.

I wiped my forehead and started jogging, saying, "See, nothing's wrong," but my voice quivered as I slowed down. The gates surrounding the other houses started blurring and melding into what I thought were other gates. The new additions were wooden with red chipped paint and weathered boards. Like a painting, the metal chain-link fence overlapped over the wooden one in a pattern that stretched my imagination. In front of me, in a bizarre haze, I saw the outlines of Keisha and Xavier. Looking behind, I saw them watching me, then in front of me again. "What the fuck?" I breathed. *Was I seeing doubles?*

Another step, and I was back beside them, still in motion. "Did you see that?" I said, scared out of my mind.

After calming down, I tried it again, this time with Xavier running alongside me. The same thing happened. It became evident that we were being drawn back to the house.

Keisha looked haunted, with dark circles forming under her eyes. "Would someone please explain what the hell is happening? Are we still awake, or am I having a nightmare?"

I began to open my mouth, but closed it, unable to find the words.

Xavier was beginning to be fed up. "Travis, do you know why this is happening, man? You look like you know something. If you do, now is the time to explain," he said, eyeing me and walking closer.

At the time, I didn't comprehend the significance of this phenomenon. Being pulled toward the house didn't make sense. Were we contained in this space and couldn't venture further? The scenario made me dizzy, and I needed a second to gather my thoughts.

Xavier, still upset, blurted out, "If she hadn't let the door close, we wouldn't even be here. We could've escaped that weird house. She's always messing things up with her funky ass."

"Hold on, bro, don't talk to her like that," I said, getting in his face. "It's nobody's fault. Calm the fuck down, and I'll explain everything. Just give me a second."

Emotions were coming at me in flurries. Regret and anger were the strongest, making me ball my fist. Xavier, taking out his frustrations on Keisha, was some hoe shit to me. My temper always stayed under control in tense situations, but I was on the verge of swinging at him. After all this time, Xavier still knew how to get under my skin. Letting the moment pass, I gained control of myself.

Keisha, on the other hand, was looking at both of us with sympathy. "See the garage over there?" She pointed at the structure behind the house. "Let's go inside, and you can explain to me what is going on in detail."

Xavier was getting on my nerves, and I didn't need his bullshit right now. Swallowing my pride, I turned towards the garage and walked. "Yeah, yeah, sure, let's go sit in the garage, and I'll try to explain to you what's going on," I mumbled under my breath.

In the distance, the house stood out with crystal clarity, as though outlined and traced with a magic marker to draw our attention. Its prominence puzzled me. Peering down the alley at the other homes, I noticed they appeared washed out and faded, resembling old photographs. Our adrenaline had masked this observation earlier, but it became evident as we calmed down. Even the sky seemed bluer over the house. My grandfather had left out this anomaly, but I chose to accept it. While Keisha and Xavier grasped that we had traveled back in time, the reason behind it remained a mystery.

Walking toward the garage, I began to shake. "Aye, before we go any further, I have something to say," I muttered into my chest. "I'm the reason we're in this fucked-up situation. I made a deal with someone," I explained, my voice trembling. "Someone who can do things," he paused. "Someone powerful and dark."

Keisha stepped back, her hand over her mouth. "I don't understand. What's going on?" she said, her voice filled with concern. "Who did you make a deal with?"

The haunting words fell from my mouth like heavy raindrops, every detail I could remember. The weird experiences from when I was in school—the creepy little boy at the arcade, everything. They both looked at me stunned when I finished, with faces of disbelief. But as I continued, their faces turned to ones of horror. When I told them about Lucky and how he could manipulate time, they looked in disbelief.

"At first, I thought the weed was laced with something, but when Keisha came along with us, I knew some fucked-up shit was going on... I just didn't expect this. Is Lucky like a god or something?" Xavier asked, jumping back in my face. "And what happens if you pull it off and save your dad? What happens to us? The money? All of it?" He stepped away from me. "It's fucked up, Travis, and a real shitty thing to do," he said, before turning his back to me.

Feelings clouded my mind as we stood in the humid heat. I had explained at last why we were here, and the situation wasn't any clearer. In fact, it seemed even more complicated. Keisha kicked at a rock and Xavier was being Xavier.

Fuck this, I thought, storming off towards the garage, furious. What Xavier was saying held a certain truth, but he was only thinking of the money. It stung when he fired off his questions. But what would he have done in my place? Let everyone die? We were talking about my family, and I had to do something, whether he understood or not. Saving my dad was important to me.

I looked at the garage, which was old and secure, but I knew I could get in. Growing up in the slums led to a pretty adventurous childhood. We'd broken into many garages, just for the fuck of it. I grabbed the knob with both hands and turned it, trying to gorilla it open, but it held.

It appeared to be locked, but frustration and despair compelled me to seek another way. Examining my surroundings, I peered into the window next to the door. With a decisive motion, I spotted an old newspaper, fixed it over the pane, and broke it with a slight tap. I slipped my arm inside and found the lock. Cautiously, we went in, driven to uncover the mysteries surrounding us.

As we sat huddled between two piles of debris in the garage, my confidence in pulling this off was dipping. I still couldn't believe all this was happening this fast, to be honest. The three of us being back in 2002 was a lot to wrap your head around, but here we were, smack dab in the middle of it.

We talked about Idrissa and the way he would die tomorrow in a rain of bullets, right in this very house. The way the old man told me the tale was like a psychedelic journey, whereas when I said it, it sounded like a jumbled mess. After answering a million questions, they understood the story and sat looking at each other.

"I understand, but a heads up would've been cool fucker," Xavier said. He paused before continuing. "But I can't believe we're in 2002. This is insane."

I looked around at our surroundings, hopeless. "I know it sounds crazy, but it's true, and I have to do this."

"So that jacked-up dude in the house was your dad?" Keisha asked from my side.

I looked into her eyes, determined. "Yeah, and I'm going to save him, so help me, God."

We all grew quiet in the messy garage, thinking and pondering what to do next. Minutes passed, and then Xavier wanted to know what would happen to us and the money he had stashed upstairs in the children's room. "So what happens to the money we cuffed? Does it go up in smoke, or do we get to keep it? A million dollars is a lot to give up."

Looking depressed and out of answers, I was out of it. "That, I don't know, bro. I didn't think that far ahead."

A look of depression fell across his face, but I didn't care. Who wanted money when they could change their whole life? I thought about how Calm and I grew up without our dad, and how that damaged us.

I couldn't lie, though; being allowed to change not only your life but everyone else's made me question who I had made the deal with. All of a sudden I became aware that this Lucky guy possessed greater power than I imagined, and the old man, my great-grandfather, had led me down a dark road without a source of light.

So here we were, stranded in the past, without a plan for something that seemed impossible to pull off. My shoulders were slumped as I sat against the wall, looking at the spot on the floor smelling of old, dried-up gas. I felt miserable, and it showed on my face and in my actions.

Next came Keisha, with her questions. "So, who is Victor?"

"A fucking lunatic," I said. "He runs things around here and my dad works for him. Tomorrow, he's going to kill everybody inside that house, but my mother."

Keisha's face grew concerned. "And you've seen this?"

"Yeah, when my grandfather drugged me or whatever," I said. "It was brutal... I wish I could forget it."

She grew silent, held my hand, and leaned her head on

my shoulder. "We'll figure it out somehow," she said. "We gotta have faith."

Sitting next to Keisha, I reached for my phone, and to my surprise, it displayed the time. In the present time, 2022, the screen had shown only dashes and asterisks, but now, in the past, it was functioning again.

"It's working," I whispered to Keisha, who still seemed upset, though not as much as before. The message "no service" appeared in the upper corner of the phone, and the battery was almost drained. The time read 4:09 p.m.

Keisha and Xavier both pulled out their phones, but neither had service. I deduced that the cell towers we were connected to in the present must not have been operational in the past. They teased me for knowing such technical details, calling me 'nerdboy,' like back in high school.

The time kept moving while we sat there, and from what I had learned from the old man's story, I knew Idrissa would soon return from the stash spot with a lump over his eye. The family would soon gather for a barbecue, and we needed to find a safe place quickly.

I ventured outside alone, not worrying about what the others might think if they saw me. This was the neighborhood, and respect for others' property was rare. If someone saw me, I'd walk away and shrug my shoulders.

The old man's vision he shared, which mirrored our current situation, played in my mind as I explored the backyard. The grill, the toys—everything was exactly as he had seen it in my mind.

I noticed a set of stairs that led to what I assumed was the basement. Their steps were worn from years of use. The air grew calmer, and I made my descent. I hesitated a second before continuing to look back at the garage.

Thinking it was time to speak with my great-grandfather, I knocked lightly on the door. Keisha and Xavier emerged from the garage just as I did, their argument seeming to have intensified during their brief separation. Keisha looked ready for confrontation, while Xavier wore a nasty sneer.

Together, the three of us stood at the door, wondering what the old man would make of us when he opened it. Would he notice our peculiar clothing, or was he beyond paying attention to fashion?

Tired of waiting, I tried the knob, and it opened. Xavier looked at me, and I looked at Keisha before Xavier tapped me inside with a light push, following me.

It stood in stark contrast to how it looked in the present. It was fully furnished with a bar, couches, and a TV. A dartboard hung in the corner, with darts hanging from it. Jazz played on an old radio at a low volume.

The horn coming out of the radio was somber and slow-paced, reminding me of how I felt. Never before had I liked that type of music, but now it sounded fitting. We all stared at the layout, impressed. It seemed my grandfather had a man cave he liked hiding in, and it was decked out. Splitting up, we peeked around, looking for my great-grandfather in the plush basement, but the only thing we found was a padlocked door and a gang of empty liquor bottles strewn throughout the area.

Now, things were getting interesting.

I walked to the door, grabbed the thick lock, and tested its durability. It was one of those Masterlocks, with a thick orange band along the bottom. I let it fall without making a sound, and I looked inside the ajar door.

With the old wood against my face, I peered into the room and saw what looked like boxes and shelves. "Shit," I whispered before returning to Keisha and Xavier, wondering what they contained.

Being industrious and street-minded, Xavier looked around for something sharp and pointy. He found what he sought on a table and went to the door.

After a few minutes of jimmying around with the ice pick, the lock was removed, and the door stood open.

The room was small, organized, and cramped. It hadn't been opened in years. Taking off our jackets and laying them down, we began to search. Opening a few boxes and seeing article after article, I was curious as to what these papers held. All through the room were papers and newspaper articles. Tattered books and folders were tucked away with dates and numbers on the side. Everything was tabbed, cataloged, and color-coded. Whoever saved all this information was organized and neat.

We all went to different areas and started snooping. Ants scurried, and dust clouded my eyes as I looked and pulled boxes toward me. I didn't know what I was looking for, but it was interesting. Just when I pushed the heavy box back in place, Keisha called my attention. "Travis, look," she said, holding an ID card towards me.

Straining my eyes in the dim room, I read it. It was some college professor's badge, tattered and yellowed by age.

It read, "Professor Johnson , History Professor." Now it was getting interesting. In the corner was a younger version of my great-grandfather, wearing a suit and tie.

The old man used to be a history professor, and I guessed these were all his records. Why they were under lock and key was still a mystery, however.

The music in the background switched to an uptempo number as I pulled a folder down and opened it. The drums and other instruments made it feel like a New Orleans festival. Xavier was nodding his head as he searched, and Keisha tapped her foot in rhythm to the music.

In my hand was an ancient article about proving the veracity of ghost sightings and first-hand accounts. It was a research paper, so I pulled down more folders, and all of them were about studies the government performed during the '60s to prove or doubt mysticism. Huge redacted sections and weird phrases ran down the sheets. I wondered what type of history the old man taught or if this was something else.

From my research in school, I knew some files were complex to come by. Some had been blacklisted to hide certain information. I found it odd, and I thought about Lucky and the strange gifts he displayed.

We stayed there for about 20 minutes, reading and trying to assemble what we were reading.

While I searched the shelves and boxes for information, I could hear my mom upstairs and the aunt I had never met. My mother's voice was light and crisp when she was younger, but it was hers. Even the pitch and tone. I felt funny at the time. I hoped they didn't hear us, but I figured we were good with the stereo playing in the background.

I was beginning to see what my great-grandfather was up to, but I still didn't grasp the whole picture. The only thing to do was wait until he returned and ask him.

CHAPTER 29

THE BARBECUE

WE STAYED in that little cramped space, sitting on top of boxes, our words just above whispers. I had a few questions for my great-grandfather after searching the room, and I couldn't wait for him to return. It was as hot as a furnace that afternoon, with the warm, sticky air clinging to us. With sweat starting to form, we all ached for a breath of fresh air. I reached for the window and opened it, letting a cool breeze blow through and cool us off. The sun was beginning to set, and I smelled meat cooking.

Careful and quiet, I maneuvered a box and stood atop it with the orange light from the retreating sun shining on my face. I pulled Keisha up beside me as Xavier grabbed a box and looked on with us. It was amazing.

Everybody was wearing extra baggy clothes, like 3 times their size, and there was not a phone in sight. Scanning the scene, I saw that this was the BBQ that my father planned earlier, and it looked like it was just starting. My eyes focused on my dad, with his bulky frame standing over the grill we passed earlier, surrounded by a group of people setting up tables. The smells gripped at our stomachs, making us bend over from hunger, while they laughed and talked.

"Smells damn good," Keisha whispered in my ear.

I ignored her and studied my father, looking at his features.

"Does he favor me?" I asked.

"Yeah... You both got big ass heads," Xavier chuckled into his palm. "He's probably a know-it-all too."

I smiled and laughed with him.

I couldn't believe it, but Calm was right there, my older brother as a toddler. He was unmistakable, with his birthmark below his eye and his odd head shape. Stumbling on shaky legs, he looked happy.

"Look at baby Calm," Keisha cooed. "He's a cutie pie."

"Crazy, right?" I muttered, looking at the past.

I watched my mother, stomach swollen with me, throw some chicken on the grill, while my dad squirted apple juice onto them. I almost cried, no lie, but swallowed the lump in my throat, remembering what we were here for.

If I prevented Idrissa's murder tomorrow, everything would be right, as it was supposed to be. And maybe—just maybe—I could experience at last what growing up with both my parents would be like.

The room was growing darker by the second, and the old man was nowhere to be found. I mean, we didn't hear him return, at least. Xavier was the first to leave the room, restless, tugging at his shirt. "Look, everybody's right there, celebrating and enjoying themselves. Why don't we stroll up and get a bite to eat?"

I was nervous and pacing back and forth. "I don't know, Xavier. It's too risky. Let's just wait for Pops to return and chill down here."

He rubbed his stomach like he was starving. "I'm hot

and hungry, dude. Plus, other cats are showing up, drinking, and kicking it. I think we can go upstairs and get something to eat, and they won't notice us. It's so crowded, we could just say we're with somebody."

I looked to Keisha, and she sided with Xavier on this one. The food did smell good, and I was thirsty.

After thinking it over, I thought it sounded like a good idea. Besides, we could look for the old man while we filled our guts and took a break for a second to think. Silently, like we were invited, we walked up the basement steps to eat and continue our search.

After being in that dark, dingy room for so long, we shielded our eyes as we entered the kitchen. Squinting, we saw a few people chatting near the refrigerator, laughing and enjoying themselves. To our right, a man sat at the table with a bottle of liquor in one hand and a cigarette in the other, drinking alone.

I tensed up, waiting to be pointed out as intruders, but when no one questioned us, I relaxed a bit and continued on our trek. It felt nice to see people in such a festive mood. Keisha gripped my hand and gave it a squeeze that made it feel even better.

As we walked through the house with the music thumping, the smells of the barbecue attacked my nose like angry men. The little children we had seen earlier waved at us as they also walked around, giggling and having a good time.

Looking like he was starving, Xavier stood on his tiptoes like a cartoon character being led by his stomach. "Man, I'm finna snap," he said, rubbing his stomach. "I hope there's still enough, because these people look greedy."

I wasn't in a rush and took my time, happy to be experiencing all of it. Pulling Keisha along, I turned my head and said, "I'm sure there is, bro."

"I'm just saying," he said, licking his lips.

With Keisha's warm body pressed against mine and Xavier back to his regular self and not so defensive, it felt like old times. Like when we all first met back in school, young and dumb. The importance of why we were here was forgotten for a moment, and all was right; we were all friends again.

The three of us walked out of the kitchen with me leading, not knowing where I was taking us. All I had to guide us was the smell of ribs and louder voices. I was on autopilot that day, taking in the sights and sounds.

Our noses and grumbling stomachs led us out back, where a majority of the people were gathered. Stepping onto the ground floor, we were greeted by a heap of people dancing and drinking. My dad and mom were surrounded on all sides, playing spades, slapping cards down on the tables like seasoned pros, while others smoked and drank from red cups.

The music was louder out here, with kids running by with hot dogs or water guns. It was a good feeling, and looking out the small window didn't do it justice. They sure knew how to party in 2002, and I was impressed and a little bit jealous. Because, in the future, we couldn't hang outside so freely without hearing gunshots from opposing crews and gangs. 2023 was a war zone.

I still couldn't believe no one held phones in their hands. It was like everybody was just enjoying each other's presence in the present and not worrying about likes and digital attention. No Bluetooth speakers playing tiny, metallic music. No one posing for the perfect picture or trying to act tough or sexy. It was a feeling I had never felt before, and looking at my friends beside me, neither had they.

It was then that Keisha took control of my hand and led us to the table with the food, a big smile covering her face. "They're too turnt... I almost envy them. And look... no one's beefing," she said. "This is a different time, for real."

Looking at the food made my stomach growl. "Crazy, right? But let's eat and sit our asses down somewhere... I want to try to spot Pops and fill this empty thing," I said, rubbing my belly.

The spread was immaculate, with dishes and drinks, paper plates, and aluminum trays of food. Xavier's eyes were bulging from their sockets. "Boy!" he said under his breath before grabbing a styrofoam plate and getting up close and personal. "Now this is what I'm talking 'bout."

We piled our plates with macaroni, ribs, potato salad, barbecued chicken, and baked beans swimming in ground beef and brown sugar. Walking to the cooler and grabbing an ice-cold pop that numbed my hand, I was ready to dig in. Everything smelled like a home-cooked meal, prompting me to remember that it was.

Under the alley's setting sun, we found a quiet spot near the same garage we had just ducked out of, ate, and tried to remain inconspicuous. My thoughts turned to how my mom and dad were an excellent duo, while I smashed the ribs and macaroni. Glancing at them between bites, I smiled.

Look at them slamming cards on the table, cursing and wiping ass. They are having a good time. Despite everything I knew of my father and his gruesome job working for Victor, I felt a connection to him. A feeling of warmth.

2002 did seem lighter, but I also knew that something was bubbling underneath the surface, waiting to come to a head. While eating and pondering over my dad, I felt something pulling at the leg of my pants, and I looked down.

Smiling with a face of pure joy was baby Calm, my 'older' brother. He had a half-eaten chicken wing in his hand and a face full of sauce.

"Now I'm the big bro," I laughed, looking at his face.

Placing my almost-finished plate to the side, I looked at him with a face of puzzlement. His chubby fingers extended quickly towards me, eager to be held by his now-big brother. He was light as a feather in my arms as I bounced him on my lap. It was like he knew we were brothers somehow and enjoyed playing with me.

"Hey, little man... How are you doing?" I said as he erupted into a fresh fit of giggles. "Is it good?" I asked, referring to the chicken wing he held curled up in his hand.

"I can just eat him," Keisha said, grabbing his stomach. "You're so cute."

While bouncing him on my knee, I felt a hand on my shoulder. Turning around, I saw my mother's young face beaming without any worry lines, unaware of her future. Tomorrow would begin her descent into darkness and addiction, but for now, she was happy.

I froze for a second before looking at her pregnant stomach, amazed at the sight. She wore a pair of shorts, a long shirt with earrings and a bright smile. Knowing she currently carried me filled me with anxiety.

She grabbed her child and asked if I was alright. "Just a little lightheaded," I said before picking up my plate from the ground.

"You sure?" she said, holding Calm on her hip.

"We're sure, Ms. Tolliver," Xavier said to my young mother, forgetting we were in the past.

She whipped her head around like a viper. "Excuse me? Who are you?" she said, looking him in the face.

Xavier stuttered for a few seconds before I spoke.

"We're Idrissa's folks from out of town; don't pay us no mind," I said, stuffing the last piece of rib in my mouth.

"Ms. Tolliver? Like I'm an old lady or something," she said as she was walking away. "You people are strange."

"That was close," Xavier said, and Keisha and I looked at each other and then at him and started laughing.

"Looking at yourself in your mother's stomach almost made you faint, didn't it?" Keisha asked me, still laughing at Xavier.

"You could tell?"

"Hell yeah, your eyes got all bugged out like a fly, dude," Xavier said, laughing. "Honestly, though, you got me wondering where my parents are; I know it was trippy as fuck."

"It could create some type of paradox or something, so we gotta be careful," I said. "What if I accidentally unalive myself... ain't no telling what may happen."

They didn't understand what I was talking about. Still, one of those late-night episodes on the History Channel said that if you went back in time and prevented yourself from being born, you could create a paradox. I didn't understand the concept, but I knew I should avoid my parents for the remainder of our trip until I had to act.

Through all of this, I was looking for Pops. When he told his story in the basement, in the present, he said he was at the barbecue. Now that I was here, I couldn't locate him. We threw our paper plates in the trash and continued our search. He had to be around someplace, and we would find him.

When Idrissa announced he had bought a house, everyone cheered and congratulated the young man on making such a bold move. I moved among the partygoers, looking for the old man, ducking hands, and dodging people who were excited for Idrissa. The music now played something celebratory, and liquor was flowing.

They were behind the table, Idrissa and my mother, happy for themselves. I had never seen her this ecstatic in all of my 20 years. She held Calm and hugged my dad with a joy I wished she carried into the future. The mom I know was first dependent on drugs, then a workaholic. Her smile was a thing to witness for me that day.

Someone turned the radio down, the screen door opened, and an older woman walked down the steps, taking her time. This was my great-grandmother, a woman I had never laid eyes on. I felt a connection to her, even without knowing her. It might've been my emotions, but I did feel an undeniable bond.

The cursing and smoking died at her arrival. She hugged everybody nearby and gave Idrissa a big smack on the cheek, which he rubbed off like a child.

"Don't be smearing my kisses, boy," she said, and the surrounding members laughed and hollered. "I'm happy for you."

Keisha, Xavier, and I were caught up in it all. My family was here, and I wished I could've gotten to know them. To see my aunt, who stood to the side with her two children, Kearah and Sam.

I envied my brother Calm this time because he at least got to be around them, even if he didn't remember. His soul did, and he got to pick up on things I never got to.

Keisha shoved me, getting me out of my feelings, and pointed to the porch. I couldn't believe what my eyes saw.

My great-grandfather was standing with a glass of something, rocking back and forth, smiling. He was younger, taller, had all his teeth, and looked handsome, almost like me.

Keisha grabbed my face, looking into my eyes. "You, your dad, and him all look alike, and... it's scary," she said.

I snatched my head out of her hands and made my way to the old man. Walking up the steps, I anticipated what I wanted to say. But the words sounded stupid in my mind.

I had to get him alone first, and that might be difficult. Although he looked drunk, he had a defiant streak about him. Like someone who stood up for himself and asked questions.

Climbing the stairs with one hand on the banister and my cohorts behind me, I was ready to confront him and grill him. Maybe even tell him who I was and ask him about the whole mess.

A few people came out of the house and down the stairs, walking past us, separating him from eyesight. The music's volume increased, and more people were celebrating, making it hard to reach him.

I turned around, and Keisha pushed me forward. "Hurry up before you lose him."

Just a few steps and I would be in front of him. My heart raced with worry. What would he say? Was he too drunk to have the conversation? It all flashed through my mind like electricity.

When I stood before him, he passed me his drink and invited me inside with a cool, calm voice that struck me as strange.

"Travis, you've made it," he said.

We all stood confused, looking at the old man dressed in a shirt and slacks with grease down the front. How did he know who I was? Xavier mouthed something inaudible and returned to the gathering, leaving Keisha and me to travel inside with my great-grandfather.

CHAPTER 30

XAVIER'S INTERLUDE

XAVIER NEVER WANTED to be anyone other than himself. And it went as far back as he could remember. Ever since he was a child, he has been like this. From how he ran to how he played Nintendo, he always did things his way. Even if he made mistakes, they were his own, and he welcomed them. There were no lies or false airs with his hustle. He held his head high when he walked into a room, confident and sure of himself.

With Xavier, what you saw was what you got.

Let him tell it; he was the last of the real ones. A young man true to the times he grew up in. He was in touch with himself and his emotions. No matter who he would offend, he spoke his truth. Harsh and unapologetic. He was the one who would tell you straight up what and didn't give a fuck if you liked it or not.

What he lacked in intelligence, he made up for with strength. Not the big buff guy in the gym type of strength either, but the gritty and get down to work and get your hands dirty kind. His mother called him her soldier of truth, getting many of the people he loved in trouble with his nuts-and-bolts approach.

Your feelings came second to the truth, and he honored that shit like a prince would. He even dressed as he felt. No flashy clothes or logos for him. No, no, he wore plain shirts and pants. The one thing he did wear that was flashy was his shoes, and that was because they didn't make plain sneakers, and the girls would laugh if he showed up wearing slips and slides.

As he spotted who he thought was the guy Keisha and Travis were looking for, he ducked and kept his distance. With how he approached the world, he knew he would only get them all in trouble if he stuck around. Staring at Travis's great-grandfather made his temper run hot. Never mind that the current version of the old geezer didn't know who they were or why they were here. All Xavier wanted to do was ask him why he got them into this bullshit. "Look at him drinking from his cup, dancing from side to side like he had it figured out," he said to himself. "If you ask me, he is nothing but an alcoholic."

Tilting his head to the side and looking around, a scent caught Xavier's attention. A scent he knew all too well. Marijuana. "Somebody's smoking," he muttered among the throng of partygoers. Noticing a group of people not far away enjoying the magical fantasy trees, he approaches with hopes of getting high and forgetting about their trip to the past. That was everybody pocketed, or put out their blunts, and crowded around Travis's parents celebrating.

So, walking around the yard, irritated, he went on a hunt to see what he could find anyone out front smoking.

Just because Xavier wasn't smart didn't mean he didn't like asking questions. Questions were how you learned anything, and reading books and researching, he thought, were a waste of time. Life taught you more than any old book could, anyway. He stopped pursuing the academic route because it was too slow, and those who did weren't who he aspired to be like. Who wanted to wait 4 years to start your life and then become a beginner all over again with some entry-level bullshit? Nope, it wasn't for him. Life was for living, and he meant to live it to the fullest.

Searching around for the weed with hungry eyes led him to a painted fence, separating the backyard from the front of the house. Unlocking the gate and opening it, he walked on the matted grass towards the orange glow of the streetlights. Voices drifted to his ears before he saw a group of young kids sitting on the steps of the house. Feeling defeated, he pulled a cigarette from his pocket and lit it.

Letting the cool evening air blow across his back, he took a big inhale and blew out his frustration. "I should just give up," he said to himself as he stood out in the front yard. Upon seeing him, the kids on the porch got up and started tossing a football between them and joking with each other, walking a couple of houses down.

Xavier's hands went to his face as he signaled for a catch with the menthol hanging from his lips. "Let me see," he shouted out, getting the guys' attention. The boy fired the ball at his head like a bullet. Without a second thought, he caught it and fired it back. "You got an arm, lil nigga. Are you on a team or something?"

"Not yet, but soon." The young man zipped it back.

"You might make it," Xavier said before firing it back.

"I hope so," the young man said, then ran off to catch his friends.

Out of the corner of his eye, he spotted an old-school Cutlass pull-up and park in front of the house. It had tinted windows and was running idle, with smoke coming from the exhaust. The windows were down, and on the passenger side, a young man around Xavier's age leaned out with his hat cocked to the side. "Yo, where did you get those shoes from? I ain't never seen those." The young man addressed Xavier.

Glancing at his feet and remembering that he was in the past, he looked surprised. "Oh, these aren't out yet; I guess I got 'em from my guy," he lied.

The young man spoke like he was up to something, leaning further out of the window. "Step into the light and let me see 'em," he said before returning to the window and talking with the driver.

Xavier, aware of what was going on, took a step back. "Hell nah, y'all look like y'all on bullshit."

The people in the car laughed amongst each other, making Xavier nervous. "Nah, for real, I want to get a closer look. We ain't on nothing, I promise," the punk said.

Xavier thought it over and said, "Fuck it." He did have his pistol in his pocket, and he wasn't scared to use it. He would give them a couple of slugs if any of them acted like they wanted it, with no questions asked.

Hiking up his pants, the steps he took were measured and calculated. With his eyes on the car and the people inside, he walked out the gate. The guys were the same in any time period. If he acted too eager, they might pull out and blast him, or if he was too timid, he'd get the same results. This was a situation in which he had to play it cool.

As soon as he planted his feet, the doors swung open in a flash, and the men stepped out, smelling like huff-ass weed. These cats were serious trouble, and Xavier was worried. Seeing that they were all massive in size with tattoos and jewelry on their necks, Xavier swallowed hard.

Stepping back out and putting his hand near his waist, he revealed his friend. The trusted companion that was always close these days. His 40-caliber pistol. It was already cocked and ready for action.

Seeing him flash his hand cannon, the largest one grabbed the other men. "Calm down, lil dude. I told you we weren't on shit. I honestly want to see your shoes," the muscular man said as he was approaching him.

"Back the fuck up; I ain't playing with your big ass."

The two little kids dropped their ball and ran away with quickness.

"Okay," they said, getting back into their car. "But for real, I only wanted to see your sneaks."

"Look at them from there," Xavier said, standing his ground. "And if you can't get a look, you're shit out of luck."

"Sheesh, could you do us a favor while you're flashing your gun?" the perpetrator said. "Could you tell Idrissa if he doesn't have my cash by tomorrow? I'm ending his bitch ass, and you too if you're around."

He then blew a kiss at Xavier and pointed forward as the car drove down the block. *That had to be Victor looking for Idrissa,* he thought. He had remembered Travis's story and just knew it. He was the one who would kill Idrissa tomorrow.

After they left, he sat on the porch steps and finished his cigarette, thinking about his predicament. Travis was so focused on saving his pops that he wasn't thinking with his right mind. The opportunity that he was given was more significant than he expected.

Going back in time and changing things would affect

everyone on the planet. Reversing things and shifting things around could fuck up everything he had ever known. Xavier was upset that his friend had dragged him along on this bullshit odyssey quest into the past.

Even though he claimed to be an average person with practical needs, he was well-informed about things and only dropped out of school because he wanted to, not because he couldn't handle the work. Although he wasn't smart, an observer might even call Xavier intelligent. Time travel was a tricky issue, and he had a few questions that he wanted to ask the old man. Still, he wanted to wait until Travis spoke about his dad, but he meant to ask his questions soon after.

With his head making sure they didn't spin the block, he brushed his knees and returned to the gathering. "Lemme go and see where Travis and his girl are," he said to himself.

Opening the dilapidated fence and stepping back to the barbecue, he saw a group of people standing by the porch, smoking and drinking. *About damn time*, he mused, making his way towards them.

After hitting the herb, he was unimpressed. It tasted terrible—awful—and reminded him of the shit he used to steal from his older brother in grammar school. "Oh well," he continued smoking, grabbed a brew, and downed it.

High from the weak weed and agitated, he stepped down the stairs and took a deep breath. The party was still in full swing, and he wanted to walk around and get more familiar with the sights and sounds of 2002. Idrissa was playing cards with his girl and looking at him.

Deep in thought, he clutched his chin and made a decision. He walked over to where Idrissa sat and approached the man they were here to save. Just thinking of leaving the money upstairs under the bed was too much. Perhaps, if he could, he would find a way to hold onto the money and change his future.

CHAPTER 31

THE OLD MAN

WE SAT ON THE COUCH, looking at the younger version of my great-grandfather pouring himself a healthy drink into an orange plastic cup, with a look of disgust on our faces. How he could drink so much without falling over baffled us, but we kept that to ourselves.

My mind flipped with questions about Lucky and how he knew my name as he lit an incense with shaky hands. Placing the match to the tip and starting the flame, the pleasant scent of sandalwood began drifting around the room, engulfing my senses. I inhaled the sweet smoke, letting it calm my anxious mind, and sat back further in my seat.

The music from the barbecue was thumping outside, making the windows vibrate as he moseyed along to the rhythm with a bop. He had a happy-go-lucky vibe about him, like nothing could disturb him. It irritated me, like we weren't of any concern to him.

Looking at his gray, beady head nodding along to the music, I had serious questions that needed serious answers.

Time wasn't a luxury we had, and here he was grooving to music, getting drunk. It was insane.

Waiting for him to have a seat and get comfortable, I looked to my right at Keisha and took a hard swallow. "Mm, I don't mean to ask too many questions, sir, but how did you know who I was?" I interrupted him as he burrowed into his recliner.

His eyes searched mine for a few seconds, then dropped to his drink. Humming along to the melody, he ignored me, taking a sizable gulp. His Adam's apple bobbed like an elevator before he set his cup down, savoring the flavor with a satisfying look. Ignoring my words, he peeked under the table and produced two identical cups, blowing into them.

"Want any?" he asked. "I don't have many guests these days," he continued, setting the cups down.

I nodded yes to his offer, but Keisha squeezed my hand, signaling for me to decline. "Well, more for me," he said, taken aback by our refusal.

A loose, drunken mind didn't seem like the right thing to have in this situation, and it was the best decision. Besides, we had started to bond, and I didn't want to spoil it by getting shitfaced.

It was like Keisha and I were a couple again. Even though I knew that we wouldn't be together if I succeeded and saved my father, at least we could enjoy our time together.

Xavier, who had walked off when he saw the old man because he was mad at the whole situation, couldn't understand. His mumbling and walking off were typical of him. I was bogus for bringing him along and not explaining or even asking, for that matter, but he was foul for leaving like that. He couldn't get that far because the time-travel effect extended around the house, making us prisoners.

As I examined the old man taking another sip and walking over to where the jackets sat, accompanied by more dancing and humming, my annoyance with him deepened. I watched as he reached into my pocket and passed across my school ID.

"Is this yours?" he asked, handing me the piece of plastic. It had "Johnson, Travis" written above my picture, along with my dormitory name and room number from my time at school. Holding the lanyard, I mused.

A feeling of relief came over me. "So... this is how you knew my name, Pops," I said to him and myself. "My old ID?"

Still no answer, just more of him humming along to the oldies playing in the background. Keisha and I sat in silence, waiting for him to address us, but he remained silent. I nodded my head, recognizing the tune. I was tempted to hum along to the smooth sounds of Frankie Beverly, my mom's favorite, but the gravity of our situation was too significant for singing. When he finished his tune, he sat down, and his carefree look was replaced with a serious one.

With his cup sitting in his lap, he at last looked me in the eyes, "Who are you," he said, "and what were you doing in my files? And don't lie; I'll know."

"Before we begin to explain, I want you to take this seriously," I said to him. "Can you do that?"

At the sound of my voice, the old man sat forward, spilling a small amount of liquor on his jeans.

"Are you alright?" I asked as he got up and grabbed a towel from nearby.

He jerked again. "Boy, you sound familiar to me," he said, grabbing the rag from me. "Are you sure you ain't related to me? Because, now that I look at you, you favor my grandson, and that funny card there has my last name on it."

Standing there surprised, I continued. "That's why we were in your files, because you won't believe this," I said. "But I am your great-grandson from twenty years in the future. I'm Idrissa's unborn child."

His eyes widened, and his voice began to crack. "Young man, please go and amuse someone else, because I don't have the time," he said, standing and wiping down his pants. "I'm going back to my grandson's party. Please take your shit and get out."

That was when I stood up, saying my piece. "No one is lying, Daniel," I said with urgency. "You sent me here from the future. You have to believe me. You told me to fix this."

"Fix what?" The old man laughed at me calling him by his government name. "And asking around the party to find out my name isn't complex. Ha, it's going to take more than that to convince me."

I had come too far to be waved aside. "If I said the name Lucky, who also goes by Lucien, would it mean anything to you?" I said, looking in his eyes for any confirmation with a forceful sense of resolve.

Pop's face froze with horror, but his eyes spoke the truth. "Lucky, you say? And I sent you back in time? Tell me more," he said, sounding meek as a fly before returning to his seat and taking in what I shared.

"It wasn't you, so to speak, but Lucky," I said. "That 'dude' scared the shit out of me."

Pops leaned to the side, grabbing his chin and tilting his head, "And you saw this Lucky character with your own two eyes? And spoke to him? There's no way that's possible. I would never align myself with that motherfucker."

"Well, you did," I replied. "And he's dark-skinned and flashy... always smiling like he knows something nobody else does," I said. "I didn't trust him, but you did."

Looking me in the eyes and setting his cup down, he uttered, "If what you say is true, we all may be in danger. Lucky isn't what you think he is, son. He's something far worse and sinister. What else happened with him?"

"From what I saw, Lucky is some type of spirit with... powers. He split himself into a hundred pieces, like it wasn't anything. Disappearing at will and even getting me kicked out of school," I said. "He's the one that sent us here."

"He did, huh?"

"Yeah," I fired back.

I explained that tomorrow Victor would murder his whole family and that he would hide in the basement while it happened like a coward. He fought back but had to accept it.

"I wouldn't hide like no coward. Whoever told you that is lying through their teeth."

"You told me, Pops. Right in this same room, 20 years in the future," I explained.

The old man sat and thought about what I said. His face went through a series of emotions, ranging from bewilderment to surprise. "The last time I saw Lucky was a few years ago. I... I don't know what to say."

"You can start with those files and books in the room," Keisha said from my side. "Are you a teacher?"

"I was... at the university. I taught anthropology," he said.

Intrigued, I asked what happened, and he explained that he was fired for drinking and insubordination. "I tried to get help for my drinking, but the private research I was doing was getting too stressful. The things I had discovered disturbed my sleep, among other things." He looked like he was breaking down. "The alcohol was a remedy at first and then a sickening crutch; it led to me getting sacked."

He took another sip. And like a masseuse, he massaged his tongue against the roughness of his mouth, savoring the fiery burn of the alcohol. All I could do was look at him with pity and hope this shit didn't run in our bloodline.

"So what about Lucky? What were you researching that drove you to drink?" I asked, breaking the brief silence.

The old man looked up, holding his glass, his eyes narrowing. "Something I should've left alone. Something that was driving me insane."

CHAPTER 32

LOST IN THE SHADOWS

I SAT FORWARD in my seat at his words, waiting for him to continue. The old alcoholic looked at me with a glance, then went back to his bottle and poured himself another drink, splashing it while doing so, having the time of his life.

Something in me wanted to snatch the bottle and smash it against the floor, but I held back. Seeing my grandfather poison himself was kind of hard to stomach. I wondered how long he had been doing this to himself and smirked at his actions.

Casting side eyes at us and beginning and starting a few times, he acted as if he didn't want to tell his story. It would hurt him to explain the things he wanted to say. A gloom hung over him, or at least that's how it looked as we sat in silence, still waiting for him to go on.

The noise from the celebration seemed distant now and not as important. The music almost disappeared into a thump against the window pane. I gripped Keisha's thigh and kissed her cheek, showing I was there with her. Minutes seemed like hours, and when I began to lose my patience with his constant hesitation, he cleared his throat.

Sensing my annoyance, he fixed his collar and picked up the almost empty liquor bottle. "Don't be angry, but this is hard, and I have to find the right words to begin." He filled the cup one last time. "I hope I get it right."

"You know how black people say they got Indian in their blood because they may have curly hair or a light-skinned cousin? I do. Those old tales were made because no one in their family knew their true origin.

All the stories I had heard growing up intrigued me, and I wanted to research them to see if there was any truth to them. With my beautiful daughter—Idrissa's mother—passing, I needed something to occupy my mind. Something to keep the devil away.

My daughter was an innocent victim, and the person who led her astray later killed himself from grief. I guess deep down he loved my baby and couldn't deal with it. Either way, I was grief-stricken.

See, when crack hit the streets, it messed up a lot of families and hurt a lot of people. And my family, my gorgeous child, was taken from us, all due to that strong, powerful drug. Who knew her boyfriend would introduce that foul substance to her and then have her sell her body for less than nothing? Me and her mother didn't.

When she was found in the hotel room, bloody and beaten to death, her 'love,' as she called him, put a bullet in his brain. Throughout this, they had two smart and rambunctious kids—Juanita and Idrissa. My wife and I took care of them while she ran the streets with the low life.

It was a sad time for us, but we made it through. Maybe a year later, Idrissa came home from school with some book reports on Native Americans. My curiosity about the old stories I heard grew like cornstalks—fast and sudden. I showed him a few of the books from the university's library as a professor of history. He got an A+ on his paper, and, well, you can say I had a new addiction. While helping him with his report, I saw something that I thought needed to be researched further—something very intriguing. Maybe I'd even write a paper and submit it to a few journals to be published.

Being in those fancy academic books was a dream of mine at the time, as I was getting older and bored with teaching. Seeing my name next to my research would feel good, and I thought this would do it. Cement my name or at least gain a little prestige or respect.

It was a footnote that started it—my descent into the paranormal—right at the bottom of the page. I found it inside an old book documenting a white family's time in a particular area. A massacre of some natives at the hands of whites. It was so brutal and final that I was surprised no one had heard of it. Someone else had to know about this assault on the natives. Researching and writing my findings down led me to a black book scribbled by someone who dabbled in occultism. A woman, to be exact, by the name of Madam Stuschskoi.

The murders were so vile and evil that the lone survivor summoned something just as evil. A spirit that would get revenge for the savage crimes committed against them.

It was said that this spirit tore apart the ignorant people and fed them to the unknown. Mangled and kept alive beyond the point of living. Burning their insides and toasting the white man's families for years. Some of the stuff I found says the spirit is still torturing the twisted souls.

Inside the book, she spoke of calamities against nature so

great that they, the occultists, would gather in spots where the most significant crimes were committed and draw on the energy left behind. Feeding on it and using it for rituals and ceremonies, they spoke to spirits long thought to be dissipated by the effects of time.

Not knowing what I was getting myself into, became obsessed with it. Spending all my time reading and collecting more information on the brutal happenings of that time, every waking moment was spent on my new obsession. Most of what you found in that room was just the ravings of nut jobs with too much time on their hands, but some of it happened, and I was going to be famous when I told the story. I even came up with a name for it: 'The Native's Last Cry.'

One particular story told of a group of Natives who lived in the Pacific Northwest near Oregon, near a great forest. A small village in the early 1900s who were living in tune with nature and building a township. Along with a couple of blacks who were living there secretly, they were doing pretty well and minding the land.

The papers I read cut off at that point, and I had to know more. So I bought a round-trip ticket and arranged a weekend visit to one such place, out in Washington, and camped out in the woods with a group I found on the internet that was sightseeing. I didn't find anything, but I discovered more about what haunted me.

I don't know why I was so possessed by this thing—this hunger—but I was like my daughter, I guess. Someone lost to addiction. It was a blank mission, however, and the only thing I found out was that Washington was sometimes miserable. But I kept searching and looking for more information about this group of people.

So for weeks, I spent time at various libraries, thirsting for more information. The few words I'd written were incomplete and needed more to shine if I ever hoped to be published. At the moment, all I had were bits and pieces of the stories, and I wanted something concrete and real.

I bought a computer for myself and my grandkids to put together school papers and to gather all my findings on the massacre I was so obsessed with. I didn't know what I was getting myself involved with, but I put one of the CDs that came in the mail inside of it, and it made an awful shrill, connecting me to the World Wide Web.

That instance introduced me to much more than porn and music. It introduced me to a world of darkness and shame. The things I saw aided in my descent into darkness.

While researching one night, I clicked a link that took me to a chatroom about strange paranormal deaths. A list of various topics made me shiver. Near the bottom, with 6 replies, I clicked it, and it sent me to a photo gallery full of pictures and journal entries. Some of them were the same as I had gathered myself.

With the screen shedding its light on my face, I spilled my drink upon seeing it. I couldn't believe what I was looking at. I shouted out to my wife, but she wasn't interested. She told me to drop it and get back to focusing on teaching. She just couldn't understand. This was what I had been looking for for months. My paper would be complete, and I could have my little academic fame. Laying my eyes on the pictures was another story. Page after page of hand-drawn pictures depicting the horrific scenes in striking detail. I'm talking about arms and limbs ripped from torsos, drawn with such realism that it made me sick. I tried to turn my head but was transfixed. This cornucopia of photos was beyond anything I had ever seen, and whoever gathered them was vile.

I scrolled down the page with the mouse, looking over the photos and enlarging the scraps from journals. When I saw what I was looking for, a couple of pages from an eyewitness who documented what he witnessed, along with a single photo of the massacre with charred bodies and burned buildings.

I read the scraps but couldn't get anything from them. But in the photos, I could. In it, dressed in fine clothes, was a man, dark-skinned with long hair and a smirk. I want to call it an evil smirk, but it was more sarcastic. The photo was washed out, but you could make it out. It took me two days to figure out how to download the picture because I didn't know how to operate the computer that well. It was the late '90s, and I was old like I am now.

When I printed the photo out, it was clearer and more pronounced, and the grin looked evil under further inspection. So my hunt began anew, and now I was looking for the man in the photo with that smirk.

A series of months passed without any luck in finding out who that man from the photo was. The only thing I had was a washed-out photo of a bracelet with the name Lucien. My friends, whom I studied and taught for years, told me to abandon it as my wife had. But like I said, this was like an addiction, something I had to have.

My search led me to become entangled with a group that had information, and they shared it with me. A dark occult group, if you want to call it that, and at the time, I didn't believe in stuff like that. Spirits and ghosts talking to loved ones from the graves were made up and a waste of time.

This group, The Children of Dim, invited me to meet with them and disclose all I knew of Lucien. They met in closed rooms with turbans and patterned tablecloths and chanted to men long dead. It was all bullshit to an academic like myself. A bunch of charlatans playing dress-up to dupe the public to make money. Little did I know it was all true, and the things they were drumming would suck me right along with them.

They didn't need candles, incense, chicken blood, or other witchcraft-related things to talk to the dead. All they needed was a belief in the ether. The substance from which galaxies were formed. Still thinking it was hogwash, I would document and write about it and put it all in my paper.

When it was published, I would be famous.

I met everyone in the group individually and heard and took oaths to keep what they told me secret for sacredness' sake. Lucien, the foul man, was already forming. Materializing in our realm with each question I posed.

At this point, it was still fun. I could continue to ignore the pain of my beloved daughter with this hobby. My wife didn't mind because she knew how my daughter's death was eating at me, and I had something to live for again.

The people I met used me to draw the spirit, but I was ignorant and unlearned in the world of the occult. When they invited me to a real-life scene, I jumped at the chance. I thought I would record it and further document my findings. I didn't know someone was tethering this demon to my soul.

The men and women who arranged the meeting told all of us in attendance to close our eyes and think of Lucien, using photos and drawings of the massacre to do so. I said the bullshit meaningless words and drank from the cup as they did. When we finished, I asked if that was it, and they said yeah, the bastards.

That's when things became all too real. The combined energy of all our thoughts solidified his spirit in the present.

Sitting on our pillows, we focused our thoughts on Lucien and how he looked in the photo with all the mental energy we had. Minutes passed with me imagining Lucien in my mind's eye. How he walked, talked, and that devilish grin.

Something happened that night that made the group of occultists and I tremble to our cores with fear. A void opening in our heads, drawing us into it. An invitation into the macabre. We opened our eyes and saw a silhouette of a man in the center of the room. Transfixed, we couldn't move; all we could do was stare. The more fearful I became of this spirit, the more solid he became. I glanced around the room, and everybody was just as frozen as I was.

My heart was beating against my chest , and I couldn't move. The figure began floating a few inches off the ground, spinning around the room, asking who called him. Over and over, his voice shrieked, and he turned in a circle.

I felt the air being sucked out of my lungs, and his voice let out a haunting shrill that raked against my nerves.

Then nothing. The apparition we had summoned with our willpower vanished. I asked everybody in attendance at the strange spectacle if they had slipped me some kind of drug, and they all denied it and told me what I witnessed was real. There weren't any such things as spirits and ghosts. The leader said they had to bind him to someone, and that someone was me. As long as I live, he can influence our world.

They believed having him walk among us would open a pathway, but the only thing that opened up was my mind.

I would stop the research and mourn my daughter. This 'seance' was all too real. We all returned to our lives; our attempts to contact spirits were null.

Months later, I started dreaming of the man in the photo,

Lucien. In it, he was dressed in the latest fashions, always in the background. The dreams would be typical, and then the next thing I know, I'm in a locked room, wandering in a desert, walking alongside Lucien. Whenever the dream would switch, I'd be chained to this spirit.

In one dream, it switched to a cave overlooking a lake with a waterfall. I walked to the water and looked to the bottom of it; it was so clear. Majestic feelings filled me, taking hold of my body.

I turned around and saw my grinning companion sitting cross-legged, hovering a few inches off the ground.

Startled by something, I woke and saw Lucien standing above me in bed, mouthing the words, 'Thank you,' and then walking out of the room.

I got up and rushed behind him through the house, unsure if I was still dreaming. By the time I caught up, he had already opened the door and was on his way down the steps.

In my mind, a voice echoed. 'We're bound to each other, to reach me. Just think of me.'

And ever since, I've been drinking. I fear that even talking about it may make him reappear.

But that night, I called out to him in darkness, thinking it was just a figment of my imagination, a fragmented memory from a stressed mind. But when he turned and smiled that devilish smirk, I knew in my soul that he was real, and somehow, my belief in him made it possible for him to travel our world. It could be that I am wrong, am crazy, and need to be checked into an asylum, but I haven't thought of that night for years.

And that was the last time I saw Lucien or even spoke about my research into the occult. I locked up everything and washed my mind of Native American killings and malevo-

lent spirits. If I were you, I'd try to figure out a way back to my current time and forget ever intertwining yourself with that foul spirit. Whether you believe me or not, Lucien is an unmistakable threat that mustn't be toyed with. If I were you, I wouldn't have come here."

CHAPTER 33

AFTERWARDS

AS HE FINISHED HIS STORY, I sat beside Keisha, feeling calmer and more informed. The story he shared didn't scare me one bit. Tales of spirits and Native American massacres didn't make me shiver or clench my teeth. No matter what I heard, I was determined to see this thing through to the end. "Forget that spirit, motherfucker, and the winds he rode in on." But as I looked at Keisha's frightened eyes and body, I could see why she was shivering.

"We got this, babe," I said, pulling her close. "Spirits don't bite."

Living in the hood surrounded by killers, thieves, drug addicts, or worse, meant that from a young age, you saw your fair share of horror. Walking to the store could lead to your demise in Chicago, or going to school, you could be robbed, or God knows what else. Even though Pop's tale was wild, it wasn't quite different from the level of craziness I experienced growing up as a kid; minus the ghost and crazy Native American shit, that is.

"Okay, okay, so Lucky, that's what I call the spirit,

Lucky, what is he? Is he a ghost, a demon? What is he? Because you never broke that part down for me."

"I don't know, boy," he admitted. "It was too evil and much too dark for me to continue researching all that occult nonsense. I never found out who or what he was."

So he was a coward then, and a coward now.

"Show us the scraps you found on the internet; they might have something we can use," I insisted. "Or at least the black book. Something to make this shit make sense."

Pops walked over to the room and, after a while, opened the door and dragged a box out across the floor. He warned, "There... Lucky, as you call him, is nothing to toy with. Be cautious." He continued, grabbing his drink. "Now, I'm going back outside to celebrate and forget this whole conversation. Good evening."

"Wait!" Keisha pleaded. "Can we sleep here tonight? We can't travel far from this place, and I'm scared."

The old man considered and agreed, "I don't see why not. Just don't make much noise, and don't touch my liquor."

After the old man agreed to let us stay, a thought crossed my mind. If I could somehow convince everyone to leave tomorrow, the future would change, I thought. Moving a few pieces around might make a difference. I kept the observation to myself, however. I didn't want to cause any unnecessary stress. But it was a nice thought that I hoped would make a difference.

Huddled in the dank basement with Keisha kneeling beside me on the floor, we searched the box for more journal scraps. Something that could tell us more about Lucky and what forces we were dealing with.

I didn't tell Pop's what I was here to prevent because I didn't want to change anything about the past. It had to be perfect for tomorrow if I was going to save my dad without a hitch. Our being here alone has no doubt changed numerous things about our present. I believed that a person could throw away a piece of paper in Connecticut and cause an earthquake in Italy, on the other side of the planet. We would have to not do or say too much, to the people here, because it was the cautious thing to do.

It was about 5 minutes before Xavier came sneaking inside the door. He moved as if he wasn't aware of what we were doing, or didn't care about what was at stake. His eyes were low, like he had smoked some weed, and his breath smelled like liquor. "Yo, what did you find out?" he asked, sitting on the loveseat with his arm over the back, and his legs sprawled in a wide stance.

"I'm still trying to figure it out," I replied, glancing in his direction, from the box I was digging into.

Xavier always was doing things to get under your skin or shit he knew he had no business doing. I guess you can say he was a wildcard. Like the time he punched the security guard at school, he knew he would be suspended, but he did it anyway. At times, he just didn't give a fuck. Concerned about his unpredictable behavior, I told him, "The idea you mentioned about changing the past, applies to you, too. We can't alter anything; we might mess around and kill ourselves, or worse. I hope you didn't do anything reckless out there, Xavier. This situation is becoming complicated."

"Relax, man. I did see the dude you told us about, Victor. He and his guy tried to pull it with me. I upped on them, though," Xavier said.

Xavier, being Xavier, did just what I hoped he wouldn't; interacting too much in this timeline, could mess some things up.

"Man, I hope you ain't done anything stupid and changed some shit," I said.

Grabbing his crotch and kicking his leg out further, he said, "Man, you're going to piss me off by calling me stupid, bro. Chill out; ain't shit going to happen."

I couldn't deal with his antics and continued to look for the scraps of the journal, in the box with Keisha.

"Here, look at this," she said, handing me a piece of paper, washed out and hard to read. I grabbed it and tried to make out the words, but I couldn't. Keisha went into her phone, took a picture of it, and zoomed in, making the words more legible. It was hard to see, but I could make it out.

"Find the other pages," I said, mouthing off the words from the journal.

The party outside was still in full swing, with people enjoying themselves. Occasionally, someone's shadows would appear in the dim room from the window. Xavier was falling asleep, and I was deciphering the journal of an eyewitness to the massacre.

June 14th, 1909

I hid behind my brother's mangled body, while the white bastards continued to slaughter us. My whole family lay dead from trying to fight back against the white men's barbarism. I closed my eyes and prayed that I would be delivered from the mess that that spirit got us in. Lucien, I hope you burn in hell if you're reading this.

What did Lucky do? I wondered while holding the page. "Keisha, this Lucky character may be more powerful than I expected. Do you think he was behind the massacre?"

Keisha managed a slight shrug. "I don't know, but this situation scares me, Travis. I'm trying not to think about what I'm involved in, but this is too much."

I didn't respond to her, and just returned to the box, and searched for more information on Lucky.

Underneath an old folder, I saw a sheet and grabbed it. It was another page from the journal. This entry was from an earlier time. Keisha took out her phone, and I began reading.

September 2nd, 1908

People always stopped by our town, on their way to better pastures, and some were weird, others dumb or wise, with good stories. Lucien, however, was the creepiest person I ever laid eyes on. The stories he spoke in the bar haunted me for nights, and that smile lasted all my days after. When he started offering deals on outrageously priced ideas, I stayed away from him. He had a way with words and the slickest smile I ever saw. I'll be happy when he leaves our town. Maybe all the bad luck that has been visiting, will stop.

Keisha dropped the phone, her eyes scanning the entry, as she absorbed the unsettling details.

"Travis, we need to think about your so-called mission, a bit further. This Lucien character sounds like the devil," she said, burrowing her eyes into a fearful expression.

"No, he isn't. I spoke to him, but he is... something," I assured her, putting my hands to my temples, and rubbing. Xavier shuffled his feet and opened his eyes. "She finally said something right."

"Why aren't you helping, Xavier? Being baked on the couch, dozing off, when you can search with us, is lame," Keisha said.

Not this arguing bullshit again: "Don't start that bickering garbage. Leave Xavier alone, Keisha; you and I got this."

Keisha and Xavier looked at me like I had committed a

major offense. "I'm for real; I need to think, and y'all arguing, is giving me a headache."

This wasn't about picking sides; it was about my family's life. The same family; outside celebrating a major achievement, accomplished by my dad.

So, I had had enough. And why were Keisha and Xavier so nasty to each other? Always bickering and shit. I didn't know what was at stake.

We searched for more information but came up empty. The box held no more information on this mysterious person, with these extraordinary abilities. Later, when Pop returned, we'd have to ask him for anything else he might've known. Our minds were intrigued, however.

I sat there in silence, imagining where it came from and who summoned the creature. Was he like the trickster god in African folklore, or something eviler and more foul? Remembering the way he smiled and grinned at me, is all I knew.

And what did Pop mean by bound to him? Were the two linked? Or was it another type of joining? All these questions plagued me. Keisha continued to look for more information, while Xavier kept dozing off.

When Keisha gave up, I tossed aside the box, irritated and annoyed. It was then that a group of men barged in through the door, angry and aggressive. I pocketed the pages and stood, pulling Keisha beside me.

Xavier stood a few seconds behind us, his hand in his pocket, his face contorted in an abrasive and screwed-up expression. His legs were stiff with a sense of security, and he was no doubt clutching his gun, ready for whatever.

I saw someone pushing through the crowd of people, and then I heard a voice say, "Who in the fuck are you, and why are you chilling in my crib like you live here? Somebody better get to explaining, or all hell's about to break loose."

A tense hush settled over the room, as someone emerged from the group of men.

Idrissa.

I tried to exit without causing a scene, trying my damnedest to walk by and get out of there before anything escalated. Xavier kept his eyes on Idrissa throughout this, unwavering in his attempt to stand his ground.

"Xavier," I said. "We should leave, and get out of these people's way."

As his chest heaved up and down, Idrissa stepped forward. "I said, who the fuck are you in my basement?" he demanded. "Somebody better say something."

This wasn't just a random encounter—it was a confrontation with the man I came to rescue. His piercing gaze demanded a response, which I struggled to form.

Head down, I took a step with Keisha in hand but was stopped by Idrissa, with a forceful shove to my chest. I looked up at his wide nose, light skin, and brown eyes. He stared back like a dog. "I'll ask again; then we have a problem."

That's when Pop's returned, shoving his way between us. "Wait, wait, they are here with me. I invited them." He was even drunker than when he left but still coherent. "This is your cousin and his friend, grandson. There is no need to antagonize them."

Idrissa looked me up and down, studying my features, then circled, watching us as his guys stood silent. "Boy, next time you better say something, cousin; you almost caught one, and you too," he said to Xavier. "Was gonna get dealt with too."

My eyes shifted to Xavier, with suspicion. Xavier never

followed the rules and could spin a lie, like the best of them. Now I had more shit to worry about.

Idrissa broke out into a hearty laugh and dragged all of us outside to enjoy the festivities, until the middle of the night. Putting his arm around my shoulder felt like an old friend welcoming me, and I smiled big and felt even bigger.

This was Dad laughing, smelling like charcoal and meat, mixed with liquor; as good times. No matter how much I tried to smooth my face and act normal, I kept breaking out into a grin. Even though he was only a few years older than me, the connection was there, and I sensed he felt it as well.

Leading us back to the celebration, he shoved a drink in my hand and put a blunt between my lips. "Celebrate with your cousin and enjoy yourself. Because soon, we're done with all this."

CHAPTER 34

THE DISCUSSION

THE SUNLIGHT DRIFTED in through the window, shining on my face and waking me. I was stiff, and my legs were sore, but other than that, I was alright. I let out a long yawn and stretched my arms, glad to be waking up and happy to have the chance to save my family.

Next to me on the floor, snuggled up, was Keisha. Her locks curled up, with a few hanging over her face, as she groaned and opened her eyes. I felt her warm breath beating against my neck, soothing my rattled nerves.

Xavier, who took the couch last night, now looked like he regretted it. After making sure everyone was awake, we all sat on the floor, feeling like big buckets of shit. As it was, we were young, and the hard floor didn't do too much damage to our bodies.

Everyone was silent, pondering our future moves in the past. Racking my brain for a solution to our problems, I kept hitting a brick wall. How could I save my dad and everyone upstairs?

The idea I had yesterday still played in my mind on repeat: How could I get everyone outside the house before

Victor showed up? That was the question that needed answering. "'Yo, we're from the future; you have to leave, or you're all going to die,'" sounded pretty wild in my mind. Just thinking of saying it out loud would be even wilder.

Sitting in that basement alone wasn't doing anything to ease the pit in our stomachs. The old man hadn't returned last night, which sucked. So getting any advice from him was out the window. Xavier was still acting strange and distant, and Keisha was scared out of her mind. If we were going to do something, we needed to come up with a plan as fast as we could.

I was the first to stand and gather my things. Looking around the room for God knows what, I sat back down beside Keisha, and put on my shoes. "We need to figure out what we're going to do. Shit, it's still early, and in a few hours, Victor is showing up, and from what I remember, he's gonna be pissed, so we've gotta be prepared."

On the verge of panicking, Keisha pulled her knees to her chest. "This sounds too dangerous all of a sudden. I'm not sure I'm cool with all this," she said, rocking back and forth, her hair swinging. "But I don't know, Travis."

She was correct; it sounded more dangerous now that we were so close to the event, but I was adamant about succeeding, or getting as close to it as possible.

I ran my hand across my head in frustration. "You weren't even supposed to be here; I didn't tell you to bring your big-headed ass in here," I snapped, telling her the truth.

My words stung her, but I didn't care at that moment. She could sit there hugging her knees; I had to save my dad.

Standing up from the floor, angry at our situation, I addressed the room. "Are you guys in, or are you chickening out?" Silence and strange looks. "I'm with Keisha.

This is some crazy shit, bro. I just went to sleep in the past. The past. Do you understand what that means?" Xavier said, looking at me. "We can mess some shit up, like erase people. You think I'm wild, but I thought about that all night. What if you prevent yourself from being born?"

"Yeah, Travis, he has a point," she said.

"None of that shit matters," I said, trying to sound confident. "I have a plan, and you know how my plans come together."

Keisha and Xavier looked at each other and smiled. "Here we go again, with this lame-ass story about how you got away from the cops," she said. "That wasn't a plan; that was luck."

"You weren't even there, and it was a plan. Right, Xavier?" I said.

Xavier knew that we would've gone to juvie without me.

He looked at me like he was balancing hidden scales or judging to see if I had worked out something. "What is it? What's the plan?"

I still needed to think of the plan Bs and Cs, so I told him to chill and give it a minute. What I was hoping was getting everybody away and hoping it would make a difference in our timeline. If I could convince my family to leave, that was. My head was hurting from the liquor I drank last night while celebrating with my family.

Xavier's eyes shifted. "See, that's why I don't fuck with you like that anymore. Always being secretive and shit, let that crap out of my nigga. If we have to be involved, tell us what you're thinking, bro," Xavier unloaded.

The pressure was mounting. "Wait, I need more time to think," I said.

"Think? It's your fault we're in this bullshit trying to save your daddy," he said.

Now he was pissing me off. "Yo, I didn't do shit. You pulled me in here, X; don't forget that. You and your super thug ass want to get over on everybody at any cost. None of this would've happened if you had listened to me in the car. None of it."

Xavier hopped off the floor and stood in my face, nose to nose. We were damn near snarling at each other like wolves. "I've been waiting for this, boy," he said, his face carved in anger.

Without any weed or alcoholic beverages clouding my brain, I was clear-headed for a chance. The hardened look on my face softened, and I took a deep breath, placing my hand on Xavier's chest like an old friend—tapping it in solidarity.

"You know I'm right. You don't want to hear it, but it's the truth. If you and Keisha don't want to help me, fine. But know this: I don't know how we get back. I was so happy to get a chance to see my father that I didn't even ask enough questions. You guys can stay down here with the old man when he returns. I'll be upstairs trying to stop a crazy man."

A silence fell across the room as the three of us thought over what I said.

Xavier's shoulders relaxed, and his face unfurled from the wrath he had just felt for me. "Man, I swear, this is fucked up, but I'm gonna help you because I ain't got no other choice."

Xavier exited the backyard to smoke a cigarette, leaving Keisha and me alone. I guess getting some fresh air would alleviate some of his worries.

"Travis, you know I'll help you; it's just that I'm scared," she admitted.

I looked at her. "I am too, but... I'm not letting that stop me."

We were now playing for higher stakes. I walked over to where she sat and said, "I want you to wait down here when it all starts, 'cause if something happens to you, I don't know what I'll do."

"Really? You don't need me to do anything?"

"Baby, if you had heard the story and seen it in my mind, you'd understand why. Victor kills everyone here— him and his guys. The only ones to escape were my mom's and Calm."

"Everybody?"

"Yes, now I know why my mom always told me my dad died in the military. I didn't know he was in a gang, taking orders from one of the higher-ups."

This was Keisha's first time hearing any of this. "Are you serious?"

"Those voices you hear upstairs, those children playing, everybody. It's going to be a massacre."

"Why'd he do it?"

"Why doesn't anybody do anything? Greed and ego," I said. "And his lying ass brother set my father up to pay a gambling debt."

She reached for me and rubbed my head with care. "Okay, if you say so, I'll wait for it to end."

We sat in silence for a few minutes, each of us thinking about what would happen in a few hours. Last night, it didn't seem so dire, but now it was a different story. Shaking my head, I felt her wet lips against mine.

"What are you doing?" I asked, but she quieted me with another kiss. This one with tongue and much more passion.

It was all so sudden, so sticky, and caught me by surprise. I pulled back to look at her, and a trail of spit hung between us. That ignited me. I grabbed her by the back of her neck and kissed her back, tasting all of her. She then unbuckled my pants, and we made love, like all depended on it.

I asked her, somewhat out of breath from our hurried session, "What was that?"

"I don't know, I feel like this may be our last time together," she uttered, pushing off and walking towards the bathroom. "Sorry for jumping you like that."

"Sorry, that was what I needed, and I know what you mean." I trailed off, feeling the gravity of her words. This might be the last time any of us see each other again.

I felt a lump in my throat and needed some fresh air. Thinking about the three of us and our fun in high school being erased with new memories felt final. It almost felt like I wouldn't be the same person. She went inside the bathroom to freshen up, and I finished getting dressed and went out back to take a piss and wipe the tears from my eyes, where no one could see.

CHAPTER 35

KEISHA'S TRIP UPSTAIRS

KEISHA LOOKED around the empty room, wondering where everyone had gone. After giving herself a speech in the mirror, she was hoping to find Travis still on the couch, where she had left him. It took a lot of coaching in there, looking at her reflection. "I'm pregnant, and you're the father," she visualized herself, stating to Travis.

She regretted making the trip now more than ever. Why did she walk up those foolish stairs? she thought. If she had stayed in the present, when Travis saved his father, she wouldn't even be aware of it. Now that she was here, grappling with the ramifications, she felt the world closing in on her. If this is a dream, then it's a nightmare, she thought.

In just a few hours, her life would get a do-over, at least in the part where she met Travis and Xavier. And she was afraid of that, panicking on the inside. Is it going to be painful to have her memories ripped from her mind? Or is it going to be gentle, like an embrace? She wondered, gripping her flats and slipping them on her feet.

"Lord, please let this experience be peaceful, because I don't think I can take it," she prayed, sitting alone in the basement. "I never asked for this, and I don't want to feel anything. So, if you're listening to a stupid 20-year-old, show her a little grace. At least grant me that, Lord."

Feeling lost and hopeless, she decided to go upstairs, reintroduce herself to Travis's family, and get something to eat. The old man had done an excellent job introducing them to everyone last night, but she didn't just want to be a guest inside someone's home and hide out. It felt wrong somehow, and her parents had raised her better.

She walked up the old stairs, smelling the wonderful scent of bacon cooking. Her stomach growled. Placing a hand on the door, she gave it a slight push. The light hit her eyes, and the full aroma blasted her. She took a deep breath and grabbed her empty stomach.

Her eyes landed on an old woman standing at a sink, cracking eggs into a big white bowl. On the stove, a fresh skillet of lean bacon sizzled, while the sound of running water filled the room. The old woman turned to turn off the faucet while two little kids sat at the table, engaged in their own little world.

"Good morning, sweetheart," the old woman said, with her back turned. "Are you well-rested?"

Keisha looked around the room. "Yes, ma'am," she said, clasping her hands in front of her.

"Good, now where are the other two?"

"Outback talking," she responded.

One of the kids shouted from the table, it was Sam. "We heard you downstairs arguing." He wore a striped shirt and had dirt on it already.

"Uh-huh," said the little boy's sister.

Shit, Keisha thought. "Did you hear everything?" she said, fearful that they might have heard the whole conversation.

"Nah, baby," said the tiny, elderly lady. "We just heard y'all fussing. Now, sit down and grab a drink of orange juice while I get breakfast done."

Keisha walked over to the rickety table, grabbed an empty glass, and poured a tall glass of OJ. Putting the glass to her lips, she took a generous sip. The cold liquid coated her insides with goodness. She put the glass back down, with a small thump on the table. "That was good," she remarked.

Taking a second to look around the room more clearly, she observed her surroundings. At the fridge were notes and kids' drawings held there by magnetic flowers, and the jars on top of the stove held grease. Dusty curtains blew in the wind, and the soft creaks of the floor as the old woman moved from side to side.

As she took in the sights and sounds, she couldn't help but feel a sense of nostalgia for the calm atmosphere that surrounded her. This was a home filled with memories and good times. Even the old rugs placed here and there all told a story.

As the old woman began humming an old tune about Light and the Lord, everything clicked for her. This was why Travis was doing all this and endangering their lives in the process. These precious people would be killed in hours, and it made her stomach turn.

Looking over at the kids playing with their toys almost made her cry. Holding back tears, she grabbed the little girl's doll off the table, "So what do I call you, Mrs.?" Her voice was raw with emotion.

"I'm Keisha, by the way."

"Baby, just call me Granny; everybody does already."

She had a sweet voice with a southern twang—a rhythm that made everything sound like a song. It reminded Keisha of Sunday mornings when her mother was home, and she would listen to dusties and clean up. She would listen to Mary J. Blige and Erykah Badu and wash the dishes, yelling for assistance.

"Well, Granny, everything smells wonderful. After all that partying last night, I need this," she said, rubbing her stomach. Granny looked at Keisha kindly.

"Do me a favor, sweetheart. Could you reach into the cabinets and grab a few plates for me?" Rubbing her arm as if it were sore, she continued, "I'm getting old and can't stretch like I used to."

Keisha gave the little girl the doll she held in her hand, slid the chair back, stood, and went over to the cabinets. Opening them, she looked at the little girl and boy, smiled, and pulled down the plates for Granny. It felt nice to think of this woman as a grandmother. She had never met her own, and she was pregnant with her great-grandchild, so it was only fitting.

A look took over her face as she thought of becoming a mother. She didn't know if she was ready to be a mother, and having the opportunity to start over was a good idea. But the thought of keeping it was strong.

"How far along are you?" Granny interrupted her thoughts, catching her off guard.

She turned, startled. "I-I don't know what you are talking about," she stammered.

Granny's eyes pierced something furious. "If you say so, child, but I know. You got all the symptoms," she paused. "Now, what's this mess I heard you talking about downstairs?"

"Oh, those two. They're just homesick, you know. They always get into it, but never trade blows or anything. They're talking it over right now."

"Hmm, hmm," she said. "It sounded serious to me. Didn't it, kids?" Without looking up, the little children both shouted out, "Yes."

"Are y'all in some kind of trouble?" Granny asked.

"No, yeah, we're fine," she said, sitting beside the children. Lying to the old woman felt horrible, but she had to. In the background, she heard steps approaching, followed by the appearance of Idrissa.

He was sober, his eyes clear, and focused. One brow was raised. "Are you still here? I thought y'all would've headed out by now." His voice was low and scraped against my ears, without any of the warmth of last night. "Pops be tripping sometimes, letting anybody stay over. Y'all should split. We don't like strangers around our kids." The children giggled.

"That child out back is your cousin, boy. Have some manners," she said, hitting him with her free hand. He ducked her swat, and his face broke into a full smile. "I'm just playing. Make yourselves at home," he said. "Pops went to the store, so hang around. Maybe later, we can all talk."

Keisha sat in silence, unable to reply. Idrissa looked at her narrowing his eyes and said, "Tell everybody I said good morning, and take it easy."

The hug Idrissa gave his grandmother as he left hit Keisha deep in her feelings. It was warm, tight, and filled with love. Her eyes drifted to his muscled frame, and she thought about Travis.

"Will do," she said, as he hugged the girl beside her.

"See ya." And he was off.

As Idrissa left, Keisha felt compelled to say something about the danger they all were in. A brief warning of the upcoming events: "You shouldn't come back today; something's going to happen."

Idrissa turned around, his camouflage jacket twisting, and looked at her. "What did you say? Don't come back," he said. "What are you talking about?"

"I had a dream, and something bad is going to happen," she lied.

Idrissa laughed, but she was telling the truth. Something terrible would happen, and if he didn't return, it could be prevented. "I'm wide awake, and so are you; I suggest you drink some coffee, and knock those dreams out of your head." He laughed. "Look after this one, Granny; she can see." He held up two fingers and pointed at his eyes, like a witch doctor.

He was a few years older than her, and from what she heard last night, he was a new homeowner. She warned him but didn't know what else to say. Later, the bright day would turn very dark. Throughout the whole exchange, Granny was absorbing it all.

She took a rag from her waist, bent down to open the oven, pulled out a pan of biscuits, and tossed them on the table. "Baby, tell me what's ailing your mind. I might be able to help." And she did. She told her all that she could, minus the time-traveling part. As she explained what was troubling her, she felt lighter.

With Granny's warm eyes listening to everything, she felt a sprout of hope grow in her chest and thought to herself. Maybe things would work out for the better.

Out in the backyard, Xavier and I were still kind of pissed at each other, even though we had resolved our issues. It was another lovely day, with a pleasant breeze blowing. I could hear the neighborhood in the background coming together.

A car started, crickets chirped, and birds shook the branches overhead.

A car sputtered by as my mind turned over the problems I was facing. The allure of being in the past had worn off, and now it was time to get down to business. It all still seemed crazy, but fuck it. Balls to the wall, I thought.

"Gimme one," I said to Xavier as I walked beside him.

Xavier dug into his pocket, brought out the pack of crumpled menthols, and threw one at me.

"So, what's the plan?" he asked.

After putting the cigarette in my mouth and taking a long drag, I enjoyed the feeling. "We'll send Granny, her daughter, and the kids out somewhere. Hopefully, they will agree. Though getting my grandmother to go with them, is going to be tough, then it's you and me and that's as far as I got."

"You and me, and what army? Between us, we have two pistols. Two. How are we going to stop them from doing anything? You learned karate while you were at school or something?"

I shook my head. "Hell nah. We're going to look around the house to make a barricade, find something, and make some traps. I don't know. It's better than just going in a blaze of bullets like we're some kind of action heroes."

Xavier thought it over: "I did see some shit in the basement we could use, and I'm positive your dad's got some heat stashed somewhere in here, but I don't think it's enough."

"We'll make it enough," I said. "Let's go and try to catch Idrissa before he leaves. Maybe we can warn him," I suggested.

Xavier cut his eyes again.

Just then, Keisha exited the backdoor. "Too late; he's

already gone," she said. "And I tried to warn him, but he blew me off. Why don't the two of you come inside and eat? We'll figure out all this wild stuff later."

▭

Keisha showed Xavier and me inside, looking nervous and paranoid. I reintroduced myself as Mike, as I did last night, and took a seat at the table. Not knowing what to do with my hands, I pulled out my phone to see the time, and one of the kids saw it and reached for it. "What's that?" Sam said.

"Oh, it's a calculator; you've seen one before. Right?" I said, putting it back, despite the kids' protests to hold it.

I looked down at the table and was surprised at what I saw. The old woman had cooked enough for a small army, and I wasn't complaining. BBQ last night, and today, a feast. Times sure were good in 2002.

Feeling famished, I reached for the bacon, but the old lady cleared her throat. "We say grace around here," she said. Chuckles spread around the table as Xavier and Keisha both laughed at me.

"That boy is greedy," Xavier reiterated, shaking his head. "With no manners," he added, laughing even harder.

Granny bent her head, her voice soft and urgent, "Lord, bless this food you provided, and guide us throughout the day. Despite the uncertainty of the future, right now," she said, her head scanning the room, "It's perfect. Amen."

I took a chance to look at her and take in all her features. The thin creases in her deep, brown skin and her broad nose. Her dark eyes and small, wrinkled hands made me feel a warmth well up inside of me. I smirked, sitting with my great-grandmother, and felt a connection that was deep, like a Malcolm X speech.

She then grabbed the bowl of eggs, made the children a plate, and then passed the bowl to Keisha before looking at me. "Young man, why are you staring at me so?" she said. "You're making me a bit uncomfortable, baby."

I jerked a little, stunned that she was so open. "I'm sorry, ma'am. I was just thinking about something and was looking in your direction, that's all," I said, with a hint of embarrassment.

She grinned and said, "It's okay, baby. Just enjoy your breakfast." I turned my face toward my plate a little, feeling uncomfortable. What a dumbass, I thought as I loaded up my spoon and prepared to dig in.

The first bite made me close my eyes and savor the rich flavor. It tasted like somebody had snatched off a piece of heaven and crammed it on a plate. The flavor and seasoning were perfect. The eggs were fluffy and fried in bacon grease and butter. Biscuits with flaky insides, which I smeared jelly in between. A heaping bowl of cheesy grits, with a dollop of butter in the center. Strips of thick bacon, with the rind still on, were crispy like an ironed shirt.

We all smashed, except for Granny. She ate a bowl of oatmeal and drank a cup of tea. After a while, I felt somebody staring at me. I tried to ignore it, hoping the feeling would disappear, but it didn't, so I looked up to see who, or what, it was.

It was Granny. Now I was feeling uncomfortable but didn't say anything. I returned to my plate, made an egg sausage biscuit with jelly, and bit into it like a hungry savage.

She placed her teacup on the table and focused on me. "You know, you are the spitting image of my grandson. I'm talking about y'all even chewing the same. Where are y'all from again?"

Keisha said, "Cleveland, we're here for a wedding."

I looked at her, as did Xavier. Both of us were stunned at her response. Keisha was a fast thinker, but to come up with that was another thing. I wanted to laugh at her but held it in.

"Yeah, we're here for a friend's wedding, and your husband told us to come by." Granny eyed us from the side. "Oh, really now, Cleveland, you say? How long you here for?"

"Just a few days," I said, stuffing my mouth.

Everyone returned to their meal without saying a word. Sam and Kearah, the two kids who helped us yesterday, got up from the table and went out back to play.

After I finished, I leaned back, forgetting the impending danger, and enjoyed the peaceful surroundings for a minute. Hell, it's nice to be surrounded by my family and friends, I thought. It all felt serene at that moment, like sitting on a porch after a hard day.

This was very different from how Calm and I grew up. My mother's dad wasn't a father figure, and my mom was on drugs in the beginning. So, for many days, we had to fend for ourselves. Eating ramen and shitty-tasting bologna sandwiches with sugary Kool-Aid was the norm. Sitting in that kitchen then made me wonder how I would grow up in this household after I saved my dad. Would I live in the suburbs and go to an excellent school? What would that be like? It was interesting to think about. A new life. We all sat in our own thoughts, thinking. Granny got up, taking her time, and Keisha helped her clean off the table.

Then she entered. My mother is 20 years younger and sparkling. Looking radiant, she wore her night clothes with a scarf around her head. On her hip was Calm, my little 'older' brother. This is wild, I thought to myself. Following behind was Juanita, my aunt.

I looked at everyone's faces, absorbing the scene, and it dawned on me. All these people surrounding me were eating, laughing, and enjoying breakfast with each other; their lives were in jeopardy. In a few hours, Victor and his group of thugs would descend on this house and destroy it all.

The emotions I felt were suffocating me. My chest was tight with worry and stress. I grabbed a glass—that might not even be mine—and took a sip. The coolness brought some relief, but if I didn't act, it was over.

I pushed my chair back and excused myself. I needed a breath to myself. The room was beginning to look unfamiliar, and I was getting dizzy. I found the door with my eyes, almost panicking. Walking to the back porch, I took a deep inhale and prayed under my breath. Not a long prayer either, just a sentence. *Send something, Lord, anything.*

The splintered wood beneath my hand was old and gritty. The birds chirping nearby gave me a moment of clarity. As if my prayers were answered, the beginnings of a plan started forming. I don't know if it was God or luck, but I was pleased. Taking a seat on the old stairs, I felt hopeful for the first time since I had come, and just maybe everything would work itself out.

CHAPTER 36

A MOMENT OF REVELATION

KEISHA SAT DOWN BESIDE ME, trying to console me, as best she could. With the way I left the kitchen, she thought I was freaking out, or having a nervous breakdown. Newsflash, I wasn't. She placed her hand on my back and moved it around, with a worried look smeared across her face. I glanced at her with a determined look, letting her know I was okay.

It was true. I was panicking at first, but I came to my senses, thinking of all that was at stake. Today was the day that I would save my father and his family and change everything. I didn't have the luxury of wigging out, not right now. The situation was too important and didn't call for a kid crippled by fear, but for a man ready to fix his future and do what he thought was right.

The vision I had, back in the present, showed me the horrible fate that my dad and his family would suffer. The senseless deaths and wasted potential were pitiful. And my mother, seeing it all, I wondered how she got along after. It appeared that violence and bloodshed were all too common in the hood, even in the past.

The cycles we learned and grew into felt designed almost. Sure, we did champion villains that upheld ways that seemed wrong, but who made us do so? Was it our fate to go through tragedy after tragedy forever? Or did my people make a bargain with the devil? Were we cursed even? It made my head swim thinking about it. To me, black life was precious and needed to be protected.

With a face full of concern, Keisha's voice was caring as she gazed at me. "Travis, what are we going to do?" she asked with care.

I let her hand rest on my back, feeling her warmth radiate into me. It wouldn't be easy, but I took a deep breath and sorted through the chaos in my mind, throwing everything I'd seen or heard at the problem and thinking of ways to fix it. As I pieced together a patchwork of half-formed ideas, the plan began to take shape, showing promise.

Turning to face her with a firm and steady voice, I said, "When we go back inside, I'll have Xavier search upstairs for any type of weapon he can find and hope it's enough. My dad looks like he has something; I know he does."

Keisha nodded, taking it in.

"Then, I want you to help me convince them all to leave before Victor shows up. Even Granny. Old people like that are set in their ways, and it might take some convincing," I continued. "Then after that, Xavier and I will wait for Victor and kill him."

Keisha shifted at the words. "Kill? Are you sure you're ready for that? Last month, you were in school running track. now you're a murderer. How are you going to do that?"

"I don't know, but I've got to try. How else am I going to stop him?"

My mind jumped around, barely thinking about

school or track anymore. That was a lifetime ago, I thought. What mattered now was saving my family and my dad from Victor and his guys. A surge of hope bubbled up in me. "I just need you to have some faith in me."

Suddenly, Keisha kissed me on the lips—not a passionate kiss, but an 'I care about you' kiss. I had never felt that from her before. I pulled back, looking shocked and amazed.

"I've got to tell you something," she said with tears filling her eyes. "Something important."

I was caught off guard by her kiss, and filled with powerful emotions, I held her hand, curious. "What is it?" I said as she stared at me.

Precious seconds passed as I waited for her to explain, but every time she tried, she would stop. "This is hard to say, Travis, but... but I'm-"

That's when Granny pushed the screen door, interrupting her. "Are y'all gonna finish y'all breakfast or not? I need to know."

Keisha stood, leaving me hanging. "We'll be right in, Granny," she answered, before looking back at me.

"Later," she mumbled. Then, wiping her eyes, she followed Granny inside, leaving me with a blank expression on my face, and a whole bunch of questions.

When I entered the kitchen, Xavier looked full from the breakfast we had eaten and was hanging out by my aunt, like a predator. His eyes were tracing her curves, and I was growing upset. I grabbed him by the arm and dragged him, along with his greasy face, to the dining room.

"Dude, you're going to make me mad," I warned. "That's my aunt, perv."

"Calm down, bro. She's just so fine; I can't help myself," he said, running his hand over his head and grinning like an idiot.

"What? She's technically old enough to be your mom."

"Not now, she isn't," he replied.

I gave him the eye. "Stop bullshitting around, and let's get down to business," I snapped. "We only have so much time before Victor arrives. I need you focused."

"Okay, okay. But I'm saying, your aunt is nice-looking."

Xavier always did stuff like this, trying to get a rise out of people. I hated it, but had to deal with it. Walking towards the stairs in the next room, Xavier turned and said, "Aye, I'm about to go get freshened up a bit. If that's cool."

A knot tightened in my stomach, the weight of our situation pressing down on me. "Fuck that; go upstairs and look for some firepower... anything that we could use to stop Victor," I urged, whispering. "We don't have long before it starts, so be quick."

"I still have this," he said, lifting his shirt and showing me the 9mm he had tucked.

I eyed it and nodded. "I still have the 40 cal downstairs. I hid it under the couch. The more weapons, the better. We don't know what Victor has."

"Bet," he said. "If I find anything, I'll bring it."

Xavier left me in the dining room by myself. That was when my mother walked by with baby Calm and a plate of food, and sat it on the dining room table.

For a moment, I was caught off-guard by her youthful appearance and her upbeat personality. "Good morning; do you get any rest down in the dungeon?" She said the baby was fidgeting in her arms.

The sunlight streaming through the cracks in the curtains, accompanied by Calm's little gurgle, was like an ointment for my stressed-out soul. I felt calmer now, and regardless of her youthful appearance, she was still my mom. My mother always eased me, even if she was 20 years younger.

"I guess we were wasted last night, huh?" I said, sort of embarrassed.

The sound of the spoon scraping the plate and Calm's laughter, which disrupted the incoming food, sounded nice to me. "We all were; don't be embarrassed, Mike." Her words carried a hint of reassurance, making me even calmer.

I couldn't get over how young and vibrant Mom looked. And to think, I grew inside her stomach at this very instant. I shook my head in disbelief at her protruding belly.

"How far along are you?" I asked.

"6 months and counting. Then I'm getting my tubes tied," she laughed. "Got any?"

Looking surprised, I stammered. "What, kids? Nah, none that I know of, at least," I said.

She peeked into the kitchen and smiled. "That's your girl?"

"I wouldn't call her that, but we used to date," I said.

My mother giggled, looking at Keisha and then at me, with a knowing look in her eyes.

"What's that supposed to mean?" I asked suspiciously.

"She can tell you," she said.

"Stop playing. If she's pregnant, she'll tell me. Do you know something? If you do, spill it."

She eyed me feeding baby Calm. "I'm just joking around; don't get your panties in a bunch. Being pregnant doesn't give me superpowers to tell if a woman is pregnant, but her face is shiny, after all," she said cutting her eyes at me. "You should ask her."

I cocked my head to the side, thinking about having a kid, then shook it. *Nah, she would've told me by now. Wouldn't she?* I thought.

Seconds passed, and I would've loved to stay and talk more. Seeing my mother as she was before the heartache and addiction and hearing her perspective was incredible to me. She was about my age now, a strange mirror to my current self, yet still, without a doubt, my mother.

I saw myself in her now, more than ever, and thought about her condition in my present time and how she was lying in the hospital bed. This strong young mother had gone through so much in such a short amount of time and survived. I saw her strength and struggled to understand where she gathered the fortitude to endure such shattering events.

But time was ticking, and we had to get them out of the house. "So," I said, "what do you have planned for the day?"

"Nothing much; I got to drop off the little one with my mom, and then go to school."

"Dang, I was hoping someone could show my girl around Chicago; we haven't been here before, and she's been bugging me."

"Shoot," she said with a soft voice. "Sorry, but I'm swamped today; maybe later, if you're still around. How long are y'all staying?"

Fuck, I still had to think of something to get everybody to stay away. In the kitchen, I heard Keisha trying and failing to convince Granny and the kids to leave the home for the remainder of the day.

Getting them out of the house was vital to my plan. Just

doing this one thing could change the whole outcome. But unfortunately, things were falling apart. With my mind racing, I tried to think of a response.

The dust motes moved in the light, streaming through the curtains, as I stood looking at her and my brother, knowing what the future held for us. I had to think of something fast. Then it came to me, like those raps I used to write in grammar school.

I took her hand, got on one knee, and begged her, "Y'all got to leave and stay away for a few days; something's about to go down here. Something terrible," I said.

She searched my eyes, looking for a joke. There were none. She saw the seriousness of my request and felt our connection. Our mother-son bond was twofold because I was swimming in her stomach at this very minute.

She felt it, but let go of my hand. "Juanita!" she yelled into the kitchen. "You hear this fool talking about something's going down?" she laughed.

Fuck, she didn't believe me. What would I do now?

I stood and walked into the kitchen, leaving my mother laughing and waiting for a response from Juanita. I scanned the room, and I saw Keisha sitting at the table, shrugging her shoulders, as if to say she had also tried.

Granny, who had been silent this whole time, sat down and took a breath, "These children come from out of town, and both are talking foolishness. One says it's a dream, and the other says. What now?" She stared at me with her wrinkled face. "Now, where did you hear about this warning mess from? A dream, too?"

"No, I heard someone mention Victor or something last night, and I also heard... What's that big dude's name? Idrissa, I think he's called," I said. "He mentioned something to me last night that has me worried, that's all. I think you all should go to the suburbs to see how the new house looks, just to be safe, you know."

The door creaked open, drawing our attention. The old man staggered in, raggedy and drunk, smelling like a barrel of beer. With the same clothes from yesterday and a bucket hat sitting crooked on his head, I thought he would fall over. His entrance brought a tense silence to the room. "Honey, he's right," he slurred to his wife. "I did something bad," he paused before stumbling. "Can't you see the signs? Everybody gets dressed... Juanita's going to drive y'all away," he said, falling to his knees and gripping the table.

Keisha's hands flew towards the pitcher of juice, to keep it from falling from his drunken actions. I rushed to help him, but he dismissed me with a wave that smelled rancid.

Granny was getting upset, with her eyes narrowing like gangways. "Alcoholic heathen, leave us alone and go back to your devilish basement," she said, swatting at him with the dishrag. The old man took the assault, too drunk to fight her advances. "I may be a fool, but there's something to their story, and I think we should listen to them," he sighed, sitting next to Keisha, who got up, holding her nose at his stench.

The old man knew everything we warned about was true. He had unleashed the foul spirit and set this whole thing in motion. Our story last night had sunk in, I guessed. Lucky was far too real, and his family might be ignorant, but he wasn't.

"I'm serious!" The old man shouted, and for a moment, he sounded sober. "Go get dressed and leave before something happens."

Even drunk, he was a force to be obeyed. His family

moved with respect, remnants of the father figure he once was before addiction. "How long do we have to wait before Victor comes?" he whispered to me.

"I didn't know for a few hours," I said, astonished that he had returned from wherever he was and was helping.

"Good, it gives me time to sober up," he said, grabbing a piece of uneaten bacon off someone's plate and tossing it in his mouth. "Honey, can you pour me some coffee, too? I think I have to be focused for the next part."

Granny looked at him, surprised, but poured him a cup of coffee and sat it before him.

"Idrissa, you did good, my boy, but at what cost?" He spoke out into the air. "But at what cost?"

———

At the old man's warning, the family hustled to leave, packing up to visit the new house. It took over an hour, but soon everyone stood poised by the door, keys in hand. Hell would break loose in hours, but we had gotten everyone to leave. Breathing a sigh of relief, I went to say bye to my mother.

They were standing in front of the van, with the side door open. Each step I took towards it felt like a small victory. My brother was running outside the van with a toy in his hand. I reached down, picked him up, and helped him into his car seat, making sure he was fastened inside and ready for the trek. His cute, little, chubby face made me smile.

"Thank you for that," my mother said, looking surprised.

"Aw, sorry for that; you just looked like you could use help."

Juanita honked the car's horn and started the car, the exhaust fumes funneling near the rear. "Come on, y'all got me excited to see the house," she said, looking impatient.

My mother looked so composed and youthful that I wanted to hug her. I gave her a deep, loving embrace to show her that I had gotten her out of harm's way. I protected her and the rest of my family from the horrific acts that would be carried out later, but I held myself back. Doing that would draw too much attention.

Hopping inside the van and strapping on her seat belt, she looked hopeful. "Idrissa is going to be so mad we left without him, but oh well." She groaned. "It was nice meeting you and the others. And I don't know if what you were saying was true, but... be careful, and God bless."

The hell with it, I thought.

My arms wrapped around her in an embrace that took her, Juanita, and Granny aback.

"Why? What was that for?"

"You looked like you needed it," I said holding my head down.

My aunt laughed. "You're weird," turning the radio up.

Gospel music played at a nice volume, and I smiled. Look at that, I thought. In the middle of all this, these people were listening to church music. Idrissa had gotten himself involved in some street shit when he had a whole family like this. God-fearing and loving.

I watched them ride off, steeling myself.

According to everything I had seen or heard about time travel, something was supposed to happen. Getting them out of the house should've changed something. I looked down at myself and waited to see what would happen. The one thing that changed was my disappointment. Sending everybody away hadn't done anything.

I was still in 2002, about to face Victor. I was thankful for getting them out, but devastated that we didn't return to our timeline.

I took the steps up the house with my shoulders down, depressed. When I went inside, Xavier clutched the money bag to his chest. "Yo, what are you carrying that around for? We can't take it with us," I said, shaking my head.

"I'm keeping this, just in case, and look at what I found," he said.

He rummaged around for a second before pulling out a substantial amount of weed along with his blunts.

"I forgot I put this here, but we can get high if you want to, and then try to put together a real plan to save your pops," he said.

I looked at the weed in the Ziploc and almost grabbed it, but changed my mind. This whole thing started because I couldn't let go of the past. Holding on to ways I should've shed a long time ago. I walked off, leaving Xavier holding the bag.

"Travis, are you cool, bro?" He asked, puzzled. "Let's blaze right quick."

"Nah, I'm good. I'm staying sober for this. It's too important. We're about to be on some Marty McFly shit, and I ain't trying to be high when we alter time."

Xavier's face worked over what I said. "You know, you're right. We're going to do this like we're running a relay race. Focused and ready to pass off at any time," he said, putting the Ziploc back inside the bag.

Time was thin, and if we peeked through the fabric, we could maybe see ourselves through it. "Where's Keisha and the old man?" I asked. "We need them here before we start."

"She's downstairs with your grandfather. He told her to follow him."

"Are you serious? I don't trust him like that, and you shouldn't either," I said, rushing towards the basement. "Time isn't a game. We got to stick together until I save my pops."

CHAPTER 37

IRONING IT OUT

I SPED downstairs to reach Keisha as fast as I could, leaping down the steps two at a time. My great-grandfather, as he was now, had changed; he was different from his future self. In the future, he possessed some sense, but in 2002, he was somewhat reckless.

Each time I had spoken to him so far, he had been drunk. Now, it wasn't a depressing stupor, but still, his habits seemed deeply entrenched in his character. I thought about some of my habits while looking at him in this condition. The weed and the occasional cigarette might have to stop if we survive this. Upstairs, when he appeared and helped us convince his family to leave, I had some hope for him, but now it was nonexistent.

All my life, trust was important to me, and yet, I still didn't trust the old man. His shirt was missing buttons, and he was stumbling all over himself. I seriously doubted he'd be much help when Victor arrived. In his condition, he'd be lucky not to piss himself.

From what I had been shown about the upcoming event, Victor was menacing, and so were his guys. They'd toss the old man to the side like a ragdoll. Thinking about my father and his association with someone like Victor made me question my motives as well. Was I doing the right thing? I couldn't tell if this event was really happening or a twisted dream.

From my expulsion from the peculiar house to the unfolding story in the basement to the mind-altering experience that led us to this point, it has been a wild ride so far, and we were just hoping our safety harness was strapped correctly.

By the time I reached the bottom of the stairs, Keisha was sitting on the couch while Pops stood over her. I don't know why I felt so protective over Keisha all of a sudden, but I didn't like the two of them together. Especially after hearing his ordeal with his daughter dying, which led to him getting involved in some freaky death cult.

I unclenched my fist when I saw nothing peculiar happening. Great-grandfather or not, if something had happened to Keisha, he was getting the business.

The room hasn't changed much since we woke here this morning. The only difference was that the lamp was on, and our sleeping things were set aside on the couch. Walking further, I saw the old man placing a cup to his mouth and taking a sip. "That stuff is strong," he frowned, sitting it back down.

The sound the cup made as it hit the table had almost a voice, and the thud symbolized the finality of it all. Maybe I was worried about pulling off what we were about to do, but everything was heightened at the time. My senses were on fire. "Are you still tossing 'em back?" I asked sarcastically, annoyed that he was drinking at a time like this.

Keisha shot me a glare. "Travis, it's not what you think," she said, looking away.

And lo and behold, my irritation turned to embarrassment when he tipped the cup, revealing it was coffee—the same cup he had been drinking upstairs. "Sorry, I just thought... you know... never mind." My lips quivered.

"It's okay; I deserve that," he replied. "I was just telling Keisha about Lucky and how, from what I've heard, he doesn't always play fair. While you were asleep last night, I did some digging, and I must admit something to you. You know how I mentioned that the spirit was tied to me? It's much deeper than that."

I was rushing to check on Keisha and probably looked stupid at the moment when nothing was happening. I shuffled on my feet before settling. "What do you mean?"

"Those cult members used me to anchor Lucky to the present. They had something planned, but never told me what. And you know, it was all too much for me, at the time. But if something happens to me, Lucky goes back to wherever he comes from."

"Where is Lucky now? Is he here? Or doing things for the Children of Dim?"

"I told you, I don't know. I would try calling him, but I'm much too scared. Lucky is powerful."

Interesting, I thought.

The old man produced papers that resembled the ones in the boxes, albeit newer. Holding them out for me to see, he said, "This is from an old hymn the slaves used to sing. If you read it, you'll see what I mean. Lucky can't be trusted."

There it was again—that word, trust. As far as I could tell, nobody could be trusted, not even myself. I thought of the many lies I had told, perhaps to save my ego or something like that. Trust was on a slippery slope.

"So what are y'all talking about?" I said, sitting next to Keisha, searching his eyes for a response.

"Have you been listening? Whatever Lucky promised is tainted. You need to think about what you agreed to do. Did he even tell you how to get back? Or did he just send you off on some fool's errand, without asking questions?"

"It was both of you," I said. "And I didn't even ask, to be honest. I just wanted to save my family."

The old man stood up. "Here, read this while I go find something."

The papers were shoved into my hands quickly. "I shouldn't be long," he said, rushing off to the side room to get more information.

"We don't have time for this. We have to get ready," I shouted to him as my eyes took in the old, crumpled sheet of paper.

After looking at it, I saw it was a poem about double speaking, or saying one thing but meaning another. It was quite creative to be so old I had to admit. A snake with a forked tongue never means what it recites. Keisha took it from me and read it for herself.

She was shaking.

"What's wrong?" I said, but tears started falling from her eyes.

"I'm scared, Travis. I was trying to ignore things and just go along, but this shit is crazy. We're in 2002? How is this possible?" She panicked, letting the paper fall. "Let's call the cops."

"Call them, and they might fuck up everything," the old man said, returning to the room.

Why did she have to be involved? I thought to myself. She didn't deserve this, and she was starting to freak me out.

I cradled her in my arms, listening to the sounds of the old man digging inside the box of documents. I was in disbelief too, but not like this. I mean, she was shivering like she was freezing, and it was contagious.

Calming her down before it got any worse was all I thought. I only knew to hold her and comfort her, hoping my presence could provide her some ease.

She whimpered and sniffled a bit as I shushed her like a child. By the time the old man returned, I had gotten her back to normal. "We'll get through this. I'm not going to let anything happen to you. We've got to be determined."

"Determined?" She scoffed. "Travis, we are about to change stuff. If it goes as you envisioned it, I won't even know you when we are done. I don't know if I'll be alive! You know how bad our neighborhood is. I could be killed, a teen mom, or worse."

"So, you're now questioning everything, after all you said earlier?" I challenged her.

"Travis, how do we get back?" She shouted.

"We go through with it, and Lucky didn't tell me how, okay?" I said. "I was too excited and just did it. Just like the old man said."

Inside, my psyche was just as messed up as Keisha's. I wanted someone to tell me it was going to be okay. But I knew no one was coming to comfort me or save me. If I wanted to be rescued, I'd have to do it myself. "If I save my pops, everything will change, is all I know," I explained vehemently. "Maybe I should've put more thought into it, but I felt driven. Can't you see that the pieces on the board will be reset? None of this will have happened, giving us a second chance," I declared.

She looked confused. "I know, but I'm still scared out of my mind," Keisha murmured. "What's the plan?"

Finally.

"Xavier is looking for weapons, and I have this," I whispered, going under the couch and pulling out the 40 cal I found. "We're going to have the drop on 'em, and since we know they're coming, I say we lay low in the backyard and surprise them. Then," I said, "we do it."

"Do what?" The old man interrupted as he entered the room carrying a box in his arms.

"We kill him," I stated bluntly. "Me and Xavier are going to hide and kill them when they come inside."

The old man looked at me and shook his head in disgust. "Travis, it's not that easy. Have you ever killed a man, let alone shot a gun before?" He asked me.

"Come on, pops, in the future, we are shown guns before girls. The whole 'hood is fucked. Shooting a pistol ain't shit."

And it wasn't. Most of the guys my age were in jail or throwing bricks at the jail. Either that, or sipping codeine and popping prescription medication. Busting guns came with the territory. It was a dark existence, but we didn't pay much attention to it. It was all we knew. Common, and if you ran with the wrong crowd, you could easily get pulled into the city's embrace.

"So you've killed a man?"

"Nah, I haven't. But it can't be too hard, right? Aim, squeeze, and fire," I snapped at him.

"Boy, I pray for you," is all he said, with a voice filled with utter disbelief.

"I'm here through some outrageous turn of events, and you're worried about that? Pray for yourself, old man. I'm standing on business."

Pops' head leaned back, and laughter filled the room. He laughed so hard that he dropped the box. The contents spilled on the floor before him.

"Business? You are barely old enough to stand on my

shoulders. Put that thing away for a second, and look at this."

He bent down gingerly to gather the papers that were scattered on the floor. His bones cracked and popped like bacon grease. Keisha and I quickly leaped on our hands and knees and helped him. "When I was younger, still looking for answers, I ran across this," he said, digging in the pile.

After looking at a few sheets, he settled on one. It was from the olden days of the Internet. Sometimes, when I was researching for a paper, I'd stumble upon old sites with names like Angelfire or Geocities. Large text dumps of information, before ads for sex enhancement pills and political jargon-filled the net.

It was unique, with weird pictures of birds and aliens, or whatever interest you were looking for.

"Lucien can be sent back, but first, we have to do what you agreed," he explained.

The paper was placed in my hand, and as I began reading, my breathing slowed. The words were faded by time and neglect but were legible. By the time I got a third way through, my eyes grew wide. When I finished, I passed it to Keisha and looked for the continuation.

Lucien was an old, primordial spirit from before man's time. The document spoke of how, when time itself was just an idea, Lucshook, the Great Force, shaped the world. Sly Lucien tricked Lucshook's creations, introducing entropy and decay, where Lucshook meant all to be eternal. For this, Lucshook bound Lucien, who was forgotten until the 1800s. That's when a group of white men slaughtered a whole town over some hateful lie. Lucien, who enjoyed playing with time and chance, saw it all as a game. He was ordained in the beginning, before shapes existed.

I read as much as I could before fear stopped me.

Lucien, or Lucky, as he was called, was a malignant force who took shape. My great-grandfather had made a deal, ensnaring me and my friends in Lucky's twisted game, that could end us all. My pounding heart rattled my teeth as I read on.

"Is this saying what I think it is?" I asked.

"Yes, and if something happens to me during this time, Lucky will roam free forever. Untied to anyone," he said. "Now, he is still bonded to me. I made the mistake and let him out of his prison. I don't know why he doesn't make himself known to me. But I have been noticing things, since I let him loose."

I sat back and listened to him explain.

"Some days something would go missing. The remote for the TV or my wallet, for instance. By this time, I was pretty much drunk all the time and chalked up the strange occurrences of my drinking. The peculiar thing was that when the items returned, they somehow looked older. The remote might have a ding on it, or my wallet would feel different when I held it. Now though, I know it was him," he said.

Keisha looked perplexed at his words. "So what? Don't stop, Victor? It makes no sense. For us to get back, we have to kill him," Keisha said.

"No, no, stop him, but do it in a way so that no one is killed. It'll be a renege on your deal. And then, I don't know what happens, but at least he will still be with me until my death."

How could I stop Victor without killing him? Since I came here, that has been my plan. I didn't think of anything else. Lucien told me to kill Victor, and everything would be alright. What the old madman suggested complicated everything.

The words I read were serious, but I didn't want to get involved with all that.

"Listen, this thing is way too intricate for me. Killing Victor should send my friends and me back to our time. What you're saying may be more dangerous to pull off."

"We can do it; you're my grandson. I believe in you and your girlfriend."

"We're not together," we both said before looking at each other.

I wasn't embarrassed, but it did feel forced, and I did have strong emotions about her. Our sudden outburst made us closer at the time, ironically.

"Regardless, you gotta have faith," he said. "Now, do you know what's going to happen?"

I recounted what I knew, and he and Keisha listened. I told them how Victor would arrive and tie everyone up later, killing everyone inside.

He froze up. "And what about me? What did I do while it was happening?"

"You hid until it was over. Your future self said, 'like a coward,'" I said.

Thoughts ran through his eyes: "Well, I'm glad you're here, because I don't feel cowardly at the moment."

We sat for a few minutes and decided on a plan that, if we could pull it off, might tip the scales in our favor. It was a long shot, and frankly, I was worried. But we were already in a situation that was beyond us. The only thing now, is to have faith in ourselves and pray to God for a victory.

CHAPTER 38

MOMENT OF TRUTH

FIRST, we heard steps, and then, from overhead, dust rained down on us. I clenched the pistol, ready for whatever. As the sounds got closer, Keisha's warm body huddled against me, causing me to tense. With sweaty palms, I extended my hand, aiming the gun.

"Be careful," she whispered, pulling at my shoulder, her breath warm.

I re-centered my focus, intent on protecting us, as the sounds from the creaky steps added to my fear. I took one final look into Kiesha's eyes as I placed my finger on the trigger, ready to blast. "Here goes nothing," I said.

It was then that I heard a voice. "Wait!" Xavier shouted. "It's only me," he said as he came inside the dim basement.

Relief washed over me. Relaxing, I placed the gun on my lap and watched him. "Sorry, man. All this talk about getting Victor and stuff got me jumpy," I explained, still amped up.

He let out a big chuckle, but was still nervous. "It's cool," he grinned. "Just be careful. That's a big-ass gun, and I don't need any extra holes in me."

We both laughed.

Inside his hand, he still carried the Neiman Marcus bag of money we found along with a sawed-off shotgun. Keisha flinched at the sight of more artillery, inching even closer. "It's cool. Gimme a little space. Okay?" I said this to her in an attempt to calm her down.

"Okay," she replied, easing back against the couch.

Looking a bit more sober and focused, Pops looked at Xavier's haul. "Where did you get that?" He shouted, his breath smelling like stale cigarettes.

"Your grandson's room. Dude was prepared," Xavier said, going into his waist and pulling out two more hand-guns. "We should be decent now."

Xavier hobbled further into the room with a smirk, drip-ping confidence, as he dropped his bounty onto the table with a series of thuds, the pistols making the loudest. Next came the ammunition, which he revealed in a slow, method-ical manner. Two boxes of bullets and a handful of shotgun shells. "So, what's going on down here? You're ready?" He looked at me, cocking a pistol. "Because I am."

He was a true friend. Even though he didn't know the outcome, he was all in. And not half-assed, either. He looked like he was ready to ride, regardless of the outcome. "I think you should forget the money; it's no use to us. It's another distraction," I said.

Picking up the bag of bills and opening it, he smelled the contents like coffee beans. "This is a million dollars here, bro," he said, savoring the aroma. "Even if we can't take it back, I'm holding on to it; feel me. By some twist of fate, we might be able to take this back with us, and I ain't leaving it."

Standing inside the cramped space, I shoved the gun into my waist. Then, I walked around the small, musty room, trying to clear my head. Everything felt claustrophobic. The dusty, faded walls were closing in on me. Unlike Xavier, I couldn't stand still. The pressure from the drunken old man made me paranoid and hesitant.

If I could summon up the courage, I would walk up to Victor and leave his brains on the floor. But I couldn't do it. I hadn't killed anyone before, and maybe the old man was right, you know? Maybe no one had to be hurt, and a simple conversation could fix everything.

I pushed the gun further under my belt, my thoughts drifting to my dad. For years, I wanted to get to know him. I wondered what he'd do in a situation like this. The tales I'd heard spun by old addicts and show-offs in the 'hood always painted him as fearless. But at the moment, fear was my constant companion.

Once, this friend told me how my dad made everybody give up their pistols and squash their problems with their fists, even joining in and knocking out a few people. I thought that was an incredible feat as a kid, with my dad being an enforcer. It made me pay attention to my words and actions a little bit. But I missed that from my father and having the opportunity to learn how to move as a man.

So, putting a slug in Victor's brain would feel good for me and my dad. But at the same time, having that cloud over my head was something I didn't want to experience. I had heard too many stories of guys losing it over doing something like that or ending up in jail.

I went through the plan the old man laid out in my head, making sure I understood the details. And I had to admit that it did sound legit, but I wasn't so sure of it yet. I took into consideration that he used to be a college professor. So, it was that to think about, and his eyes were clearer now as he sat there, calculating the situation he had designed further.

Maybe talking to Victor and explaining everything wasn't such a bad idea. Breaking down how his brother, Derek, took the money to pay a gambling debt and blamed it on Idrissa sounded like it might work. I was still on the fence, but when I thought about it, it was our last shot at avoiding spilling blood.

I'd lost a few childhood friends to gun violence, and I know how it made you feel. Knowing the person who was responsible was right around the corner, maybe a few blocks away, made retaliation much easier. And the guns that flooded the city from freight trains or niggas going to Indiana made Chicago feel like Vietnam.

Looking over at Xavier, I knew what to do. "Yo, there's been a change of plans." My voice was solid and firm. "We're going to do some different shit. See if we can carry it out, without killing anyone."

Xavier's face froze as he stepped into the sunlight beaming through the window, as if I had just said something blasphemous. "How in the fuck are we going to do that?" he asked with a look of confusion.

"I don't know, but I ain't a killer, dude. And I don't think I could live with myself if I killed them in cold blood," I explained.

"But, Travis, if we don't kill him... What will happen to us? Are we going to be stuck in this backward-ass time, dude? 'Cause if so, I ain't with it," he said as he walked towards me, clapping his hands for emphasis. "How are we going to get back? If you don't close off the loop?"

I didn't have an answer, and he was beginning to annoy me. "Let him explain," I grunted, pointing at the old man. "I'm still processing it all." Keisha's soft breath in the cramped basement was milder. No longer shivering on the verge of tears, she was calmer and more herself. Pop's voice, like crinkling paper, went over the plan again for Xavier.

Keisha and I looked at each other, confused because Xavier wasn't feeling it. "That's it? Talking... You got to be out of your rabbit-fucking mind." Xavier took a drag. "I saw Victor and his homies, you know. They looked like some 'real' hitters. Y'all are crazy if you think a conversation is going to stop them." He was mad and had a right to be. I was hesitant at first, but maybe guns wouldn't have to be drawn.

"Bro, calm down and think... That spirit dude, Lucky, is dangerous. If we kill Victor, he's free. Do you understand what that means? The only thing keeping him bound now is him," I said, pointing to the old man on the couch. "Something he did when he first met him."

"Man, all this spiritual mumbo-jumbo is giving me a headache, Travis." He blew the smoke in my face. "Why did I come inside this house? Come to think of it, all of this is your fault," he argued, aiming the cigarette at me. "That loop we were talking about, I'm closing it the first chance I get."

I waved the smoke from my face and grabbed him by the shoulder, "Xavier, stop overreacting. Let's try the old man's way first. And then, if it falls to shit, we go out fighting, guns and all." I held my hand on his shoulder and gave it a shake. "We got this."

Xavier shrugged me off. "I don't know; getting the drop on him and laying him out is simple and clean." He started pacing. "We won't get a chance to do something like this, but once, and you want to waste it listening to some... alcoholic... You're crazy, bro!"

"But we have to try, don't we? Aren't you tired of this cycle we're living in? We traveled 20 years back into the past, and it was just more of the same shit," I raged. "Shooting and killing. I know you said you might've popped someone, but damn. How did you sleep after that? Or are you a mindless thug, like the rest of them... It's time to grow up, dawg!"

Xavier's shoulders slumped as he thought about what I said. He knew the world we grew up in. Death and violence. "I know you can feel it. Let's at least give it a shot," I added.

"Man, Travis, you're gambling with our lives. What do you think, Keisha? You have been over there, quiet as a hooker in church."

Keisha looked surprised that Xavier asked her what she thought. Still a bit shaken, she told him. "What do I think? Now you ask me what I think? I think it's all crazy. I thought about having another chance at my life and more opportunities, but this whole thing is confusing," she said, pondering the question.

"Well, should we kill Victor in the raw, or try to talk to him? Your opinion means something," I asked her.

Keisha hesitated and then responded. "I don't know; talk to him, I guess. Killing ain't always the answer."

Somebody was thinking, or at least I thought.

"Are you stupid?" Xavier fired out.

"Aye, motherfucker, watch your mouth. If you wouldn't talk to your mother that way, don't talk to me that way!" She shouted, jumping from her seat.

I calmed her down as best I could while she scolded Xavier. Watching her fly off the handle made me start thinking. Her mood had been off all day, ever since she got involved. And that conversation I had earlier with my mom added to my curiosity.

Pushing my thoughts of Keisha to the side, I stood in Xavier's face. "Dude, you're pushing it... Time is of the essence," I said, ready to snap. "You're with me or not?"

We stood face-to-face. Two men with two different viewpoints. I didn't want to resort to violence; he was all for it. I braced myself, my fists balled, and my muscles were tense. Thinking about Xavier's flippant mouth throughout all this, I was ready to swing. I raised my fist, and I paused, thinking about what I was doing. Stop violence with more violence? I took a step back and gave him some space. Keisha grabbed my hand and reassured me.

"It's the right thing," she consoled my angry mind.

Xavier's face went through a series of expressions, as he played with the idea. After a few minutes, he looked at us, and a smile cracked the corner of his face. "Fuck it, I'm down," he smirked. "But if anything looks funny, I'm shooting somebody."

Our hands came together in a deafening clap as I brought him close for a brotherly embrace. Keisha looked at Xavier with a side-eye, and Pops, who had been silent throughout the whole mess, rose from his seat. "Now that that's settled, let's go get in position."

CHAPTER 39

WHEN SHIT HITS THE FAN

THE ROOM we were in was nice, featuring a big-screen TV and DVD player on a stand on the hardwood floor. A couple of couches were positioned against the wall, surrounding the entertainment setup, making for a cozy environment. From the window, we watched the porch through closed curtains as we waited for Victor to arrive.

Daniel, or Pops, as I still thought of him, sat on the porch, a black cloth draped over his lap. With his button-up shirt and dress shoes, he looked pretty cool, I must admit. This cool cat was definitely my great-grandfather, I thought, looking through the curtains.

Xavier, the wild card, hid by the side of the house, near some bushes. Equipped with a sawed-off shotgun in hand, he was doing security, just in case things didn't go as planned. I needed to go check on him in a minute to make sure he was staying cool.

The operation was well underway. All that was left now was to wait for Victor to show up, which I knew from my vision would be soon. Just thinking about what I saw made me sick. The way they killed everyone was brutal and uncalled for.

A breeze blew under the slit in the window, moving the curtains. I slid one of them back to see how Pops was doing, and upon closer inspection, we realized he was sleeping. "Look at his chest, Travis," Keisha whispered. "See how it rises and falls? I bet you he's asleep." She shook her head in disbelief.

Annoyed, I tapped on the window to wake him. "Hey!" I shouted through the glass at his oblivious form. "What are you doing?"

He waved me off, taking a sip of his beer and mumbling something unintelligible.

Under normal circumstances, he would have looked peaceful sitting there in the afternoon shade. However, the impending threat changed my perception. He glanced over his shoulder and shooed us away, wiping his mouth with his hand.

"Think he'll be alright?" Keisha asked.

"I hope so," I replied, taking a seat.

In my hand was the chromed-out pistol, its weight a reminder of what was about to go down. Keisha gripped her gun as well, though she was unfamiliar with how to use it. "Hold it with two hands and fire when you need to," I instructed her.

Handing her the pistol earlier had emboldened her. "Don't shoot anyone you don't mean to," I cautioned as she practiced removing and reinserting the clip. "I didn't make a mistake giving this to you, did I?"

"No," she assured me as she placed her finger near the trigger. "You did right. Now I feel protected."

Her constant reloading made me nervous, but I refrained from commenting. "Remember, nobody dies. This is just for show, to intimidate Victor and his goons. Don't pull it out unless you have to. Understand?"

"I got you," she said. "Why don't you go check on Xavier? I'll alert you if anything happens."

She was back to her usual self—alert, sarcastic, and quick-witted. I smiled at her, and told her to be careful, then headed out the back to see what Xavier was up to.

Around the back, ducked down in the yard, peeping the scene, lay Xavier. He was lying on his stomach, in a tall patch of grass, with a hoodie he found lying around somewhere.

The hood was up, and he had a cigarette in his mouth. From the front of the yard, nobody could see him. He had picked a good place to conceal himself.

Everything boiled down to the conversation between the old man and Victor. We'd already saved my aunt, her kids, and my great-grandmother from the upcoming assault. Now my great-grandfather had to play his part.

"You straight?" I whispered, crouching down beside the stiff grass.

"Pretty much, I can see everything from here," he said, looking to the porch. "Now all we have to do is wait and see what happens."

A car drove down the street, and we both waited to see if they would park. The slow-driving sedan kept going, and we both relaxed.

"Man, I hope the old man can pull it off... this morning, he looked fine. Now, though... It's looking kind of iffy."

The cigarette was down to its last puff, and Xavier flicked it a few feet in front of him, sitting up beside me.

"I'm ready if shit hits the fan... I figure I should be straight, regardless of whatever happens," Xavier said. "I have a backup plan."

I looked at him, my voice stern. "What are you talking about now, Xavier?"

"Don't worry... It's nothing like that," he said, smiling. "But they ain't going to know what hit them."

I grabbed him by his arm, shaking him. "Xavier, now is not the time for surprises, bro. Tell me what you're cooking up."

"Calm down," he said, snatching away from me. "You gotta trust me."

I didn't know if I did. Xavier always followed his own rules. Even when you thought he was following orders, he'd always pull some half-assed maneuver at the last second. I looked at him one final time and prayed that he wouldn't pull his typical bullshit.

That's when we saw an old-school Buick Regal pull up with a nice paint job and gold rims, followed by another nondescript vehicle. I hit Xavier on the shoulder, "And it begins," I said, and ducked my way back inside to Keisha.

From behind the curtains, Keisha and I stood still, blood pumping. Through the crack in the window, we kneeled, so they couldn't see us, with narrowed eyes and open ears.

The big brute, dressed like an old-school rapper, had to be Victor, as I vaguely remembered. He was also buff, like one of those wrestling guys I used to watch as a kid. He had a scary look in his eyes and was grinning.

"Damn, he's big," Keisha mouthed to me, but I hushed her, focused on what was about to go down.

Walking up the steps with two henchmen and his brother, he fixed his eyes on the old man. I had never seen someone so serious before. The goons beside him stood shorter and less aggressive than he did, but they still looked like killers.

"Where's Idrissa?" Victor asked, standing over him. "He has something of mine, and I'm here to retrieve it."

The old man, scared and fidgeting in the presence of the menacing Victor, placed his beer beside him. He grabbed his clothes and tried to stand, but was held in place by one of the henchmen.

"Not so fast," he said. "Is he here? A simple enough question, right?"

"Young man," the old man uttered. "My grandson isn't home, but is all this necessary? You coming here with all these thugs, like you're Al Capone or somebody."

Victor let out a laugh. "I like you, old man. Comparing me to Al Capone is a compliment," he said. "Now tell me when he'll be back."

Pops, looking nervous and drunk, replied, "That, I don't know, but maybe we can talk about why you are here."

"Somebody get this old fool before I slap him," one of the thugs addressed him.

The old man leaned forward and tried to stand again; that's when Derek, Victor's brother, pulled out a gun and stuck it to his ribs.

"Aye, you two, go inside and see if you see our money. And hurry up," Derek ordered the men.

Everything the old man said he'd do failed as he sat there, bug-eyed and frozen from fear. I pulled Keisha away from the window, as we heard the menacing men approaching. The screen door opened, and I pulled out my gun, ready to unload on anyone dumb enough to enter, when, from outside the window, I heard the old man's rebuttal.

"There isn't any money here," he said, halting everyone.

"My grandson doesn't have it. He's loyal to you, for God knows what reason. Please leave here before he arrives."

"What's he going to do?"

"Nothing; it's what you do that concerns me, young man," he said, now standing up. "You're wired up now; going off a half-assed story, you know, is bullshit. Am I right?"

Victor wiped his nose with his hand. "No, you aren't. But I am high as hell, I won't lie, but the story isn't half-assed. Right, Derek?"

Derek ground the gun into the old man's ribs, but Pops didn't budge. "Your brother's got a habit, and I'm afraid he's playing you. Tell him, Derek. Tell him how you took the money to pay off your debts."

Wham! He took a blow to the side of the head, and the force of the blow made me shudder.

The old man fell forward into Victor, who let him fall to the floor. But the old man caught his balance, looking surprised. Keisha and I eyed each other, still aiming our guns at the door. The old man stood up, taking his time, and dusted off his clothes.

The look on his face was filled with drive as he planted his feet. "Why did you hit me? Is what I'm saying true?" he asked, rubbing his head and addressing Derek. "Just tell your brother what happened, and let's put this behind us. It's only right."

Tension was high, and it looked like we would have to resort to Plan B. Adrenaline, fear, and stupidity welled in my chest. I mapped out in my head what I'd do, and it only took about three seconds. I'd open the door and let loose the whole clip, right into Victor's chest. I was young, anxious, and ready to end this.

I kissed Keisha; her eyes were frantic at the moment.

Just as I was standing, readying myself to unleash havoc on the thug, she whispered in my ear, "Travis, I'm pregnant. Please don't do anything stupid. Please."

It was like a loud, high-pitched sound went off in my head at her words, disorienting me. I couldn't think with a rational mind. Damn, this changes everything. If I went out and shot Victor, it should take us back to our present, as Lucky said. But she had our seed in her stomach. I looked at her, surprised and unable to talk because of the situation.

Question after question infiltrated my mind in that small window. Indescribable feelings screamed at me to make a decision. In Keisha's eyes, I saw her plea. But if the old man died out there, our future would die with him. My head swirled with the implications.

No matter what, I had to get out there and save him. I moved the curtain to check, and he still stood against the small mob. That's when I saw Derek ushering the old man inside with the rest of the goons.

I scrambled, pulling Keisha along like a rag doll. Escape was the only option. Through the dining room, around the table, and into the kitchen. Aiming for the back door, I ran with the speed of a cheetah. No one was catching us today, not if I had a choice.

Putting my hand on the knob, I twisted and pulled the door towards me. We both froze in our tracks. Two more goons stood, holding Xavier by the collar. I tried to raise my pistol, but the next thing I felt was cold steel meeting my scalp. Then darkness.

CHAPTER 40

THE NEGOTIATION

WHEN I AWOKE, my arms were bound with old television wires, inducing near panic. Beside me lay the rest of our squad, unconscious, with Keisha lying on her side, and Xavier and Pops tied up on their stomachs. I felt a little woozy and disoriented but was fine otherwise, except for the big, throbbing lump on the back of my head.

"Shit," I hissed under my breath, my heart pounding against my ribcage.

The entire plan had fallen apart at the seams, and I didn't know what to do. Pops was supposed to convince them not to kill Idrissa, but that fell through. I guess we put too much pressure on the old man, and now we were paying the price. Xavier's plan had sounded much more feasible at the moment, but that moment had passed as well.

Straining, I heard footsteps, combined with voices, coming from the front of the house, feeling the vibration through the old, splintered wood beneath me. They sounded like they were celebrating our capture, deepening my sense of hopelessness. I had come all the way here from 20 years in the future and fucked up everything.

Twisting my neck, I found that we were being held in the dining room. Looking out the window, I saw the sun hadn't moved too much, so we still had time. To do what, though, only God knew.

Grit from the unswept floor smashed into my face as I rolled closer to Keisha's sleeping body. Her face looked peaceful and more comforting to me now that I knew she was pregnant. Just thinking that inside her stomach was our unborn child made me determined to get out of this situation.

I took my foot and tapped it against hers, waking her. Keisha's eyes opened, taking in everyone, then grew wide with panic. She started flipping on her belly and squirming, ready to scream. I alerted her to be quiet until I figured out what was going on. She came to her senses, to our strange predicament. With her hair a mess and the eyeliner a little runny, she calmed her breathing and looked me in the eyes. While I took it all in, it made me want to get revenge on Victor.

I turned my head to see the plate my mother had eaten out of earlier, forgotten in my family's rush to vacate the premises. The scent of piss coming from the old man stung my nose. His drunken ass couldn't hold his liquor, and was stinking up the place. Time was running out for us, and we needed to get out of here fast. I've got to figure something out, I thought.

Trying to play it cool, I looked to Keisha, who was calm and ready to speak. Her voice trembled, "What happened? Did they kill your dad?"

I shifted my eyes around the room to see if someone was watching us. "Shh, not yet, but I think we messed up and got caught," I said, turning my face toward her. "Are you okay?" I asked her with a voice full of concern.

"I have a headache, and these cords are cutting into my wrists. Travis, I'm scared," she whimpered, fidgeting with her wrists.

Panic was setting in, and I ached to comfort her but couldn't do anything, tied up against the floor. "It'll be okay," I said, feeling the hot air from my mouth blow against my face. "Can you wiggle yourself free?"

I tried to move my bound wrists, under the strain of the cords, to free my hands. "They tied me up pretty well," I whispered to her.

She glanced at me with a shameful look in her eyes. "I'm sorry, Travis. I should've told you as soon as I saw you that I was pregnant," she whimpered. "Now we're in this weird house, and we may..."

"Don't say it." I cut her off, fearful of what she was going to utter. "I think I can get out of this," I assured her, looking into her eyes. "And you don't have to be sorry," I said as I scooted closer to her. "We'll figure this out."

She looked at me with eyes full of tears, and it all made sense. Her talking with my great-grandfather in the basement and his 'plan' to get out of this without hurting anyone was all about saving his family, even his unborn family.

I looked at Pops' sleeping form and felt a connection to him. Yeah, he was an alcoholic who played around with some dark things, but he did it for his family. I guess saving my unborn child was more important than saving my dad, the old fellow.

The younger version of him wasn't racked by regret and was able to see things for what they were. Twenty years of who knows what and addiction unhinged him. And all I wanted to do was see my dad, but I only went along with him out of ignorance. Because if I had known that Keisha was pregnant, I never would've come here.

I tried to manipulate the cords that tied my wrists, trying to loosen them with every bit of strength I had. They weren't too tight, just overbound. If I could just move my hand to the side, I could free myself. The hard plastic of the extension cords was burning my wrists, but I was determined to get out of the predicament before anybody decided to check on us.

The voices were getting softer, and then the footsteps stopped. That's when Xavier shifted around and woke up, looking disoriented. "Travis," he said.

I shot him a glare, whispering, "Dude, shut up. You want them to find us?"

"Too late for that. Ain't it?" he replied.

Ignoring his smart comment, I continued wiggling free. The wires were cutting into my wrists now, but I think I had it. Just then, something gritty stamped on my wrist, forcing me to be still. A voice laced with menace cut through the silence. "What the hell do you think you're doing?"

Struggling on the floor, I tried to turn over to get a better look, but was kicked in the stomach. The pain made me shout out. "Argh, what was that for?" I yelled at our captors. "Let us go. Please," I said, still in pain from the boot that struck my side.

"Victor!!!" echoed a thug's shout, betraying a hint of triumph, in the other room, "They're awake."

Keisha's eyes were the size of dinner plates, while Xavier, with his face against the floor, just chuckled. Pops was still unconscious and incapacitated. I began to grow sorry, but he eventually woke to more shouts from the goons standing over us.

The slow footsteps vibrating the floor had to be Victor's. "Pick them up and set them on the couch," the voice said. "I want to ask them a few questions."

Hands gripped me, pulling me to my feet. Blood trickled onto the floor from the gash on the back of my head. "Untie them too... They're not dangerous... I don't think."

And just like that, we were escorted to the living room and sat on the couches, with the old man taking a chair near the window.

The room was a mess, with couches, pillows, and the carpet ripped from the floor. It looked like they were looking for the stash that Derek had stolen. The front door was open, and sunlight spilled inside.

Xavier, Keisha, and I filled the couch, rubbing our heads and picking at our newfound scars. I whispered in Keisha's ear, "Don't worry," and she obliged.

Derek and Victor looked like twins, standing before us. One menacing, and one with a devilish look in his eyes. The other is smaller and impish.

"I remember you from last night," he said, bent over Xavier, and grabbed his face. "You upped the strap on us."

Xavier retorted, pride swelling in his chest, as he jerked away from Victor's grasp, "Hell yeah, I did. Call it intuition."

"Who are you, and where are you from?" Victor demanded.

I spoke for all of us: "We're from out of town, and we don't know what's going on."

-Slap-

"Stop lying, and tell us the truth," Victor said.

I rubbed my cheek, looking him in the face with fiery eyes. "I told you already, and cool out with all the violence. Didn't your mother teach you any better?"

Derek looked at Victor and laughed. "Dig this one. He thinks he's in control of something."

My feet tapped against the carpeted floor in a fit of

nervousness. "I don't think anything... I just want to go home," I said, admitting the honest-to-God truth.

"We turned this house upside down and can't find the money. Idrissa is going to get all of you hurt," Victor sneered.

I looked over to Pops, who was still dazed and confused. Unable to understand what was going on, he looked out of it. His shirt was now half-buttoned, and his graying, nappy chest hair was visible. His bloodshot eyes met mine, filled with remorse.

"Where the fuck are y'all from again?" Derek asked, sizing us up.

"Milwaukee," Xavier blurted out, his voice sounding confident. "We don't even know what you are talking about. We haven't seen or heard anything about no money, dawg."

Xavier was sitting like he was sitting on some secret information, with his arm slung over the back of the chair. I sat up and motioned for him to chill. This was not the time for him to go flying off. He looked at me and smiled.

That's when Derek grabbed him by the collar and bent to his face. "I don't like you, little nigga. You think you're slick, with this smug little smile on your face. I'll give you something to smile about."

"Hold on," I uttered. "Calm down, please. We just got into town yesterday; we're innocent and just want to go home. Let us go."

Victor walked to an empty chair and took a seat, his arms looking like cannons, draped over his legs. "Ain't nobody going anywhere, till I get my money. Somebody is lying, and I'm going to find out who and deal with them," Victor said. "Derek, leave them alone for now, go on the porch, and keep an eye out for our pal Idrissa."

Derek looked at his brother with contempt in his eyes, then let Xavier's collar go before he left the door.

Keisha slid closer to me, while Xavier kept that smile on his face. Xavier's voice had a casual flippancy as he scanned the room. "Anyone holding a blunt? No?"

Victor went to his pocket, pulled out a pack of Swishers, threw them in Xavier's lap, and chuckled. "Unlike my brother, I like you, and under different circumstances, I'd offer you a job," he said, sitting back in his chair. "Might as well get high before it's over. Right?"

Keisha dug her nails into my arm and gasped. "Calm down," I whispered to her.

In the future, the weed was stronger than what they smoked here, and the smell was beautiful, if you liked weed. So when Xavier pulled out the small satchel, the two goons standing beside us perked up, lit up by the aroma of the bud.

"Damn, that smells good," one of them said, looking down at Xavier.

Xavier was already splitting the blunt and licking it. "I have enough for you, if you want," he said between his teeth. "Want some?"

The bigger of the two reached for it, but Victor halted him. "That's not regular weed. Where did you get it from?" he said.

"This is why we're here. We got pounds of this back home. We came to let our cousin try it out, right, Travis?"

I looked surprised for a bit, but I kept up the ruse. "Oh yeah. Idrissa told us about you and how you might be interested in buying a few pounds. We didn't expect all this to be going down."

"Ah, yeah," Victor said. "Let's see it."

The man standing over Xavier snatched the satchel from him and smelled it before handing it to his boss.

He eyed it with a weird look and took a nugget out of the bag. "Damn, this shit is high-grade and potent, by the looks of it. How much of this shit you got?"

"Lots... But we didn't bring much. Just a few ounces."

Xavier was in control now, and he knew it. The weed was pretty good, even for our time. Every time we smoked it, we couldn't stay awake. I didn't know what Xavier was cooking up, but I hoped they would smoke it.

I glanced at the old man sitting on the floor, with a huge wet spot darkening the front of his pants. He looked defeated and pretty much out of it. His part of the plan had backfired, and I guessed he felt embarrassed.

My empathy was running high, and I felt it with him. Not being able to convince Victor to question his brother's motives stung Pops, and I could see it in his face.

I tried to perk him up with my eyes by narrowing them and then looking at Xavier, hoping he hadn't given up. We needed everybody firing on all cylinders, and even though he was drunk, he proved to have an exceptional mind. I guess it's where I got my intelligence from.

Keisha reached behind her while they were distracted with the weed and showed me she still had her pistol tucked in her pants. How she had it baffled me. I grabbed her and leaned her back onto the couch with wide eyes.

We just might be okay, I thought.

Looking around the room at our captors and making sure they didn't peep us, I took the gun from Keisha and squeezed it inside the cushions. Xavier watched us with a smirk on his face, then nodded and lit the blunt.

I noticed he wasn't inhaling the smoke and was just blowing it out. We had both smoked it and knew what it could do. It tasted divine and knocked you on your ass. The potent stuff had to be handled with care, and I hoped these idiots threatening us smoked it like Xavier and I had done.

"Ooh wee!" The smaller goon said this before snatching it from Xavier's grasp. "This shit smells good as hell," he said, putting it to his lips and taking a deep drag.

His eyes widened, and he put his free hand to his mouth and coughed. Deep, hurtful coughs shook his body. Wheezing, he tried to take another hit but couldn't. "What is this shit-" he continued coughing. "It tastes so good."

"Gimme that," the other goon said, and took a hit.

Keisha eyed him, while Xavier just sat back in his comfortable seat and cracked a wicked smile. "This that fire, boy... you might want to take it easy," he said.

"Shut your lame ass up," the goon coughed, passing the blunt to Victor.

"I'm good; that shit will make you lazy." Victor declined his partner's hit of the powerful marijuana.

Xavier's smile disappeared when he saw that Victor didn't hit the weed.

"Are you sure you don't want to try it?" I said. "It's worth it."

Victor went into his waist and pulled out a gun with a very big barrel. "Yeah, I'm sure that weed be fucking with me. But these two seem to enjoy it. How much, and how quick, can you get this shit?"

I lied, my face staying calm. "If you let us go, I can get it back up here in a matter of days. But you got a nigga worried, with that cannon on your lap."

"Oh, this is just for making sure y'all aren't up to anything funny." He picked up the gun. "If you can get me some of that, I could make some major bread in the hood."

"Hell yeah, boss. This shit is fire," the bigger henchman

said, now able to hit the blunt without coughing. "What do they call this shit?"

"Kush. It's from some Arabs, and back in Cleveland, we are the only ones with the connect," I said.

Victor stood up, "When Idrissa gets here, and if he gets my money, we can definitely do business. If not," he cocked the pistol. "You're dead, all of you."

CHAPTER 41

A DANGEROUS BARGAIN

IT DIDN'T TAKE LONG for Victor's lazy henchmen to find themselves a seat and doze off. The weed was much too potent for this period, and it knocked them out. The stories I'd heard growing up were that the weed they smoked in the past was from Mexico and bricked up. Most of it was old and moldy and sold in small $10 bags. This good stuff could easily be sold for $50 for the same amount.

Both of their eyes were glazed, and one even started drooling himself to sleep. Even though Victor had told them to watch us, they just couldn't. With both their sleepy heads bobbing to make sure we weren't moving, they clearly were failing to carry out his orders.

From where I sat, I could see Victor and his brother, Derek, lounging on the porch. Outside, I heard more soldiers, and from the sound of it, he had called his whole crew.

My heart hammered, looking at the group of young men assembled to send a message to anyone dumb enough to steal from Victor. Every now and then, I'd see a few stepping on the porch with their hands near their waists, gripping pistols, while others surveyed the scene with careful eyes. Many were kids our age, and it made the situation feel different somehow. It made me think that blacks had been facing the same hurdles for far too long. Regardless of whether we survived, I knew that staying in this environment was not ideal for me.

"Wait til your pops get here. All hell is going to break loose, I swear," Xavier said, breaking my train of thought.

I shifted my eyes over to him as he slid the pistol out of one of the men's hands. "What did you do?" I whispered across the disheveled room.

"That's what I told you earlier. My backup plan," he said. "They'll never see it coming."

I knew he had done something, but I wasn't expecting this. It caught me unaware as I clenched my fist.

"X, don't be playing around," I quipped, forgetting about the men hearing me.

"Boy, you better be; you're going to wake 'em up," he whispered. "But I saw your dad last night. We kind of had a conversation."

I tried to stand, but Keisha's sweaty hand, gripping my shoulder, halted me before he continued. "I told him something was going on today, sort of, but not quite."

"Shit, Xavier, you more than likely fucked some shit up. What else did you say?"

He was full of surprises, it seemed. "I told him I saw Victor and that if he ran across him and his brother, they would be on his ass," he said. "He didn't believe me at first, but your old man is smart like you. He asked me a couple of questions before coming around. He said he'd be prepared."

I clenched my fist and considered screaming, but I didn't want Victor and Derek to return.

"Travis, what are we gonna do?" Keisha spoke from

beside me. "I don't want to die in the past, regardless of whether I'm carrying your baby."

Xavier chuckled. "I knew something was up. Congratulations," he said with a hint of sarcasm. "And now I know why you weren't doing shit when you had the chance. Kissy boy's in love."

I leaped out of my seat and caught Xavier right across the jaw, my temper boiling. Heaving and breathing hard, I waited for him to stand, but he didn't. The two henchmen grunted, alerting all our attention. Everyone stiffened. When they continued sleeping like someone had slipped them melatonin, I calmed my temper.

Xavier's hand went to his jaw, and his face screwed up. "I deserved that," he mumbled. "But the next one, I'm beating your ass, and I don't care who wakes up."

I didn't know what to do. I mean, I could open the door and let Victor have it, but then we'd all go back to our present, with different lives. The money we had found, my difficult life, and my baby with my high school sweetheart would go up in smoke, or whatever events like this did.

It appeared that I had put too much on my plate and now had to eat every painstaking morsel. If we waited too long, we'd all die today, in the early 2000s, as unknowns. The thought was unsettling. I was frozen from misdirection and needed an answer. I looked at everybody's faces, even the old drunken mess of a man on the floor, and sat back down, defeated.

Xavier leaned forward, "What's your problem, bro? I just helped us. A lot. Idrissa doesn't know who we are, so that part is good. Right? And just think about what your dad's going to do when he gets here. I mean, I was thinking about getting back with the money and all, but killing Victor is the best option. There's too much at stake."

"He's right, Travis. I don't know if I'm ready to be a mother yet, and you're so focused on living a better life and getting back to school. Let's kill Victor and forget all this ever happened," she said to me, almost pleading. "I can't even get my head around all this anyway."

It was confusing, I had to admit. Fooling around with time and spirits was too complex and made my temples throb. If we hadn't killed Victor and still saved my father, what would happen? Lucky told me the rules, but they were foggy now. It felt like trying to look through a murky bowl of soup. Plus, Keisha was carrying our child, and that meant something, didn't it?

"But this is different," I said. "I could be the father that I never had. Teach our child important things, and you want me to forget them? Do you know how much that means to me? I don't think I would ever forgive myself, and you couldn't either; otherwise, you would've never told me."

She paused and looked at me in a loving way, with the beginnings of tears in her eyes. "I-I don't know-"

Victor and Derek strutted into the room like bosses, interrupting her. We all fell silent and alert; our conversation left hanging. I communicated with Xavier through my eyes, shaking my head to signal him not to take any action. Would he listen? Or fly off and do his own thing, like he was known to? Keisha held her head down and said what sounded like a prayer under her breath. I kissed her on the cheek and hoped she said a few words for me as well.

"What the fuck?" Derek said, looking at his homies, as he dozed off on the couch. "Get y'all goofy asses up, Idrissa will be here in a few."

The two men rolled over and continued sleeping. That was the moment I rose, grabbing the gun from between the seat's cushion and cocking it, with Xavier rising with me.

Neither of us had planned on doing this, but something about the moment said that this was it. An unexpected rush of feeling was accompanied by youthful ignorance. Even though we didn't know how this would play out, we were in this together.

We both aimed our guns at Victor and Derek. "Don't open your mouths, or you know," I said with confidence, betraying my nerves. The pistol was heavy in my hand, and I was fearful of using it, but I couldn't let them know. I had to man up and take control of the situation.

My best friend from childhood had done something that would screw up everything we had been trying to achieve. The news Xavier shared with my father could unravel our whole trip to the past. The ramifications were too intricate to wrap my mind around, but I knew it could spell our doom.

Keisha slunk out of her seat, unable to speak, and, like a small mouse, went over to the door and closed it without alerting anyone outside.

The old man rose from his position on the dusty floor, with the huge wet spot on his pants almost dried and the gray area resembling an insect on those psychology exams. He wobbled a bit, but kept his balance, holding the wall for support. The lines on his face showed worry and concern.

The smell he exuded was horrible, but he was paying attention and silent, watching how this drama would unfold with bloodshot eyes.

"You know your brother took the money. Don't you?" I spoke to Victor as I grabbed him by the arm and escorted him to the kitchen.

Derek tried to scream out, but Xavier unleashed a cracking blow to his mouth with the butt of the gun. He clenched and grabbed his gaping jaw as blood and teeth sprayed onto the floor.

"Little muthafucker," Derek shouted, holding his mouth.

Victor just smiled and kept walking, looking at me with a fit of anger in his eyes that made me skip a step.

"So you do know," I said, regaining my footing. "All this is for show, isn't it?"

He didn't do a good job of hiding his anger. "Who are you, really?" Victor chuckled. "And how long do you think you'll live pointing that gun at me?" he said, with curled veins, shooting from the side of his neck.

"Long enough."

Keisha, the old man, Xavier, and I walked past the dining room, into the kitchen and out into the garage. It looked different from last night, now draped in tall trees. The radio was here, and there were a few chairs around, but it looked empty and devoid of life. With the greasy spots, from God knows what on the floor, and scraps and bits of metal, it filled me with a sense of dread.

Derek was wiping blood from his mouth, from Xavier's blow, as we sat him and his wired-up brother in the two plastic chairs next to a dilapidated window. Derek put up a fight, twisting and turning, while Victor just accepted it. They were very different in mood and appearance. Derek had a look behind his eyes, now beginning to sweat like a prisoner. Victor is like a Rottweiler.

The way I felt was a mix of things. I looked Victor in the face with a serious expression, trying to get across to him. "Do you know your brother has a gambling habit? And that he took the money? The old man wasn't lying, you know. Why are you doing this?" I inquired.

Victor sat, looking at me in the face, with a small

smile, playing on the side of his mouth. "Well, somebody has to cause trouble to keep things interesting. Especially in the hood. With all the obstacles in our way, sometimes it feels good to make someone else's life hard. Mostly to send a message, though. And why does it matter to you? You're just visiting, right? What does this have to do with you?"

Now, it was my turn to strike someone, and I was eager to do so. With the pistol in my hand, I raised it and brought it against the side of his head with force, letting all my frustration out in a single blow. I made his head turn from the power.

Keisha cringed from behind, and the old man smiled a toothy grin. Victor's head bent over from the force I exerted. "I'm asking the questions now, coward," I said, breathing through my mouth. "Are you that fucked up that you'd kill just for the hell of it? To have control?" I raised the pistol. "You're sick."

"I have a reputation, and it has to be lethal. Derek confessed last night, but I had already threatened his grandson," he pointed at the old man. "And I always keep my promises... It's how I keep my power."

Blood started to trickle down his brow in straight lines that he ignored. In the light from the window, he and his brother sneered, and spat on the floor at our feet.

"How can you take something that isn't yours? Life is a gift," Keisha said. The pregnancy made her more emotional. "God gave it to us-"

"And men like me... Well, we take it," Victor snarled.

"Someone is gonna know we're gone, stupid asses. What are you gonna do, then? Have a shootout with that one pistol?" Derek squealed, looking around and fidgeting.

After the blows I dealt Victor, I guessed Derek felt he

was next. I heard someone rustling and turned to see Xavier bringing out the bag, with the pistols from earlier.

"Nah, motherfucker. We got some heavy-duty weaponry, courtesy of your homey, Idrissa. If things get too crazy, we're lighting this place up," Xavier said, pulling out the huge assault rifle and cocking it back.

The smell of the unused garage was getting to me, making it hard to make a decision. Pacing back and forth over the large stain on the floor, I was petrified. If I wanted to, I could pull the trigger and take us back to the present. Just 4 pounds of pressure against the trigger of this pistol, and we'd be back, or so Lucky said.

It was hard to believe that it was this simple, but it was. The rules I had been given were clear. Kill Victor and come back home, changed. Knowing the new information about Lucky being set free and my unborn child, froze me again in my tracks.

Learning about Lucky's origin frightened me more than Victor or becoming a father. Lucky was something that neither of us had ever encountered before, and I feared freeing him from his ties to the old man.

Even now, I felt his presence, and it gave me shivers. Was he watching us now, waiting for us to make a mistake?

From outside the door, I heard Victor's lackeys scrambling, looking for their boss. Xavier, always ready for action, glanced at me with a smile and a wink. Keisha's frantic eyes shot across the oily garage before dropping to the ground in a fit of exasperation. "I'm tired, Travis, and at this point, I don't care what you do," she said. "Send us back or whatever... I'm done with it."

This was the moment, and my chest heaved as I breathed in the dank air of that sweaty garage. Victor and Derek were mumbling to themselves as I held my finger on the trigger. Gritting my teeth and sucking in oxygen, I had made a decision.

Standing on shaky legs, I planted them both on the slick surface, and raised the gun. It felt like forever, but I had decided that killing them was the best bet. Xavier's dreams of getting back with the money and Keisha's pregnancy would mean nothing.

The baby hadn't even developed a brain yet, and wouldn't even know. None of us would, for that matter. I had decided to experience a life I had always envied. The only thing stopping me now was fate, I suppose, because as soon as I got ready to pull the trigger, Derek lunged out of his seat and tackled me, making me drop the gun.

In the brief amount of time, both Victor and Derek, due to my indecision, had knocked me to the floor, forcing Xavier to shoot and miss his mark. Keisha screamed as I scrambled to recover the gun that was knocked out of my hand. In seconds, both of our hostages had fled the premises, leaving us panicked inside a dirty, dark garage.

CHAPTER 42

IN THE GARAGE

POPS STOOD IN THE CORNER, emanating the stench of urine, as I retrieved the gun from the floor and embraced Keisha. In the dim, humid garage, fear engulfed us, and options seemed scarce. We had depleted our resources, so to speak. It felt as though my life hinged on the intimate bond between us, and as Keisha's body pressed against mine, time seemed to slow down.

The silence was deafening, broken only by the sound of our labored breathing and the distant shouts of Victor's men. The garage felt like a tomb—a final resting place for our shattered dreams and failed attempts at altering the course of our lives. The weight of our decisions pressed down on us, suffocating and relentless.

"What do we do now?" The old man's voice shattered our momentary respite on the garage floor. "You messed it all up," he wheezed. "Now it's all gone to hell."

I remained silent because, deep down, I knew he was right. We had indeed ruined everything. But in our defense, we were still just kids—not even 20 years old yet. This venture had proven too daunting for our young minds. At first, I attributed it to us being young, but now I believe it was destined to unfold this way.

The glare I shot at the old man could have melted steel; it was seething with heat. At that moment, I craved someone else to blame besides myself. This was all the old bastard's fault, I thought. If I'd had the time to feel anger, I would have been furious. But Victor loomed outside the door, commanding his men and cautioning them against rash actions.

Xavier still clutched the weapon, his bravado diminishing, his eyes lowered, muttering to himself in disbelief. "Shit," he whispered over and over again, unraveling before my eyes. As I observed his agitated demeanor and whispered curses, I realized he was lost. As a product of the streets, I should have recognized it sooner. He was all talk, without substance.

My foolishness had led me to believe everything he said about guns and violence. How could I have been so naive? Xavier was, after all, a novice in this dangerous world, relying on his brother's reputation. Had I not been ensnared by his delusions, I might have sought another path. Now, trapped in the confines of an old, greasy garage, we teetered on the edge of ruthless demise, at the hands of a heartless criminal. It was the epitome of despair.

Feeling ashamed, I hung my head, bracing for the inevitable end. Our actions had boxed us into this precarious situation, with no way out. Time travel was more complex than I had imagined, and it left my mind spinning in confusion.

Someone peered through the window, and I fired a warning shot. "Don't try that again!" I shouted. "We just want to go home."

Derek and Victor murmured as they positioned their men, their hushed commands lost on me.

"God forgive us," I whispered, drawing Keisha close.

All we heard were the guns cocking behind the door as we prepared to meet our maker. The tension was thick, like a promiscuous lady of the night, and our time travel misadventure neared its conclusion.

Why I ever thought I could pull off something so complicated was beyond me. All I wanted was to experience life with both my mom and dad as a family, like it was meant to be. Such familial unity was rare for black kids in our neighborhood, and I longed to know that feeling. Keisha's pregnancy tangled things further, and the enigmatic Lucky added more to the confusion.

As the final moments approached, a collective realization dawned and was exchanged among us, marking the end of our time here. Keisha's calm eyes darted around the room, now filled with terror, while the old man and Xavier stood on alert.

Everyone here knew our fate, yet I clung to a vestige of hope with all I had. Perhaps something would intervene, or God would arrange a hidden miracle. While I hugged Keisha in my arms, I knew it might be foolish to hold onto such thoughts, but I couldn't give up so easily.

The seconds ticked by, each one an eternity, as we waited for the inevitable confrontation. The air grew thick with the scent of fear and desperation, mingling with the pungent odors of the garage. Our hearts raced, pounding against our chests, as if trying to escape the confines of our bodies.

Suddenly, a loud crash echoed through the garage, followed by the sound of splintering wood. Victor's men had breached the door, their footsteps thundering against the concrete floor. We huddled together, our eyes wide with terror, as the shadows of our attackers danced across the walls.

I raised my gun, my hands shaking as I aimed it at the approaching figures. This was it—the moment of truth. We had come so far, risked so much, and now it all hung in the balance. Would we emerge from this nightmare unscathed, or would our lives be forever shattered by the consequences of our actions?

As the first of Victor's men rounded the corner, his eyes gleaming with malice, I steeled myself for the fight of my life. There was no turning back now; there was no escape from the hell we had created. All that remained was the primal instinct to survive, to protect those I loved, and to face the demons that had haunted us for so long.

With a final, desperate cry, I pulled the trigger, the sound of the gunshot reverberating through the garage like a thunderclap. And in that instant, as the world exploded into chaos and violence, I knew that nothing would ever be the same again.

CHAPTER 43

IDRISSA'S ARRIVAL

OUTSIDE, sitting in the car, was Idrissa with an arsenal of guns strewn around him. From A-K's to sawed-off rifles and handguns. Each firearm was a deadly component needed to save his family from the clutches of Victor and his gang. A bead of sweat rolled down his head as he thought about the odd conversation with Xavier last night. Finding the young man talking to Victor outside his house seemed suspicious. Having his jaw bruised by Victor's meaty hands a few hours earlier made it all feel shadier.

With his arms crossed, Idrissa had listened to the scrawny, dark-skinned kid's story with skepticism. The things he claimed to know and warned against made Idrissa's skin crawl. Victor was volatile and could erupt at any moment, but how did this random kid know that?

When he heard "murdered," Idrissa grabbed him by the shirt collar and shook him by the collar. Victor wouldn't just kill him like that, he thought. Victor only wanted to scare him into delivering the money that his devious brother had taken at gunpoint. But murder him in cold blood and his family? The thought of it reverberated inside his skull. How did the skinny kid also know about Derek's gambling problem and other inside information? It was all unnerving.

Xavier had warned that Victor would kill anyone left inside when he came for Idrissa the next day. He sounded so confident that when Idrissa sat him down, he listened but scrutinized every word. Xavier claimed that a friend of an out-of-town relative would help Idrissa escape this predicament tomorrow and that if he took his advice, he should come in with guns blazing.

The kid was in over his head, but for some odd reason, Idrissa believed parts of his outlandish story. Knowing Derek had a gambling problem and was trying to pin it all on him rang true. Now, sitting in the smoke-filled car with sweaty hands sliding along the Desert Eagle as he observed the gang outside, Idrissa believed every word. Thinking he might be overprepared, he grabbed the assault rifle and slung it over his shoulder before getting out.

He was parked a few houses away, watching the group gathered in front of his place. Most were his friends, and he felt bad for what he was about to unleash. Victor was the boss who gave orders and rewarded his top men generously —a new car or a few grand trumped any ties they had to Idrissa.

Being in a gang demanded loyalty to the one running things, and Victor demanded it daily. Idrissa was just a henchman when it came down to it, even though he had come through for the guys many times, even saving a few. None of that would matter when they saw him turn on them.

Breathing calmly and trying to slow down his erratic heartbeat, he was ready to begin. His cousin from last night, the one they called 'Mike', was supposed to help, but he looked out of place as well. The clothing he wore was wrong and too tight. No one wore pants that close to their nuts. This wasn't the 1970s with disco music and spinning lights. It was 2002. They wore 'em baggy with room to hide the drugs they sold from the cops or pistols. How would he help? And his girl looked scared and useless. But if the scrawny kid said they would help, he'd welcome it.

Idrissa's mind raced as he considered the gravity of the situation. He knew that turning against Victor and the gang would have dire consequences, not just for himself but for his entire family. The thought of his wife and children being caught in the crossfire made his stomach churn with fear and anxiety.

Now, as he sat in the car, armed to the teeth and ready to take on his former brothers, Idrissa couldn't help but question his choices. Had he been blinded by the allure of the gang, or was he a product of his environment, doing what he needed to survive?

He thought of Xavier, the scrawny kid who seemed to know more than he should. How did he fit into all of this? Was he there to help, or did he have his own agenda? Idrissa couldn't shake the feeling that there was more to the story than met the eye.

As he stepped out of the car, the weight of the assault rifle heavy in his hands, Idrissa took a deep breath and steeled himself for the battle ahead. "I can't believe I'm doing this," he uttered to himself. There was no turning back; if he fired a shot, there was no way to undo the choices he had made. Derek had set all this in motion with his no-good, dirty-talking ways. The pummeling Idrissa received yesterday drove home the fact that today may be his last day on earth. Deciding that all he could do was fight, he set his mind on protecting his family, in any way he knew how.

So with a hard, steely grimace, as he opened the car

door, he secured the pistols in his waistband, pointed the rifle at his old crew, and unleashed a barrage of shots that sent them all running from his unexpected onslaught. A couple of people hit the pavement with chaotic thuds, squirming from being hit. Here, they thought they were providing security when they were in fact being picked off by a seasoned killer.

Idrissa's eyes were determined and filled with a callous hatred for the men. The remorse he thought he would feel was nonexistent at the moment, and in its place was a hatred for the men who dared to harm him and his family. With the rifle under his arm, he squeezed round after round as the small crowd dispersed and ducked behind cars. Friends who were just here last night celebrating with him returned fire.

It was cinematic as Idrissa walked towards his house untouched and unbothered by the poorly aimed guns missing him. "Just go home!" He shouted as he mowed down three men in order from left to right. "I don't want to do this."

A lone bullet clipped Idrissa's cheek, but he was too charged to notice it. "I warned you," he said before letting the empty rifle fall to his side. "Those were flesh wounds and nothing serious. Please stop shooting at me before I get angry."

And by some strange twist of fate, they did. The few people he shot limped and crawled to find help, while the rest ran off, leaving him alone in front of his home. The skinny kid said he would try to get his family out before Victor arrived, but he wasn't sure. Did he convince them to leave? He wondered as he ran up the rickety steps.

Just then, someone who was ducked down behind the porch grabbed him by the shoulder. Turning with a look of surprise, he lifted up the pistol and tried to fire a shot at the assailant. Unable to shoot him, he took a punch to the face, which dropped him to his knees.

Breathing hard and caught by surprise, he was dragged off the porch by the ankles by a few men who hadn't run off yet. "Get down, motherfucker." That was all he heard as he was kicking and flailing as they drug him down the stairs.

Kicks and punches followed, blinding him. But he somehow found a way to get to his feet. With his gun out of reach, he would have to handle this the old-fashioned way. With his fists.

He took a swing and connected with the first goon nearest him, breaking his jaw upon contact. All those pull-ups and his natural, big-framed body did the rest.

In the front yard of his childhood home, he braced for a fight. "No weapons! Okay?" He yelled. "Let's see who's really good with their hands. And I don't want to kill any of y'all punks anyway. I actually like a few of you."

Somehow they agreed, with a few of them even passing their pistols to their men to hold. They respected him and were loyal in a sense. He guessed it was all the work he had put in that made them realize that they were friends. And when you treat people like human beings, they respond like human beings.

Idrissa took off his shirt, revealing taut muscles underneath a wife beater, toned and full of vigor. "Let's do this," he said bouncing on his feet.

One of his boys stepped up. A tall man with a reputation for being a knock-out artist. "I'm about to lay your bitch ass out, Idrissa," he laughed, balling up his fists. "And then... I guess let Victor and Derek handle you," he charged in a fighting stance.

Maybe it was all the dirt Idrissa did or just a bit of luck, but he simply sidestepped and came crashing down with an electric blow to his temple. The men surrounding him each made a sound as the man fell on the floor, like a bag of dirt. "Who's next?" Idrissa yelled. "I can handle all of you." He flexed. "Remember who your big homie is and who saved many of you from these cold streets."

It was light work as he toppled man after man. Years living a vicious life had honed his body and reflexes. Charged and feeling like Muhammad Ali in his prime, he bobbed and ducked punches, tussled and wrestled with all his 'friends' one-on-one, with no one getting the best of him. "I'm getting bored and tired of this shit. Why don't y'all just give up and let me inside to see about my family?" He said almost out of breath.

"Because we just can't." A cock-diesel man approached, cracking his knuckles. "If you get the best of us, we'll let you inside. Right Jigsaw?"

"Yeah, right," Jigsaw said, pushing his way through the small crowd.

Idrissa's mind flashed back to earlier times when he and Jigsaw had butted heads and traded blows in front of a liquor store. Although Idrissa had bested him, it had been close. With another big dude fighting beside him, they just might whip his ass and end his attempts to save his family.

"A small thing to a giant," Idrissa said, full of bravado. "I can handle you two stupid motherfuckers, easy."

CHAPTER 44

APPROACHING DANGER

HERE WE WERE, huddled in silence, as the gunshots rang out in the distance. Someone had turned on the overhead light, bathing us in a dim orange glow. Outside the door, Victor shouted out to his men to get out front and protect him, as we heard footsteps signaling their departure.

"That's your dad, Travis. I know it... And he sounds angry," Xavier explained to me while creeping toward the window. With a cautious hand, he moved the rags that served as curtains, peering out the dusty glass. "Everyone is gone... For now, at least," his words rang out, sounding relieved.

Feeling relief, Keisha sat up, with a look of hope on her face. "Where did they go?" she asked.

"It looks like the thugs went out front," Xavier reported, as we heard more shots and screams in the background. "But Victor and Derek ran inside."

"Come on, let's follow them before something happens to my dad," I cried out. I couldn't let anything happen to my father, no matter what. This whole trip was because I wanted to save him, and everything was in jeopardy. So with nervous legs, I stood and pulled Keisha up alongside me, and we hurried out the door to follow Victor and Derek. I knew it was dangerous to do so, but everything was hinged on our next actions.

The old, thick door opened with ease as we fled behind the bastards, who had just threatened our lives with violence. I could still hear the door creaking as my foot stomped on a patch of matted grass with Keisha's hand in mine, determined to catch them and put a stop to this madness.

I inhaled and smelled the gunpowder in the air, and later I heard the voice of my dad, giving a warning, and then silence. I could only hope that the break in the gunfire would continue as we ran through the yard, towards the house.

Xavier carried the rifle behind him, breathing hard, while the old man trudged behind him, as if none of this mattered.

I didn't know what we were running into, but I was prepared to unleash my pent-up feelings. Getting kicked out of school and followed by a malevolent spirit for weeks had reached its peak, plus seeing my mom through her horrific ordeal had almost destroyed my resolve. Along with the disturbing dreams and Keisha's pregnancy, it felt like I would explode at any minute.

Looking back on it, I don't know how I held it together for so long.

———

When we entered through the basement door, Xavier ran to his hiding spot and pulled out the bag of money we had found earlier in the day. All the bills were still there, and he let out a breath of relief. "You still on that?" I asked him as we headed up the steps to the kitchen.

"And you know it. I'm holding on to this, just in case," he replied. "But what's the plan? Enter and start shooting? Or have you cooked up something else?"

"Hey, Pops. Is there a hiding spot we could duck into?" I asked, but didn't get a response. I turned my head to see if he had heard me, and I was surprised to see the old man wasn't there. I surveyed the room, looking for his presence, but he was missing. How could he leave at a time like this? It was beyond me, but he feared for his life.

"Fuck him. He was falling apart anyway. Let's come up with a quick plan, before we go up there," Xavier said.

Upstairs, we heard Victor and Derek rummaging around. Their voices, like whispers in the depths of the basement.

"No plans, just action," I whispered, and I ran up the steps with my pistol drawn. It had reached the precipice—or crescendo, so to speak. I had decided what to do and didn't want anybody saying anything to interfere.

Victor and his selfish brother had to go. I hoped fate was on my side as I raced up the old steps, towards the light peeking in through the door. We had traveled here from the future, ready to change it. Save my father and change my fate, as predicted. Change the way my brother and I were brought up and fix our troubled childhood.

I looked at Keisha in front of the door, feeling remorse. Remorseful for the child in her stomach, she was willing to throw it away because she loved me. *Or did she*, I thought? If she loved me, she wouldn't be so willing to do so. I was confused and filled with contempt in that moment.

I wish I had more time to sift through my thoughts and talk them over with Keisha for some clarity. Knowing that once I pulled the trigger and killed Victor, it would be all over made me shiver. I took her hand in mine and squeezed it. I was hoping she felt the love, and other mixed-up feelings that were pummeling my mind.

She returned the look with worried eyes, letting me know that she too was confused. *But what could we do?* This whole mission was a wild ride, filled with decisions and life-altering consequences. Every choice was a fork, without sustenance. One way was to live with my parents and their families—a life I missed out on due to the greed and ego of unscrupulous men. The other was money and my unborn child. And Xavier, a friend who showed me that it was cool to be a nerd, pulled me out of my shell. Keisha and I wouldn't even have met if it weren't for him.

I wonder what he felt while he clutched the bag of money to his chest. Did he tell my father to come here with guns blazing, hoping to save my family as well? He was a true friend, and I appreciated him. From the fights to walking around the neighborhood doing nothing, it filled me with the saddest, most fucked-up feelings I had ever felt.

I swallowed the frog in my throat while standing there with my friends at the crossroads. In a matter of seconds, we would confront Victor and his evil-ass brother and put an end to this. Two men deserved it. *But were they victims as well?* Chicago never pulled punches on the South Side, as far as black lives were concerned. All of us were pushed to do things we didn't want to do in order to survive the harsh environment. We were all brought up in troubling times, doing our best to ensure stability in our lives.

Staring at the door, determined to change our fate, I put on my big boy clothes and drew the gun. This moment was what I had come back to this time for. Victor's and his brother's lives were in my hands. And even though I didn't know if I could pull it off, one way or another, our fates would be decided.

◻

As I pushed open the door to the kitchen, my adrenaline surged, making me feel braver than I was. Every sense was alert and tuned in as I scanned the bright room for any signs of Victor and Derek. It appeared they had fled before our arrival, although we had just heard them here mere seconds ago.

The stove, with its oily skillets perched on top, almost fell as Xavier brushed against it. Wired with adrenaline, I grabbed the slick handle before it could fall. I gave Xavier a silent reprimand with my eyes, and he lowered his head in embarrassment. Keisha, on the other hand, remained glued to my side, her breath warm against the back of my neck.

The only sounds were the gentle taps of our feet against the clean linoleum tiles. I heard more chatter emanating from deeper inside the house, causing us to freeze in our steps. It all felt surreal upon reflection. None of us were prepared for what was about to unfold. I was an athlete who had returned home from school, unable to let go of the 'hood. Keisha and Xavier were just young adults, striving to carve out better lives. This wasn't our world.

Creeping, we reached the dining room undetected. Crouched beside the door, like bumbling amateurs trying not to be seen, we were scared for our lives. I held the gun, with Xavier behind me, with the AR. We left Keisha in the kitchen, armed with a .38 for protection. I focused on Victor, watching him sneak a peek through the window as the gunfire subsided.

This was it. My final opportunity to end it once and for

all. Flashbacks of intimacy with Keisha flooded my mind; her pregnancy was a consequence I chose to ignore. Shaking off the distraction, I stood and entered the room, the gun trained on the back of Victor's head.

Derek reached for my gun, but it was too late, his arms grabbing at the air. I mean, it all happened so fast that it didn't register what was happening, but as I began shooting, I thought I saw someone enter the room. Two someones, but I was filled with so much anxious energy, I couldn't be sure. Time froze as I squeezed the trigger, firing bullet after bullet, turning my head at the bright flashes coming from the nozzle.

I had done what I came here to do: kill Victor. The pompous piece of shit asshole who was the cause of all of this. Round after round, went into his skull. Those few seconds felt like hours. When the gun started clicking, due to me emptying the clip, I turned to face the aftermath.

I lowered the pistol, and what I saw staggered me. On the floor was Pops, my great-grandfather, with Victor and Derek fleeing the scene. Then came Idrissa, barging in through the open door, his pistol flailing.

The gun fell from my hand, and my shoulders slumped. Mouth opened; I hadn't ever seen anyone so hurt by my actions before. Surprise and astonishment flooded his face as he bent beside his grandfather, sobbing. "What the fuck just happened?" he cried out, forgetting about the ordeal with Victor and Derek.

In a foolish attempt to kill Victor, I missed it. My mind flashed back before I fired the gun and glimpsed two figures jump in front of Victor. Those two figures were Lucky and Pops. Amidst the confusion, Lucky appeared and pushed my great-grandfather in front of the pistol, allowing me to kill him.

My breath caught in my chest as the room seemed to swirl around me. The breeze blowing through the door brought no relief as I dropped to my knees and crawled towards the old man. Blood spilled from his mouth, and his chest heaved as Idrissa held his hand. The holes I had put in him gushed crimson floods of death as he struggled to speak his final words.

"Now you have to get Lucky. I fear what he's capable of," he gasped out, between scarlet drips escaping his lips.

Looking at my father, I shouted out, "What did I do?" Grabbing Pop's bloodied shirt.

No one had seen this coming. No one had prepared for the old man to die. If he dies now, everything will be erased. My meeting him, getting kicked out of school, and Keisha's pregnancy. Everything would be swept clean by the hands of fate, and Lucky would be freed.

Keisha rushed out of the kitchen, clutching her pistol, before dropping it and kneeling beside me. "What does this mean? Is everything going to return to normal?" she asked, her voice cracking with stress and tears threatening to spill.

I was too devastated to respond. Keisha shook my shoulder, attempting to pull me away, but I remained rooted in place. Meanwhile, Xavier rifled through the Neiman Marcus bag, tossing money into the air and cursing under his breath. However, money was the least of my concerns.

As the old man, Daniel, drew his last breaths, we would all be freed from the past. His ragged chest fell up and down, and my gaze remained fixed on him. The lines on his face were just like mine, and the afternoon light reflecting in his eyes filled me with grief and sadness. At that moment, as I looked into my father's youthful face, I saw a reflection of myself. Three bright, intelligent men, at a crossroads.

I reached for my father's blood-soaked hand and offered

my apologies before pulling away. *What would this mean? Would he remember this in the future, or would it all fade into foggy oblivion?*

Standing, I let out a melancholic chuckle and waited to be transported back to the present. I had messed up everything, but at least I would return to school. Anxiety gnawed at me as Xavier continued to scatter money around the room.

"So, this is it?" Keisha said.

"I suppose so," I murmured, heading towards the kitchen. The sunlight filtering into the room seemed to shift, and I wondered if this was the beginning of our journey back. Back to everything we had altered—back into the unfamiliar.

"It would've been nice to, you know, have your child," she said, with her head down. "I wonder if it would've been a boy or girl. It kind of makes me sad thinking about it."

I lifted her head, gazing into her eyes. "Yeah, and if we had pulled this off, I would've asked you to marry me. The feelings I felt over the past couple of weeks grew every day, I think."

Pulling her closer to me, I kissed her deeply and passionately, followed by a loving embrace, on the verge of something I couldn't describe. I wanted to say sorry for what couldn't be, but it was deeper than that. I nearly broke inside when I released her. Wiping tears, I whispered, "I'll miss you." She hugged me again, sobbing, unable to speak.

I held her against my chest and whispered in her ear, "Maybe we'll see each other, or I'll call, or something. I don't know. But this isn't the end. I feel like we were meant to be."

After our tender embrace, I was empty. My insides

were torn apart. Looking at Xavier, I stumbled towards him. "Come on. We've got to go." My voice cracked with regret.

"Maybe your dad can use the money," Xavier replied half-heartedly, scooping the bills from the floor. "Anyway, it was... something."

"Yeah, it was. I thought for sure we were about to be rich."

"You and that damned money." I laughed. "But you know what? We were already rich, bro."

"Already rich? You tripping again, Travis," he said, looking puzzled.

"We were, once you think about it. Our money wasn't the hundred-dollar bills, but the life we lived," I said, clutching his hand in mine.

I took one last look at my great-grandfather's body, and I felt the weight of destiny like a noose around my neck. Then, with heavy steps full of dread, I walked with Xavier and Keisha into the kitchen and into the hands of fate.

As soon as my feet crossed the threshold into the kitchen, everything dissolved into a black void, pulling us all inward. At first, screams pierced the air, the distorted cacophony reminiscent of how a DJ scratches at a party. But soon, the chaos gave way to silence, as my mind was torn asunder. Memories were ripped from my consciousness, like children pulling blades of grass from the earth; each handful was a string of thoughts, with consequences unraveling.

It was as if reality itself was coming undone. In moments, all of this would fade into oblivion, and I would be back at school with Amina. Relief washed over me. Though I would miss Keisha and Xavier, I welcomed the end of our harrowing ordeal.

Standing in the vortex of nothingness, I felt a strange

sense of peace. The old man's dying wish of finding Lucky faded into oblivion, more memories uprooted from the tender soil of my mind. Perhaps he wouldn't be so terrible, unleashed upon the world. I pondered as lights and matter began to coalesce around me. Soon enough, everything faded away, and the only remnants were fragments of Keisha's and Xavier's laughter.

CHAPTER 45

AT THE CROSSROADS

THE LIGHT WAS BLINDING and forced me to shield my eyes from its rays. I felt the heat on my exposed flesh, burning my skin. It was the weirdest, most intense feeling I had ever experienced. Each second there was torture, and all I wanted was to be released from its agonizing hell. It was then that the blaze started to die down, relieving my flesh from the scorching heat. When I felt it was safe, I lowered my hands with great care and surveyed my surroundings.

Cautiously taking a step forward, I called out into the blackness. "Yo!" I yelled. "Where am I?" I asked but didn't get a reply. My thoughts turned to me, and I drew a blank. *Who was I?* I thought. *And where did I come from?*

I extended my hands all the while, thinking something was wrong. Fear was inherent and inside of me, pounding against my chest like two 15-inch woofers. *Am I a ghost? Or maybe nothing?* I later thought about walking in that strange void.

A name echoed around my brain. It was small and

distant, but eventually, I grabbed it like it was life itself. "Travis. My name is Travis." I said it out loud.

At this realization, a flood of thoughts poured into my mind. A school, my girlfriend, and a short man with gold chains draped around his neck were the most prevalent. But the more I remembered, the more it all became clear.

I had messed everything up. Allowing my great-grandfather to be killed. The demon Lucky had double-crossed us, and I was sent back to an uncertain present. Keisha and Xavier were both gone, leaving me to navigate this dreamscape.

My trip to the early oo's felt like it was for nothing. It was nice to see my father and the rest of my family, but I didn't fix the past. In fact, I had bungled up everything. Learning of Keisha's pregnancy further complicated matters. The chance of being a dad and having the opportunity to be the man I never had was great, even now.

Looking down at my feet, my heart dropped.

The floor, or what was the floor, was transparent, and I was staring at myself in the anthropology class the day Lucky first made himself known to me. The whole scene paused and was immovable, like a video on YouTube. "What the fuck is going on?" I cried out to the haunting scenery. "Lucky, if you're here, come on out and show yourself."

A laugh cascaded around me, breaking my nerves like wafer bars. "So you figured it out, huh?" He said, moving the darkness, with a bluish light encircling him.

"Where's my family? And why am I seeing myself in the class below me, Lucky? What is happening here?"

He smiled with the same sick grin as before, gold chains clinking against his chest. "Let me explain, and you can decide how you want to approach the situation," he uttered. "You have a decision to make. Choose right and... go to your new future, which has been altered. Choose wrong, love through the whole ordeal again, and try to change it."

"Let me guess, you pushing my grandfather was not in the rules."

"Bingo. Somebody give this man a treat." His eyes were glowing like charcoal bricks.

Something told me to look up, and I saw the bottoms of shoes and one face staring down at me. My own. What I was doing and what I was looking at perplexed me.

"What's up top?"

"Your new present. The life you always wanted, of course. Make the right choice, and it's yours, but with a catch." He said. "Choose that one, and I'm free. Choose to have another go, and well, you know. Try it again."

Go back and do all this over, hoping to get it right this time. Or living the life I always wanted, both parents living in the suburbs. Both decisions carried a weight that I wasn't strong enough to lift.

"How many times have I done this? It feels all too familiar." I said, moving closer to the specter.

"A few hundred times at least. You're adamant that you can change it, and somehow you always end up right here."

I was frozen with indecision. "A few hundred, you say, and I always choose to go back?"

"Yes, though this is the first time you've looked up or down on the matter. The previous times, you fought me or listened to your conscience. What will it be?" He pressured me.

I thought about a world where both my parents were alive. I also thought of Keisha being pregnant with my child and her friendship with Xavier. "I had friends and a child on the way. Why wouldn't you go back and try to make that a reality?"

Lucky chuckled, and the phantom images above and below rippled. "Because you never do it. Not for the last few hundred times at least." He said.

"How do I know you aren't lying?"

"Because you don't. But know this: Pick the wrong one, and I'm free. I am free to go and do what I want without being bound to anyone. A being the world hasn't seen in millennia," he smiled. "Your time draws near."

A clock materialized in front of me, causing me to panic. "Decide," he said.

My mind worked out the ramifications of each choice. Could I do it this time? Lucky said it a hundred times, and each time I messed up things. The clock was ticking in front of me in its transparent form. "Time is of the essence, young man. If you don't choose, you and I both cease to exist. You must hurry." Lucky said.

The decision was simple.

"Well, you know what I want to do. Send me back. I have to try, right? Maybe this will be the time I get it right. And we can fix everything and bind you back to your prison. I choose below."

Everything froze. Lucky's sick sneer and my form. All of it.

Just as I arrived. I left the black emptiness to return to the bleak present. Hoping that this was the time I would get it right and live happily ever after. Hoping I had a chance at life.

With the weird dream still lingering in my mind, I walked the university halls like a character in a novel. I couldn't vividly remember the late-night visions I had, yet I did recall an unsettling echo that shaded my thoughts for the remainder of the afternoon—a feeling I desperately wanted to shake.....

ABOUT THE AUTHOR

Jimmie Watkins is a unique storyteller from the city of Chicago. With an uncanny ability to wield words, he cuts through emotions and explores the depth of human emotions. Jimmie possesses a rare ability to walk between genres with his masterful stories, which amplify his talents as a writer.

Whether it's hip hop, urban fiction, sci-fi, or fantasy, Jimmie demonstrates a high command of language. His tales are witty, immersive, and mind-bending, inviting readers to walk on journeys with him across thought-provoking plateaus and mental vistas.